Reprecussions

Reprecussions

WILLIAM GIBBS

Copyright © 2019 by William Gibbs.

Library of Congress Control Number:		2019901001
ISBN:	Hardcover	978-1-7960-1251-4
	Softcover	978-1-7960-1250-7
	eBook	978-1-7960-1249-1

All rights reserved. No part of this book may be reproduced or transmitted in any form or by any means, electronic or mechanical, including photocopying, recording, or by any information storage and retrieval system, without permission in writing from the copyright owner.

This is a work of fiction. All of the characters, names, incidents, organizations, and dialogue in this novel are either the products of the author's imagination or are used fictitiously.

Any people depicted in stock imagery provided by Getty Images are models, and such images are being used for illustrative purposes only.
Certain stock imagery © Getty Images.

Print information available on the last page.

Rev. date: 01/26/2019

To order additional copies of this book, contact:
Xlibris
1-888-795-4274
www.Xlibris.com
Orders@Xlibris.com
782388

CHAPTER ONE

"I'm almost done making this Frappuccino. Give me a second, okay?" She says as she hurries to finish one of her regular's coffee order.

Anika Washington has been working at the Coffee Shoppe for over four years. She started working there full time since she graduated from high school a little over two years ago. She didn't go to college like some of her friends, but she also didn't fall into the trap of winding up with the wrong man and having a bunch of little mistakes running around either.

It's not that she's not smart and can't do more with her life; it's more to the point that she hasn't found out what she wants to do as of yet. One of her short-term goals is to become assistant manager of the Coffee Shoppe and get a new car. She figures that once she becomes manager, everything will fall into place.

Today has been tougher than most for her. The girl who was supposed to be working today didn't show up, and Patrick, the store manager, asked if she wanted to pick up a few extra hours. Seeing how she needed the money and wanted to show the manager how dedicated she was, she took him up on his offer.

Anika is a lot of things, but stupid isn't one of them. She has known for quite some time that Patrick has a thing for her. She smiles and bats her eyes at him, and he usually leaves her alone. She figures as long as he's giving out the hours, she's gonna keep smiling.

She has two problems; they're down one person, and Patrick is utterly useless. Not to mention the fact that it's "Coupon Tuesday," and the lines have been out the door. She has tried to pick up the pace but her added effort has been less than successful.

"I'm sorry about the wait. Can I take your order?" Anika said with her award-winning smile.

"How about a coffee black and you for dinner?" the customer said with a lewd smile plastered on his face.

Anika is anything but unprofessional, but she has her limits. "Well, I can get you a small coffee with two creams and a sugar with a side of disappointment?"

"Bitch."

"Look, you see the line is out the door and I'm the only one working. I don't have time for games right now." She gives Patrick a withering stare. "What can I get you?"

He smiles and she knew the words that were about to come out of his crooked mouth weren't going to be good. "Well, if I can't have you, I guess I'll just settle for your smile."

"Get the fuck out."

"Come on, boo, why you gotta be like that?" the smug customer said as Anika began to fume.

Anika Washington is one of the nicest people who will give the shirt off her back and her last bite to eat to a stranger and always has a kind word to say on most days.

Today isn't most days.

"Look, you come in here almost every day and just mumble to yourself or just stare. I'm cool with that because I was just letting you do you. But when you start with the disrespect and you know I don't want your ugly ass, that's just too much. This is my place of employment, and I don't need you coming up in here messin' with my money."

She knew that she was gonna have to go there with him eventually. He's been coming into the Coffee Shoppe for weeks now, and he would just stare. Lately, his staring was causing her to feel uncomfortable. She has been reading on the news about women getting robbed and even raped in the area. She didn't know if it was him, but if it is, she wanted people in the shop to get a good look at him so if anything went down, they would remember him and hopefully he would get arrested.

"*That's not doing much for me though,*" she thought as the customer continued to stand there and just smile as he looked her body up and down.

"Anika!"

She turned to see Patrick standing next to her, fuming. He gave her a glare as he turned to the customer and gave him his best smile. "I'm sorry sir, she didn't mean what she said."

"The hell I didn't! I'm tired of you bringing your ass up in here looking at my body. I'm not a fuckin' wet dream for you! If you keep coming up in here, I'm going to have my brother fuck you up!"

She didn't have a brother or sister for that matter. She was an only child who was raised by her grandmother. Her mother used to come see her when she was young. The visits were often but became more infrequent over the years until she stopped coming around when she was eleven. After that time, it was just her grandmother and her. Her grandmother wasn't in the best of health, but she did the best she could. Her grandmother told her something all her life that she tried to adhere to, "If you can't do nothing right, you can love yourself. No one is going to truly love you unless you love yourself first."

That was something she took to heart and tries to live by daily. Sometimes it gets her into trouble like she's in now.

"Into my office. Now!" Patrick said as he grabbed Anika by the elbow and led her into his office. He pointed at a chair and told her to sit. Anika plopped down into the chair as she waited for the lecture that she knew he was going to give.

"What's going on with you today? You've been edgy all day, and now you're cussing out customers? Talk to me and I'll see what I can do."

Anika sighed inwardly. She knew he meant well, but what is she going to say? "*You suck at being a manager and I'm tired of you always rubbing up against me?*" She knew that wouldn't go over well. "I'm just having a bad day."

"I can't have you mistreating our customers, Anika. I'm going to have to write you up and send you home."

"What?" Anika said as her mouth hung open in shock. "Patrick, I'm your best employee, and I came into today because you asked me to as a favor." Anika sat up and put both hands on the desk as her eyes began to swell with tears. "You know I need the money. Please don't do this."

"I'm sorry, Anika, but I have a business to run here, and I can't let you interfere with that. I'm placing you on a week's suspension. We can talk after that."

Anika sat in the chair in shock as tears began to run down her cheeks. Since her grandmother had gotten sick, she has been the only source of income for them. Her grandmother applied for SSI, but they keep giving her the runaround and they can't count on that money anytime soon. Missing a weeks' worth of pay would put them too far behind. Anika began to sob "Come on Patrick. There has got to be something else I can do. I'll clean the bathrooms. I'll work over-time at straight pay; anything."

Something passed through Patrick's eyes as a ghost of smile crept across his face. He sat back in his chair as if he was contemplating something. "I'll tell you what I can do; I can cut your pay by two dollars an hour and I won't suspend you. If you're agreeable, I'm sure we can work out something," he said as he looked at her chest to confirm his meaning.

Anika in most scenarios would be livid and ready to call corporate and file a complaint. She has been working here for years and she valued her job. She has aspirations to become assistant manager, and if things went right, even store manager. But in the end, all she could do was laugh.

At first she just smiled, and then once she could no longer contain it, she began to laugh. She sat back in the chair and laughed until she lost her breath. Eventually, she pulled herself together and looked at him and smiled.

Patrick didn't know what to make of the situation. He assumed, at best, she would take him up on his offer and at worst, she would cuss him out and threaten to call corporate, which would fall on death ears. Rumor has it that more than a few members of the hierarchy had their hands slapped for similar, if not worse, offenses. He knew ultimately she would take the pay cut and work her ass off to get the money back. In the meantime, he would save on his budget and take her up on the offer to work overtime at straight pay. It was a win-win situation. But her response was totally unexpected.

Anika stood up once she composed herself. Turned and headed for the door. She stopped and turned to regard her boss. "You know what, I think I'll pass. I'm straight on working here. I don't know what I'm going to do, but I will land on my feet. You take care."

She turned back to the door to leave when suddenly Patrick said, "And where do you think you're going? Come on, Anika, what are you doing? We both know you're not going to really quit. You said it yourself that you need the money, and jobs just don't grow on trees anymore."

Anika said without turning back "Patrick you have got to be the worse manager I've met since working here, and that's saying something. You don't see the forest for the trees. Let me ask you something; if you and I are the only one's working today, and you and I are both right here in your office, who's watching the store?"

Patrick's eyes became big as saucers as he ran out of the office, pushing past Anika.

"Exactly," Anika said as she calmly gathered her belongings to leave. She knew that Patrick was going to have a hard time explaining why he and a female employee went to his office with a store full of customers. He more than likely will lose his job over this and she couldn't be happier.

Once Anika had gathered her things, she opened the door to leave, and when she did, the scene before her was worse than she imagined. The store was in shambles, and Patrick was in the process of trying to put out a fire. People were behind the counter trying to open the register. A fight broke out as people began to fight over the ill-gotten gains.

Anika walked toward the door with determination. She glanced and saw Patrick give her a look on the verge of desperation. She gave him a wink as she walked out into the night.

She felt a moment of panic as she stepped out into the unknown. The Coffee Shoppe had been a part of her life, and she felt a pang of guilt as she left it behind. Deep down inside, she knew it was for the best. There was a part of her that spoke to her in her grandmother's voice, *"You can't get to the high ground without climbing over a few bumps."*

Anika steeled herself as she made her way to her car. It was dark outside, and the employees always had to park in the back by the brush. It was the darkest part of the lot and she complained frequently that it wasn't safe for the people who close to park there, but her complaints always fell on deaf ears.

She got an uneasy feeling as she felt eyes on her. She quickened her pace as she headed toward her car. She didn't want to let whoever was possibly following her know that she was on to them. She went to use her remote control to unlock the door. but it didn't work. She silently reprimanded herself for not changing the battery in it after the repairman told her what was wrong.

Anika got to her car and began to fumble with her keys, and she started to panic for some unknown reason. She dropped the keys on the ground and scrambled to pick them up. Then she felt someone standing directly behind her. She didn't turn around and tried as casually as she could to unlock the door when she suddenly felt hands grab her roughly.

He didn't turn her around but kept her facing toward the car as he had her pinned from behind. She kept her hands on the top of the car because she didn't want to give him a reason to hurt her. If all he is after is money, she had roughly $80 on her, and she was more than happy to give it to him. Her life is worth more than a few dollars.

"If you don't want to get hurt, give me all of your money."

Anika expected for him to ask for her money, but once he voiced his intentions, his voice sent her into a whole other level of panic. He sounded as if he didn't have an ounce of sympathy, and she knew without a doubt she was going to die.

Tears began to run down her face as she resigned herself to her fate. She reached down and grabbed her wallet and handed it over to the thief. He took it from over her shoulder as he released her to see what he gained.

She heard a sharp cuss as he grabbed her and spun her around. She looked him in his eyes and saw nothing but hatred. She wanted to scream, but her mouth wouldn't move. Fear had completely taken over her.

"This all the fuck you got?!" He reached behind his waist and pulled out a gun with the barrel pointed directly at her face.

Anika's eyes became big as saucers as more tears ran down her cheeks. She was visibly shaking as he cocked the gun.

"I know you got more than that. Empty your pockets and lay it on the ground."

Anika did what he said as quickly as she could. She emptied her pockets out and laid it all out on the ground.

The thief sifted through Anika's things. He grabbed her purse and turned it upside down, looking for any remaining items of value. He threw the purse to the ground and let out a scream of frustration as he turned to her with a menacing stare.

The thief raised the gun to Anika's head, and she said a silent prayer. The barrel of the gun pressed against her forehead, and she knew she walked her last steps on the earth.

"Hold up, you sure you totally checked her?"

Anika's head shot up as she looked to see where the second voice was coming from. She couldn't make out who it was as he was shrouded by the shadows of the brush next to the parking lot. She saw a bright flash as he lit a cigarette and took a long drag and let the smoke out slowly.

The thief grabbed her roughly by the arm and dragged her to her feet, slamming her roughly into the side of her car, causing the air to rush from her lungs. He ran his hands up and down her body in an effort to find any hidden treasures. He ran his hands all over her body, turning each pocket inside out. He ripped any pockets that he couldn't get his hands in.

To add to her humiliation, his hands lingered over her breast, ass and other places that she tried to struggle from, but he held her firmly in place. He pulled her closely to him as she felt his breath on her neck. "You feel really good, boo, I'm gonna enjoy playin' with you."

A stab of fear ran through her body as she struggled for all she was worth to get away. If he was going to have his way with her, it was going to be over her dead body. As she tried to struggle her way to freedom, she felt a blow to the side her head that sent her senses reeling.

Anika fell hard to the ground and her head spun. She realized that he must have hit her with the butt of the gun. She tried to stand but the blow had caused her to lose all sense of balance and she just sat on her knees, defeated.

She could hear the man from the brush speak again "Stop playing with her. Somebody is going to come out here. If she doesn't have anything else, kill her so we can go."

Upon hearing her death sentence pronounced, she came fully to her knees, dropped her head, and said a silent prayer. She felt him hovering over her and heard him snicker. She waited for what seemed like an eternity. As the moments passed, she waited for the sound of the gun but was greeted only with silence. She began to become angry. She knew that she was about to die, but she wouldn't be made a fool of in the process. She opened her eyes and raised her head defiantly, ready to face death head on. She looked around and no one was there. She was afraid to move, fearing they might still be around, but after a few minutes, she knew they were long gone. She fell back against her car and cried.

The drive home was a silent haze as she recounted the events of the night. She was robbed, almost killed, and if things had gone differently, raped. Not to mention that she quit her job today. In short, she's had better days.

Anika pulled up to her grandmother's home and just sat in the car as the tears flowed. She didn't know what she was going to do to make ends meet. Her grandmother had given her all to her, and she would be damned if she didn't return the favor. All the sacrifices she made just to see that she was brought up right is something that she could never repay. She knows that it could have easily gone the other way. Just thinking about some of her friends that weren't so lucky sent chills up Anika's back. Hooked on drugs, multiple children without a father by their side, disease; or worse just to name a few. This sent a chill up her spine as she thanked God for the grandmother who cared enough to see her through to adulthood.

Anika sat in the car for a long time trying to compose herself. Her grandmother has been going through a lot of trying times lately, and she didn't want to add to them. She sat in the car and composed herself as she made her way into the house.

Anika walked through the door to find her grandmother sitting on the couch watching her favorite game show. She was fully engaged in the show as she yelled at the contestants as they got the answer wrong.

"How did you not know that? You're a professor of history, for crying out loud!" Anika's grandmother threw her hands up in the air in frustration as she noticed her granddaughter standing at the door with a smile on her face as she looked on at her.

"What's wrong, love?" she said as she could tell that something just wasn't right.

"Nothing Grandma. I just had a long day, is all. I think I'm going to go upstairs and just lay down for a few, okay? I'll come back down and make us something to eat."

Evelyn Washington has known her granddaughter since birth. Unlike her mother, she loved her from the start and would give her life to see her smile. If anybody knew Anika, she would be a foremost expert on the subject. "You and I have been through too much for you to stand there and lie to me. I know something is wrong, and it will do neither one of us any good if you hold it inside."

Anika ponders what her grandmother had to say and braces herself as she prepares to tell her grandmother the events of the evening. "Mama, I lost my job tonight, and I was robbed."

Her grandmother was silent as she stared at the television motionless.

Anika didn't know what to think. Her grandmother sat on the couch motionless as she tried to digest the information that she just heard. The show continued until it went off and still she sat motionless.

Anika waited and began to worry until her grandmother stirred. "First and foremost, are you okay?"

Anika nodded.

"Good, I don't know what I would do if something happened to my baby." Evelyn turned off the television and gave Anika her full attention. "Tell me everything that happened."

Anika felt tears come to her eyes as she recounted the evening's events. She told her grandmother how she lost her job and what she wouldn't do to keep it. She told her how she was robbed in the parking lot and how she thought she was going to die. Her grandmother listened in silence as she recounted the events as Anika told them to her, not leaving out any details.

Satisfied that she got the gist of the situation, her grandmother pondered the dilemma her granddaughter found herself in. She looked over into her eyes and saw a myriad of emotions. Fear, embarrassment, confusion and possibly hope?

She stood up and walked over to her granddaughter and pulled her into a hug. Anika fell into her arms and dissolved into tears and she began to cry uncontrollably. This went on for a few minutes until Anika began to compose herself. She leaned back and looked into her grandmother's eyes. "I'm so sorry Grandma, I let you down!"

She gave her a quizzical look. "Why would you think you let me down?"

"Because I lost my job and we both were depending on that income to get by," Anika said as she began to cry again.

"Don't worry about that, honey. We'll find a way to get by. God doesn't give you more than you can handle, though sometimes it seems like it."

Anika smiled. Her grandmother always knew what to say to make her feel better, and this was no exception.

Evelyn leaned back to get a better look at Anika. She looked her in the eyes to see if she was doing better and noticed something.

"Tell me," was all she said as she waited for Anika to respond.

Anika got ready to lie, but her grandmother knew her too well. She didn't want to add more burden on her than she already had. "I really don't want to talk about it right now, if that's okay with you?" she said with a hint of hope that she would let it die for now. No such luck.

"Baby, if we're going to pull off the Band-Aid, we might as well take it all the way off. There's no need to let it fester. It'll do more harm than good in the long run."

Anika pondered it for a moment then said, "I don't think I'm ready to talk about it just yet."

"Don't do this to yourself, Anika. I've raised you better than this. What's the one thing I always told you no matter what?"

Anika knew instantly what she was getting at which caused her to lower her head in shame. She thought to herself, *Is that what I'm really doing? Not loving myself?* She knew the answer before she even thought it. She steeled herself and took a deep breath as she met her grandmother's gaze. "When I told you how he held the gun to my head, what I didn't say was that if things had gone differently, he would have raped me as well."

Evelyn visibly stiffened at hearing that her only grandchild was almost raped. "Are you okay?" Evelyn said as she pulled her granddaughter into another hug.

"Yeah, I'm okay. I think I was more scared of being raped than dying. I know it doesn't make sense, but that's how I felt at the time," Anika said as she hugged her grandmother back. She looked up with tears in her eyes. "I didn't mean to let you down, and I'm going out first thing in the morning to find another job. I'll do just about anything to get food on the table for us."

Evelyn looked her granddaughter in the face, and the realization of what has happened to the dynamics of their relationship left her speechless. She didn't know when it began, but over the last two years or so, she has come to rely on her granddaughter more than she was willing to admit.

Since she became sick, she let her take care of her. At first it was to appease Anika because she was sick with worry, and just being able to contribute helped to alleviate some of the anxiety she felt. Then slowly as her illness worsened, she began to rely on her in a more real and tangible way.

"No, baby, I'm the one who needs to apologize to you. Your mother left you in my care when you were a baby not because she didn't love you in her own way, but because she knew you would be better off with me. Lately that hasn't been the case," Evelyn said as tears began to run down her cheeks.

Anika leaned back in her grandmother's arms and had an odd look on her face. "Grandma, you've been sick lately. We're family and it's my responsibility to take care of you after all of the years you've been doing it for me."

She just shook her head as she looked down at the ground. "That's the problem, Anika. You're always looking out for me but never taking time for yourself." Anika began to protest, but she held up her hand, cutting off the objection. "I know you were about to say some nonsense about it would be selfish for you to think about yourself during a time like this." Anika shook her head vigorously in the affirmative. "Did you ever consider what would happen if I continue to be sick? What if I'm ill for the next twenty years? God willing, that won't be the case, but what happens to you?"

Anika looked off into space as she searched for the answers but eventually gave up.

Evelyn continued, "I'm a grown woman and I can take care of myself. It's my responsibility to take care of YOU, not the other way around. I'm not gonna lie to you and say it's going to be easy, but I'll be damned if I let you throw your life away taking care of me!"

Anika took an involuntary step back as her grandmother's voice raised with charged emotion. She hasn't seen her grandmother like this in a long time. She was worried for her, but she knew deep down inside that she was right. The thought of not being there for her was gut-wrenching. Her grandmother is all she has left, and she would be lost without her. "I hear you, Grandma, but without you, I would be lost. Please let me take care of you." Anika said with pleading eyes as the tears began to fall again.

"No" was all she would say. Anything other than that would spark a whole new conversation and would just be a repeat of everything that was just said. She walked over to the couch and sat back down and patted the seat next to her indicating she wanted Anika to do the same. She took her hands into hers and said, "I want you to go back to school. You are honestly one of the smartest people I have ever met, and it would be a true sin if I let you waste your time taking care of me. You are a truly beautiful woman who can do anything she sets her mind to. You were born with an honest soul that few can hope to attain. I want more for you than what I have."

Anika is a truly beautiful woman. Her skin is caramel color without a mark upon it. Her eyes are the color of amber that many have complimented her on but fell on death ears as Anika never considered herself that good-looking growing up. She has long hair that she has been growing since she was a little child that runs down past her shoulders because she wanted to have hair like Beyonce's. She has an hourglass shape that causes more than one man to turn his head to get a second look. She is well proportioned, with large firm breasts and a behind that's round, but not overly large. She eats right and exercises daily because she doesn't want to lose her edge, she says.

Anika was ready to argue her position as she had a myriad of points that she could use to counter her grandmother's argument but she stopped. The realization of what she was doing was sobering, to say the least. What she wanted was actually being selfish, contrary to what she thought. She wanted to keep her grandmother all to herself so she will always be there for *her*. The thought left her feeling small.

She looked in her grandmother's eyes and saw a look of determination. As she was beginning to speak, she saw her grandmother lean forward, ready to fight for her future. Anika held up her hand this time and her grandmother leaned back slightly, letting her speak. "I know you love me, Grandma, and I know you want the best for me. I listened to what you had to say and every part of me wanted to fight you tooth and nail on this. But then I took an honest look at why I was doing this, and it brought things into perspective. I really don't want things to change." Her grandmother began to protest, but she indicated she wasn't done. "You taught me many things one of them was that everything changes. No matter how much I try, I can't stop time from moving on. I've been trying to hold on to some part of my life that has and will forever be important to me; you. You have shown me love from Jump Street and I can never repay you for what you have done."

Her grandmother beamed.

"I want so much to show you the love that you have shown me since I was born, and I realized the way to do it is by honoring your wishes."

Her grandmother looked at her with a leery eye, "And what exactly do you mean by that dear?"

Anika got ready to say something smart but thought better of it, "I'm going to go back to school. I will honor you by being the best black woman I can be. I'm going to start looking for a school to attend. I always wanted to get a degree in business."

Anika stood up and walked away with a purpose. Evelyn looked at her actions and began to laugh to herself. "Where are you going?"

Anika stopped as she began to climb up the stairs to answer her grandmother, "I'm about to go look for schools to attend. I'll come back down and cook dinner in a few." She began to go up the stairs and then stopped to look at her grandmother with a worried look. "It's okay if I cook from time to time for you, right?"

Evelyn broke out in laughter as Anika looked at her with a look of puzzlement. Not knowing what to think about the situation, she shrugged and continued bounding up the stairs.

Evelyn laughed as she grabbed the mail that had been piling up for the last few days. As she sorted through the pile, she stopped when she noticed a letter from social security. She rolled her eyes as she figured it was another letter asking for more documentation that she has provided on numerous occasions or just another out right denial with no explanation at all.

She sat back expecting the worse, but as she started to read the letter, she realized this one read a little different than the other ones. As she read, her heart began to jump in her chest. She continued reading as her hands began to shake when she got to the line that said, "*We regret the delay in your payment for the last three years. To compensate, we are giving you an extra payment in the amount of....*"

Evelyn dropped the letter as she looked at the check amount. She hasn't seen that much money at one time in her life. She dropped to her knees as she praised God for the fortuitous turn of events as tears of joy ran down her cheeks.

After praising God for all he has done, she jumped to her feet and made her way over to the stairs. She yelled for Anika. Moments later, Anika came running down the stairs with a clear look of concern on her face.

Anika looked at her grandmother sideways as she began to smile, "What is it?"

Evelyn could barely contain her smile "God is good. I just got a check in the mail." She handed the letter over to her granddaughter. Anika quickly read over the letter, and her eyes began to grow large as she saw the amount of the award. Her eyes began to swell with tears of joy as she realized that many of their problems had just been solved.

"I can't believe it Grandma. You did it!" Anika said as she grabbed her grandmother in a fierce hug.

"It wasn't me, babe. It was you and all those letters you wrote on my behalf. I don't think this would have ever happened without you." Evelyn started to laugh again as she hugged her granddaughter again "Tonight we eat well. Get dressed. We're going out to dinner and for once, it's on me!"

They both laughed as they made their way upstairs to get dressed to celebrate their sudden change in fortune.

CHAPTER TWO

Anika Washington, true to her word, did honor her grandmother's wishes.

Over the next seven years, Anika went to school at the University of Louisville and got her bachelor's in finance. She went on to get her master's in business management when she was offered a position at one of the top online banks in the world.

She started out working in the call center, making collection calls. She would go home every night dejected because she felt she deserved a better position than what she had. She would constantly complain to her grandmother that she has better credentials than her boss and her boss's boss.

Evelyn would quietly listen to her granddaughter vent her frustrations about the injustice of it all. When she was done, she would explain to her that anything worth having takes time and dedication. She explained to her that her opportunity would come and when it does, she needs to be ready.

Anika didn't feel particularly buoyed by the conversation, but she followed her grandmother's advice, and one day there was an opening for a financial buyer. She applied for this like she did every other position that opened up; she wanted out of the call center life.

Unlike the other times, she got an interview and nailed it. A few weeks later, she was formally offered the position of retail buyer for the auto division. Just a few short years later, she made senior buyer and then was promoted to corporate area manager.

Anika was the youngest manager in the industry and she had her share of troubles, but always found a way to preserve.

Now at twenty-seven, she had the career she always wanted, but something seemed to be lacking and she couldn't put a finger on it. She figured she would go see the one person who hasn't led her astray yet; her grandmother.

Evelyn was sitting on her couch watching "The Price Is Right," yelling at the television as always as Anika made her way into her childhood home. She smiled as she felt a twinge of nostalgia as the scene brought back a flood of memories from a long time ago.

Evelyn finally noticed her granddaughter standing, there smiling at her, and tried her best to hide her excitement at seeing her but with mixed results. "Why don't you sit down? I see that those expensive shoes you're wearing is killing your feet. You ain't gotta look cute for me."

Anika smiled as she made her way over to the recliner. She had to admit, the shoes she was wearing were hot, but they were murder on her feet. She sat back in the chair and promptly kicked her shoes off and let out an audible sigh.

Evelyn smiled at her granddaughter. She hadn't seen her in almost three weeks and was beginning to worry about her. She wanted to call, but she fought the urge. Anika was a grown capable woman who would let her know if anything was wrong. "You're looking good, sweetie. That color is nice on you." She turned the television off so she could give her granddaughter her full attention. "Now, tell me, what's wrong."

Anika was surprised but quickly realized that her grandmother could always tell her moods. "I don't know what it is; I'm doing great at work. I'm in line for a vice president position and the money is good where I'm at now. I just feel something is missing, you know?"

Evelyn chuckled as she looked at her only grandchild. "When was the last time you went out and had any fun?"

Anika sat up in the recliner ready to answer the question, but found herself at a loss. Then a smile crossed her face as she turned to face her. "I went out with co-workers for drinks just last week. I had two martinis and a shot of some drink I couldn't tell you what it was. But I had fun, " she said triumphantly.

Evelyn chuckled as she smiled at her granddaughter. "Baby, I don't think you understand what I'm saying. I'm asking you when was the last time you went out with a man. I know you've been focusing on your career, and I can't begin to tell you how proud I am of you, but we all have needs…"

Anika began to flush furiously; she didn't even consider what her grandmother was saying until just now. *When was the last time I went out on a date? It couldn't have been that long, could it?* Anika thought to herself.

Evelyn waited patiently while her granddaughter came to terms with what she just told her. Anika is an extraordinary woman, but she can sometimes get tunnel vision to say the least. She remembered a time while she was in school that Anika was studying for final exams and collapsed on the floor, almost giving her a heart attack. Come to find out that she forgot to eat for three days! Yes, her granddaughter has tunnel vision, sometimes to her detriment, and this isn't any different.

She continued to sit patiently while her granddaughter ran through a gambit of emotions. She almost laughed out loud as she saw her struggle to remember the last time she actually let her hair down and had fun for herself. She saw her eyes sparkle as she seemed to come to a resolution.

Anika stood up from the chair with a triumphant leap. "I remember when I went to New York last year with some of my college friends and we went to a club and I met Idris Elba! He shook my hand and I almost died!" she said as she smiled and fell back in the chair, full of giggles as she reminisced over times gone by.

Evelyn let out an audible sigh, "Girl, when was the last time you got some ass?!"

Anika's mouth fell open in utter astonishment. In all her years she has never heard her grandmother speak in such open terms.

"I'm sorry I had to put it out there like that, but sometimes you can't beat around the bush and in your case, the bush hasn't been beaten in a while."

Anika was beyond embarrassed. She never thought in a million years her grandmother would be so "raw" with her opinions. But once she thought about it, it wasn't so farfetched. Her grandmother was a woman just like her and she had to have needs too, right? She shuddered at the thought of picturing her with any man.

As if reading her thoughts, her grandmother went on, "I don't talk about my personal life because it's personal, but I think this warrants an exception."

Anika looked on with confusion displayed across her face, but she remained silent as she waited for her grandmother to continue.

Evelyn saw that she had her granddaughter's full attention and she continued. "You remember Mr. Crowder who used to tend to the garden out back?"

She did. She remembered how her grandmother's garden was the envy of the neighborhood. She remembered how all the ladies and some men would come and ask her what her secret was and her grandmother would only respond with a smile. "It's not a secret if I tell you, now is it?"

She continued "He and I were seeing each other for years. I finally cut it off when he started *pruning* other gardens." Evelyn sat back as she reflected on the past "He sure could *prune*," she said out loud as she continued to reminisce about the past.

"Wait, you and Mr. Crowder?" Anika said as she tried to make sense of what she just heard.

"Yes, me and Mr. Crowder. What, you think I don't have needs too? I want . . . . no, need the touch of a man. It doesn't make me weak; it makes me human." She noticed the look on her granddaughter's face and quickly added, "I'm not saying you should go out and lay with every man you meet. I'm saying that you shouldn't shut yourself off to the idea of love. I'm not getting any younger and I would like to know my great-grandchildren and they remember me as I am now. Not someone who is too feeble to remember their own name or unable to keep from crapping their pants."

Anika made her way over to her grandmother and took her hands into hers. "You're not going anywhere any time soon. We are too tight.

I'm for you and you're for me." She grabbed her grandmother in a tight embrace as she tried to banish any thoughts of her not being in her life.

Evelyn enjoyed the moment as brief as it was. She reluctantly pulled away from her and gave her a melancholy look with a sad smile. "Sweetie, I am going to die at some point in time."

Anika began to panic as tears formed in her eyes. Evelyn put up a hand to stem off any emotional outburst.

"I'm not dying any time soon, God willing. What I'm saying is that you will outlive me. I would love to be around in my right mind to see you grow old, but that is a childish wish. I know I have more years behind me than in front. I wouldn't even try and kid myself, nor would I lie to you." She ran the back of her hand down the side of Anika's face. "I love you more than I dare express. You have surpassed any reasonable expectations I might selfishly have had for you. You are a lady of the highest order. Any real man would consider you a treasure." She pushed Anika back so that she could look her in the eye. "But I need you to be weary of those niggas out there that will try and win you over. They will try and breakdown your confidence and put a baby in you the first chance they get. They need someone like you to take care of them, to validate their reason for being on this earth. And they will systematically destroy you from the inside. They want to be more than what they are, but they don't want to achieve it themselves."

"They want what you have, what you have achieved, but they don't want you to achieve it."

Anika looked on with a perplexed expression, and she went on as she tried to clarify things for her. "They want you to be on the top of the mountain because only you can get them there, but they don't want you to lead. They want all the accolades but don't want to put forth any effort to achieve it themselves. They want you to carry them, but when it comes time for the praise, they want you to fall back to the shadows and let them bask in the glory, alone."

"I'm sorry Grandma, but I don't understand."

Evelyn continued, "A real man is comfortable in his own skin. He doesn't need you to raise his profile. He just needs YOU. He wants to be there to carry you, not be the instrument of your failure. A real man wants to bring joy to your life, not bring problems that didn't exist before you met him."

Anika nodded as understanding began to dawn on her face.

"Now don't get me wrong, he doesn't have to be successful in the manner that you are. He needs to be a man that can stand on his own two feet, who can carry you if need be. Don't judge a man by the size of his wallet; judge him purely by his actions. Once you turn down the volume on life, you can see the heart of the matter."

Anika took to heart the wisdom that her grandmother had to impart to her. As long as she can remember, her grandmother has never led her astray. She has always put her best interest first and foremost to whatever would be easier or beneficial to her. She knew her grandma could have taken the easier path on countless occasions, but not once has she forsaken her. "So what do I do?"

Evelyn looked at her like she had two heads "You need to go out and enjoy your youth. You don't get a second chance, believe me."

It's been a month since Anika had her heart-felt conversation with her grandmother, and things have had mixed results to say the least. Either the men she would meet at the club were trying to get laid, had a girl, or they were married. The married ones were the worse; they were always smooth with their words, and if you didn't keep up your guard, you could easily wind up a booty call.

She remembered with bitterness Jay. He had told her everything he thought she might want to hear, and she ate it up like a starving orphan. He told her she was beautiful, intelligent, and he always paid when they went out. She thought he was being a gentleman when he didn't try to get the goods. Now looking back, she realized he was after bigger game.

He would drop her off at her door and give her hand a simple kiss. Then caress her cheek and drive off, leaving her swooning. She would go in the house walking on clouds until she tries to call him later that evening, only to either get his voicemail, a quick reply, or he would pick up the line and then immediately hang up.

He would always have an excuse. It was either his phone was messing up or he didn't hear it, in the shower, or just sleep thinking about her. He had an excuse for everything. He was so good that he had her doubting herself. She would go talk to her grandmother and she would just nod with a knowing look but would never give advice. She would always say, "I could tell you, but you wouldn't learn nothing."

She would ask over and over again, but she would dodge her questions until she became fed up and just flatly refused. She knew then that she was left to her own devices.

It was by pure luck that he was finally revealed to be a dog in sheep's clothing. She was out with her girls at a bar celebrating Iliana's engagement to her high school boyfriend. She was telling the tale of how they broke up, and years later, he came back to her saying how he never forgot about her. He said that he knew she was the one many years ago, but he wasn't the man he needed to be at that time and he had a lot of growing up to do before he was worthy of her love.

All the women at the table had mixed emotions about the whole story. Some were genuinely happy for her and Carl; they gave congratulations and showered her with hugs and buying rounds. Others were quiet, reflecting on their decisions and how they got to this point in their lives.

She on the other hand was over-joyed for them. She told the waiter to keep the drinks flowing as the ladies let their hair down. Numerous men came over trying to holla, but they either flirted and sent them on their way or pointedly ignored them.

Kenya was the most ruthless. An unsuspecting victim came up and asked her to dance. She told him that she didn't know how. Not one to be deterred, he told her he would teach her. She didn't know when things went bad, but all of a sudden, she was asking him if he could support her and her three children (she doesn't have any) and if he was educated.

Before Anika knew it, Kenya was throwing her drink in his face. She was clearly intoxicated, and to his credit, he just shook his head and walked away, finally getting the hint that if he was sober, he would have gotten long ago.

As the drinks kept flowing, the evening got more interesting. She finally had more than she could handle and excused herself to go to the rest room. As she was walking to the bathroom only to stand in a long line, she saw a familiar face.

Sitting in VIP, she saw Jay huddled up in the corner having an animated conversation with a woman. From the looks of it, the woman wasn't very happy with him and tried to get up to leave. He would grab her hand and gently lead her back to her seat.

She didn't know what they were saying and oddly enough she felt guilty listening to their conversation. As she stood in line, she wanted desperately to walk away, but her bladder wasn't having it. After numerous drinks, she had to go or she was going to explode.

She tried not to look, but curiosity got the best of her. She looked out the corner of her eye and was shocked by what she saw. Jay had his hands around her throat, and the woman was struggling to get free. Anika began to call for help and then she saw the strangest thing, they started kissing passionately.

He had his hands up her dress and began pulling down her thong. She began to straddle him and before long they were having sex in the club, oblivious to those in attendance. Anika looked around to see if anyone else noticed and to her amazement they didn't. The session was short but fulfilling as both partners disengaged and fell back on the couch spent. The woman he was with discreetly grabbed her underwear and placed them in her purse while Jay being Jay, stood up and chose to straighten his clothing, not caring who saw.

He looked around and froze when he saw Anika. The woman he was with didn't notice his reaction as she made her way out of VIP to stand in line to the bathroom with her. Jay began to panic as he raced down from VIP and grabbed the woman roughly and yanked her out of the line as Anika stood there just staring at them as he pulled her away. The woman looked profoundly embarrassed as she looked back at Anika with a look of embarrassment.

Anika was more shocked than anything as she finally made her way into a stall and relieved her full bladder. As she stood at the sink washing her hands, she looked in the mirror and saw a beautiful, successful woman looking back at her. *His loss, I was gonna fuck him tonight too, dumbass nigga,* she thought to herself as she made her way out of the bathroom and back into the club.

Her girls gave her a questioning look as she sat down. *Did they know?* She thought to herself as a myriad of emotions ran through her mind in an instant.

"Damn girl, what the hell took you so long? We thought you got snatched up or something," Kenya said as she took a sip from yet another drink.

Anika, relieved, said, "Shit, if I was, you bitches didn't move!"

The two looked at each other with a bewildered look and said in unison, "Bitch, the bottle ain't empty yet!"

All the women burst out in laughter as the evening continued. Anika's problems were put on the backburner as she enjoyed a night out with friends. She could hardly remember when she had this much fun. Sure, she has gone out plenty of times, but she always had to have her guard up and put her best foot forward. But when she is hanging out with her girls, she is just Anika.

The night wore on and they continued to share laughs, love, and tears as each let their hair down and opened up like they haven't done since high school. At one point Iliana broke down into tears as she yelled how much she missed hanging like this and she would cut off her soon-to-be husband's balls if he didn't let her hang with her friends.

Anika looked up and noticed Kenya recording the whole emotional outburst. When she noticed Anika looking at her, she said with a perplexed look, "What? Like you weren't going to do it."

She thought to herself and laughed as the thought didn't cross her mind, but after a moment, she pulled out her phone and began recording as the show continued. Iliana continued on, oblivious to her friend's impromptu recording session as she bared her soul.

As the night wore on, the club began to do last call. The waiter, who had been so nice to them, came over with the bill and a funny look on his face. Kenya grabbed the bill and once she saw the amount, she visibly stiffened. Iliana, forever nosy, grabbed the bill next and let an audible squeak. Now it was Anika's turn and when she saw the bill, her eyes bugged out of her head. *Did we actually drink that much?* She thought as she tried and failed to remember how many drinks and bottles they purchased. Cold reality set in when they played the "cute guy game." Whenever they saw a man who was exceptionally hot, they would send him a drink. By that time, they were pretty wasted and pretty much any guy with a pulse was getting a drink. They had a few situations where the women who were with them came over to voice their displeasure, but once they explained the game they were playing, the ladies for the most part let it die although they left them with a wary eye.

Anika sighed to herself as she reached into her purse to pull out her wallet. The waiter came over and leaned in where only she can hear. "Just drop me $20 and I will forget I ever saw you. I will just say that when I was helping the bouncers break up a fight, you ladies slipped out."

Anika couldn't help but smile. This young man couldn't be any older than twenty-one and he was willing to put his job on the line for them, people he didn't know.

"Don't worry about it, I got this," she said as she pulled out her black card as her girls said, "Damn, baller!" Even the waiter was visibly impressed. Anika, not one for attention, began to blush. The waiter took the bill away to be processed. She looked up and both her girls were looking at her with open astonishment.

"So what exactly do you do and are y'all hiring?" Kenya said as she saw dollar signs.

"I'm gonna keep it real; how much do you make girl?!" Iliana said as she leaned in, trying to be secretive as she was clearly still feeling the alcohol.

"I work for this automotive firm and to answer your question, I do a'ight."

"So, you got a black card?"

"No" Anika said as she lied. "That's my company card that I'm supposed to use for clients only. I'll just tell them that I took out two potential clients," she said as she gave them a wink.

The waiter came back and handed her receipt to sign and her card. She gave the slip and pen back to him. He looked at his tip and then looked at her with awe as she put her finger to her lip, indicating to him to keep it on the low. He quickly caught her hint and remained silent.

The club had closed by this time, and only the staff and they remained. The waiter walked them to the door to let them out. Iliana and Kenya walked out first, but Anika remained behind to talk to the waiter. The two women gave her a knowing look but continued on to the limo.

She turned to the waiter who was trying to give her his most seductive smile. "It's not that kind of party," she chuckled. He gave her a confused look as she continued on. "How old are you?"

"Twenty-three" he said as he tried to figure out what her angle was.

"Did you go to school?"

"Yes, I just graduated from the University of Cincinnati with a degree in accounting. I'm out here looking for a job, but it's hard out here, you know?" He looked her up and down as he appraised her. "Maybe you don't."

She reached in her wallet and gave him her business card. "I want you to show up at this address on Monday at 9 a.m. If you're late, don't even bother."

"Aren't you even going to ask me my name?"

"I will if you show up on time."

He looked at the card as she walked away to join her friends in the limo. He stood at the door until they drove off wondering what she had in mind.

CHAPTER THREE

After they stopped for an early-morning breakfast, she finally arrived home to her apartment. She waved as Gus the doorman greeted her. He gave her a chuckle indicating that she was gonna be feeling that in the morning. All she could do was smile as she made her way into the elevator.

It seemed like an eternity as the elevator slowly crept up to her floor. She could feel her stomach starting to churn from the motion, and it threatened to empty its contents on the floor of the elevator.

Thankfully, Anika was able to keep herself from throwing up as she exited the elevator and stumbled toward her apartment. She took more than a few minutes to open the door as she struggled with the keys as she was seeing double.

Finally the door opened and she fell through, almost tripping over the couch table in the process. She threw her shoes in the direction of her bedroom as she had discarded them long ago. As she stumbled her way over to her waiting couch, she froze as she felt someone else in the room.

"Did you enjoy the show?"

Anika sat up bolt straight as she heard the voice from the shadows. She slowly slid away from the direction of the voice as her heart began to pound in her chest. "W-who's there?" she said as her fear began to cause her to panic.

"Oh, so now you don't know me, huh? You bitches are all the same. . ."

Anika tried to peer through the darkness "Jay, is that you?" she said tentatively.

She was rewarded by a flash of light, and he turned on the lamp next to the chair he was sitting in.

"So, you don't even know your own man's voice? Just how many men do you having coming through here? You're a slut."

She began to argue that she wasn't his girl when she felt herself becoming angry. "What the hell are you doing here, Jay? And just how in the fuck did you get into my house?!"

He gave her a lecherous smile. "I had a key made a while ago. You never know when I might have to come over and let myself in to make sure another car isn't parked in my spot."

"Nigga, you crazy!" Anika said as she began to stand.

"Sit yo ass down!"

She yelped as his voice suddenly rose and she promptly sat down. She noticed he had something in his hand and realized it was a belt. He had it wrapped tightly around his fist with the buckle sticking out. *Is he gonna beat me?!* she thought as panic began to rise in her anew.

"I see you're just like the rest. . . You just not gonna learn. . ." He began to rise as he tightened the belt around his fist. "But I'm gonna teach you!"

Anika jumped up and ran towards the kitchen with Jay quickly following. She tried to get to the knife drawer, but Jay intercepted her. She was rewarded with a blow across her arm as Jay struck her with the buckle of his belt.

"Oh so you wanna make this hard?! I got yo hard right here, hoe!" Jay swung again and hit her across the back as she fell to the ground.

Anika looked up at Jay with tears in her eyes. He slowly made his way toward her, feeling triumphant. She could see the smoldering hatred in his eyes, and she knew he was going to hurt her.

Anika grabbed the cabinet door and slammed it into Jay's knee as he crumbled to the ground screaming in pain. "You gonna pay for that!"

Anika tried to scramble to her feet, but Jay caught her by her ankle and pulled her roughly down to the ground. "You thought that was funny, didn't you? Yeah, I can see you laughing, but I bet you won't think this is funny!" he said as he slammed her head against the kitchen floor.

Anika's vision swam as her head bounced off the floor. She knew that if she didn't do something quick, he was going to kill her. She reached down and grabbed him by his testicles and squeezed for all she was worth.

Jay let out a savage scream as he released her head and desperately tried to break her grip on his manhood. He squeezed her wrist painfully, but she knew if she released him, it would be all over.

Anika gave one final muscle straining squeeze and scrambled to her feet. Jay lay on the ground moaning as she rushes to the coat closet, looking for something that would turn the tide.

"Asshole," she said under her breath as the stun gun she was looking for was gone. She knew he must have removed it. Knowing what he probably had planned for her further fueled her anger as she went to one of her many other "safe havens" and retrieved the object she was looking for.

She found the stun gun she was looking for and gave a ghost of a smile when she realized it was fully charged. She made her way back into the kitchen where Jay lay on the ground moaning. He looked up and gave her a chuckle of disbelief. "So what you gonna do with that? You gonna shoot me?" He staggered to his feet and took a tentative step toward her. "Think this through Anika, if you kill me, what are you gonna tell the police? Who's gonna take care of your grandma?"

At the mention of her grandmother, she began to see red. "You weren't thinking about my grandmother when you were beating me."

Jay took another step toward Anika and began to smile. "You don't have the balls to kill me. Just hand the gun over to me, and I'll forget this ever happened."

It was Anika's turn to smile. "What makes you think I was going to kill you?"

Jay was feeling emboldened as he took a confident step toward her. "Give me the fucking gun and I won't beat your ass *that* bad."

Anika didn't respond as she shot Jay in the chest with the stun gun. The look on his face was priceless as he gave her a questioning look as 10,000 volts coursed through his chest. He dropped to the ground like a sack of potatoes. She stood over him as his body shook uncontrollably. She looked down and noticed that he wet himself as the currents continued to run through his body. He looked up at Anika with a look of pleading in his eyes. She gave him a look of total contempt as she pushed the trigger again, sending another 10,000 volts of current through his body that caused him to convulse anew.

Jay lay on the floor in a pool of his own bodily fluids, totally unaware of his surroundings as the stun gun did its job. She casually made her way over to her phone and called the police.

Jay sat up and gave her a pleading look "You don't have to do this. I promise I won't bother you again." He began to sob as his body shook with the effort. "My wife will leave me if you do this. She's all I got."

She gave him a cold look. "Then what was I? You told me that I was all you ever wanted, remember?"

"I-I was wrong to have done that. If you let me go, I promise I will never bother you again, please!"

"Nope, if I let you go, you won't learn anything," she shrugged.

"You bitch!" he said as he lunged toward her. She nimbly moved out of his way and shot him with another round of voltage.

She laughed as she filled him with another round of voltage as he convulsed with the new wave of pain. "You act like you're the only one with friends. If you had bothered to take a look around, you would have seen all the cameras in my apartment. I have the footage downloaded to an undisclosed site that I alone have the key to. I don't think your friends will touch you with a ten-foot pole. You are officially persona non grata, my dear sir."

It was Jay's turn to smile. "You think you're so smart, don't you? Cameras are a double-edged sword. If I go down, you go down. What do you think a jury will say to you torturing me on your kitchen floor? I'm a defenseless man totally incapacitated, being held hostage by Anika Washington!" he said the last part for the cameras.

She gave him a look of astonishment, "Either you're stupid or you think I'm stupid. What makes you think I won't just simply edit the footage or destroy it all together? You really haven't thought this through. . ."

The doorbell rang and they both looked up. Anika made her way over to the door casually and when she opened it, Jay began to scream for help. The police officer walked through the door, followed by a plain-clothes man who must be a detective. Both of the men looked at the screaming man on the floor and turned back to Anika with a questioning look.

"So you gonna tell us what happened or just let me guess?" the plain-clothes detective said as he stared at her. Before she could answer, he began to speak. "He forced his way into your apartment and you struggled by the front door. You managed to free yourself and made your way over to a stun gun and were able to incapacitate him and call for help. Tell me I'm right."

Anika smiled. "Close, but this ratbastard was smart enough to make a copy of my key, and he was waiting on me when I came back from the club for Iliana's bachelorette party."

"Oh, how's she doing? Is she really going to go through with it?"

Anika shook her head. "Yeah, it appears so. Love is blind."

"Love is fucking retarded, if you ask me."

Jay's hopes died on the vine as he observed the casual tone between Anika and the plain-clothes officer.

The two laughed like old friends as they reminisced about old times.

Finally the officer's stare fell on Jay and his blood ran cold. "So what's his story again?"

Anika rolled her eyes. "I told you before. He broke in my apartment and tried to *teach me a lesson*. I fought him off and got to my stun gun and lit his ass up."

The plain-clothes officer began to scratch the back of his head "I'm sorry, Anika, I'm gonna need more than that."

Anika gave a dramatic sigh as she made her way over to her desk and brought back her laptop. She brought up a program and waited for the officer to make his way over. She replayed the footage from the cameras to about twenty minutes before she came home. The recording showed

Jay entering her apartment and removing her stun gun from the closet and turned off the lights, waiting.

As he watched the rest of the events unfold, he looked out the corner of his eye at Jay with a murderous look. Jay began to panic as he looked to the officer in uniform and only saw open contempt on his face.

They watched the events to their conclusion until they arrived. Everyone remained silent as the tension in the room began to build. The detective looked at Anika. "So what do you want to do? You want to press charges? We have enough evidence here to guarantee that he will do time. Attempted rape, assault, breaking and entering; any one of these things is enough to put him in jail for a minute."

Anika thought for a moment and then her eyes fell on Jay. He had tears streaming down his face, and he silently begged her not to press charges. "Nah, I don't want to press charges at this time, Officer." Jay let out an audible sigh as he began to visibly relax. "I want you to beat the breaks off of him. Don't kill him; just beat him enough to make sure he never does this again."

Jay was holding his breath as he saw his fortunes balancing on the tip of a razor's edge. He knew that even if he was convicted, he wouldn't do jail time. His lawyers would pick the authenticity of the video apart and more than likely get it dismissed. But what she was proposing was a different animal altogether.

The officer stared at Jay as he contemplated her decision. Then he gave a wicked smile. "I think we can arrange something to your satisfaction."

Jay looked at the officer in uniform in hopes of finding mercy, but once he saw the look of pure rage on his face, he knew that all hope was lost.

Anika made a copy of the video for the detective and erased all footage of their conversation and then turned off the feed. "When you're done, drop him off at his address in whatever condition you see fit so his wife can see what a piece of shit he really is."

The detective walked over to Jay, and he immediately started begging for them not to hurt him. "Hey, bruh, don't start crying now. We haven't even hurt you yet. You see my friend over there? Well, his mom had a boyfriend when he was growing up who used to beat her and his brothers and sisters. One day they came home and he was touching their little sister. She tried to stop him, and he beat her to death with a chain. Me personally, I just don't like bullies. So, do yourself a favor and just be quiet. Take it like a man or a bitch. Really doesn't matter but know this: this is happening."

The police officer walked over to Jay and brought him roughly to his feet. Jay began to snivel, but he saw the hard look on the officer's face and he quickly fell silent. The officer turned him around and placed handcuffs on him. Jay offered no resistance, resigned to his fate.

Anika made her way over to the door and opened it. The officer began to lead him away when the detective stopped him for a moment so he could place his jacket over Jay's head.

She gave him a questioning look and he said, "The fewer questions asked, the better."

The officer led Jay through, and the detective followed when she touched his arm and he looked at her questioning, but before he could make a comment, she grabbed him in a tight embrace and began to cry.

He wasn't sure if she was or not, but when he felt her body shake with the effort, he knew that she couldn't contain the emotions anymore. He held her gently, letting the feelings run their course.

"Thank you, Anthony, I don't know what I would have done if you didn't come."

"Come on now, you were there for me when nobody else gave a damn about me, including my family. You are closer to me than any family member, and I will always be there for you no matter what. That's what we do for each other."

She handed him the disc with events of the evening on it, and as her face hardened, she said, "Make him hurt."

The smile faded from his face "Oh no doubt. This shit won't happen again, I promise you that."

After everyone was gone, she felt the events of the evening crash in on her, and she collapsed on the couch and the tears fell with earnest.

Sunday morning came and Anika was still on the couch wrapped in a bathrobe and the doorbell rang. She made her way over to the door, but before she could open it, she heard a key turn and the door open. Her heart jumped in her throat as she pulled out the stun gun, thinking that somehow Jay escaped and was now coming back seeking revenge. This time she would be ready.

As the door opened, she saw her grandmother Evelyn walk through the door and nearly fall over at seeing Anika standing there pointing a stun gun at her head.

"I'm sorry. I thought you were going to church with me this morning. If you didn't want to go, all you had to do is say so!"

Anika threw the stun gun on the couch and ran to her grandmother's side. "I'm so sorry Grandma. I thought you were someone else."

Evelyn looked around the apartment and saw that it was a total wreck. She saw the bags under Anika's eyes, and she knew something had to have happened. "I'm fine, dear. Why don't you tell me about all of this?" she said as she waved her hand around at the utter carnage.

Anika gave a sheepish grin. "It's nothing, I just had a few friends over and things got out of hand, that's all."

"Uh-huh. . ."

"I'm fine Grandma. I'm a big girl, and I can take care of myself."

Uh-huh. . . I don't know what's worse: you lying to my face or the fact that you're so bad at it."

"Like I said Grandma. . ."

"JUST STOP IT! If you don't want to tell me, that's fine, but don't disrespect me by lying about it. I can plainly see that something happened and I'm pretty sure I know who it happened with."

Anika looked around her apartment, and she hardly recognized it. There were broken picture frames, turned-over furniture, and glass everywhere. She looked down and noticed the belt that Jay used to beat her with, and the tears began to flow again. Her grandmother grabbed her into her arms, and Anika let her as the tears continued to flow. "It was Jay."

Evelyn's jaw tightened as she thought about him putting his hands on her. "Now I understand why you had that stun gun. I'm so sorry, babe. I should have seen this coming. I knew he wasn't about nothing, but I knew if I told you every time without letting you see things for yourself, you would never learn to trust your own instincts." Evelyn began to cry. "This is my entire fault! I'm gonna get some big jailhouse brothas to kick his ass!"

Anika said in a whisper of a voice, "No need."

Evelyn leaned back, causing Anika to raise her head and look her in the eye. "What did you do?"

"I did pretty much as you suggested; I called up Anthony and he took care of it for me."

Evelyn was starting to become nervous, "What do you mean he took care of it?"

"Well, I told him to beat the shit out of him but not to kill him. I asked him to drop him off at his house so his wife can see what a piece of shit he really is."

"Oh." was all she could say.

Both women just sat there on the floor, holding each other for comfort. When Anika sat up and began to stretch, she started to rise and head towards her bedroom.

Evelyn looked at her with a look confusion. "Where are you going sweetie?"

Anika gave her a strange look "I'm going to get ready for church. The last thing I need to do is sit around here feeling sorry for myself. That won't make my situation any better, and besides, what better place to go than church to receive the good word?" she said as she ran to get ready.

Evelyn could only shake her head in wonder as she watched her granddaughter pull herself up by the boot straps and continue on. She doubted if she herself had that much strength.

"What a remarkable woman," she thought.

CHAPTER FOUR

It was a sunny Monday morning as Anika made her way into the office. She was greeted by several employees, and she just smiled and nodded back.

Anika made her rounds to her staff and greeted everyone personally. She was about to go into her office but was stopped by Shawna, her personal assistant.

"Good morning, Ms. Washington. There is someone here to see you."

"I thought I told you to stop calling me Ms. Washington. Just call me Anika. Ms. Washington makes me sound old. Do you think I'm old, Shawna? Do you?"

Shawna began to look around sheepishly "I'm sorry."

"Oh, for heaven's sakes, I'm just messing with you!"

Shawna visibly relaxed, "there is someone here to see you. He was here when I got here, I told him to wait in your office, if that's okay?"

Anika got ready to tease her some more, but she knew it would only make Shawna even more uncomfortable so decided against it. But it was tempting. "It's fine"

She peeked into her head into her office and saw the young man from the club sitting on her couch reading over something, no doubt his resume. He didn't notice her watching him as she slid back out of her office. She turned around and asked Shawna if she knew his name.

She shook her head. "No, he wouldn't tell me. He said he was only giving that to you. He said he was the waiter from Saturday night."

Anika gave a smirk. "Figures."

She waited for Anika to give some clue of the evening, but nothing was forthcoming. Shawna may be shy and quiet, but she was a notorious gossiper. Anika really liked her and she did excellent work. She figured the best way to deal with her would be to tell her nothing. She can't gossip if she doesn't have anything to gossip about.

"Hold all my calls. I'm going to be doing an *interrogation* for the next hour or so."

Shawna knew the meaning of that statement. Most people who do interviews want to know what you have done and what school you went to. But Anika wants to know if you can do the job. It doesn't matter what school you attended, how many awards you've won, or who you know. The bottom line is: what can you do?

More than a few have left one of her interrogations mumbling under their breath that they thought they had the job in the bag, only to leave humiliated. On more than one occasion, people have left in tears, man or woman alike, it matters not. She wants the best person for the job because mistakes are frowned upon and work ethic is something that is held in the highest regard. She doesn't ask for more than your best, but your best is what she demands.

Anika walked into her office, ignoring the young man sitting on her sofa as he rushed to his feet as he notices her entering the room. He extended his hand in greeting, but Anika blatantly ignored it. He stood there, uncertain what to do next.

It took everything within her not to bust out laughing, but she held it together. She had to know what he was made of. She read a few emails and, made a couple of calls when she noticed out of the corner of her eye the young man picking up his papers and slamming them back into his briefcase, heading for the door.

"Where do you think you're going?"

He turned around to regard her. "Look, I don't have time for games. I thought you were about your business, but I see that I was wrong. You have a blessed day," he said as he made his way out the door.

"Come back."

"Nah, I'm good."

"Please?"

When she said that, he took a deep breath and closed the door. He waited a moment before turning around, gathering his composure. Finally in control of his emotions, he turned around to face her. "I know I may not be your first choice. Hell, I might not even be on your radar. But the only thing I ask of you is to treat me with the same respect that I imagine that you would like for me to treat you with. If that's something that is within your doing, I will stay, deal?"

Anika couldn't help but smile. "Deal."

"A'ight cool. My name is Deshaun."

"Pleased to meet you. Why don't we get this interview going, shall we?"

It was Deshaun's turn to smile. "I think I would like that."

The interview went on for more than two hours. Shawna was bursting at the seams to know what was going on in there. She called on more than one occasion to "check on her", but Anika told her everything was fine and she will call if she needs anything.

The temptation was to the point that she couldn't take it anymore. She knew she would get yelled at, but she had to know what was going on in there. As she reached out for the handle, the door opened and both them walked out laughing. Anika shot her a blazing glare, and she could tell by the look that she was in trouble. She dropped her head and went back to her desk.

Shawna felt her heart drop in her chest as they both made their way over to her desk. "I can explain. You see it was so quiet in there, I wanted to make sure you were okay," she said as she shot Deshaun an apologetic look.

"We'll discuss that later. In the meantime, I would like to introduce you to Deshaun. He will be the new buyer."

"Pleased to meet you," she said as Deshaun greeted her in return.

"Oh and Shawna, could you please cancel the rest of the interviews?"

"Yes, of course." Anika could tell that she was upset. But she didn't know that Anika knew one of the candidates was her boyfriend. She thought that she was able to slip the application in unnoticed, but she couldn't have been more wrong. Anika knew the moment she had Shawna setup the interviews.

We have all done stupid things for love, she thought. An image of Jay crossed her mind, and she felt a shiver run up and down her spine and the events of the other night started to play throughout her memories. She quickly suppressed the memory and continued on her original line of thought. There are two things she hates: a liar and a person who doesn't have enough decency to tell her a good lie. Shawna was there with her from the beginning, and she would hate to let her go. She figured she would give her the chance to come clean and then see if she could rebuild the trust they once had. At this moment, she wasn't so sure.

"Do me a favor, Shawna, and show Deshaun to the empty office down the hall, will you?"

"Yes, of course," she said as she began to walk toward the office, not seeing if he was even following.

"Did I do something wrong?" Deshaun asked, a little concerned by the expression on Shawna's face.

"No, it wasn't you, it was me," she said as she stood with her arms crossed as she watched her walk down the hall. "You should probably catch up with her."

"You're right," he said as he hurried to catch up with the angry assistant.

Anika shook her head as a smile crossed her face as she headed back into her office to attack the mountain of work. And for once she was happy for the distraction.

The weeks went by without any incidents. Anika was able to get Deshaun up to speed, and he was doing well. Everyone seemed to like him with the exception of Shawna, who still held a grudge with him getting chosen over her boyfriend. The argument that she and Anika had over her trying to get her boyfriend a job at the firm was one to remember as the office staff still are talking about it.

The situation came to a head when Shawna stormed out of the office, cursing and yelling at anyone who was dumb enough to get caught in her crosshairs. Shawna stood by the elevators with her arms crossed. Anika came storming out of the office behind her, determined to get the last word in. They were both at the elevator screaming at the top of their voices, trying to gain an edge in the battle of words. They both began to feel self-conscious as everyone was watching them have it out and the elevator still wasn't there.

The seconds ticking by felt like hours as neither was willing to give ground. The elevator finally came, but as the doors opened, both women stood with their mouths agape as it was packed tight. Neither woman was able to get on, nor did either one wanted to try and look foolish in the process.

"Oh come on!" Shawna said as the frustration came to a head. She looked at the stairs, but the thought of climbing down seventeen flights to the ground didn't appeal to her. She turned to face Anika with a withering stare. "You could have at least given him a chance. He might have surprised you!"

"I might have considered it if you didn't try and play me! I thought we were better than that. Haven't I always been there when you needed me?"

Shawna's anger waivered when she thought about all the times she was indeed there for her. She remembered when her parents put her out for dating a man they didn't approve of. She knew it was because he was black, but they never would admit it. She is a blonde-haired, blue-eyed southern belle, and it would seem unseemly for her to be seen with someone other than from their circle.

She remembers how she let her stay with her until she could get a place of her own. She even bought most of the furniture for her place. She called it a loan that she could pay back with loyalty. Shawna began to get angry all over again, but she knew it wasn't directed at Anika this time. This time, it was at herself.

She knew that she should have asked her to look over his resume instead of trying to sneak him into the pile of potentials. Hindsight made her feel even smaller when she considered that Anika trusted her, but she always double- checked everything. But like a true southern woman, it was hard for her to admit her fault. But with the preponderance of evidence staring her in the face, how could she not?

"I think I might possibly be wrong. I'm not saying for certain, but possibly." She said with a sheepish look on her face.

Anika had a look of stone as she stared at Shawna. Anyone that didn't know her would think that she was about to explode. But Shawna knew her better than most. She could tell her eyes were smiling. And when the corners of her mouth began to twitch, she knew that maybe there was a chance to salvage this situation.

"I guess I'm sorry too for calling you all those names and possibly other things that you might not have noticed yet?" she said as she walked up to whisper in her ear.

No one knows what was said, but the look of shock on Shawna's face was priceless. She whispered in Anika's ear, and it was her turn to look on with shock. "Delete it" was all that was said. Shawna only nodded.

Anika began to walk back to her office but turned to see Shawna with her arms folded staring at her.

"I'm going to delete it. Get off my back."

Shawna could only smile as she followed her back to her office.

"Hey, Shawna, is Anika in her office?" Deshaun gave her his best smile. He was rewarded with a frown and her rolling her eyes.

"Yes, she's in her office."

"Thanks," he said as he made his way towards her door.

"Wait, I didn't say you could go in."

"But she's expecting me. I told her I would be right there."

Shawna paused for a moment, looking up at the ceiling. Deshaun wasn't sure what she was looking at, and he began to look up at the ceiling as well.

"What are you doing?"

Deshaun looked down and saw Shawna just staring at him. He got ready to explain, but she cut him off.

"You can go in. She's been expecting you."

He got ready to say something nasty but thought better of it. "Thanks," was all he could muster.

"Uh-huh"

Deshaun entered Anika's office and saw that she was on the phone. She waived him over to take a seat. He did as he was bidden as he began to look around her office. He's been here numerous times, but every time he comes in, he notices something different. This time it was the stun gun sitting in a case. He wondered how he missed it all those other times that he was in her office. He wanted to ask, but one thing she made very clear during his interview: private lives are private for a reason. He took her at her meaning at once.

Anika finished her conversation and hung up the phone. She turned to Deshaun with a smile on her face.

"I was looking over your proposal for increasing numbers in the New York territories. I must say, they were pretty good. The only fault I see is in the delivery or more to the point, the person delivering it."

"I don't follow."

"I want you to do it. You've been here long enough and you have excelled at everything I've asked of you thus far. You know the business better than some people who have been here for years, and I think you're ready."

Deshaun sat back in shock. "Don't you think I'm too young for this? I mean, do you think they will take me serious?"

"Don't be ridiculous. You got me to take you serious within ten minutes and anyone who knows me knows that isn't possible."

Deshaun's face began to blush as he doesn't handle compliments very well.

"Oh stop, being a little girl. You know that you're perfectly qualified for this. We're going next week, so make sure that you're packed and ready to go."

"We?"

Anika had a puzzled look on her face "You thought I was going to send you by yourself? This is your first time going out. I have to make sure you know what you're doing. Can't have you fucking up on my watch."

"Uh, thanks, I think."

She gave him a wink "Have Shawna make travel arrangements for the first flight out on Monday."

Deshaun had a funny look on his face. "Uh, I don't think she really cares for me."

Anika smiled. "No, she's just confused and really, really stubborn. Trust me, she doesn't dislike you. If anything, she probably. . . never mind. Just tell her. If she gives you any trouble, tell her to come see me. That'll shut her up for a minute or two," she said as she laughed.

Deshaun shook his head as he left her still laughing in her office. When he walked out, he noticed Shawna staring at him with an intense look. He felt slightly uncomfortable, but this time, he wasn't going to let her get the best of him. He kept eye contact as he walked over to her desk and was rewarded with her looking away first. "I need you to book two first-class tickets for Monday to New York for Anika and myself."

She just stared at him. "Okay" was all that she said as she gave him a funny look.

He was starting to feel uncomfortable, and he walked away before it became apparent to her.

She watched him walk away until he went into his office. A smile crossed her face.

This didn't go unnoticed as Anika was watching the whole exchange from her doorway. She crept back in her office quietly so as not to be seen and silently closed the door.

The afternoon wore on as Shawna was finishing typing up the proposal for Anika when she heard her swear and come storming out the door.

"Why didn't you tell me I had an appointment this afternoon?!"

Shawna had a look of puzzlement on her face. "You never told me you had any appointments today."

Anika paused as she considered her words "You might be right, but you still should have known."

"Okay. . ."

She stared at her assistant for a moment and then an evil smile spread across her face. "When you finish that report or whatever it is that you're doing, I want you to take Deshaun out for coffee and bury the hatchet. When you're done, you can go home. How does that sound?"

An evil smile of her own spread across her face "Can I use the corporate card?"

Anika thought for a moment. "Yes, but don't get ignorant with it. I will be reviewing the expense report."

"Fine."

Anika turned to leave but stopped and turned back to Shawna. "I really need you to ease up on him. He's really is a good guy. If you're mean to him, I will find out," she said as she let the threat hang in the air.

CHAPTER FIVE

Anika came rushing into the lecture hall like a tornado. She ran to the podium and looked at her watch and smiled. "I made it on time!" She looked up and felt like a deer caught in headlights as the auditorium was packed and they were all looking at her as if she had two heads.

She projected an air of confidence that she really didn't feel at the moment and removed her coat and laid it across the stool behind her. "Hello, my name is Anika Washington and I will be subbing for Professor Wynn today."

She silently cursed herself for letting him talk her into subbing for his class. "Pay it forward" was his motto, and he instilled that into her when she was just a young clueless freshman trying to understand the world around her. He not only said, but he lived the ideology. He was always willing to help those who were willing to put forth any type of effort, even if it was half-ass. He believed as long as there was effort, there was something to work with.

She looked over his notes and just sighed when she saw his lesson plan. Just strike up a conversation and let them do the work for you. *Is that what he did with us?* she thought.

"As I was saying, my name is Anika Washington and I'm vice president at Indies Financial. I'm head of the automotive financial division. I oversee financing for large dealerships and for subprime buyers. So, does anyone have any questions?"

"Actually, yes, I do," a voice says from the crowd. Anika was unable to locate them due to the light shining in her face and the lack of light on the audience.

"Okay, what's your question?"

"What does this have to do with journalism?"

Anika was annoyed by the obvious attempt to throw her off, but she wouldn't take the bait. "Journalism, you say? If you don't know what you're talking about, how are you going to write about it? That's the quickest way to lose credibility."

Another voice spoke up. A woman's, was the next to ask a question. "If you're not in the journalism field, how is it that you're qualified to teach this class? I don't mean any disrespect, but, what can we actually learn from you?"

Anika was starting to fray at the edges, but she would be damned if she lets a class full of kids who don't even know what the real world is like get the best of her. "I'm glad you asked, whoever you are. Less than one out of a hundred journalism students will actually make a career out of it. And looking around your class, I would say there are not even a hundred people in here. So the odds are not one of you will actually be a journalist, so who is wasting whose time?"

There was a murmur among the class as they weren't expecting that type of response. Anika's eyes were beginning to adjust to the light, and she was able to make out her audience. She could see small groups of students huddled together conversing among themselves. The spotlight that was shining on her was beginning to annoy her so she looked around to find the light switch. She located it on the far wall and made her way over. She turned, the light off and the whole class turned to see their advantage had been taken away.

"That's better. Nice to be able to see you all at last. So where were we?"

Among the chaos, Anika saw a man sitting in the front row with his hand raised causally. She had to almost do a double take because he was absolutely beautiful. From what she could tell, he had a low-cut hairstyle, with dark caramel skin and brown, penetrating eyes. She found herself subconsciously playing with a small tusk of hair as she admired him. She became aware of her actions and quickly started straightening papers on the podium, hoping he hadn't noticed.

If he noticed, he didn't give any indication as he waited with his hand raised as if he had all day. He noticed that she was looking and gave her a smile.

Anika felt her chest rise quickly as he had the nerve to have a smile that could light up a room. She noticed that he had a goatee that was perfectly trimmed that framed his full lips that deviously concealed his smile that she was sure tortured many a woman with the promise of more. Quickly putting her walls back up, she acknowledged him. "Yes, you with your hand raised. What can I do for you?"

At hearing her speak, the class became quiet. They noticed who asked the question, and there were a few cat-calls and several grunts. She couldn't tell where they were coming from, but she knew it was a man's voice.

At having been given the floor, the young man stood to address her. Anika swooned on her feet as he stood over six feet tall, with broad shoulders and a defined chest. He wore a long-sleeved pullover shirt, but it did little to hide his physique. Anika noticed other women in the class staring as well, and she felt a twinge of jealousy. She pushed those thoughts to the side as she drank in more of his appearance.

She could tell that he must be an athlete of some kind because no man usually looks like that who isn't. Anika stared at his arms, and she saw the promise of bulging muscles underneath. She wondered absently what they would feel like wrapped around her waist as he raised her up against his body as she wraps her legs around his back and. . . She caught herself as the room seemed to heat up with sexual tension.

Anika waved him back to his seat, but he remained standing. "I'm sorry, I was raised to respect those in authority." He looked around the room, and his classmates diverted their gaze from his. Satisfied that his point was made, he turned to address Anika once more. "I have been reading up on the possible merger of your company with Alliance Financial. If this is true, how does that affect your department considering they're in the same line of business that you previously mentioned?"

Anika was absently thinking how deep his voice was when she realized he was speaking to her. She thought for a moment about what he had said and realized he had a valid point with his question. She really hadn't considered all the possible ramifications of the merger. She wasn't worried about her position with the organization; she knew if they were stupid enough to let her go, she would have another job before the close of business making more money than she was presently. The people Anika worried about most was those "caught in the middle." Deep down her concern was with the people who have been with the company ten-plus years, making double the amount in salary of the new employees to the position. If they were to start letting go of the people on her staff, that's where they would start. She knew a lot of them had families, and it's hard out there in the workforce. She felt her heart go out to them.

Returning her thoughts to the present, she answered, "At this point in time, the situation is still fluid. We are currently weighing our options and trying to make the best decision for the company as a whole with an eye toward the future."

He regarded her for a moment, "So basically, you don't know."

Anika's mouth fell open with astonishment. *Who does he think he is to make such assumptions about me!* she thought to herself. "To say I have a concrete answer at this time would be premature at best, but to say I don't know or don't have a clue is rather irresponsible, don't you think?"

She felt a slight smug smile attempting to crack the corner of her mouth as she saw him fumbling for an answer. The rest of the class was looking on as he suddenly became quiet, not seemingly knowing what to do next. She was ready to move on to the next question as a number of students had their hands raised when she noticed he looked up at her with those damn penetrating eyes again.

"I never said you didn't have a clue. Those were your words, not mine. I simple asked a question that was hardly a secret, but your response was rather interesting. Sometimes what you don't say, says more than what you ever would have thought."

"Excuse me?" was the only response she had at the sudden turn of events. She thought she had him effectively silenced when he skillfully turned her throw-away statement into an indictment of her knowledge. If she wasn't so pissed and profoundly embarrassed right now, she might actually be impressed.

"Well, I asked a question that I knew you had prepared based on your position and your obvious involvement with the merger. I wanted to gauge your response to the question so as to get an idea or possibly a clue as to what happens next. I didn't mean to offend you; I just wanted to try out an interview technique that I learned a while ago."

Anika was curious about his education. "And where might that be?"

"The streets." He looked on without a hint of shame or embarrassment.

She wondered if she felt the same way when she was in school. That was a question for another time as she wondered about the man in front of her. He was certainly pleasing to the eye, but now she knew there was more to him than just good looks and a chiseled body.

The class went on for another half hour or so. Anika couldn't tell as the questions kept pouring in, and she found herself truly enjoying the experience. She looked up and noticed that the hour had passed by and she was rather disappointed that it was over so soon. She dismissed the class and began to gather her things.

She noticed everyone leaving except for the young man still sitting in his seat casually as his classmates left to attend other classes. Once everyone had left, he stood up and walked toward her. Anika felt her heart skip a beat as he made his way over.

"I wanted to wait until the class was over so I can apologize to you. I honestly didn't mean to show you up. It was just as I said; I wanted to gauge your reaction, that's all."

Anika momentarily lost her voice as the man she has been silently admiring since she entered the classroom was standing not more than six feet from her. She felt like a school-girl all over again and she didn't like it. "What makes you think that you showed me?"

He cocked his head slightly to the side as he began to smile. "Okay, if you say so. . ."

"I just did," she said as she folded her arms.

"Okay."

"You know, you really think you are so smart, don't you? Using your charms and sex appeal to try and intimidate me. That won't work on me, mister." She immediately regretted the words as they spilled out of her mouth.

He began to laugh. "Sex appeal? Intimidate? I'm going to leave it at that before my sex appeal causes you to faint. We can't have that."

Not knowing what to do now as the situation got away from her, she resorted to her only option, she stormed off. She heard him chuckling behind her as she headed toward the door. The fact that he got the best of her annoyed her to no end.

Anika turned around to try and gain back a measure of pride but was stopped in her tracks as he was standing closer to her than she realized. He wasn't more than three feet away, and she could smell his manly scent that sent a shiver down her back. She didn't dare to speak as she didn't quite trust her voice at that moment.

He didn't expect her to turn around so abruptly, as he nearly came crashing into her. He took a step back, giving her personal space back. "Look, I shouldn't be teasing you since you are my instructor and I don't know you. I was totally out of line."

Anika regarded him for a moment. "Nah, you're good. To be honest, you did kind of catch me off guard."

He sighed, relieved that he didn't make the situation worse. He looked down for a moment, not sure of his next course of action. Anika looked at him quizzically when he looked up with a determined look on his face. "Look, I'm done with classes for the day and I don't have to be at work anytime soon and I was wondering if you would like to have coffee with me. I know a place on campus that isn't too bad, and it will give me a chance to make it up to you properly."

Anika felt her pulse racing yet again at the young man addressing her. "That's a tempting offer, but one, I'm much older than you. Two, I don't think it would be a good look for us to be seen together outside of class. Your classmates might get the wrong idea."

He nodded his head as he looked her in the eye again with those damn penetrating eyes of his. "My name is Kendrick, Kendrick Watts. To respond to your statements in order: one, that wasn't an offer, it was for coffee. If I made an offer to you, it wouldn't be in that manner, trust me. Two, you're not my instructor. Professor Wynn asked you to cover for him because we ran off all the other student aides and he was desperate; and lastly, I don't give a damn what anyone has to say about what I do or don't do."

She felt her defense weakening as his logic was winning her over. She held on to her last line of defense. "I'm too old to be hanging out with someone of your age. I'm probably old enough to be your big sister."

He chuckled. "You're probably, what, twenty-seven? I'll be twenty-eight next month, and again, it's just coffee." He stepped past her to open the door for her. "I'm not in the business of asking someone more than twice to do something with or for me. If you don't want to, that's fine, but just say it and stop making excuses."

Anika knew she shouldn't, but at the moment she couldn't think of another reason not to. "So where is this coffee place you were going on about?"

They walked a short distance to the coffee house and they sat in a quiet corner talking. Anika felt extremely comfortable just talking about the school and some of the professors they had in common. She completely forgot about the reasons why she shouldn't be there and that little voice inside of her head was all but mute at that point. If anything, it was urging her on.

She began to giggle as he talked about his encounter with Professor Woods. She was notoriously known for seducing her finer-looking men in her class in exchange for a better grade. He talked about how she subtly made advances in the beginning, but as the class wore on, her tactics became more bold.

One time she had him come to her office because there was a "*discrepancy*" with one of his papers. He went on to explain how she offered to make the "*problem go away*" in exchange for special services that only he seemed to be able to provide.

Anika was sitting back, subconsciously twirling her hair with her legs crossed and chewing on a coffee stirrer. "I can understand where she's coming from." She immediately realized that her statement wasn't said in her mind but came roaring out her mouth before she realized it. She sat up stone straight and prayed that he wasn't paying attention.

If he noticed, he had enough graciousness to not let on that he knew as he continued with his story. "So I simply told her 'no'. She threatened to go to the ethics board and bring up charges of plagiarism. I called her bluff and reminded her that she herself had a reputation of the very thing I was going to bring up myself. I told her I wonder which one they were more likely to believe."

"So what happened?" Anika was curious to see the outcome of the events.

"Nothing. She stopped making advances and she graded me based on merit alone."

"What grade did you wind up getting? An A+, I imagine?"

"Nope, I got a well-earned B+. I was late on an assignment because my computer crashed at the house and didn't have time to get a new computer until the next day. I think my grade was fair."

"Well, I'm glad that you didn't get too bad of a grade. I know how hard it is to bring up a bad grade. Believe me, I had a few in my time." Anika laughed as she took another sip of her coffee.

Kendrick laughed in turn as he looked at his watch. He looked disappointed. "I'm sorry, but I have to go. Work calls. I really enjoyed the cup of coffee. I hope you did as well."

"But of course."

"Good." Kendrick got ready to say something else but thought better of it as he grabbed his jacket to leave.

He gave her a smile as walked past her. Anika turned around suddenly as he was about to walk out the door. "Would you like to have dinner tomorrow?" She realized she said it louder than she intended to as the people next to her stopped to see what his answer would be.

If he noticed the people at the other table, he didn't acknowledge them as he never took his eyes off hers. "I'm sorry I won't be able to do dinner tomorrow because I have to work, but I only have one class tomorrow, so I will be available for lunch if you have time?"

Anika said yes quicker than she wanted to. *What's wrong with me?* she thought to herself. He smiled and walked out the door into the chilly afternoon air. She realized that she didn't get his number and grabbed her jacket to follow after him. She walked outside and saw him waiting for her with a smile on her face.

"You aren't used to this, are you?"

She giggled. "Is it that obvious?" She buttoned her coat up as the air began to bite.

"Just a tad bit," he said as he held his figures an inch apart.

"Listen, I came out here to. . .,"but before she could answer, he gave her his number on a piece of paper.

"Hit me up when you know what time you'll be free. Like I said, I'm free after my morning class."

She smiled again as she turned up the collar on her jacket as the wind picked up. "Okay." A gust of wind blew her scarf off of her shoulders and fell to the ground. Before she could bend over to pick it up, Kendrick had scooped it up and placed it around her shoulders. She felt a flutter in her stomach as he slowly draped it across her shoulders and tied it loosely around her neck.

"Don't worry, I got you," he said as he whispered in her ear as the wind began to blow more gustily.

Anika felt her mouth dry up as excitement rushed through her. She felt him pull away as the moment was gone. She wanted more than anything at that moment for him stay close to her a little while longer. Maybe a lot longer. She didn't know, but she knew it wasn't long enough. For once that day since meeting him, she was able to control her urges and was glad.

She stood there as he walked away toward wherever he was going until he turned the corner and was gone. Anika was left with her own thoughts as a torrent of emotions ran through her. Like many times in the past, she would over-analyze a situation until there was nothing left. But this time she fought the urge and won as she let the feelings wash over her and basked in the thought of him.

Anika tried to go back to work, but she found it next to impossible to concentrate so she decided it was better to leave than mess up something that she will only have to fix later. She knew she was too wired to go home so she decided to go see her favorite lady, her grandma.

Evelyn opened the door and Anika all but floated into the room. She wondered what had got her granddaughter so excited and she was swept up in an embrace as Anika hugged her and laughed at the same time. Soon she found that she was laughing as well. The two women made their way into the den, and they both sat on the sofa.

Evelyn finally caught her breath and was able to talk. "Child, what has got you so happy? Did you get another promotion at work again? I swear you spend more time at work than you do anywhere else. You're going to work yourself into the ground."

Anika had a bright glow on her face as she smiled. "I met a guy!"

Evelyn thought of Jay for a moment but buried the thought. She didn't want to get caught in the trap of thinking every man was the same, and she was glad to see that her granddaughter didn't pick up that destructive trait. She smiled patiently. "So tell me about this young man you met. Is he hot with a hard body?"

"Grandma!" I didn't know you thought like that."

"Hey, I might be your grandmother, but I'm still all woman." She ran her hands up and down her sides, letting her know that she still had a shape.

And indeed she did. Her grandmother always believed in taking care of herself and worked out regularly, a habit she thankfully passed on to her. Anika continued. "To answer your question, yes, lord his body is banging! He has a smile that can melt ice and he is smart too. I was subbing for my old, Professor Wynn, today, and he was in the class. He had the nerve to try and show me up! Can you believe that?" Anika thought back on the moment and a ghost of a smile crossed her face.

Her grandmother took the opportunity to tease her. "So you're robbing the cradle now? Don't you think you're a little too young for that? I mean, you should at least wait until your forty!"

Anika waved her hand, dismissing the jab. "No, he's my age. Actually, his birthday is next month, and he'll be older than me then."

Evelyn felt her curiosity rise to the surface. "So tell me more about him. Did he start school late because he was in the military?"

Anika thought for a moment and then she realized that she didn't know that much about him. They had talked for hours and she really hadn't learned anything about him. She felt a moment of doubt, but she quickly buried it. She wasn't going to let doubt ruin her fun. She wanted to have fun for once, and he seemed like he would be ideal for that. She let her mind wonder for a moment and then she thought about his body and she felt her body start to get warm. She looked up and noticed her grandmother looking at her, waiting for answer to a question that she forgot was even asked.

"I'm sorry, Grandma, I got lost in my thoughts for a moment."

Evelyn patted her hand. "Don't worry dear, it happens to us all at some point." She gave her a knowing smile.

Anika thought for a moment that maybe she had read her thoughts and she felt her cheeks flush. She pushed the thought aside to answer her question. "To be honest, I don't know all that much about him. I know that he's getting ready to graduate from school with a degree in journalism. I know that he has a job after work. I don't know what he does because I didn't think to ask him that, but don't worry, we're meeting for lunch tomorrow."

Evelyn's heart soared at finally seeing her granddaughter smile again. She just hoped it wasn't fool's gold.

CHAPTER SIX

Anika arrived at work with a bounce in her step. She walked up to Shawna and gave her a hug, leaving the other woman with a look of shock and confusion. Not knowing what else to do, she hugged her back.

Anika pulled back with a smile on her face. "I need you to cancel my afternoon appointments. Just reschedule them for tomorrow or something. Whatever you think is best."

Now Shawna was starting to get worried *whatever I think is best? I hope she hasn't finally cracked up,* she thought to herself. "Yes, of course."

Anika walked into her office and Shawna followed closely behind. "You wanna tell me what's going on? Are you sick or something? I know a good doctor who can help you with this sort of thing, and he's very discreet."

Anika raised her eyebrow. "What sort of thing do you mean?"

Shawna looked as if it was the most obvious thing in the world. "You're having a nervous breakdown. I knew it would happen sooner or later. You spend so much time here and you never go out, so it was just a matter of time."

Anika frowned. She didn't like where the conversation was heading. "I'm not cracking up or having a breakdown." She moved to stand next to Shawna, which caused her to take an involuntary step backward. Anika ignored her reaction as she moved close enough to whisper in her ear. "I want to tell you something and if you tell another person, I'll fire you and then the real fun will start. Do you understand?"

Shawna was offended at the negative connotation that was attributed to her, but she ignored it for the moment as her curiosity won out. "Okay, what is it? Are you pregnant or something?"

"No!" Anika said into her ear which caused Shawna to jump back. She apologized quickly for yelling into her ear. "I'm sorry for that, but that was stupid. I would have to be seeing someone, and we both know that isn't the case."

Now Shawna was truly confused. "Then what is it?"

Anika was almost bursting at the seams when she yelled "I met someone!" She looked around quickly to see if someone might be listening.

Shawna couldn't help but laugh. She has known Anika for more than three years, and she can probably count on one finger how many men she has gone out with. She went out with that one guy named Jay, but she had a bad feeling about him. She didn't want to overstep her bounds and butt in where she doesn't belong, so she kept that to herself.

She didn't know when that ended, but she knew something had happened because Anika was quiet, withdrawn for a few weeks, but she didn't want to pry so she let her be.

But this was different. This time she wanted to tell her, and she was more than happy to hear her boss's good news. She figured that if she got out of the office, she would finally get a life, and in turn, she would stop being so overbearing. But if she was truly honest with herself, she knows that Anika is the best boss she has ever worked for. She respects her opinion and she only gets on her when she messes up. She treats her as a friend. She doesn't know if that's just her personality or not, but that's how she chooses to see it.

Shawna reached out to hug her, and Anika jumped at the chance to hug her back. Both ladies stood there giggling like two little schoolgirls as they rocked from side to side with excitement.

Anika whispered in her ear. "Now remember, don't tell another soul or else."

Shawna was brought back to reality as she extricated herself from Anika's embrace. "Yeah about that, what makes you think I ever tell your business?"

Anika looked at her as if she had told a joke. "Come on now, everyone in here knows that you're the biggest gossiper in the company."

Shawna stood wooden at hearing that someone she considered a friend would say something like that. She fought back the tears as she gathered herself. "Let me ask you something, Anika. Have you ever heard something about you? Have you ever heard something about someone else that you told me?"

Anika thought for a moment, but she couldn't remember a time.

"Just as I thought, you're no different than the rest of them. You know why people always attribute gossip to me? Because I don't give a damn what people say or do. Did I listen to the gossip? You better believe it, I wanted to make sure that nobody was trying to cut you off at the knees and you didn't know about it. I come here to do a job for you, and I make damn sure I do my best every damn day. Do you think I care what those other losers have to say? Hell no, you wanna know why? Because I thought I worked for the strongest woman I've ever met. I truly looked up to you, did you know that?"

Anika was left speechless. All this time she naturally assumed that Shawna was at the heart of all the gossip in the office. She never once thought to question it. She knew she had truly hurt someone who had considered her a friend, and in truth, she consider her a friend as well but never really thought about it in that sense until now. "I-I'm sorry, I just assumed that what I heard was true. I honestly never considered that you were actually looking out for me."

"Anika, I'm proud of the woman you are and in truth, I want to be like you. Why would I ever do something like spread your business out in the streets? I'm trying to get where you're at, not pull you down to my level. That only shows that I can destroy, not grow."

Anika didn't know what to say. She felt profoundly guilty over her assumptions and actions toward Shawna. She knew without a doubt that she was wrong. Her grandmother told her that anyone can say they're sorry but to show it takes those words to a whole new level. "I have an idea on how to fix this, but give me a few days to see if I can make it work, okay?"

Shawna thought for a moment as she weighed her options. Anika could probably tell that curiosity was threatening to get the best of her. She knew if she asked now, it would totally undermine her whole grand speech. She was having a hard time trying to control her face, but once she saw sweat beading on her forehead, she had to turn her head and feign a cough to keep from giving herself away.

Shawna noticed Anika had turned her head suddenly and she became instantly suspicious. She stared at her for a moment, silently trying to figure out what she was up to. She knows Anika, and with that, she knows that whenever Anika apologizes for something she has done wrong, she follows it up with an act of kindness that is both sweet but nerve-racking at the same time.

She remembers one time when Anika apologized for spilling coffee on her new jacket. The next thing she knew, they were at Saint Matthews Mall buying a brand-new jacket with an outfit to boot. She tried to stop her, explaining that just simply dry-cleaning the jacket would have been more than enough, but Anika wouldn't hear of it. She threatened to demote her to janitor if she didn't take it. Of course, she said yes. Who wants to waste a great manicure on scrubbing toilets?

Shawna finally relented. "Okay, fine, but do me a favor: don't go over the top this time, okay? You know how that makes me feel."

Anika opened her mouth in shock as she made an exaggerated motion of putting her hand to her chest. "My dear, why would you ever assume I would do anything of the kind?"

"Uh-huh. . ."

Anika dropped the act and turned to look at her friend with the most sincere look she could muster. "I really am sorry and I will take your feelings into consideration before I do anything this time, okay?"

Shawna smiled. "Okay'.

"Cool, let's go get some coffee. I need some caffeine and a double shot of espresso. I didn't get any sleep last night!"

Shawna had to know so she asked. "Why not?"

Anika looked down at the ground, almost too ashamed to tell her. "I was up all night picking out a song for us."

She stopped walking and Anika stopped to turn and see why. "You're serious too, aren't you? And he hasn't so much as kissed you yet, has he?"

Anika shook her head.

Shawna threw her hands up in the air in disbelief. "Come on, boss. Let's get you some coffee so we can sit down and talk about the birds and the bees because obviously you weren't paying attention the last time!"

Anika lowered her head even further due to the embarrassment. Shawna looked at her and felt sorry for the predicament that she has gotten herself in, and she placed her arm around her. "Come on, let's just get you some coffee and see where you're at after that, shall we?"

Anika nodded as they got on the elevator. Shawna couldn't help but smile. It's not often that a woman as strong as Anika needs her help. She was glad that she confided in her, and she wasn't going to let her down.

Anika was waiting at the Japanese restaurant for Kendrick to arrive. She picked a location close to campus but not too close, and she wanted to make sure that it was upscale but she didn't want to come off as uppity. She looked at her watch for what seemed like the hundredth time when in actuality, it wasn't more than five times at most.

She arrived thirty minutes early because one, she wanted to make sure they got a good table because this restaurant doesn't take reservations and they're crowded around this time. Two, she was extremely nervous and wanted to try and sneak a drink in before he got there so she could calm her nerves.

She had the bartender bring her the strongest shot they had. He kind of looked at her funny when she asked. He tried to explain to her that it wasn't a weak drink, but she hushed him up with a twenty-dollar bill to just make it and not explain it. He shrugged and made the drink without further comment.

He passed her the drink, and when he saw that her intentions were to down it in one gulp, he tried to warn her, but it was too late. "Ma'am, let me get you a pitcher of ice water because I fear you're going to need it."

He brought the pitcher of water over to the table, and she shot him an annoyed look. But as the moments passed, she felt the drink taking effect. Her mind became somewhat sluggish, and she felt her tongue begin to hang from her mouth. In short, she was drunk. She was probably drunker than she had been in years; maybe since college.

The bartender noticed her head swaying and rushed over discreetly but with a hint of urgency. "I tried to warn you. That drink ain't no joke. Please tell me you didn't drive here?" She gave him a sheepish grin and shrugged her shoulders. The bartender rolled his eyes and poured her a cup of a hot, dark drink.

Anika noticed him pouring her another drink, and she tried to wave him off. She tried to voice her objections, but the words didn't seem to come out right.

"It's not alcohol. It's coffee. It's a rather strong brew that we don't sell in the restaurant. Drink this and you'll feel better soon." "He looked at her and felt sympathy. "Are you meeting someone here?"

She nodded meekly as she took a sip of the coffee. She took a swallow and her eyes grew big as saucers. She got ready to speak, but he placed a hand on her arm. "I know it's strong and most people can't handle it but it's what you need right now."

Anika's eyes were still as big as saucers as she pointed at the cup and gave a thumbs-up sign. The bartender was surprised by her response. People have had all sorts of reactions to his special coffee, but that was the first time that someone actually liked it. Seeing that his job was done, he turned to walk away when Anika placed her hand on his arm. He turned with a curious expression on his face.

"That. . . is probably the best coffee I've ever had in my life! Do you know how I can possibly buy some?"

He smiled at the compliment. "Actually, I make it at home. I can do up an order for you if you're really serious."

"Hell, yes!" she whispered so as no one else can hear. "That coffee really took the edge off of that drink. I'm sorry I didn't listen to you originally. I could have saved myself the embarrassment and humiliation if I wasn't so nervous." She thought for a moment. "Nah, it worked out like it was supposed to. I wouldn't have gotten this delicious coffee if I had." She handed him her business card and thanked him again.

He turned to leave but stopped to regard her. "It truly was a pleasure to meet you" he looked down at her business card---"Ms. Washington." He smiled as he walked away.

Anika sat there sipping on her new favorite coffee. She was lost in her thoughts when she felt someone looking at her. To her surprise, Kendrick was sitting across from the table looking at her with his penetrating eyes. "When did you get here?"

"Not that long ago. I was just sitting here watching you think. Do you know that when you're thinking, your eyebrows go up and down? It's kinda cute."

Anika felt the familiar butterflies in her stomach. She remembered the questions that her grandmother asked and she couldn't answer. She wasn't going to make the same mistake again. She wasn't going to let her physical needs triumph over her logic. "Thank you. I was thinking and I have a few questions for you."

Kendrick gave a slight smile as he looked down at the table. "Ah, I take it that you've talked about me to friends or family. You've come to the realization that you don't know anything about me." He looked her in the eye to make a point. "I don't have anything to hide. I'm an open book. I don't play games. I'm a grown-ass man. I want you to judge me by the man that I am, not by who I used to be or what your perceptions or fantasies portray. Agreed?"

She was taken aback by his boldness and candor. Anika doesn't date often. She can count on one hand how many times she's been on a date in the last seven years. They all seemed nice in the beginning but inevitably let her down. She always considered herself a practical woman, a woman who accepts a person's limitations and shortcomings. There were times when all she wanted a man for was sex, but they always seemed to put their foot in their mouths and ruined the moment. She chose to focus on her career, and her love life was what suffered as a result.

She remembered Jay and it brought a chill. The thought of their last encounter brought an unsolicited shiver down her spine. She took a sip of wine, trying to control her nerves. She set the glass down carefully, fearful that she would spill its contents.

Kendrick noticed her hands shaking, and he placed his on top of hers, giving silent support. Anika gave him a bright smile that she really didn't feel. The moment became too much for her, and she gently removed her hands and placed them on her lap.

He could tell something was bothering her by her actions. It wasn't something that she wanted to discuss. Not wanting to pry, he poured himself a drink and offered to refill hers, which she readily accepted.

They sat in silence for what seemed like forever. Anika knew the date was going south, and in her current emotional state, she didn't know what to do to bring it back. She silently cursed herself for letting him get to her after all this time. She had gone to see a therapist, and he helped her through the worse of it. He had warned her that there will be times when thoughts of the event will come up but not to let it consume her. She was less than successful.

Anika felt her stomach drop as she realized that she had let herself down and probably turned off what seemed to be a good guy. She was ready to admit defeat when he did something totally unexpected. He stood up and walked over to her chair and gently grabbed her hand, bringing her to her feet and gave her a hug.

She stood woodenly for a moment, totally taken off guard by the gesture, but she warmed up quickly. She felt herself melt into his embrace as he held her gently, content to just be there for her. She noticed the restaurant had stopped their conversations briefly as they eyed the two of them standing there in an embrace, but Kendrick totally ignored them, giving his full attention to her, and she couldn't express at that moment what that meant to her.

He didn't know her, and he damn sure didn't owe her this. There was no ulterior motive; he didn't try to cop a feel, not that she would have minded in the least. He was simply there for her. She found him to be a decent human being, and that solicited a powerful emotional response from her that she wasn't ready to deal with.

She regretfully disengaged herself from his embrace. She was unable to make eye contact at the moment, not quite trusting herself at that time. She looked down and found her seat. She felt him sit down across from her. She chanced a quick peek and saw him looking at his menu intently.

Anika suspected that was more for her benefit than anything else. "Thank you for that."

Kendrick never looked up from the menu. "Think nothing of it. That's what friends are for."

Friends? She thought to herself. *I guess I'm not good enough to date? Well, his loss. He probably isn't on my level anyway!* Anika picked up her menu and raised it so that he couldn't see her pouting.

Kendrick smiled to himself. He hasn't met a woman quite like her, he lamented. She was strong and determined while being vulnerable and unsure all at the same time. She was a woman who was truly worthy of getting to know.

"So, I can tell you got a lot on your mind and you don't seem that interested in eating. I have an idea, if you're up for it?"

Anika wasn't sure what he had in mind, but she was open to pretty much anything at that moment.

"I haven't done this in years, so don't you dare laugh at me!" Anika said as she stood with the bat on her shoulder, waiting for the first pitch. She saw the ball coming at her, and she ducked quickly out of the way.

"I think you were supposed to swing at the ball, not run out of the batter's box," Kendrick said with a grin on his face as he tried not to laugh. Another pitch came, and this time she swung at it, missing badly and making a full 360-degree turn in the process. That proved to be too much as he burst out in laughter at the scene before him.

Anika heard him laughing, and she became more determined to hit the ball. She saw another pitch come her way and she swung with all her might and the bat flew out of her hands and hit the cage in front of her, which brought a renewed round of laughter from Kendrick.

Anika was fuming by this time. She wasn't going to let this stupid ball get the best of her. Another pitch came and another miss. By now she was cursing under her breath as she was unable to hit the ball.

"Try relaxing and stop trying to murder it. You want to try and make contact, not hit a home run," Kendrick said as he was starting to feel sorry for her.

Anika took his advice as the next pitch came. She did a controlled swing and was rewarded with contact. The ball jumped off her bat and landed between second and third base. She jumped up and down, and she beamed with pride.

"You might want to pay attention because you still have a few more balls left."

Anika was brought back to reality as Kendrick's words reminded her that she wasn't done yet. She hit three more balls by the time she was done. She was sweating as she walked out of the batting cage toward Kendrick with a big smile on her face.

He saw her walking towards him with a giant smile and he couldn't help but to return it. "You did really well for somebody who hasn't done this in a while."

"Second." she panted.

"Second what?"

"Second time I've ever done this," she said as she sat down at the table and took a drink from her bottle of water.

"Now I'm really impressed," he said as he looked at her with open admiration. He grabbed a towel out of his gym bag, and he began to wipe her brow. He noticed her looking at him with an unreadable look on her face, but she didn't object. He noticed sweat was dripping down between her breasts, and he felt his cheeks reddening and he looked away. He placed the towel around her neck, and not knowing what else to do, he grabbed his bottle of water and took another drink.

Anika was pleasantly surprised when Kendrick had begun to wipe the sweat off of her brow. She felt her body start to tingle as he touched her, even if it was with a towel. She didn't want to let on just how much his touch was affecting her so she kept her mask up. The simple act of him wiping sweat from her was bringing waves of pleasure as she felt her mask starting to crumple.

Thankfully he stopped. She wasn't sure how much more she could take as the act of him touching her was exquisite torture. When he placed the towel around her neck, this gave her the excuse to turn away so she could regain her composure and wipe the sweat from between her breasts.

They spent the rest of the day together just enjoying each other's company. They went and ate hot dogs in the park, and went for a long walk while simply getting to know each other. Time had gone by faster than either one of them wanted, but it was time to part ways.

They both stood at her car door in awkward silence, not knowing what to say or do. Neither wanted to say goodbye because that would bring an end to an enjoyable day that neither wanted to end just yet but knew it would have to eventually.

Anika was just standing there like a school-girl, which was becoming the norm when around him. She found the time she spent with him to be so natural that it was almost like they had been friends for years. *Friends,* she thought to herself again. She was definitely feeling a connection, but she didn't want to seem too eager so she would let the next move come from him. After all, she asked him out to lunch!

A look passed across Kendrick's face, but she wasn't sure what it was as he finally spoke. "I really had a great time with you today, Anika. I'm really glad that we took some time out of our busy schedules to just chill. We should do this again soon."

Anika didn't know what to expect from Kendrick, but she was profoundly disappointed. She thought he would at least set a date for the next time or even give her a hug, something. "I really had a nice time too. Yeah, we should probably hang out again." She couldn't totally keep the disappointment out of her voice.

"Look, my work schedule is gonna be crazy the next couple of weeks and I got these classes that are kicking my butt. I'm sure we'll work out something." He smiled as he opened her car door for her.

"Okay," she said, crestfallen. She thought that maybe there was more there between them, but she guessed she was wrong. She sighed silently to herself as she remote-started her car.

When she started her car, Kendrick took it as his cue to leave. He didn't want to do too much too soon. After all, she was a big-time finance lady working at a top firm and he was . . . just a guy working at his cousin's repair shop who hasn't graduated from school yet. He knew he was selling himself short but not by much.

Kendrick got a late jump on life due to decisions that he made in his past. He wasn't a choir boy by no stretch of the imagination, but he was a decent person. He woke up one day and he knew he had a decision to make . . . get on the right track or keep doing what he was doing. He decided to make more of himself, and he made a change. It was as simple as that.

But nothing is ever that simple. There are always obstacles. He cut off all of his old friends he used to run with and the women he used to deal with. He learned quickly that those who don't see a future for themselves don't want you to see one either. They will go to great lengths to keep you down. He thought back on all that he went through and where he is today.

I'm a better man, he thought to himself. At that moment, he made his decision.

Anika watched Kendrick turn to walk away when she started her car. She wanted to turn it off, hoping he would stay just a little longer. But what was the point, she thought. He seemed to have made his decision.

She watched his back for a moment longer before turning to get in her car.

"Hey."

Anika turned around and Kendrick was standing before her. She was getting ready to say something when he grabbed her in his arms and began to kiss her. She was shocked at first but quickly rebounded as she returned the kiss.

He lifted her up in the air as he held her around the waist. Her feet dangled in the air as his powerful arms held her aloft. Their tongues fought for supremacy as they kissed each other passionately. They both lost track of time as they continued to feed off each other's passion.

Kendrick finally lowered her back to the ground as Anika's feet met concrete for what seemed like for the first time. They continued to give each other light kisses as their lust started to ignite again. It was he who finally broke away, but she could tell that he wanted more, much more.

"I have to say something," he said through a lust-filled voice. He took a moment to gather himself and then he spoke again. "What I was saying earlier wasn't bullshit. I do have a lot going on right now, but I will make time to see you very soon, I promise. The reason why I didn't say that earlier was because I didn't want to make it seem like I was making excuses."

Anika had to agree with his assessment. She was all but convinced that he wasn't that interested in her, and she would have taken it as him making excuses.

He grabbed her into his arms and lifted her off her feet again, this time so she could look in his eyes. "A person always makes time for things that are important to them. I will see you soon."

With that, he lowered her gently back down to the ground. She was hoping for more kisses but was slightly disappointed as he took a step back. "Good night, Anika," he said as he held her car door so she could get in.

He waited until she was in and buckled up before he closed it. She immediately rolled down the window, and he bent over to rest his chiseled arms on the door frame. He reached inside of the car and gently extracted her hand and placed a soft kiss on the back and then rolled it over and placed one on her palm.

When he kissed her palm, it was like she was being shot full of electricity. She felt her body go weak as he stroked her palm with his finger. Anika had to pull her hand away because her body was responding eagerly to his whims.

Kendrick gave her a knowing glance as he smiled at her. "You drive safely and let me know when you get in so I know you're okay."

She gave him a nod and a smile as he stepped back and she drove off. The drive home was full of thoughts of their kiss and the promise of more. She remembered how strong and safe his embrace felt. She remembered how he lifted her into his arms as if she weighed nothing. But most of all, she remembered his words.

He didn't have to explain himself, but he wanted to, which is what stuck with her the most. He laid himself bare before her, and let her know what his intentions were. She knew that took courage for him to expose his emotions like that. Too often people take advantage of vulnerability, and she appreciated that he felt comfortable enough with her to show it.

She arrived home after a long day. She considered taking a bath but decided against it due to how exhausted she was. She planned on doing some work that she had put off, but once she sat down on her bed, she knew that just wasn't going to happen. The last thing Anika remembered was receiving a text back from Kendrick letting her know that he had received her message that she made it home safely. He wished her a good night's sleep, and she drifted off with a smile on her face.

Kendrick had every intention of calling Anika, but he barely had time to breathe, let alone talk on the phone. This is his last year at school, and he is due to graduate in the fall. He could have waited until the spring to graduate, which would have been easier on him, but he didn't see a good reason to put it off. Figured he could sleep when he was dead.

To make things even more hectic, his cousin, Rich, had to fire one of his longtime employees at the shop because he caught them stealing from him. It was problematic due to the heavy clientele, but he was happy for the additional hours. Kendrick tried to get Rich to bring someone else on, but he really didn't have time to interview anyone.

Kendrick also has been planning for his future. He really didn't know how to break into the journalism business so he did the next best thing: he hired a headhunter to find him a job. His only criteria was somewhere in the Midwest and enough of a salary that he can pay his bills. He'd figure the rest out as it came. No point in worrying about something until you know what exactly you're worrying about.

Kendrick has always been a laid-back person ever since he was a child. His nickname was K-Smooth growing up, because he always had a plan. It was seldom that you would see Kendrick without a smile, but when that did happen, it was because someone violated his cardinal rules.

There were three things you didn't do in his world: fuck with his family, his neighborhood, or his money. As long as you stayed on the right side of those three things, you would never have a problem. If you didn't know any better, you would think he was the kindest, most mannerable person you could have ever met. He would give his last dollar if he thought it would help you, regardless of the inconvenience to him.

There was this dealer who moved into his neighborhood trying to move crack. He found out because he had heard from one of the dudes who was locked up with him. His name was R. G. and he had a reputation for eliminating his problems. Most people tended to steer clear of him whenever possible. But Kendrick was never one to shy away from doing what he figured was right.

He went to him man to man, showing respect and asking him nicely not to deal in his neighborhood. R. G. clowned him and threatened to put a bullet in his head while he was asleep. This didn't faze him as Kendrick said what he had to say and left, totally ignoring the man's threats.

The next day, Kendrick got a call from his aunt saying that his niece is in the hospital because she overdosed on some drugs she got from a new dealer on the block. He immediately started checking around on who it could have been, but deep down inside, he already knew. From that point, he was on the hunt for R. G.

It didn't take long for him to locate where he was. In truth, he wasn't hiding. If anything, he was open about the fact he intended to run this neighborhood like his own personal kingdom. It didn't bother him in the least that he was putting bad product out on the streets because he figured that if he was the only dealer in the area, they won't have any choice but to use his regardless.

Later that night, R. G. was home with his new girl, an underage girl that he got hooked on his product. Among other things, he was a pedophile who liked them young. Often-times if his advances were rebuffed, he would simply kidnap them and get them hooked on his product. If they were lucky, he would put them to work on the streets . . . if they were lucky. Those less fortunate wouldn't be heard from again, and no one would speak up for fear of disappearing themselves.

Kendrick knew all this and more in his search to find him. As he entered the house, he found R. G. in the bed, sleeping with his new victim. No one knows what happened from that point, but to this day, they still haven't been able to locate him. The police didn't consider it a great loss and quickly gave up trying to locate him, if they even tried.

It wasn't long after that when R. G.'s lieutenant turned up missing. The word on the street was that he was hiding out in a cabin in the woods. They found him with his throat slashed and a look of total shock on his face. No one knew who did it, but from that point forward, there hasn't been another drug dealer who tried to get a foothold in the neighborhood.

The girl who was in his bed, who had been missing for over a week at that point, was found at the neighborhood rehab clinic. She had gone into shock, and the doctors had said that it was from the drugs in her system. Others thought it was from the traumatic events that she was exposed to.

She never spoke of what happened that night, but from that point forward, she was a different person. No longer did she spend her days skipping school and her evenings trying to get high. Now she was a committed student who spends her evenings at church or helping out in the neighborhood. She's due to graduate from school on time and enlist in the Navy to serve her country.

From that point, Kendrick spiraled down a road of alcoholism and depression. He had distanced himself from his friends and family and started keeping company with an unsavory crowd. He was rumored to be involved in one violent act after another, but no one could definitively link him to it. He would go missing days at a time, and when he returned, he never mentioned his whereabouts.

Kendrick was brought out of his thoughts by a knock at the door. He tried to ignore it as he felt his mood growing dark yet again as thoughts of his past came back unbidden. They knocked again, but this time they pounded on the door with their fist. He looked through the peep-hole and sighed once he saw who it was. His first instinct was to leave them knocking at the door, but he knew eventually it would grate on his nerves and he would open it anyway. *Why put off the inevitable,* he thought.

Kendrick opened the door and stepped aside so they could enter. He could tell from the look on her face that it was going to be one of those conversations.

"I know you heard me knocking out there. What took you so long?"

Kendrick felt his nerves beginning to fray, but he wouldn't give her the satisfaction. "And hello to you too. What do you want, ShaBree?"

She could tell that she struck a nerve, and it brought a smile to her face. "Nothing. I was just stopping by seeing what you was up to. Oh, and you know I hate when you call me that. Call me ShaSha, please, and thank you."

"Whatever."

"I just got in from work, and now I got to knock out my schoolwork as well." He opened the door and pointed toward the exit. "Now you know so you can leave."

She ignored him as she walked into the living room and took off her coat. She plopped down on the couch, putting her feet up on the table, and grabbed the remote. Kendrick moved his table out of the way, causing ShaBree's feet to drop to the floor. Not one to be deterred, she put her feet up on the couch, which caused Kendrick to lose his temper.

This is what she was waiting for.

Kendrick stormed over and rudely grabbed ShaBree's feet and threw them to the floor. But before he could act, she spread her legs wide, revealing that she was naked underneath her already short dress. She saw him glance at her womanhood, and she bent her legs seductively. "What's the matter, boo? I remember a time when you would have already had me bent over the back of your couch screaming for you to stop, but we both knew I really didn't want you to," she said as she winked at him and ran her tongue seductively over her lips.

He rolled his eyes. "Look, ShaBree, I don't have time for your games. I got work to do."

"So will you have time to play later? I need you to beat it up. Nobody, and I mean nobody, has ever fucked me the way that you used to." A smile played across her lips, but underneath her smile, there was a look akin to desperation.

"That was in the past. I'm a grown man, and it's time for me to put away childish things." He gave her a knowing look. He tossed her jacket at her, and it landed in between her legs, effectively ending her seduction.

She could tell by his mood that play-time was over, but in reality she got exactly what she wanted. She needed to know if she could still get a rise out of him after all this time, and she was satisfied with her answer.

ShaBree made her way over to the door, and Kendrick opened it to help her along. As she walked over to the door, she took the opportunity to let her eyes roam over his body, and she wasn't disappointed. He was standing there, and she could see muscles bulging beneath his shirt and then she let her eyes roam down to his man region. Her breath caught in her throat and she remembered more than saw how he felt between her legs. She almost missed a step at the memory of him stroking her to ecstasy and beyond.

She stopped in front of him and looked up into his eyes. She felt herself becoming aroused just being next to him. His scent had drifted into her nose, and she began to swoon. Her hands started to caress his chest. She could feel the hard muscle beneath his shirt as she moved her hands farther down to his pants. He grabbed her hands, ending her impromptu exploration. His body is still as incredible as she remembered. She had a mini temper tantrum and the abrupt end to her fun, but she took it in stride.

ShaBree looked past him out the door and noticed that it was pitch black outside. She gave him an innocent look. "It's pretty dark outside Kendrick. Why don't you be a gentleman and walk me home?"

Kendrick stepped past her and looked out the door. "Yeah, it's pretty dark out there, but it was dark when yo ass got here. Besides, isn't that your car over there?"

ShaBree looked down at the floor which gave her away. "Hey, I had to try." She went to her tiptoes and kissed him on the cheek. "I'm not giving up on us."

"Good night, ShaBree."

"It's ShaSha."

"Whatever," he said as he closed the door.

Kendrick knew his day was going too good when she showed up. It never fails that she always comes around when he's feeling good and hopeful. It's like the universe is conspiring against his happiness.

He knew he could do one of two things: sit around pouting and complaining about his situation or do something about. He chose the latter.

Kendrick spent the rest of the evening working on his school assignments. It wasn't until he was on his third or fourth cup of coffee that he realized what time it was. He looked at his watch and moaned inwardly. There was no point in going to sleep now; he has less than two hours before he was due to get up, so he figured he would get his workout in early.

He quickly changed clothes and grabbed his headphones. He was going to drive to the gym but thought better of it. He needed to clear his head, and there was no better way for him to do that than to go for a short run. The gym wasn't more than a couple miles from his house so, he figured he would incorporate it into his workout.

Kendrick arrived at the gym feeling rejuvenated after his short run. He made his way to the counter to check in and was greeted with a smile from the office staff. He had been going to this gym since he was a kid, and he was familiar with everyone who worked there.

After making small talk with some of the staff members, he made his way to his locker to retrieve his workout gloves and belt. Today was going to be a heavy-lifting day.

He walked over to the area with the free weights and saw a few familiar faces. He had known most of them growing up from the neighborhood, but a few moved there recently and they quickly got along.

"Sup, Kendrick! You here kinda early, ain't you?"

"Hey, Josh I was up all night and it was too late to go to bed so I figured I would get it in early today." Kendrick said as he walked over and to greet his longtime friend.

"You was putting in work huh?" Josh gave him a knowing smirk.

"Nah, bro, I was finishing up my schoolwork. This last semester has been tough! Between that and work, I barely have time for myself. Good thing I'm almost done."

"Hey, I feel you on that, but like you said, you're almost done."

Kendrick gave him a nod as he went over to the rack and retrieved two dumbbells and began doing hammer curls. Josh came over and grabbed a wooden staff and began doing upper body stretches with it.

"Hey, Kendrick, have you heard that Lawrence is back in town? My boy saw him the other day at the pool hall with two other dudes. I guess he's doing well because he said he was buying drinks for everybody and flashing money."

"Oh yeah? I'm glad he's doing all right for himself," Kendrick said as he continued to do his sets, never stopping to acknowledge him.

Josh noticed Kendrick's odd response. "Just like yo ass, always taking the high road. I remember what you said the last time you saw him."

"That was a long time ago. We had a fundamental difference of opinion at the time. It's been a while. Let's just let that shit lay where it is . . . the past," Kendrick said as the frustration was becoming apparent on his face.

"Oh, that's cool. Whatever gets you up in the morning." Josh noticed the turn of Kendrick's mood and realized he touched a nerve. He tried to change the subject. "I saw you at the batting cages yesterday with a fine-ass lady. Me and my wife were going to come over and speak, but I didn't want to kill y'all vibe. You two looked like you were really enjoying each other's company."

This time, Kendrick did stop his workout and turned to regard his friend. "Yeah, she was cool," Kendrick said as he couldn't stop smiling.

"She must have been more than just cool because yo ass hasn't stopped smiling since I mentioned her. She must have put it on you or something."

"Something like that," Kendrick said as he continued to smile.

Josh put the bar down and walked over to stand in front of Kendrick.

Kendrick saw that he wanted to get serious and set aside his dumbbells as he gave his longtime friend his undivided attention.

He waited until he had his full attention before he continued. "You know how I was before I met Marile. I went from one woman to the next, not really giving a fuck about tomorrow. I'm not gonna sit here and pretend all of the women before her were no good. They were fine women who would have made any man happy, but they weren't my happiness. It wasn't until I met her that I realized what I was missing. God blessed me more times than I can count when he placed her in my life. What I'm trying to say is that if you find that in someone, don't let that pass you by. That type of love can transform the hardest man into something more."

Kendrick knew what his friend was saying was true. He had known Josh since elementary school and he always had a temper topped off with a mean streak that more often than not got him into trouble. They used to run the streets together, and people gave him a wide berth because they didn't know what if anything was going to set him off.

He once broke a man's legs because he stepped on his shoes in the club. His only response was that "I bet he won't do that shit again." Needless to say, he was a ticking time bomb.

It wasn't until he met Marile did his life begin to change.

He was set-up on a blind date with her through his aunt who said, "All he needed was a good woman in his life." But he always countered with, "All I need is my money, my niggas, and my weed. Everything else will work itself out."

The first thing he noticed was that she wasn't impressed by his clout, nor was she afraid of him. This was something that he wasn't used to. He would normally tell a woman who he was, and they would want to be with him on name only. This woman was different and something inside of him wanted to get to know her better.

For weeks she would blow him off. First it was because of his approach, and then it was because he always came over to her home smelling like weed. He even resorted to threatening her, which she dismissed as a child's tantrum. It wasn't until he showed up at her door in a suit bearing flowers did she finally acknowledge him. They have been together ever since.

"I'm just saying, she must mean something to you because yo ass is always running around up in here with a frown on your face like somebody ate yo big piece of chicken. Now you giggling like a little bitch at a Trey Songz concert."

Kendrick tried to hide his smile but failed miserably at it.

"Look, nigga, I can't be hanging with no soft dudes. You gonna have to correct that shit pronto."

Kendrick knew his friend was joking when he started smiling. "So when we gonna get to meet this lady? I have to see what all the fuss is about."

"Yeah, we gonna set something up real soon. I wanna take it slow with this one. I'm not trying to rush into anything just yet, but I do wanna know what she's all about."

"I feel you. Now if you done being a little sensitive bitch, maybe you can spot a real nigga on these weights."

Kendrick rolled his eyes as he got ready to come back with a crack on his boy when Josh held up his hand asking him to hold up.

He fished around in his pocket and retrieved his phone. He looked at the caller ID and smiled when he saw who it was. "What's up, boo?" he said as he got up and walked a short distance away outside of earshot.

Kendrick smiled as he watched his friend transform before his eyes into the doting husband. He went back to doing his workout as he occasionally heard his friend laugh out loud at some perceived joke.

He finished his last set as Josh walked back over. When he finally reached Kendrick, the familiar scowl was back. "Nigga, I thought I asked you to spot me? We got a problem?" Josh said as he sat on the bench impatiently waiting on Kendrick.

It took Kendrick a second to reconcile the man who was just smiling and laughing on the phone to the hard-as-nails dude in front of him now. "Yeah, I got you, but you gone need to correct your tone for real," he said as he grabbed the weight to help him lift it off the stance.

"You know I'm just fuckin' with you. Half these dudes in here run around scared, but you keep it real and I respect that. Besides, we go back to diapers and baby bottles."

Kendrick just shook his head at his long-time friend's viewpoint. "I gotta ask you, how do you turn it off?"

"Turn what off?"

Kendrick was struggling for a way to articulate his point. "I mean how do you go from being like how you are now to all sweet and loving with you wife?"

Josh looked at him as if he lost his mind. "It's simple: I love my wife and I made a promise to her that I would honor her above all else. I never promised that for the rest of you."

Not knowing what else to say, Kendrick just muttered, "Oh."

"So you gonna keep talking like you on Oprah or are you going to spot me?" Josh said, looking clearly annoyed with the line of questioning.

"Yeah, I got you."

CHAPTER SEVEN

Anika woke up with a smile on her face as the sun rained down on her, gentling nudging her to begin her day. She hopped out of bed, ready to conquer the world. She had enough foresight to lay her clothes out for the day last night before she went to bed. She made a pot of coffee and quickly jumped in the shower. By the time she was dressed, the coffee was ready, and she headed out the door to start her day.

She arrived at the office earlier than normal, which caught Shawna off guard. "You're here earlier than normal. Did you accidentally set your alarm clock early?" she said, clearly trying to get a rise out of Anika as she followed her into her office with a cup of coffee in tow.

Anika shook her finger at her with a smile on her face as she knew what Shawna was trying to do. "Not going to work. I'm in too good of a mood for your foolishness today!" she said as she took the offered cup of coffee and beamed. "You got that coffee I told you about?!" she said as she smiled while leaning back in her chair, enjoying the taste.

"But of course, what type of assistant would I be if I didn't?"

Anika closed her eyes to enjoy her unexpected cup of coffee. "I take it you want to know what happened yesterday," she said as she opened one eye to look at her assistant. "Buttering me up with a cup of coffee? Please, I thought you would come with something better than that. . ."

Anika was cut off as Shawna presented her with a warm sticky bun. "You think that was all I had? You don't know me very well," she said as she topped off her cup of coffee.

"You know bribes will get you everywhere, right?" Anika said as she took a long sip of her coffee yet again as it elicited an audible sigh. "Well, it worked."

Shawna smiled as her plan worked. "You thought it wouldn't? I've been working for you too long not to know what your weaknesses are. So spill, what happened?"

Anika burst out laughing. "I was going to tell you anyway, but thanks for the gifts. They are much appreciated!"

"Whatever, I was going to do them anyway," Shawna said with a pout as her plan was thwarted. "It's my job to make you happy, boss."

"Uh-huh, let you tell it," Anika sighed. "I guess I can tell you if you're interested." In truth she couldn't wait to tell her. She did her best to compose herself as she tried to hide her smile. She paused for effect until Shawna started twirling her hand, prompting for her to reveal her secrets.

"Look, bitch, you going to tell me or what?" Shawna said as her patience was clearly at their end.

Anika was going to tease her about the bitch comment, but she knew she was going too far with the teasing so she let it pass. "Well, if you must know, the lunch was a total disaster. I started drinking before he got there, and I was pretty hammered when the waiter came over and gave me that delicious coffee." Anika smiled as she took another sip of the delicious brew. "Anyway, the coffee helped sober me up, and that's when he showed up."

"Okay, keep going . . ." Shawna said as she topped off Anika's cup yet again, who readily accepted.

"By this time I started feeling sorry for myself and was ready to call the whole thing off when he did something totally unexpected." She leaned back in her chair as she reminisced on the experience.

Shawna clapped her hands in front of Anika's face, startling her. "Focus, damn! You can get all wet and gooey later. Some of us actually have to do work to make a certain someone look good!" She looked at her pointedly.

"Sorry, I was just . . . never mind. As I was saying, he stood up in the restaurant in front of everyone and . . . hugged me. I know that doesn't seem like much, but I was really freaking out and it was like he just knew what I needed. He didn't want anything: acknowledgment, sex, money, favors . . . nothing. He just wanted to be there for me. I have never had a man do that for me before."

Anika looked up from her cup of coffee to see if she still held her attention, and she noticed Shawna had a faraway look on her face. She didn't say anything as she continued. "I thought the date was over at that point and likely would be the last time I would see him. But he surprised me yet again."

"What did he do?" Shawna said as she sat forward in the chair, hanging on her every word.

"He took me to the batting cages. He said I needed to blow off some steam because he thinks I carry the world on my shoulders. Can you believe that?"

Shawna said nothing as she quickly took a suspiciously long sip of her coffee and avoided eye contact. Anika knew there was a story behind her actions, which she filed away for another time, when she least suspected. She knew she hated that as she hid her devilish smile inside. "Anyway," she said as she rolled her eyes, "we just sat around and talked as we ate. We just sat back and had a normal conversation until it got dark and he walked me to my car."

Shawna had a smirk on her face as she waited for the story to get juicy. She could tell Anika was holding out on her, and she was bursting at the seams to find out what. "Look, I'm gonna need you to do better than what you're doing. When telling a story, you need to tell the whole story and stop glossing over the juicy bits!" Shawna said, clearly annoyed by Anika's deliberate pace. "If this is how it's going to be, I'm sure I can tell just as bland a story as you when it comes to my love life. Get to talking!"

Anika burst out laughing as she saw that her friend's face was now beet red with frustration. She noticed that she was struggling to regain her composure, which caused her laughter to renew in force. She noticed Shawna getting up to leave, and she did her best rein in her laughter. "I'm sorry, please stay. I just couldn't help but tease you a little bit. You make it way too easy."

Shawna tried to hide her smile. "That's not funny. You know I hate when you do that!"

"You're right, I'm sorry. You still want me to tell you? I'm going to be serious this time, okay?"

"Yeah, aight. Hurry up 'cause I got stuff to do."

Anika instantly put on her boss hat. "What do you need to do? Do I have any meetings this morning?"

Shawna quickly threw up her hands to ward off the barrage of questions she knew would soon follow. "Not literally! It was a figure of speech!" She gave Anika a weird look as she leaned back in her chair, which she didn't realize until then that she was halfway out of it. "I think I need to choose my words more carefully from now on. You really need to get laid." She shook her head and smiled in amazement. "Speaking of getting laid . . .finish your story, please?"

Anika switched back into girlfriend mode, and she continued with the story. "So he walked me to my car, and we stood and talked some more. I was feeling all kinds of chemistry with this man. He was wiping sweat from my forehead, and it was all I could do to stand still!" She paused to take another sip of the delicious coffee and relish in the memory of his touch. She felt another smile creep across her face but quickly regained her composure or risk Shawna's wrath.

"Anyway, we were standing at my car door and neither of us was saying anything. I remote-started my car hoping, that would give him a little push to make a move."

Shawna laughed. "Oh, that was real subtle. I'm sure he didn't notice at all."

Anika began to feel nervous as she started straightening papers on her desk. "Well, shit. I had to try something. I could tell he was feeling me too, but he was being too nice, if you know what I mean?"

Shawna just gave a knowing nod as she went to grab both of them one of the delicious pastries that she brought in. They went nicely with the coffee, which gave another layer of flavor to the impromptu meal.

Anika took a small bite and then continued on describing her date.

"I was ready to chalk it up as a loss. I figured he thought I was just too much of a headache or something like that when he simply said good night."

"I'm sorry, girl," she said with a look of sympathy.

"I'm not finished."

"My bad, I thought you were done."

"It's okay. Anyway, I turned to get in my car and then he called my name. I turned back around, and he was right there standing in front of me. I was getting ready to say something, but for the life of me I couldn't remember because he kissed me."

"Awww shit!"

"I know, right! It kind of came out of nowhere. I'm not complaining at all, but I was a little surprised. He told me he didn't want me to think he wasn't into me, but he has a lot going on with school and what-not. He said he was going to make time so we can go out again."

"Wow. That must have been some kiss."

"Yeah it was. But why you say that?"

"Because you crushed the hell out of that pastry."

Anika looked down and noticed that she had smashed the sticky treat in her hand. *Damn, that really was some kiss,* she thought as she tried to clean up the mess. She looked up and noticed Shawna coming with a stack of wet wipes, which she gratefully took.

Shawna gave Anika a smirk. "You might want to call him sooner than later. I'm just saying."

"You might be right," Anika said as she absently wiped the sticky goo from her hand.

Shawna was shocked by her candor but wasn't one to pile on. *We've all been there before,* she thought. "Hey, if you're not busy later, you wanna grab some drinks at the bar downstairs?"

"Sure, I got this great corporate credit card!" Then she held up her card to prove her point.

Anika just shook her head. "That's what I get for giving you a corporate card."

Shawna started to giggle "You gave it to me because I'm the best assistant you've ever had. Plus you were in a really good mood and didn't know any better."

"You keep telling yourself that." Anika looked at her email and saw a ton of new messages and sighed, "Okay, enough fun for now. We have a lot of work to knock out today."

Shawna took it as her Cue to get professional. She gathered up her things as she made her way back to her desk. Anika called after her, "If you're using that card, it better be top shelf!"

She smiled as she started her day.

CHAPTER EIGHT

Deshaun rushed toward the door as it began to close. He stuck his foot in to catch it and pry it open with his free hand. He nimbly stepped by the person who wouldn't hold the door as he scrambled toward it with a briefcase and a box full of donuts. He made the elevator as the door was beginning to close. He shrugged his shoulders at the person who wouldn't hold the door for him, and he was rewarded with a cold stare as the elevator doors closed shut.

Normally, Deshaun would have let the rudeness pass and held the elevator. People always said he was nice to a fault. But today he was running late. He kept pushing the elevator button, hoping it would go faster. He glanced at his watch and felt his pulse quicken. Anika was very clear when she hired him that she could over-look a lot of things, but showing up late for work wasn't one of them.

The elevator doors finally opened, and he rushed into the office. In his haste, he didn't see the mail cart and almost tripped over it. Thankfully he had athletic balance from his days playing high school basketball and was able to avoid an embarrassing fall by spinning on his heel and swerving around the cart.

"Nice moves. You didn't even drop the donuts" Shawna said as she clapped mockingly.

"Ha ha, you got jokes," Deshaun tried to glance around Shawna, but she purposely blocked his view. "I was wondering, is Anika in yet? I'm pretty sure she's been busy this morning. Probably hasn't had a chance to make her rounds this morning," he said with more worry in his voice than he intended.

Shawna just stared at him for a second longer than she needed to, then a wicked smile crept across her face. "She walked around twice this morning actually. She asked me to call you and make sure you were okay." She gave him a condescending glaze up and down. A weird look crossed her face but quickly disappeared. "I guess you're alright. You want me to let her know you're here?"

"No need to trouble yourself. I think I can manage."

"Are you sure? It's no trouble at all."

He knew she was messing with him, but he didn't want to let her know that just yet. He figured it would be smarter and a lot less troublesome to let her have her pound of flesh. "No, that's okay, really." He handed her the box of Anika's favorite donuts. "Do you think you could give these to her? You know, as a show of contrition?"

"You mean as a bribe."

"Yes. I see we agree on something finally."

Shawna took the donuts from Deshaun "I'll give them to her but I'm not sure she's going to want them considering I brought her favorite pastries in from the deli across town" she said smugly.

Deshaun absently rubbed the back of his head "could you give them to her anyway? She may not eat them but at least she'll know I had good intentions."

"You mean the bribe?"

"Semantics."

She gave him that weird look again. "Whatever".

"Thanks, Shawna. Let me know if there's something I can do to repay you."

She started to say something, but thought better of it. "Oh, I'm sure I can come up with something."

She watched him walk toward his office and then hurried to catch up. Deshaun turned around and stopped when he saw her hurrying toward him. He could tell she wanted to say something, but she seemed to be struggling with her words. Finally, she seemed to come to a decision. She looked him in the eye with a fierceness that he wasn't expecting. He fought the urge to take a step back from the intensity of her glare.

"Look, she never left her office. We spent the first part of the morning talking, so you're safe." She turned to storm away but felt someone touch her arm, and she froze in place.

"I really appreciate you telling me. I know we have our verbal jabs. Okay, you have your verbal jabs, but all and all, I think you're pretty cool."

Shawna tried to fight the smile that was threatening to spread across her face but finally gave in. "I think you have your moments too," she said as she looked down at the floor, unable to meet his gaze.

"Hey, I meant to tell you, I had a great time yesterday. You have the oddest sense of humor, but I actually get it."

Shawna gave him that look again, which he still didn't have the foggiest idea what was going through her head. "Thanks, I think".

"As odd as this sounds, I think we could be really good friends." He smiled as he playfully touched her on the arm.

Shawna's awkward smile melted away, leaving an unreadable mask once again. Without a word, she turned and walked away.

Deshaun didn't know what to make of what just happened. He started to follow her but thought better of it. He figured she would tell him when she was ready. He made his way into his and placed his briefcase on his desk. As he was removing his jacket, Shawna stormed into his office. Without a word, she punched him in the arm. He was more shocked than hurt by the punch.

Without a word yet again, Shawna stormed out of his office but stopped when she reached the door. She turned around and made her way back toward him. He braced himself for the next blow. Shawna didn't hit him but she went on her tippy toes and whispered into his ear. "We are not friends. Don't ever touch me again." With that, she turned and stomped away from his office.

What the hell was that all about?! He thought to himself. He didn't know what to make of it as he made his way over to his chair. He had a lot of work to catch up and not a lot of time to do it. He began to roll up his sleeves and noticed that one of his arms had wet spots on it. They look a lot like tears. *Nah, that couldn't possibly be it,* he thought to himself. He dismissed the idea as he quickly buried himself in his work.

CHAPTER NINE

Anika was excited to hear from Kendrick. He had promised to call her soon, and he lived up to that promise by inviting her out on a "respectable date," as he put it. Anika spent the day swamped with work. She had numerous meetings, conference calls, and a business luncheon that took way too long with clients. Thankfully she got the invitation toward the latter part of the day, or she wouldn't have been able to concentrate.

She spent the rest of the day in a closed-door meeting with her assistant, working on a "strategic client proposal," as she put it, and they were not to be disturbed. Actually, they were trying to find something to wear for her date.

"I gotta say, Shawna, this was the best idea ever!"

"Well, duh. This is what you pay me the big pennies for."

"We might have to change that to dollars. This idea could revolutionize prepping and take it to a whole other level."

"I'll remember you said that when it comes time for my review," Shawna said as she pretended to absently brush dirt off her shoulders.

Both women were hovered around Anika's computer, trying to put together outfits from her closet. This whole idea came about one day when Shawna was over her to home and she was trying to plan her wardrobe for the week. Shawna suggested that she photograph all her articles of clothing so when she has free time she can look over what she has available and put together outfits.

At first Anika was skeptical about the idea until Shawna laid out a top on the bed against a white sheet and took a photo. Then she took another photo after she removed the top and placed first a pair of slacks, followed by jeans and then a skirt. She uploaded all the photos to a grid and then opened them up and compared the items. Once Anika saw the potential of such an idea, she was all aboard.

They had spent the rest of the day and part of the next cataloging her entire wardrobe. She then spent the rest of the day organizing items by color, style, and article. Eventually she had her entire wardrobe uploaded into a file for her convenience.

As the two women went over the numerous articles of clothing, Anika jumped up and walked away in frustration as the sheer number was starting to work her nerves. "Damn, I didn't know I had that many clothes! Why didn't you tell me it was hopeless?" She said as she leveled an accusatory look at Shawna.

If her glare bothered her, she didn't let on. "You weren't saying this when you were out shopping for all these clothes," she said as she shrugged.

Anika got ready to launch into another round of complaints when Shawna held up her hand to quiet Anika, which caught her by surprise which caused to go silent, which was Shawna's intent. She quickly clicked a few buttons and then turned the screen around toward Anika.

Anika looked down and a smile slowly crept across her face. "I never thought about wearing a dress. That cuts research time in half. But what about my accessories and shoes?"

Shawna had anticipated her request as she made a few more clicks on the computer and brought up a few selections of shoes and two selections for accessories.

Anika turned her face in a less-than excited expression. "That's all I have? I guess I haven't been shopping as much as I thought," she said, clearly disappointed by her limited choices.

"Nah, you have a shit load of clothes and other stuff. I'm sure if I left you to your own devices you would have figured out something to wear;__ in about a week."

"You're probably right"

"Of course I'm right. You doubt my skills?" Shawna said as she took a long drag of her coffee that Anika just now noticed she had. She was tempted to ask for a cup, but she stopped herself. She already had more than she should and was feeling more nervous than she thought she should already. That was the last thing she needed.

With more than a little prodding, Anika finally settled on an outfit for the evening. She picked out a form-fitting black cocktail dress. It was strapless, and it had a low but not-too low cut that showed her cleavage, but still left some things to the imagination. She had decided to wear pearl earrings and a pair of six-inch black heels.

Normally she would think twice about wearing such high heels. Men sometimes tend to feel self-conscious when she wore them because she would, more often than not, stand a lot taller than her date.

On one occasion she remembered a date asked her if she brought any other shoes to wear because she was making him look bad in front of his clients. She politely excused herself and left. After a string of less-than-flattering messages, he got the hint and fell off.

One of the things she liked about Kendrick was that he was tall, _very tall, in fact. But the thing that stood out the most about him was his utter confidence in himself. It wasn't arrogance but an intimate knowledge that he knew exactly who he was and he had accepted himself for who he was, faults and all.

This is something that she struggled with her whole life, but Kendrick made it look as simple as breathing. He seems as if he's in complete control of any given situation. She would worry and stress over a situation, hoping that it turns out in her favor, while he would seemingly walk into a chaotic situation and things would immediately calm down. She was more than a little envious.

As the day wore on, Anika found herself watching the clock. She knew that she should probably be doing something more productive but as hard as she tried, she couldn't concentrate. Finally, she gave up and packed up her things to head home and get ready. She had instructed Shawna that she would be leaving the office to meet a client. She also instructed her to tell her other clients that she would be returning to the office tomorrow morning. Shawna gave her a slight smirk but said nothing as she left the office.

Anika came into her house running. She had dropped her briefcase on the sofa as she began stripping off clothes on her way to the bedroom. She made her way into the closet as she pulled out the outfit that she had decided on earlier and laid it out on the bed.

She went into the bathroom and ran her bath water. She searched through her bath salts until she found the proper scents she was looking for. Women ask her all the time what she uses, and she would always give a vague answer. She liked to keep some secrets to herself. The trick was to mix the scents until she came up with the right combination.

Today she was going with a scent she made up called "subtle seduction." This mixed well with the perfume that she had picked out. They say that scent is the strongest link to memory. and she wanted to make sure she left an impression with Kendrick.

Now that she finally had her clothes together, she noticed that the tub was full. She carefully slid into the hot water until it was up to her chin. She exhaled softly as the hot water worked out knots of tension from her body that. until now, she wasn't fully aware of.

As the soft scents and heat did their magic on her tense body, she closed her eyes and let them do their work. As she drifted in the luxurious bath water, she let her mind wander to Kendrick. She wondered to herself if she was putting too much stock in the little that she knew about him. It was an uncomfortable truth that she knew held more than a little mystery in it.

She had only known him for a short time, and until now, this is their first real date. She ran down the list about things she didn't know about him. She knew he was in school and was set to graduate at the end of the semester. She knew that he had an exquisite physique that more than held her attention. She also knew that he was a thoughtful man who tended to contemplate his words before he let them carelessly slip from his lips.

She caught herself drifting away with the thought of him and silently admonished herself for being so childlike. She suddenly opened her eyes when she realized that outside of the few things she loved about him, that was it.

At that sobering thought, her mind started to travel down darker paths. She began to wonder if he was secretly into men or if he did a stint in prison. She wondered if maybe he was married with kids and he didn't know how to tell her. She wondered if maybe he beats his women.

A chill ran down her spine as memories of Jay in her apartment began to flood her mind. She remembered the way he looked at her and how every word he uttered was designed to tear down every aspect of her being. She remembered how he hit her, repeatedly.

A single tear ran down her cheek as she wrapped her arms around her legs and began to rock back and forth. She allowed her self-pity to fully engulf her as the tears began to run freely from her eyes.

She didn't know how long she sat there in the water, but she realized that it had turned cold. She pulled herself out of the water and wrapped a towel around her curvy frame. Anika made her way toward her bedroom as she dried off.

She glanced out the corner of her eye and caught her reflection. Her first thought was to turn away, ashamed that she would allow someone to hurt her like that. But despite the self-loathing that she felt and the memories that brought her low, she walked over and looked herself right in the eye.

"I am Anika Washington. Although something bad happened to me, doesn't mean that I will let it dictate my life. My grandmother raised me to be a strong, competent woman who may fall, but she will also rise again and again" she said out loud to herself.

Although she was only speaking to herself, the words helped lift her up and provided a much-needed boost. She went into her room and got ready with a smile on her face and a song in her heart.

CHAPTER TEN

Anika arrived at the restaurant a few minutes early, hoping to get a quick drink to calm her nerves before Kendrick arrived. She made her way over to the bar and signaled for the bartender "I'll have a glass of vodka and orange juice, top shelf, please?"

"I'll have a rum and Coke. You can put her drink on my tab."

Anika turned around and smiled as she saw Kendrick standing behind her. He looked at her as if he hadn't seen her in years. "So you came early to get a drink too, huh?"

"Yeah, how did you know?" she said as she laughed. She always seemed to be able to let loose and laugh around him, she thought.

"Probably the same reason as you, I guess. I was a little nervous about seeing you again, and I figured that a drink would help calm my nerves." He rubbed the back of his head nervously.

At that moment, Kendrick looked like a nervous school boy. She didn't know why, but that set her immediately at ease. She figured that if he was nervous, why shouldn't she be?

They both sat at the bar enjoying their drinks and making small talk. He was telling her about school and how this last year was a lot tougher than he had originally anticipated. He was going on about how his cousin said he didn't have time to hire more people at the shoppe, but he knew that he was just being cheap.

Anika sat back and listened to him tell her about everything that was going on with him since they last met, and all the fears she previously held were melting away. But something told her to err on the side of caution and find out anyway.

"Are you married?" she said a little too loud, as several people at the bar looked up to see who she was speaking to. Anika dropped her head as she felt all eyes on her.

"No, I'm trying to finish school before I even think about that."

"Do you have a girlfriend or boyfriend, for that matter?"

"No, I haven't had one of those for a long time. I'm referring to a girlfriend. I'm not into dudes," he said as he smiled at her questioning. "I don't do drugs, I have a clean bill of health, and I live alone. Anything else I might have left out?"

Anika started to say no, but then a thought came to her. "You said you don't have a girlfriend, but are you seeing someone?"

"I'm trying to, but she keeps asking questions and won't let me get a word in edgewise," Kendrick said as he began to laugh.

"Well, I'm sorry if I'm being so forward. But I really like you and I'd rather find all this out now than be surprised later," she said as she realized that she had been holding her breath. She let it out and felt a lot better about the situation.

"So, tell me, do any of the questions you put to me apply to you?" he asked as he took a sip of his drink. He looked relaxed, but she could tell he was paying close attention.

"Not married and haven't been married . . . wait, were you ever married?" Anika said as she realized she never asked him that question.

He shook his head no as his smiled grew bigger as she began to flush.

"Good to know," she said as she returned his smile. "No kids, drugs, mental issues, no long list of boyfriends, although I'm embarrassed to tell you how short it really is." He gave her a skeptical look as he took another sip of his drink. "You can ask my grandmother if you don't believe me! Hell, I'll take a lie detector test if that'll convince you." Anika noticed again that she had gotten a little too loud as some of the men began to chuckle.

She turned to look back at Kendrick and saw that he was trying to hide his laugh. "So you don't believe me?" she said with a hint of hurt in her voice.

"I believe you. From the way you're acting tonight, I just can't see it being too long a list," he said as he began to laugh again.

Anika folded her arms and looked away, embarrassed that he was able to read her so easily.

"But you never told me if you had a man or not."

Anika looked up when she noticed that Kendrick had asked another question. "No, I'm not seeing anyone presently. It's been a few months since I last dated anyone. I don't know if you can really call it dating because we would go out but nothing ever happened between us. I mean we would make out and stuff but we never actually . . . did it." She started to blush again as he didn't say anything except smirk as he continued to sip on his drink.

"No, I don't have a man," she said as she looked away, uncomfortable with his gaze.

Kendrick noticed her change and immediately began to apologize. "I'm sorry, I didn't know. How long has it been?"

"How long has what been?" she said as she was confused by his line of questioning.

"Since he passed away?" Kendrick said as he was clearly unsure where he went wrong.

Anika gave a sad smile. "Oh, he's not dead. At least the last time I saw him away."

"I'm sorry, I didn't mean to stir up anything. I thought we were just having fun with the quid pro quo. I would completely understand if you wanted to call the evening off."

But before she could respond, the hostess had announced that their table was ready. Kendrick gave her a friendly look, but he didn't betray which way he was leaning, leaving the decision completely in her hands. She figured it was because he felt he made a mistake by asking an emotionally charged question.

Without looking in his direction, Anika said, "Great, lead the way. I'm starving."

Kendrick followed without comment as the hostess led them to their table. As they made their way to the table, Anika looked back and wondered what was going through Kendrick's mind. He still had that friendly expression on his face, which she couldn't read. She wanted to say something, but now wasn't the time. She figured she will find out soon enough.

They finally reached their destination in a quiet little cozy corner of the restaurant. Kendrick nimbly stepped around the hostess to pull the chair out for Anika, which brought a smile from her and a more-than-admiring glance from the hostess. A spark of jealousy welled up in Anika but she pushed it back down. It still simmered just below the surface. If she was going to be with Kendrick, this was something she would have to get used to.

For what it's worth, Kendrick didn't even notice the hostess look as his attention was totally focused on her which brought a smile to her face.

Before she could say anything, Kendrick jumped. "Look, I know I struck a chord earlier and I will understand if you want to call it a night. I don't want you to be here now if you don't want to. We can do this night again, no sweat."

"Are you trying to get rid of me?" Anika said with a smirk on her face.

Kendrick was totally caught off guard as he nervously rubbed the back of his neck again. She loved when he did that. It was so cute.

"No, no. . . I just didn't want you to feel obligated to spend time with me."

"Did we just step into a dimension where everything is opposite? Maybe we should walk out and come back in. This is getting weird," Anika said as she started to giggle.

Her laughter became infectious as he started to laugh as well. That seemed to break the ice as they began to relax and be themselves again. Kendrick leaned across the table and touched her hand. This sent waves of pleasure up her arm and throughout her body. Before the pleasure became too much, she took the opportunity to speak. She placed her hand over his, which elicited a smile from him in return.

"I was dating a man that, up until a few months ago, I was really starting to like. . ." She had never told this story before _not the whole story. She felt embarrassed and until now she didn't understand it. She took a deep breath "I'm going to tell you the whole story. . ."

Kendrick sat back without comment as Anika told him everything. She left out the part about her knowing the officer who came to help. She didn't want to get Anthony in trouble if Kendrick somehow let it slip. He didn't interrupt her as she spoke, but his jaws clenched as she told him how this coward put his hands on her for no other reason than he thought she might be upset that he was fucking his apparent wife in a club in front of her. The conversation went on as she told him the whole story. After she was done, she felt as if a weight had been lifted off of her shoulders and she was finally able to breathe.

Kendrick sat back as he processed the whole story and turn of events. He leaned forward and finally said, "So. . . is that it?" She nodded. "So Jay got mad at you because he thought you saw him and then broke into your apartment and beat you because YOU might have been upset." Kendrick let the words hang in the air as his anger began to boil to the surface.

Anika placed a reassuring hand on his. "I'm fine now. It's in the past. If anything, it made me a stronger person."

Kendrick looked her in the eye with dead seriousness. "If you so much as see this man walking on the same side of the street as you, you call me. People like that just don't go away, Anika, unless you give them a reason to."

I'm sure he had ample reason to she thought to herself. After what Anthony described to her went down, she felt reasonably sure she wouldn't hear from him again.

Kendrick stood up and walked over to Anika and wrapped his arms around her. She immediately felt safe and secure within his grasp. She felt as if the world couldn't touch her as long as she held on.

He begrudgingly released his embrace as he stood. She looked up and saw the oddest belt buckle. Without thought, she gently traced her fingers along its edges. Realization sat in as she became aware of what she was doing and quickly pulled her hand away. "Sorry" was all she could say as she couldn't meet his gaze.

He gentled lifted her chin until she met his eyes. "It's cool. This is my lucky belt buckle I won in a game of basketball." He looked down and readjusted it, something he might have done a thousand times out of habit. "This belt buckle has gotten me out of more scraps than I can remember."

"Who knew black dudes still wore belt buckles?" she said as she began to giggle again.

"Only the coolest of the cool, I'm guessing."

"Apparently."

He bent down and gave her a gentle kiss on the cheek. "If you'll excuse me, I have to go to the little boys' room."

"From what I can see, you're definitely going to the wrong room. You might want to ask where the big-boy room is," Anika said as she looked him directly in the eye, making sure she conveyed her meaning. Kendrick didn't say anything as he returned her look. He gave her a wink and he was off.

Anika sat at the table as she looked around and began to take in the ambiance of the restaurant. She saw that the majority of the patrons were couples. They could be on dates or married, she couldn't tell. She looked down at the table and was pleasantly surprised to find a bottle of wine chilling in a bucket of ice. She was so focused on her conversation with Kendrick that she didn't even notice that it was there. She pulled the bottle out of the ice and noticed that it was one of her favorite bottles of wine with a very good year. She started to pour two glasses; she hoped that he liked wine as much as she did. As she poured his glass, she couldn't remember him ever drinking wine or mentioning that he liked it. She figured that if he didn't, she would be more than happy to take care of it for him. It's against the law somewhere, she figured, to waste wine, she was sure of it.

As she took a sip, her lips parted into a content smile as the flavor was divine. The wine had sent a warm tingle throughout her body. She sat back and savored the moment. She felt hands touch her shoulders, and she carelessly placed her hand over one of them as she gave it a gentle squeeze. "Your hands are pretty dry. I hope you washed them," she teased as the grip became less than pleasurable. "I was just joking. You don't have to squeeze so hard. I don't like that," she said as the feeling started to feel unnerving.

"Oh, so now you don't want me to touch you? You're such a fuckin' tease."

A cold chill ran down Anika's back as she recognized the voice. She tried to turn around but his grip tightened and prevented her from doing so. *Please don't let it be him* she thought to herself. But she already knew deep down inside that it was.

"Did you miss me?" Jay said as his hands began to grope her in a sexual manner. He ran his hand down inside of her dress and began to twist her nipple hard. Tears began to well up in her eyes as she looked around to see if anyone was paying attention. Everyone was going along with their evening, oblivious of what was taking place.

She was tempted to scream for help, but she knew that he would make her pay if she did. He moved his hand over to her opposite breast and twisted her nipple again, only this time he did it so hard that she let out a yelp. One of the guests noticed the noise and looked to see what was happening. He made eye contact with her then glanced up past her only to see the murderous look Jay was giving him he and quickly looked down at his plate, cowering.

Jay wasn't a physically imposing man, and she couldn't help but wonder what scared the man. She looked up and saw that he was visibly shaken. He was so disturbed by what he saw that he reached in his wallet and pulled out money to pay for his dinner as he and his guest promptly left.

Anika tried to steal another look, but this time he wrapped his hand around her throat as he started to squeeze. "Bitch, did I tell you that you could move?"

Tears ran down her face as she shook her head no. He released his grip and thankfully placed his hands on her shoulders again. "Why won't you leave me alone?" Anika mumbled as fear claimed her voice.

Jay let out a sadistic soft laugh next to Anika's ear. "Now why would I do that? You and I have unfinished business." He moved his hands down to her upper arms and gave them a mockingly sweet rub, then he bent down and whispered in her ear again. "I don't think your officer friend will be coming to save you this time."

Anika quickly turned around, oblivious to the danger that action may hold. "What did you do to him?" Tears began to run down her cheeks anew.

Jay casually used a finger to scoop up one of her tears and placed his finger in his mouth, enjoying the fear he brought out in her. "I was able to find the big silent one. He wasn't too smart or aware of his surroundings. I thought he never talked. But before it was over, he was begging me to make it stop. Do you want to know what I did?" Jay said as an evil smile slowly slid across his face.

Anika shook her head as she was too afraid to know. Then something struck her. *He said big and silent,* she thought to herself. Anthony wasn't very big and he was anything but silent. She wanted to let out a sigh of relief, but she didn't want to give anything away to Jay.

"You shook your head no, but I really know that means yes. Well, after we started cutting off his fingers, he started to open up to us a bit. He told me all about your friend Anthony. He gave me his name, the hours he works, where he goes for drinks, address _pretty much everything except his blood type although I'm pretty sure he would have if he knew."

New tears fell down her face as she thought about the torture that they put him through and she began to worry about where Anthony was and if he knew that Jay was after him. Anika's breath caught in her chest when the realization that he kept saying *we* sat in. Anika gave Jay a hard look, which momentarily caught him off guard, causing him to release his grip slightly, which enabled her to take a deep breath. "Why do you keep saying *we*?" Was all she could say before he suddenly cut off her by squeezing her throat even harder this time, which caused her to struggle to try and pry his fingers free. His grip was like a vise. She found her vision beginning to blur at the edges as she felt herself losing consciousness.

Jay ignored her attempts to remove his hand as he continued. "As I was saying, what we did was cut off both his hands and feet, and then tied him to a tree in the woods. By now I'm pretty sure anything and everything that smelled his blood has had a feast and he was the main course."

"Hey, Anika, who's your friend?" Kendrick said as he casually took his seat. If he noticed the scene before him, he didn't give any indication as he took a sip of the wine. "Oh, this is good. . ."

Jay gave a nod behind him as two large men dressed in black suits took up positions on each side of Kendrick. Kendrick tried to reach for his glass, but both men placed a huge warning hand on his shoulders, causing him to place his arms at his side.

Anika saw the two huge men take up positions on either side of Kendrick, and she began to fear for him as well. Tears began to well up in her eyes as she mouthed the word "sorry" for getting him into this situation. Kendrick just gave her a smile, and he did something totally unexpected: he winked at her. That caught Anika off guard and apparently Jay as well. She glanced up and she noticed the look on Jay's face probably thinking the same thing. *What's wrong with him?*

Jay turned Anika's face toward him as he squeezed her jaw painfully. "Who is your friend, boo?"

Anika began to shake her head furiously. "Nobody. We just met today. He has nothing to do with this."

Jay began to shake his head as he laughed. "You know, one thing I always prided myself on is that I can tell when a whore is lying to me, and you, my dear, are lying. Too bad, I might have let him go, but since you lied, I guess things are going to have to get messy."

"Anika, are you ready to go get another drink, say somewhere less crowded?" Kendrick said as he looked her in the eyes with his penetrating stare. Gone was the relaxed nonchalant attitude and was replaced with a look that she hadn't seen before on him. It was a look that she hadn't seen before from anyone. It was the look of a man who wasn't use to someone getting in his way and would remove them if they dared.

"No, Kendrick, you don't understand. . ." she began. At the mention of his name, the two huge men shared a nervous glance at one another but said nothing.

Jay was oblivious to the sudden change in the air. "I think it's time we go somewhere where no one can hear you scream. It's a pity I couldn't find your friend Anthony. It would have been nice to get this all over with at the same time." he mused.

Jay gave a slight nod, but neither of the huge men moved. He gave another nod, this time with more animation, but again neither man moved. Finally he threw his hands up in the air in frustration. "What's the problem? I'm not paying you enough?"

Both men shared another glance and one of them finally said, "We can't boss."

Jay gave them a withering stare. "What do you mean you *can't*?"

The man who had spoken was starting to sweat profusely.

"Anika, are you ready to go or do you want to stay here with them? Just so you know, I'm not paying for all y'all." Everyone looked at him and for a moment both Jay and Anika had forgotten he was even there as they were so focused on the huge men and the obvious fear they were experiencing.

"Are you going to tell me or do I have to guess? Don't tell me you're afraid of a girl. I know you're not afraid of him." Jay pointed a mocking finger at Kendrick.

By now the man was on the verge of tears as his eyes began to well up. "You don't understand, this is Kendrick _*the* Kendrick." By now the man had dissolved into tears.

Jay looked at him with open astonishment. He had hired the two most dangerous men that he could find, and they came highly recommended. He looked at the one who remained silent, and he was starting to shake. "Will somebody please explain who this Kendrick is supposed to be?" he said, obviously getting fed up with the whole situation.

"I think I can explain it better than they can. Two things: first, I am not a man who takes kindly to someone interrupting my dinner and messing with those who I care about. Secondly, I have two blades that have punctured their carotid arteries in their thighs. I'm pretty sure they're paying more attention to me than you at the moment." Kendrick kept his eyes on Jay as he spoke to his bodyguards. "I'm gonna pull these blades out, and I suggest you go see Nancy and have her look at those for you. I didn't push too deep, so you should be aight." He pulled the blades out, and both men let out a grunt and a sigh of relief. Kendrick reached into his pocket and gave one of them a card. "Give this to her and tell her I told you it was okay."

Both men took the card and turned to leave when Kendrick stopped them. "As of now, you no longer work for him. If I find out otherwise. . . don't make me come looking for you." Both men nodded and quickly left.

"*What the hell just happened?!* Anika thought to herself as she tried to process what she just saw. She glanced up at Jay, and he was standing there motionless, stunned, with his mouth hanging open.

"So, are you going to let go of my date now or do we need to go have a long talk?"

There was a moment of tension when Anika didn't know if he would let go or if Kendrick would act. By the look on his face, she was sure he wasn't bluffing and that scared her. She looked at Jay's face and it was a picture of indecision. She could tell that he was weighing his options. She turned back to look at Kendrick, and there was clear certainty on his face as if he knew the exact path he would take either way. Finally, Jay released his grip on Anika, and she quickly moved out of his reach.

Kendrick reached out and grabbed Anika's hand. He looked at her to make sure she was okay and then turned his attention back toward Jay. "You can go now."

Jay was full of bottled-up fury as he turned to leave. He reached for something, and Anika's heart got caught in her throat when she realized that he was reaching for a cane. He turned to leave, and he labored as he moved to leave. He stopped next to them and without looking in their direction, he said. "This isn't over by a longshot."

Kendrick gave Jay a menacing stare "It is if I ever see you again or if I hear that you so much as put her name in your mouth. . . I hope I made myself clear."

Jay shook with rage, but he didn't utter a word. Anika watched him until he was gone from the restaurant and even then she waited, just to make sure that he didn't come back. Once she realized that he was gone for good, she visibly relaxed. Now that the immediate danger had passed, she began to assess the situation.

Everything that happened was so surreal. Not more than ten minutes ago, the only thing on her mind was is she going to have the filet mignon or the Chilean sea bass. The next thing she knew, the man she thought she would never see again, is threatening to kill her in a most unpleasant way. Then like out of a movie, Kendrick comes in sexier than ever and saves the day by doing some ole gangsta/ninja shit to Jay's two hired guns, all without getting out of his seat. Where they do that at?

This was almost too much to try and process at one time. It was then that she finally noticed that Kendrick was talking to her in a hushed yet somewhat urgent tone. "Anika, if you can hear me, please sit down. Everyone is starting to stare and we don't want to make a bigger scene than we probably already have."

At hearing that, she numbly moved over and reclaimed her seat as she continued to run through the evening's events. Through the haze, she thought about how the evening began and how things have progressed. It seems like light years ago when the only thing she considered was if maybe he had a girl-friend or wife. Oh, how she longed for simpler times.

Now she is replaying the events of the past twenty minutes. *"Was it just twenty minutes?"* she thought as she looked down at her watch to confirm. She thought about how Jay had obviously been keeping tabs on her. Stalking would be the more appropriate term, she thought ruefully. She remembered the two large men who looked like they eat steel for breakfast and the emotionless expressions that they wore on their faces. But what really stood out was how these men seemed to be terrified of Kendrick and in direct opposition of his carefree approach that he took in the obviously dangerous situation.

What scared her more than anything was that she had no idea who he was. With Jay, looking back on him, there were signs. How he used to pull her to him a little too forcefully or how he would argue down her opinion even though he hid it behind corny humor, but now she knew better.

She looked up at Kendrick, who seemed to be waiting patiently with a blank expression, but she could tell by his posture that he was hoping that she would give him the chance to explain. "Who are you? I thought that I had a pretty good read on you but obviously I was wrong," she said as she waved the waiter over to their table. "Bring me a bottle of your strongest wine. I don't care what it is." The waiter left with a strange expression on his face, which she didn't pay any mind to.

"So are you going to tell me or am I going to have to wait until something else happens? I wonder, if I threw myself off the roof, would you fly up and save me?" Anika said as she laughed bitterly.

"It's not what you think, Anika. . ."

"Oh, really? Tell me, Kendrick _if that's your name_, what do I think? Do I think that you're some crime lord? Yep. Do I believe that there is a truly dangerous side to you? Pretty much. How about that you had a secret life that I want to have nothing to do with? You better believe it!"

By that time the waiter returned with a bottle of red wine. He was getting ready to pour her a glass when she took the bottle from him and waved him away. Kendrick reached over to hold her glass while she poured and she stared daggers into him, which prompted him to let go.

Anika poured her first glass and downed it quickly. She was getting ready to pour herself another but gave up on the idea as she removed the middle man and turned the bottle up to her mouth. She took a long drink as a guest of the restaurant gave her disapproving glances. Finally she sat the bottle down and gave a loud belch into her hand that caused people to sigh audibly, which she quickly gave the middle finger to as she waved both hands around herself, making sure she let everyone know exactly what she thought of their opinions.

She turned back toward Kendrick and it was obvious that she was starting to feel the effects of the wine. "That really hit the spot! So, I know you're full of shit, but please continue," she said as she leaned forward on both elbows.

Kendrick leaned forward so as not to be overheard. "It's not that simple Anika, I have a past, that's obvious, but it's not what you think."

"Uh-huh... You know what the worse part of this is? After all that has happened and people wanting to kill, rape, feed me to animals, I still want to fuck the shit out of you. Isn't that absolutely hilarious?" she said as she reached for the bottle again.

"I don't know what to say about that last part, but-..." Anika held up her hand indicating that she wanted him to stop as she took another long drink from the bottle.

Kendrick waited patiently for her to finish and when she slammed the bottle back down on the table and let out another loud belch, but this time she didn't cover her mouth, he took it as a sign that he could go on with his explanation. "When I was younger, there was trouble in my neighborhood and I had some . . . issues." Kendrick looked around and saw that he had an audience, thanks to Anika's loud belching, among other things. "Why don't we get out of here and go somewhere more private so we can finish this conversation?"

Anika looked at him a longtime with a blank expression. She just stared at him as Kendrick was beginning to worry if maybe she zoned out. Suddenly she looked up at him "Okay, let's go but on one condition."

"And that would be?"

"Promise you won't hurt or kill me."

Kendrick couldn't help but smile. "Now why would I do that?"

"I don't know, maybe I know too much and you have to get rid of witness? Shit, I don't know how this works," she said as she waved her hands in the air comically, which caused even more people to stare.

One of the patrons, finally fed up with Anika's antics, spoke up. "Why don't you two go somewhere else? We all are trying to have a nice dinner here."

Kendrick leaned over so only the person who spoke could hear. "Mind your business before you upset me."

The patron saw the dead serious look on Kendrick's face, and he quickly found his food to be a lot more interesting. After seeing how he had quickly cowed the person who spoke up, everyone decided that they rather do something else than gain his attention.

Kendrick turned his attention back to Anika. "I would never do that to someone such as you." He reached an arm around her waist to hold her up as they made their way towards the exit. The waiter came up with a questioning look on his face. Kendrick reached into his pocket and handed him a wad of bills. "Keep the change." Whatever the amount was, the waiter had a huge smile on his face.

"Why me?"

Kendrick noticed that she spoke through slurred speech. "Huh?" was his only response as he struggled to understand what she was saying.

"Why wouldn't you kill me?"

He gave it some thought as they made their way outside. "It's because you don't deserve it."

Anika shrugged. "Huh, makes sense. . ." Kendrick opened the car down and she plopped down in the seat. He started to close the car door when she reached out and pulled him closer. "One more thing, I promise."

He started to laugh. "What's up?"

"If I like what you have to say, you have to fuck me, deal?"

He was caught totally off guard by her bold request but quickly recovered. "Let's just see how the conversation goes before we make any hasty request, shall we?"

She obviously didn't hear what he said as she continued. "I'm not talking about one of the nice-and-easy fucks. Nope, I want one of those nasty fucks that when you sitting in church and it crosses your mind, you have to pray twice as hard."

All Kendrick could do was shake his head as he got into the car and strapped Anika into her seat as they drove off to a more private location.

They had to make a few stops as the alcohol within Anika's stomach was causing it to churn. He was barely able to pull the car off to the side of the road before she threw up. As her stomach emptied, she was starting to sober up.

They finally reached their destination on the other side of town. It was a small bar that was set far off from the road between two buildings. If you weren't paying attention, you would miss it. They made their way inside and found a quiet spot in a corner so they could talk more privately.

A waitress made her way over to their table, and Kendrick ordered a rum and Coke while he glanced at Anika and ordered her a coffee, which she quickly changed to a scotch on the rocks, causing Kendrick to raise an eyebrow. "I have a feeling that I think I'm going to need it," she said as she turned towards him expectantly.

Before he could speak, Anika chimed in. "Don't lie. I'm a big girl."

Kendrick couldn't help smile at that. He cleared his throat and started. "A lot of what was said back there was true. I do have somewhat of a reputation. I'm not going to lie to you, Anika. Most of it is true, but some of it is so off the wall that I can't help but laugh. I don't dispute it because it helps me out when I need it. Take tonight, for example, if the reputation that I built up over the years wasn't in effect, there would have been a lot of unnecessary violence."

Anika gave him a deadpan stare. "So you saying that if you didn't have this well-deserved reputation _your words not mine_, then there would have been unnecessary violence? Come on, dude. You got to do better than that. You strike me as an intelligent guy, I know you got a better story than that."

Kendrick didn't say anything at first as he tried to gain his composure. He's trying to be totally honest with her and he keeps running into dead ends. "Look, I'm being straight up with you. I'm not about bullshit. I don't give it nor do I allow it around me."

"Uh-huh. . ." Anika said as the waitress came back with their drinks. She quickly took a long sip.

Kendrick waited patiently until she was finished and he was sure he had her full attention. Confident that he did, he continued. "Let me ask you a question, do you believe actions speak louder than words?"

"Yes." she said immediately.

Kendrick decided to take a different approach. "I agree. So tell me, when did I ever lie to you?"

Anika slammed her glass down and leaned forward on her elbows as she looked Kendrick directly in the eye. "I'm glad you asked. I'm going to tell you exactly how you lied. You lied when you said. . ." She leaned backed slightly as she tried to remember a time that he actually lied to her. The scene in the restaurant was totally surreal. She had never seen anything like that in her life. The way he just sat there so calm . . . he had to have lied to her at some point. Didn't he?

Kendrick leaned in a little closer. "I'm waiting."

All the many times that they've spent together and all the conversations they had played out in her mind, Anika couldn't think of one time that he lied. If anything, he has been completely open with her, which was something that she never experienced before. She figured that he was just better at it than the others. But she was starting to doubt that assumption.

"It must be the liquor, but I can't think of a time that you have ever lied to me. But that doesn't mean you won't."

"Anika, to say that I will never lie to you would be a lie in and of itself. No one can ever say what they won't do. We don't know what the future holds. But I'll tell you this, I will be as honest as I can even if it hurts, deal?"

She just sat there as she pondered his offer. She couldn't find any loophole that he could later use against her, so she relented. "Deal, but I'm going to hold you to that."

"I wouldn't have said it if I had no intention of upholding my end of the bargain."

After he said that, Anika couldn't help but smile. As crazy as the last couple of hours have been, she felt as if she couldn't believe what he was saying. "So you going to tell me how we got to this point?" she said as she looked at him with complete openness.

Kendrick nodded his head as he let her know that he could. As the waitress passed by, he stopped her and ordered more drinks. He knew this was going to require more alcohol than they currently had to get through it all. He waited until the waitress returned and left before he started because he wanted to make sure that there weren't any ear hustlers lurking around who might take the opportunity to listen in.

Confident that no one was listening, he looked at her. "Are you sure you want to know? Once you learn all there is, you can't put the genie back into the bottle."

She looked him directly in the eye. "If I had doubts I wouldn't be here."

Kendrick let out a long sigh as he began to tell her who he was. . .

Once Kendrick had finished, he saw the look of shock on Anika's face and his heart began to drop. Not so much as he was worried that she would go and tell someone, but that it might be too much for her to overcome. Sometimes it's easier to pretend than to actually know the truth.

Anika started to come out of her haze and then she stood. Kendrick's eyes followed her as she stood. She didn't look at him as she scanned the bar and then immediately left. He sat there in stunned silence as thoughts ran through his mind. He was crestfallen as he reached for his drink and downed it.

Not knowing what else to do, he reached into his pocket and peeled off a few bills to pay the tab. Kendrick turned around to grab his jacket and then turned back when he heard Anika walk up behind him.

"We leaving already?" she said as she stared at him with a quizzical look. "I was hoping to get another glass of scotch. Whatever it was, it was pretty good." She saw the look on his face and was starting to get worried. "What's wrong?"

Kendrick couldn't seem to meet her eyes. "I figured you were done with me after what I just told you. Look, I trust you to keep my secrets, but I can completely understand if it was too much for you."

The last thing he expected to hear from her was laughter, but when he finally looked up at Anika, she was giggling softly at him. "You really thought I was leaving? That's cute. But I really really had to go pee. I didn't want to embarrass you by asking in the middle of your story."

Kendrick was at a loss for words. "But I thought. . ."

"You thought I was going to leave and never see you again? Hardly."

Kendrick didn't know what to think at this point. He was hoping that she would give him a chance in spite of everything that has happened in his life, but he didn't actually believe that she would. It took him a moment to come to terms with what that actually meant. He sat down in the chair again as his mind raced and Anika joined him.

"You know what we need? More drinks!" Anika said as she waved the waitress over and ordered more drinks. She turned back to Kendrick and saw a totally confused look on his face, and it took some effort not to start giggling at him. "So you wanna tell me what's going through that beautiful head of yours?"

Kendrick took a moment to gather his thoughts as he tried to put everything into perspective. "Well, to be honest, I didn't think you were going to stay," he said, being completely upfront. "I thought once I told you everything that happened and how we got to this point, you would politely excuse yourself and never come back." He shrugged as he laid everything on the table.

Before they could say anything, the waitress arrived with their drinks and they both took a moment to take a long sip. Anika let out an audible sigh as she set her glass down and turned her attention back toward him. "I would be lying if I said some of the things you told me didn't scare the shit out of me. But what I did notice was that you are essentially the same man I thought you were when I first met you. You're strong, honest, and a man of your word."

"When we first met, you told me that you weren't a saint and at that point, anything that happened before then frankly wasn't any of my business. You never tried to portray yourself as something you were not. I think in some ways you are too hard on yourself and don't give yourself enough credit for making it this far. I grew up with guys who were in situations that weren't nearly as serious as yours and things didn't end well for them."

Kendrick finally found his voice. "So where does this leave us?"

"Hopefully another date, and this time, I can do without the excitement." She couldn't help but laugh.

He took her hand and placed it within his. "I'm serious. This is new ground for me and I don't know how this works."

She thought on it for a moment and shrugged. "You asking me like I know. I told you about my love life, and it was nothing much to speak of. You unfortunately got to meet the worse of them."

As Kendrick thought back on the night's events, his jaw started to tighten as he remembered how Jay had put his hands on her. Anika touched the side of his face as she saw how he began to tense up. He reached up and rubbed the back of her hand. "I'm sorry you had to go through that. I promise you I will never treat you in that fashion."

"I would hope not. You're too cute to be that bad."

Kendrick began to smile, but then it started to fade. "Promise me if you see him, to call me. I don't want you going anywhere near him. He's the type of man who doesn't understand when to let things go."

"I'm going to be fine. I think he's learned his lesson."

"I don't. If it's all the same, I think I'm going to go have a talk with him."

A chill ran down Anika's back at the icy tone Kendrick used. She was pretty sure he wasn't just going to talk. She was certain that if he saw Jay again, Jay wouldn't be heard from again. A small part of her was repulsed at the idea of Kendrick doing something to him, but her rational mind had a different train of thought.

He already tried to hurt her once, and the only thing that stopped him was that she was able to get her hands on her Taser gun. She would hate to think what would have happened if she failed. Then she had Anthony and his friend talk to him and that just made matters worse. He showed up at the restaurant with two dudes ready to do God-knows-what to her and Kendrick. The only thing that saved them was that Kendrick's reputation preceded him and the two men left. Even after all of that, she knew that if given half the chance, Jay would kill her.

Kendrick gave her hand a light squeeze to bring her out of her thoughts. "You okay in there? You kind of just zoned out on me."

Anika shook her head slightly as she remembered how scared she was. "I'm scared. I don't like to admit it, but I don't know what to do."

Kendrick lifted her chin until her eyes met his. "I do. I don't want you to think about this anymore. I promise you that you won't have any more problems from him; you have my word."

At hearing his words, she started to feel better knowing deep down inside that he will protect her. At first she felt sorry for Jay, but that quickly started to fade as she thought about the realization that he had probably done this before. You don't get like that overnight. "Thanks for having my back. I've never had a man or anyone do that for me before, outside of my grandmother."

Kendrick didn't say anything as he raised her hand to his lips as he softly kissed the back of her hand, which sent chills up her arm. She thought he was finished until he kissed her other hand and the pleasure continued. It was becoming too much as she pulled her hand away. Her chest was rising up and down heavily as she tried to regain her composure.

"Truth or dare."

It took a moment for Kendrick to realize she had actually said something. "Huh?"

"Truth or dare. Pick one."

He looked her directly in the eye. "Truth."

Anika pretended as if she was thinking then said, "What's your favorite color?"

Kendrick was caught off guard at such an odd question, but he played along. "Blue".

"Yay, you win!" She began to clap. "I'll pay the tab." Before he could protest, Anika had already flagged down the waitress and cashed out. She turned to look at him. "I do believe we made an agreement?"

Now he was totally lost as she grabbed her coat and made her way purposefully towards the door. Not knowing what else to do, he followed. He increased his pace as he stepped past her to open the door. "Where are we going?"

Anika turned around to look at him like it was the most obvious thing in the world. She turned around trying to get her bearings. "I don't know where I am. You live near here?" Kendrick nodded. "That'll work, let's go."

"Wait, what?"

Anika was totally exasperated. "As smart and sexy as you are, you can be totally clueless. I told you if I liked what you had to say, we was fuckin'. Well, I'm still here, aren't I? Lead the way." She said as she waved her hand letting him know to hurry up.

"You sure about this?"

"Oh, yeah, I'm sure."

The ride to Kendrick's place was quiet. Kendrick focused on the road while Anika sat quietly in the passenger seat. She stole a glance out the corner of her eye as her eyes raked up and down his body. She let out a slight quiver as her body began to anticipate what was ahead.

They arrived at Kendrick's place before she knew it. He lived no more than ten minutes away from the bar, which somewhat surprised her. She had assumed that he lived farther away for some reason.

Kendrick pulled into the driveway of a modest town-house in a poorer part of the city. He told her during one of their many conversations that he grew up in the hood. He had said that while he was in school and trying to get himself together, he never found a reason to actually leave.

Kendrick opened the door to his town-house and stepped aside so that Anika could enter. It was dark so she waited by the foyer for him to turn the lights on. He slid by her and she smelled his cologne as his scent sent a momentary thrill up and down her body.

As the lights came on, she quickly looked around. What she saw wasn't quite what she expected. His home was tastefully decorated with creams and an assortment of colors that wouldn't normally be associated with this neighborhood or a man for that matter. She noticed that the furniture was of high quality and the lighting set the perfect mood for a cozy, quiet sanctuary.

"Whoever decorated your place, tell her she did an outstanding job." She gave a start as the fireplace came to life as Kendrick had turned it on to try and knock the chill off the room.

"Why does it have to be a woman's touch?" he looked at her quizzically as he stepped behind her and gathered her coat. "Men happen to have excellent taste as well."

"I haven't met a straight man with taste this good."

"Well, congratulations, you've met one."

Anika cringed slightly as she realized her mistake. "I'm sorry; I was trying to be funny." Her eyes couldn't meet his. "You have really nice taste."

He tried to keep a neutral expression on his face but failed as he burst out laughing. "Girl, you need to lighten up! That's not the first time I've heard that. You think you were bad, you should have heard what my boys had to say. Needless to say, they haven't been over all that often. I don't make excuses for my taste, and I'm willing to try different things. I like what I like." He shrugged.

She asked him where the bathroom was, and he pointed her in the right direction as he went in the kitchen to make them drinks. She wanted to freshen up and possibly brush her teeth or at the very least gargle.

When she came out of the bathroom, she noticed that Kendrick was sitting on the couch fiddling with something in his hand. Suddenly smooth music started playing through speakers that she didn't notice were mounted in the ceiling.

As she made her way over to the couch, Kendrick stood as she approached and handed her a class of scotch on the rocks. She took a sip and her eyes lit up. "This is good _so smooth."

"I'm glad you like it. A friend gave it to me as a gift a while back."

She closed her eyes as she savored the taste of the scotch as it left a warm pleasant feeling in her stomach that began to spread throughout her body. She opened her eyes and saw Kendrick looking at her with a penetrating glance. She sat her glass on the table and brought her lips to his as they gave each other a slow kiss.

Anika felt his hands run up and down her back as she felt chills run through her. She slipped her tongue into his mouth, searching for his as they tangoed in a sensual dance. Kendrick broke the kiss as he ran his tongue across her neck and was rewarded with a soft moan.

As he kissed her neck, he ran his hands up to her breasts and gently massaged them through the fabric. Anika let out a gasp as she loved to have her titties played with. Kendrick reached behind her and began to unzip her dress. She took a step back and let the dress fall off of her, revealing her soft, caramel skin that lay beneath. The only thing that remained was the G-string she wore, which she regretted at this moment.

Kendrick rose to stand before her and before he touched her, she began to undress him. Anika removed his shirt, and she gaped at his chiseled chest. She knew that his chest was hard underneath, but it was better than she ever imagined.

Anika began to run her hands up and down his chest as she lightly stroked his abs as her fingers traced the ridges along his chiseled abdomen. Kendrick did a sharp intake of air as she started to suck softly on one nipple and then the next. He reached his hand up to stroke her head, but she grabbed them and placed them at his side.

"Uh-uh, this is my show, if I remember correct?" He gave a slight nod, which caused slight smile to appear on her face.

Anika continued to explore his chocolate-covered steel frame as she reached around and gripped his firm ass cheeks. She started to kiss his stomach which quickly turned into long licks as she began to taste his flesh. She could tell that he was starting to pant as his breathing started to pick up. She smiled to herself as her teasing was starting to drive him crazy.

She looked up and searched for his eyes until they met. Not breaking eye contact, she started to remove his pants. He was down to his underwear, and she placed her mouth on his dick and blew warm air through the material, and she was rewarded with a soft moan.

She knew her teasing was starting to be too much so she reached up and pulled his underwear down to the floor as he stepped out of them.

As she looked up, she saw his large manhood jump. It was at least nine inches _probably closer to ten, _with large veins running along the length of it. The head was large with a dark, angry purple shade to it. She took the opportunity to explore him, placing wet kisses up and down the side of it, which caused it to lurch even more. She finally reached the head and ran her tongue around it, slipping the tip of her tongue inside of the slit, slurping up the pre-cum. She decided that she liked the taste. It had a smooth silky taste to it that she now wanted more than anything to drink.

She opened her mouth as wide as she could as she struggled to take in his huge dick. She started to suck on the head as she tried to take more of him in. It jumped in her mouth, and she was rewarded with more pre-cum as she eagerly slurped it, tasting more of the delicious fluids. She closed her eyes and tried concentrating on taking more of his dick. She felt the tip tickling the back of her throat. She started to breathe through her nose as the head started to push past her tonsils and make its way down her throat.

She kept trying to get more of him down her throat until regrettably she couldn't go any farther. She opened her eyes and was slightly disappointed as she realized that she was a little past half-way in her attempt to take him whole. She silently vowed to herself that she would get there.

For now she would try and please him with what she had. From the way he was breathing and his legs were locked out, she knew she must be doing something right. She ran her tongue along the bottom of his shaft and stroked the portion that she couldn't get in her mouth with her hand.

Kendrick's hips began to thrust back and forth slightly in rhythm with her stroking. Anika grabbed both of Kendrick's hands and placed them on the back of her head. He immediately grabbed the back of her head, but he didn't force her farther down on his dick as she continued to administer her loving.

She felt him jump in her mouth and that was all the warning she got as he exploded down the back of her throat. She let go of his shaft and grabbed his ass as she let him face fuck her. She trusted him not to slam his dick down her throat, and he didn't disappoint her.

Stream after stream flowed out of him as she tried desperately to keep up. She pulled back a little so that she could taste him. She let the last few gobs explode in her mouth as she swallowed them happily. Anika continued to lick and suck on his shaft until it was completely drained.

Kendrick collapsed back on the couch, totally spent from her thorough ministrations on his member. She started to get up until she saw a small glob on the head of dick and she greedily licked it up. She saw him staring at her intently as lust showed clearly on his face, and to her amazement, he started to rise again.

Not one to look a gift horse in the mouth, she stood up slowly and peeled off the now-drenched panties that she had on and let them fall to the floor. She looked down and noticed that Kendrick was completely hard again and she knew he was a keeper. He reached for her, but she gently pushed his hands away.

She didn't need his help with this. She was about to take a big-girl ride, and she needed to go at her own pace until she got used to it and then it's all good. She straddled him as she felt his tip touch her lips and a shiver of pleasure ran through her body. She knew this was going to be good, and she wanted to savor every moment of it.

Anika grabbed his huge shaft and rubbed it up and down the length of her lips. She knew lubrication wasn't going to be an issue considering she was absolutely gushing with sexual excitement. She rubbed the tip against her clit and jumped slightly from the intensity of the pleasure it was bringing her. She continued to move it against her clit in small circles as she reached a mini orgasm.

She couldn't remember the last time she had cum. She was never one to sleep around and she really never got into masturbating. Anika felt her legs shaking as the orgasm took more out of her than she thought. Not wanting to waste any more time, she positioned the head against her drooling hole and began to slowly lower herself on his rock hard shaft.

She fought the urge to bury it to the hilt inside of her, but she had two problems. One, she hasn't had sex in who knows how long and two, but more importantly, he had an absolute monster. His length was more than she'd ever had, and the girth was larger than a cucumber. Not to mention the head was larger than the shaft, which presented its own challenges. All in all, this was going to take some time.

Anika grabbed the base of his staff and began to twirl her hips slowly as she worked the head in. After what seemed like forever, she felt it break through and as it did, she had another orgasm which was bigger than the last. This caused her legs to give way and half of his dick was buried inside of her. Anika's mouth opened wide with a mixture of shock, surprise, and pain, accompanied by waves and waves of pleasure.

The pleasure clearly outweighed the pain as she began to rise and fall on him with little mini thrusts, not wanting to take in more than she was currently ready for. She looked down at Kendrick and she beamed. He couldn't have been a more accommodating lover. He was patient as he let her get used to him and take things at her own pace. She could tell he was fighting the urge to do more, but he wanted to make her as comfortable as possible and she really appreciated that fact.

Anika began to move slowly up and down on Kendrick's dick. She rode him from the tip to the point that she felt comfortable, which was slightly more than half. She looked into his eyes and saw the smoldering lust burning deep within. His body began to tense and she increased her pace as little by excoriatingly delicious little, more of him made his way deeper into her wanton body.

She felt another orgasm, this time much bigger than the last one starting to take hold. She bent over and whispered. "Cum in me". That was all the encouragement he needed as he unleashed torrents of cum inside of her tight pussy.

Anika felt his hot fluid shoot into the depths of her womanhood, and it triggered a mind-blowing orgasm that shook her whole body down to its core. Her mouth hung open as her legs gave way as she started to swallow the rest of his staff, which remained amazingly hard inside of her. She didn't stop until she felt his balls brushing up against her ass.

A single tear ran down her cheek as the pleasure and pain was almost too much to bear. She began to giggle as she started to ride the full length of his dick. She started kissing Kendrick deeply as she buried her tongue in his mouth, and he responded in kind. She bit his lower lip as she felt another orgasm approaching. This time, Kendrick wouldn't be denied. He didn't take full control of the situation as he desperately wanted to, but he did begin to meet her, stroke for stroke. This brought new waves of pleasure for Anika as she came yet again. She rested her head on Kendrick's shoulder as he grabbed her ass with both hands as he began to drive deep into her, which brought another orgasm from Anika. She began to moan loudly as he continued his assault. Kendrick let out a primal growl as he unleashed another load deep within her. Anika kissed his neck as she shivered from the sheer ecstasy that he was giving her.

They both collapsed on the couch as they lay entangled in a sweaty heap. Anika rolled off of Kendrick as their combined juices ran out of her. Kendrick grabbed a towel off the coffee table and laid it down on the couch. Kendrick sat back down, and Anika lay across his chest as she placed her head in between the crook of his neck. They lay there as they tried to recoup from their intense love-making.

"Damn, is it always going to be like that?" she said as she kissed his chest. "I think I might have to take more vacation days in the future if this keeps up." She laughed.

"I was about to ask you the same thing." He said as he kissed the top of her head. "You sure you haven't had more practice than you were originally letting on?" He couldn't help but laugh as she set up and playfully punched him in the shoulder.

"No, smartass, I wouldn't lie to you. To be honest, I've never done anything quite like that before." She said as she lightly bit his nipple.

He let out a content sigh as she began to lick his nipple. "Done anything like what before?"

"Turned into a slut bunny," she said as she continued to lazily lick his nipple. "What can I say, you bring that out of me."

"Uh-huh. . . you keep that up and neither one of us will be getting any sleep."

She lifted her head as she looked at him with a confused look. "Who said anything about sleeping? I plan on getting my fill of you tonight."

Kendrick just chuckled. "All right, why don't we take this upstairs then?"

Anika shook her head. "Nope, not tonight. You think you slick, you want to get me upstairs so you can put my legs behind my head and fuck the shit out of me. I know how you men think." She straddled him as she felt his rapidly rising manhood join the conversation. "I wouldn't mind that, but tonight, I want to have my way with you, if that's okay?" She didn't wait for him to respond as she slowly lowered herself on to his now rock-hard staff.

"No wonder you're so damn good at business," he said as he slowly gave in to her desires.

"Well, yes and no. I am rather tenacious when it comes to work; I don't give an inch nor do I give up until I have what I want. But you, _you are something different." She said as she started to grind on him.

Not meeting his eyes she said, "I wanted to fuck you the first day I ever saw you. The night after we met, I went home and fucked myself to sleep with the thought of you being the last thing that crossed my mind before sleep took over." Now she was going full bore as she was grinding up and down on the full length of his dick.

"Wow, I thought I was the only one who did that. I wanted you badly. Not just your body, I wanted a place in your life."

Anika felt a massive orgasm building, but she stopped when she realized what he said. "You want a place in my life?"

He looked at her with pure sincerity on his face as he shook his head. "I've never met a woman like you before. I've known empty promises, lies, deceit, and all-around bullshit, but you are none of those things. You allow me to see past all the clutter this life has to offer on a daily basis and just see . . . you. When I'm with you, the noise fades away and I'm left with an undeniable truth that you are who you say you are. That is something I don't want to give up."

Tears ran down her cheeks as she started kissing him slowly yet passionately. She started to ride him again as her orgasm flowed through her body, causing her to clamp down on Kendrick, which brought on his own orgasm. They both lay in one another's arms, drinking in the moment as the silence held them in an embrace that they won't soon forget.

Kendrick rose with Anika in his arms. This time she let him carry her up the stairs as she wrapped her arms around his neck. He brought her into a large bedroom with windows that surrounded the whole room. He had a large king-sized bed that sat in the center of the room.

She noticed that there weren't any curtains as she gave him a quizzical look. He looked around trying to find the source of her consternation then he realized what it was. "Oh, don't worry. No one can see in. I have one-way windows. The only thing that can come in is light," he said as he gave her a reassuring smile.

He laid her on the bed, but as he began to pull away, she kept her arms wrapped around his neck as she looked deeply into his eyes. "I love you. I know I'm probably violating some girl-code law or whatever, but I don't care. I love you." She released her arms, allowing Kendrick to sit up. "I heard what you said downstairs and I want you to know, I feel the same way. I think any man other than you would be a step down for me. I know all about you. But more importantly, I know who you are and what you stand for. You say what you mean and mean what you say. I know you would never betray my trust. I would consider it an honor to stand at your side."

Kendrick stood and walked over to the window. Doubts began to sway throughout his very core. He thought about what would happen when she outgrew him. He thought about his past and all the blood on his hands. He thought he didn't deserve love. Love was something that people who lived this life never experienced, especially for someone like him who was neck deep in it.

He didn't notice Anika walking up behind him as she wrapped her arms around his waist. She rested her head against his back as she held him in a silent embrace that said more than either could at that moment.

The silence almost became palpable when she whispered, "Why are you trying to make this harder than what it is? Why won't you just let this be what we both know it is?"

"You don't understand. . . I. . ." he was cut off as she stepped around in front of him and placed her fingers against his lips, silencing him.

"I don't think you're really hearing me. I know who you are, Kendrick. Those things that happened in your past were the actions of someone else. Your past relationships were the way they were because of the acts of selfish people."

She looked him deeply in the eye and leaned in to kiss him, never breaking eye contact. "I love you, and there's nothing you can do to change that. I'm not going to leave you, and I damn sure ain't trying to get any other dick than yours. Just the thought of it is making me want you again." She pushed him back to arm's length yet not breaking eye contact. "Now tell me."

"Damn, woman, you're like a dog with a bone! You know I love you!" He scooped her up in his arms, and she squealed as he carried her back to the bed. He placed her on the bed and then hovered above her body as he kissed her again. "I love you and nothing is going to change that."

"Damn, Skippy," she said as she began to kiss him as their passion began to rise anew. She broke the kiss and shook her finger at him. "Oh no, you don't! You think you're slick, don't you?"

Kendrick was thoroughly confused as he froze in his tracks. He didn't move a muscle for fear he would make a wrong move. "Uh, what happened?"

"Don't pretend like you're innocent! You know damn well what you were about to do." Before he could say anything, Anika quickly threw her legs behind her head. "Oh great, now you're just being mean." She put the back of her hand to her forehead in mock despair. "I can't believe that you would use your chiseled body and all-around sexiness against me like this! Oh, whatever will I do?!"

At first he was totally stupefied, but realization began to dawn as his manhood caught on quicker than he did as he became even harder, if that were possible. "Well, I guess you're going to have to pay the price!" he said in his deep menacing voice, which almost caused him to break character as he began to giggle, but quickly fought the urge.

"Oh no! Please don't put that huge monster into my tiny, little honey pot. I don't think I could handle another dozen orgasms!" She threw her hands up in mock fear as she spread her lips exposing her overflowing juices that ran freely down her ass crack.

"Just remember you brought this on yourself!" Kendrick said as he slowly, but gently, feed her his shaft. He noticed her toes beginning to curl as he inserted more and more of his cock into her eagerly awaiting love tunnel. They both became quiet as they watched his dick slowly disappear into her nether regions until his balls rested on her ass.

He started out with short quick thrust as he kept his shaft buried to the hilt inside her as she began having numerous mini orgasms that felt like tiny explosions going off. He was worried that maybe the position was uncomfortable for her, but she looked completely at ease. It seems that she was just as comfortable with her legs behind her head or sitting in a chair. The thought of her flexibility caused his dick to become harder as he increased his stroke. Now he was working with more than half, which caused Anika to begin moaning as he was starting to bring more intense orgasms out of her.

He felt himself getting close and she noticed too as he began to swell inside of her. "Can you fuck me a little harder please?" she said in a baby voice, which seemed to do something to him as he began to fuck her with an animalistic urgency.

Kendrick pulled it all the way out to the tip and then buried it in her depths as he pistoned in and out of her love box. He let out a grunt as he exploded inside of her as his seed filled the farthest reaches of her womb, which triggered a massive orgasm inside of her. Anika began to come down from her orgasm and to her amazement; he was still pounding her tight, little pussy.

They fucked for another half hour, each of them having two more orgasms before they collapsed on top of each other. Kendrick kept his dick buried inside of Anika, trapping their combined fluids from their love-making.

Eventually he started to go sof, and he fell out of her with a slight popping noise as their fluids began to pool on the bed. Kendrick hopped up from the bed and laid a towel down so neither one of them had to sleep in the wet spot, which she appreciated.

They got under the cover and cuddled in each other's arms and legs and fell fast asleep. Anika didn't tell Kendrick that she had to work tomorrow, but after tonight, she deserved a break. She kissed his chest lightly as she drifted off to sleep.

CHAPTER ELEVEN

"Look, I told you like a million times she isn't coming in today because something came up."

Deshaun looked at Shawna with a strange look. "I only asked you like once, and that was just now. Are you okay?"

She rolled her eyes, not bothering to look at him. "I'm fine, I couldn't be better. As a matter of fact, I think I'm too happy that, I'm afraid you might ruin my day if you keep hanging around me." She waved her hand at Deshaun, indicating that he should leave her station. Not knowing what else to do, he walked back to his office, shaking his head.

He walked into his office and slammed the door behind him in frustration. He's been working on the proposal to the largest car dealership on the East Coast for over a month. The plan was for Anika to shadow him on his first major deal but she's been M-I-A for the last week. Even when she's in the office, she seems to be a million miles away.

She told him he would do fine, just use his better judgment and there shouldn't be a problem. He didn't know what was going on with her. She would never have said that before. Whatever the case, he knew his career could be made or broken over this deal.

He walked over to his desk, brought up his proposal and went over the numbers for what seemed like the millionth time. From what he could tell, the numbers were perfect. What he needed was a second set of eyes. Normally, he would turn to Anika, but that obviously isn't a choice at this point.

He had an idea, but he knew he would be setting himself up for abuse. He could have gone to one of the other buyers, but frankly he didn't trust them. Besides that, he's seen some of their work, and frankly, this might be over their heads. He looked at his watch and sighed as it was way past business hours, and everyone has probably already gone home.

He stared at the phone, dreading what came next, but he knew in the end that, he didn't really have a choice. He took a deep breath and then dialed the number.

She answered almost immediately, "What" was all that she said.

"Can you come to my office, please?"

"Why?"

"I need your help with something."

"Can't you just tell me what it is so I can decide if I want to help you or not?"

Deshaun was quickly becoming irritated, but he held his tongue as he continued, "I need your help with this report, and you're the only person I could think of who could actually help me with it."

There was a long pause as he waited for Shawna to respond. "Give me a sec, I'll be right there."

Deshaun was a little dejected because of her attitude. He thought things were admittedly a little rough in the beginning, but eventually they became quite cordial toward one another. They would even crack jokes and have lunch, then all of a sudden, nothing. He tried on several occasions to broach the subject, but she flatly refused to talk about it.

He even sent her flowers anonymously in hopes that it would brighten her mood. He spied on her out of his office door as her face brightened when she got them. She smiled as she inhaled the scent, but when she saw him looking, an odd look came over her and she immediately dumped them in the trash. She must have figured out they were from him.

It's been over a month since she stopped speaking to him, and he resigned himself to just being strictly professional. He was happy that they were friends once and even secretly wished for more. But now, the only time he can see her is at work.

Something is better than nothing he thought to himself. There was a knock at his door and he was brought out of his increasingly depressing thoughts. Before he could say "Come in," Shawna walked right in before being given permission.

He ignored her breach in protocol if not in manners and got straight to the point. He put on his most sincere, pleading smile. "I know you're probably busy, but I could really use your help with this proposal. I don't know who else to turn to."

Shawna stood there with her arms folded, not making eye contact while staring at the wall. "Let me guess, you couldn't find anyone else to help you so you came crawling to me?"

He was taken totally by surprise with the odd statement, but he quickly recovered. "You were the first person I came to. I know you don't like me, but I think you're smart and you really know your stuff."

At hearing that, she finally turned to look him. "Why would you think I would be busy?"

It was his turn not to meet her eyes. "Well, seeing how beautiful you are, I figured you would have more offers for dates than you would know what to do with them." He waved his hand up and down in her general direction, indicating her whole appearance. He looked at his watch. "Not to mention, it's after 6:30 and you should have already been gone by now.

When he said that, she looked at her watch and swore under her breath. "Hold on, I have to send off this report for Anika or she'll have my ass. Give me a couple of minutes, I'll be right back." She ran out of his office to finish up her duties.

He moved his laptop over to the small conference table he had in his office that he normally used to eat his lunch. It allowed access all the way around, so it would make it easier for both of them to look everything over at the same time. He grabbed a bottle of water out of the mini-fridge as Shawna came rushing back in.

When she came back in, he froze. She came in sporting a smile and it looked as if she let her blonde hair down and it was now falling over her shoulders. He started to say something witty, but he didn't want to inadvertently ruin her mood again so he kept it to himself.

She noticed his staring but said nothing as she walked over and sat down in the chair breathlessly. "So, let me see what's got your panties all in a bunch." She turned the laptop towards herself and started reading.

Deshaun just sat there not knowing what to do. He was almost afraid to talk for fear of saying the wrong thing. He began to look her over and he had to admit that she was sexy as hell. She had large, supple breasts that strained against her button-up white dress shirt. He was sitting at an angle that allowed him to steal a peek of her shapely legs. They were thick, but not flabby. He could tell that she worked out regularly. But the thing that stood out the most was her shapely ass.

He always considered himself a gentleman, but the first time he saw her, it took everything in him not to try and ask her out right then and there. He knew Anika offered him an opportunity that he may not have gotten on his own, and he didn't want to mess that up even if it meant that he had to put his love life on hold. Not that he had any issues in that department.

He was tall and slender with a well-defined physique. He works out five days a week to keep in shape. Ladies always found him to be charming, and he could be very persuasive when he wanted to be.

"Hello, you still here?" Deshaun snapped his head up when he noticed that Shawna was talking to him. He could tell by the smirk on her face that she knew what he was doing. "I got a few pics you could have if you think it would help."

Now, he was totally embarrassed. Not knowing what else to say, he blurted out. "You hungry?"

She started chuckling. "Sure, Chinese sounds good. Don't order from the one across the street, as theirs taste like shit. Order from Sung Paw's and get me chicken and broccoli, extra spicy."

He called and placed their orders, ordering himself chicken fried rice and two spring rolls. He grabbed a bottle of water for Shawna, and she smiled as she took a sip.

"I think I know what your problem is," she said as she waved him over to her side as he slid his chair next to hers. She noticed his intoxicating scent and felt a slight shiver. She quickly looked at him and to her relief, he didn't notice. "Your problem is that you're giving away money."

Deshaun was ready to argue that he clearly thought out everything, but she held up her hand, cutting him off. "Your proposal is great, but you are offering things that shouldn't be included in your initial offer. You want to leave room for negotiations. If you start out high, you have nowhere to go, which makes you look like a rookie, which unfortunately you are."

He sat back in his chair with his arms crossed, feeling slightly defensive. He sighed, "What do you suggest?"

They sat down and got to work. They argued over what to take out. Deshaun said that several items were the linchpin of the whole deal, while Shawna contented that he could take them out and just change the approach. They went back and forth like this until the food arrived.

They decided to take a break to eat. He went over to the mini-fridge and grabbed a couple bottles of water to go with the meal. Shawna took the bottle and smiled her thanks. They sat down and made small talk to past the time. They started telling stories of their childhood and how they tried to cover up when they got in trouble.

He told her about a time when he was in high school and took his mom's car out while she was sleep and somehow got a scratch on the door. He told her how he began to panic when he finally, in his desperation, grabbed a magic marker and colored it in.

"So, what happened, did she find out?" Shawna said around a mouthful of food.

"Nothing. It wasn't until later, about a month if I remember, she sent me to the store to pick up some eggs because she was making my graduation cake. She was standing on the porch when I pulled in the driveway and she noticed a slight discoloration on the door.

She didn't say anything as I went into the house and sat the bags down in the kitchen. I turned around and she was standing in the doorway. By this time I forgot about the whole painting-the-door thing and just shrugged. She just nodded and walked away."

"A couple of days later, I asked her did she see my Jordan's I just got, and she looked me dead in the eye and just shrugged and walked away. I knew then that she knew I did it and got me back big-time. I had to run the stadium stairs for like a month until I could save up some money to replace them because they were part of my basketball uniform and we got a technical every time I came out on the floor out of uniform."

"My mom just set in the crowd and gave me a smirk every time my team yelled at me."

Shawna was laughing so hard that she started snorting. She tried to fight it, but wound up doing it all the more. Her laughter became infectious, and soon they both were laughing so hard that they were tearing up. "That was messed up! I guess you learned your lesson huh?"

He just looked at her as she laughed and all he could do was smile. "You know, this was really fun."

She returned his smile. "Yeah, I'm glad we did this."

"I'm glad we can be friends again. You don't know how much I missed hanging out with you, homie."

At hearing his words, her smile began to falter. She tried to pretend his words didn't hurt, but she couldn't hide it as tears began to run down her face. She turned away so he couldn't see how much his words hurt her as she stood to walk out of his office.

Deshaun saw that he did it again. He saw her stand to walk away yet again and leave him clueless. This time, he wanted to know. "Shawna, what did I do this time!"

Shawna stopped at the door and turned around with tears in her eyes. "Why do you keep doing this to me? One minute I think maybe you like me, and then the next minute you pull the rug out from under me. I don't know what type of joy you get out of this, but I do have my pride." She turned around and placed her hand on the door to leave. She spoke without looking back. "Please don't speak to me unless you absolutely have to. I don't think I can take any-more of your games."

"You like me?"

She didn't know if it was the genuineness in voice or false hope, but she turned around to regard him. "Isn't it obvious? I always find a reason to talk to you. Sometimes, I can't believe how handsome and funny you are and I just clam up."

"I always wondered why you did that." Things were starting to finally make sense as all the pieces were starting to fall into place. "The funny thing is, I've been crushing on you since the first time I saw you.

I wanted to say something, but I thought Anika would frown on that sort of thing and I didn't want to blow this opportunity." He just shook his head and started to laugh. "I just assume you had a man waiting at home. I figured that if I couldn't be with you, I would be your friend."

It was her turn to laugh. "No man at home. We broke up a while ago. He didn't think I was worth cherishing."

"I would," he said as he gave her a deadly serious look.

Shawna's breath caught in her chest as she noticed how serious he was. Before she knew it, she was walking toward him. She couldn't stop herself now if she wanted to, which at this time she really didn't want to as she cupped his face with both hands and kissed him deeply.

He saw her walking toward him with a look of determination. A part of him wanted to brace because he thought she might hit him again, which, if he were being honest with himself, he probably deserved it. He knew she wasn't going to hit him when she cupped his face in her hands and kissed him. All the longing he felt for her bubbled to the surface as he pulled her closer to him and kissed her back with equal fervor.

Their hands were all over each other as their passions began to ignite. Their tongues were fighting for supremacy in each other's mouths as their hands began to explore more sensual regions. Deshaun gently placed his hands on shoulders and pushed her back.

The look of hurt and embarrassment played across her face. She tried to move away, but he held her firmly in place. "I have to ask you something." He wrapped her in his arms when he noticed that her lips began to quiver, which was a clear sign that tears were soon to follow. "I wanted to know if Anika would be cool with all of this. I don't want to lose my job, but I also don't want to lose you."

She leaned her head back to see if he was playing with her emotions, and once she was satisfied that that wasn't the case, a smile crept across her face. "What makes you think she doesn't know already?" She had to fight the urge to laugh when she saw the bewildered look on his face. She gave him a peck. "Believe me when I tell you that if she had a problem, she would have told you and me, more than likely at the same time."

Deshaun began to visibly relax when he realized that there wouldn't be any issues at work. He grabbed her hand and pulled her toward him, and she let him as they found themselves in each other's arms once again.

They quickly picked up where they left off without missing a beat. Their mouths found one another again as they became lost in their passion. Deshaun was running his hands up her back as he then started to caress to the small of her back. Shawna broke away and looked deep in his eyes as she removed his hands from her back and slid them underneath her blouse so that he could caress her ample breasts.

"I love to have my breasts played with, do you think it would be okay if I remove this hot blouse?" Before he could say anything, she had the shirt unbuttoned, over her head, and on tossed on the couch.

She stood before him, topless with the exception of her lace bra, which gave little if any support as her breasts stood proud and firm on their own. Deshaun leaned against his desk with his mouth held open in utter shock. He knew she wasn't shy, but he didn't expect this. She stood with her hands on hips in all her glory. She had a flat, well-defined stomach with light freckles on her otherwise unblemished exposed skin. He could just make out her dark nipples through her sheer bra.

"You know I could just leave a picture if you like." She was still standing with her hands on her hips. "I want you."

That was all the encouragement he needed. He reached behind her and released the clasp of her bra with one hand. She was ready to make a smart comment, but was cut off as the only sound that came from her was a loud intake of air as he began to suck on her breast.

He started out by simply licking each nipple in turn, rotating back and forth between them all the while as she began moaning softly. He continued administering pleasure to her breasts as he began to suck on them lightly. He knew he struck the right chord when she began to stroke the back of his head as she gently pulled him closer.

He had a feeling that "gentle" could turn into something more forceful if he tried to pull away. He didn't want to risk her anger by trying even though he was somewhat curious. Landing on the better side of caution, he continued pleasuring her breasts.

A loud moan escaped her throat as her body began to tense and shake slightly. "I can't believe you made me cum. That hasn't happened in a month of Sundays." She pulled his face toward her and began peppering it with small kisses, her way of saying thank-you.

It was her turn to please him. She began by kissing him on the neck as she unbuttoned his shirt. She removed it and began kissing his chest. She worked her way down to his pants and started removing his belt, followed by his pants. She squeezed his dick through his boxers, and it was rock hard. She tried to find the tip and found it near his hip. "Damn," she said under breath as she started to remove away his boxers.

She grabbed his third leg by the base and could barely get her hand around it as her middle finger and thumb struggled to meet. She buried her nose between his shaft and balls and inhaled as the scent became intoxicating. She started to lick his balls and his dick jumped, and it would have slipped from her hand if she didn't have a firm grip on it. She sucked on his balls lightly for a few minutes until his staff began to pulse angrily in her hand, demanding the attention it so richly deserves.

All the time she spent on his nuts caused his dick to become jealous, she thought. Little did he know that the best was yet to come. She has had a few boyfriends over the years and they all, for one reason or another, have turned out to be jerks of the highest order. But if you were to ask them, not one would ever say that sex was the problem. If anything, the sex is what made them try to be something that they weren't.

Her views on sex were simple: anything but children or small animals. If it was to please her man, it was on the table. Anal? Yes, please. Threesome? As long as she went first. Anytime, anyplace was her motto.

One time, a boyfriend she thought might be the one kept hinting at a threesome with her best friend at the time. She knew his birthday was coming up, and she had something special in mind for him. She invited him over for a quiet evening at her house considering he never liked making a big deal about his birthday. He considered it one step closer to death, he would say.

He came in and the lights were off. He called out tentatively for her, but there was no response. He made his way to the bedroom and opened and the door. He saw Shawna and her best friend, Megan, were waiting on the bed in various enticing lingerie. Megan was on the bed in a matching bra-and-panty set that left nothing to the imagination while wearing a dog collar and holding a tray of grapes. Shawna had on a white lace body-suit that accentuated all of her best features as she stood by the bed holding Megan's leash.

They all enjoyed the evening together as she pleased her man in all the ways he's been begging for and even a few he didn't. They fucked him until he begged them to stop, and even then, they tried to get just a little bit more just to make sure they got every last drop.

It wasn't until a few weeks later that she went to her man's house to surprise him with dinner that she found her best friend and the man that she loved more than anything fucking on the sheets she bought him because he had a thing for silk. They were so caught up in each other that they didn't even notice her there watching them with a look of betrayal and hurt. She left, and they never saw her again.

Since then, she has gone from one failed relationship to another, with all of them ultimately breaking her heart.

Even with all of the heart-aches she's experienced in her life, the thought of giving up on love has never been an option. One thing she has always given herself credit for was never falling for the same trick twice. But like anything else, men have been rather creative with their lack of commitment.

To say all men cheat, wouldn't be doing them justice. She has had to deal with cheaters, thieves, and liars. She even had one guy fake his death because he didn't want to commit (actually, he faked his death because he owed some guys a lot of money, but it still counts).

Her last boyfriend loved spending time with her, but he loved spending time with her trust fund more. Her parents gave her a sizable sum when she turned twenty-one that she never intended to tell anyone that she had. As far as the world knew, she was struggling like everyone else. She wanted to make it on her own and find out her true worth before leaning on mommy and daddy for assistance.

It was a total fluke that he found out about her previously unknown wealth. She had been checking her monthly statements online and her computer crashed. She told Craig, her boyfriend at the time, and he offered to help. Since the computer was turned off, she assumed that all the information had been erased. But somehow when he brought it back up, there it was.

From that point forward, their relationship had changed. He became more doting toward her, but he stopped going to school and doing pretty much anything else. She tried to motivate him by getting him a job through Anika, but he didn't have any experience. After that, the relationship just fell apart. When he left, he blamed her for being selfish, not sharing with the person she supposedly loved. He totally neglected the fact that she worked since she met him.

Her thoughts were brought back to the present when she felt his dick jump in her mouth, and that was all the warning she was given as he started to cum down her throat in gushes. It wasn't until then that she noticed that he had her head in a death grip and his cock continued to shoot torrents of cum down the back of her throat.

She absolutely loved it.

Shawna loved when a man takes control in bed, especially in an office at work. He had the full length of his dick buried to the hilt as the hairs on his balls tickled her chin. She stuck her tongue out as he began to fuck her face as the last vestiges of his orgasm poured in her hungry mouth.

As he began to go limp, he fell out of her mouth. She noticed a drop still hanging precariously from the tip and she quickly licked it up. *"Waste not, want not,"* she thought.

Thinking their session was over, she reached down to grab her clothes that were thrown around the office, she felt a hand pull her arm, turning her around. She looked up and saw a confused look on Deshaun's face. "We're done already?" Was all he could say at her attempted departure.

Shawna stared at him with a look of bewilderment. *"How can he still be ready for more?"* she thought to herself as she looked down and saw that his dick was slowly rising again.

"Can you turn around and place your leg on the desk, if you would please?" You would think he was asking her to pass the sugar at an office breakfast meeting and not asking her to assume the position, on a desk no less. She couldn't help but smirk as she quickly obeyed his commands.

She waited with eager anticipation as she waited on both knees with her ass turned up in the air. Her excitement caused her fluids to begin to flow as she waited for the first stroke. She was wondering what the holdup was when she felt his hand slap her across her ass. To say she was surprised would be an epic understatement.

Deshaun has always been somewhat reserved, but she always attributed that to this being his first real job, and they, more often than not, only saw each other in a work environment.

She was brought out of her thoughts as he slapped her ass again, which caused her to wiggle, waiting for the next slap. She wasn't disappointed as he slapped her ass yet again, but this time a little harder. This was followed by another and then another.

With each stroke, Shawna could feel her arousal grow. One of the things she always wanted was to be spanked. She doesn't know when the fetish started, but it's one she loves to be done to her. There were boyfriends who she approached with the idea. Either they flat-out refused or others said they would, but were too timid to make it count.

Deshaun slapped her ass yet again and she orgasmed.

Her body began to quiver all over as she is racked with a massive orgasm that seemed to last longer than she thought possible. Her body became like jelly as she fell forward which caused her to unintentionally raise her ass higher and her legs spread even wider.

She felt the head slide in easily as her pussy was drenched from her orgasm. She flinched slightly as the thickest part of the shaft started to spread her almost to its limit. She never had someone so big inside of her before and she thought she was up to the challenge, but now she was having second thoughts.

He was starting to enter virgin territory, and she was trying to reach back and place a hand on his stomach to keep him from going any further. He gently placed her back on the desk as he continued to feed her more than she could handle.

Her eyes were shut tight as the pain was almost too much to bear. Then, her body began to shake as another orgasm ran through her. Her juices coated his dick, which made it a little easier for her to handle. She felt his balls brush up against her as he finally, mercifully, got it all the way inside of her womb.

They stayed in that position for a few moments, allowing her to become accustomed to his girth. He grabbed his shirt and placed it under her knees, and she was thankful because they were starting to hurt. She looked back and gripped him with her pussy, just to say thank you, and she swore he blushed.

Deshaun started to move slowly with small strokes. After a while, Shawna noticed the pain began to subside as the pleasure was starting to win out. She wiggled her ass, urging him to pick up the pace.

He was fucking her with the full length of his manhood, pulling it out to the tip, only to fill her up until he was buried balls deep. The pleasure was building as they were both becoming lost in the act. Deshaun was now slamming his full length inside of Shawna, and to say that she was enjoying herself would be an understatement.

The orgasms were now coming back to back to back. She can't remember ever coming this much. He had both of his hands on the small of her back as he continued to drill her with no end in sight. He was pulling her back to meet his stroke, which was causing her to moan.

The inklings of a massive orgasm were on the horizon, and Shawna was meeting his stroke as she more than welcomed it. She felt it deep inside as the pressure built to a delicious crescendo. When the first wave hit, it took her breath away.

This orgasm was unlike anything she had ever felt before. Her body shook uncontrollably as the pleasure was more than she was prepared to handle. All the while, Deshaun continued his assault on her pussy which caused the pleasure to be prolonged with no end in sight.

A tear escaped her eye as she continued to ride the waves of ecstasy. Her pussy involuntary clamped down on Deshaun's staff, which caused him to grunt which was the only warning she received as he began to pour copious amounts of his man seed into her tight little pussy.

This triggered another orgasm, which caused her to black-out momentarily, and when she came through, he was stroking her slowly as he came down from his orgasmic high. He took a step back and his still semi-hard dick reluctantly left her. She now felt empty and had a strong desire for him to fuck her again as crazy as it sounded.

The evidence of their love-making began to flow from her as it settled on his shirt. She tried to move, but her legs were too weak. She didn't have enough strength to even sit up as she collapsed down on the desk spread-eagled.

Gentle hands began to help her off the desk and over to the small couch in his office. Deshaun brought her a bottle of water from the refrigerator, which she gratefully accepted. She downed it in a few gulps and he had another at the ready, which she took and sipped this time now that the urgency had passed.

She looked down and saw that she was covered in sweat and she could only imagine how she looked. She subconsciously began to fix her hair, then he grabbed her hand and said, "Please don't. I think you look beautiful."

Not knowing how to take it, Shawna just stared at him. She's not used to someone being so frank with her. Usually, guys will say anything to get in her pants, but he already has so. . . what does he want? Everybody wants something, right? She thought to herself as she just stared at him with gratitude and more than a little skepticism.

As if he could read her mind, Deshaun said, "Don't read too much into it. I just think you look beautiful regardless of the situation." He shrugged as if it was the most obvious thing in the world.

Sitting up suddenly, Shawna stared at him intently. "I don't want to read too much into anything, but, what are we doing here? Did you just want to fuck me, add a little cream to your coffee? Or was this more than a one-time deal?"

Now, it was his turn to look at her with regard. He saw an intense look on her face, but he also saw . . . fear? He took her hand into his. "I'm gonna have to say this can only be a one-time thing." Her eyes got big as saucers as tears threatened to form. She tried to pull her hand away, but he held tight. "What I was going to say was that we can't do this in the office. I was hoping maybe at my place? I can cook dinner or we can go out. I was thinking Mexican; I haven't had that in a while."

Shawna turned her eyes away from him as she started to blush. "I guess that sounds cool, when you wanted to go?"

"I thought we were going to go now? After messing around with you, a dude needs to eat. Next time, I'll be better prepared," he started laughing.

"So, what are we, fuck buddies or something?" she said as her guard slowly started to creep back up.

"What are you getting at? Just tell me exactly what it is you want to know and I'll answer honestly." He starts to put on his clothes, and she couldn't help but admire his form. "If you're asking if we're fuck buddies, then I would probably have to say no. . ."

"Oh" was all she could say as she began to get dressed. She was hoping for more, but she was glad he was being honest as much as it hurts.

"Look, I think I can have pretty much any woman I want. I'm not trying to blow my own head up because if I don't believe it, who will, right? It's just that if, I can have any woman, why would I have just any woman? Shawna, I want you. I've had one girlfriend throughout high school and most of college, that's it. I don't know what we are, but I'm not trying to muddy the waters with other women. I want to give you my undivided attention and see where this goes." He walked over and grabbed a polo shirt out of a bag he keeps in his office. "Did I answer your question?"

Now, she was really blushing as she smiled. "Yes, I believe you have."

"Cool, let's go eat," he said as he opened the door. She walked out and he slapped her ass as she walked by. She looked at him questioningly. "You better get used to it. You have an ass that needs attending to," he said as he closed the door behind them.

"I'm going to hold you to it." she said as she grabbed his hand as they made their way to the elevator.

CHAPTER TWELVE

He kept looking at his watch and noticed it's going on two o'clock and he has an important meeting in an hour. He keeps mumbling to himself that this is no way to do business. Jay had half a mind to leave, but he knew he went through too much and called in pretty much all of his favors just to get this appointment. Now was not the time to let pride get in the way.

The waiter came over to see if there was anything else he needed, and he just waved him away. The less contact he had, the better chance that he won't be able to remember his face if things went sideways. He paid in cash, which made it harder for anyone to place him at the restaurant.

He chose this location purposely because most deals that took place here were off the books and more than likely illegal in nature. There were no cameras in the restaurant and none on the streets surrounding the area, and he was pretty sure that wasn't by accident.

He glanced at his watch again as his impatience began to fester. The war raging inside of him on whether to leave or stay was causing his anger to rise. He downed his glass of merlot in two gulps and slammed it on the table. He grabbed his jacket off the chair and prepared to leave.

"Jayson Perry, I presume? I do apologize for being late. I rather had an unruly situation where my previous client decided he didn't or couldn't pay. I think I believed him when he said that he didn't have it. It matters not really; my pockets were still empty in the end. I rather liked him actually; he will be missed. So what is it that you need?"

Jay didn't like being addressed by his full name in public, especially considering the nature of their meeting. "My friends call me Jay." He extended his hand in greeting.

"We're not friends," he said without a hint humor. Where once was a warm smile now held a strictly business demeanor. "I don't eat and shit in the same room. I may have to kill you at some point." He pointedly ignored his handshake.

Jay was somewhat taken aback by his words, but he really wasn't all that surprised. Even though he worked in the corporate realm, it wasn't beyond the pale if someone decided they wanted to take his business. This way, they wouldn't have to buy him out. He fought the urge to look around, seeing phantom dangers lurking around every corner.

He pushed such foolish thoughts out of his mind and dismissed them as unfounded fears. He regarded the man that sat casually before him in a very expensive, blue, three-piece suit. He had tattoos of intricate designs on the back of his hands, and he could tell that they ran up his arms. He noticed that the man was tall and very muscular. He exuded confidence and menace all at the same time without even trying. The last thing anyone would want is to cross paths with a man like him.

He was perfect.

The man snapped his fingers, which brought Jay out of his deep thoughts. "I thought you wanted to offer me work, not admire me. For the record, I don't go that way."

Jay was embarrassed and wanted to argue that he wasn't, which would only have made things worse. "Are you wearing a wire? Are you the police?"

"You're wasting my time. I'm outta here."

The man rose to leave, Jay wasn't about to start all over again. He banged his hand on the table which caught the attention of those nearby. The well-dressed man glanced around and noticed that he was being watched. Jay noticed that he didn't like that, so he sat down so the eyes would leave him.

"Do that again and I'll kill your whole family and send you the video," he said in a low menacing voice.

Jay knew he was playing a dangerous game that in all likelihood he could wind up dead. Now was not the time to turn back. His life and possibly his families hung in the balance. "You never answered my question."

"After I leave here, your family is dead." his voice dripped with venom.

Jay couldn't help but swallow back the fear as he looked at him in a way that made him want to run out of there and hide, but he fought through. "I don't think you will unless there's money to be had. The only money involved in this is with me. Answer the question."

They stared at each other intently, then the well-dressed man broke into a smile. "I think I might get to like you if this all works out. To answer the question, I'm not wearing a wire and I'm not a cop or the police."

"Thank you."

"Just so you know, I really would have killed your family just to prove a point. Of course, I would have changed clothes first; this suit is too nice to mess up for free." he said as the smile never left his face. You would have thought he was talking about the wine selection at how easily he talked about murdering his family. "My name is Lawrence Mikelson." He extended his hand.

Jay shook it in turn. "I appreciate it. Now if you're amendable to possibly adding let's say. . . my wife to the list, I'm sure we can work something out."

He knew his wife was planning on leaving him and taking the kids. He didn't really care one way or the other, but she also had a secret account and found that she was hiding money for years apparently. It just so happen that he was on friendly terms with the top divorce lawyers in the city and one let it slip over drinks one night.

He needed her death to look like an accident, and if that meant the kids too well. . . you sometimes have to break a few eggs to make an omelet.

Jay pulled out a manila folder and slid it over to the man. "I need you to make it messy and if you can add her apparent boyfriend to it, all the better."

Lawrence opened the folder and began to look them over. He knew the woman wouldn't be an issue. Something about her seemed vaguely familiar. He turned his attention to the man and knew it would be something altogether different.

That was Kendrick Washington. They have known each other for the majority of their lives. He got him out of more scraps than he could count and in a pinch. He was always there for him when he needed help with money or just to talk.

"You're gonna have to find yourself someone else. I'll return your retainer."

He got ready to leave, but Jay's words held him in his seat. "I thought you were supposed to be the best. For some reason, I can't find anyone in this town to take my money. I offered them double their usually fee, but they all turned me down flat. Oh well, on to the next, I suppose. . ." Jay mumbled to himself, clearly perturbed.

Lawrence became lost in his thoughts as he remembered how things ended. He didn't understand what the big deal was; they've been through worse than that. Even as he tried to explain himself, Kendrick said that if he ever saw him again he would kill him. At first, he thought he was joking, but once he put the word out, he knew that they were done.

"I'll pay you triple if you take the job and double if you can kill them both. I'll give you half now and the rest when the job is done" Jay said as a last-ditch effort.

He smiled. "I think we might be able to work something out." *I guess we're going to settle this once and for all* he thought to himself.

Both men shook and ordered drinks to celebrate their arrangement.

CHAPTER THIRTEEN

The music washed over her as she closed her eyes, letting the last few days of stress fade away. She knew when she decided to take those two weeks off, she would pay for it. In her position, she could only delegate so much, and that was part of the problem.

The few people who are in her position rarely take vacations. And if they did, it wasn't more than two, maybe three days at a time and they all said they spent more time than a little bit working through the night to stay on top of their workload. Most of them said they don't like surprises, and others feared for their jobs.

She thought she was above all of that; reality showed her otherwise. Everything they said was true, and she wasn't prepared for that. The first day, everything seemed fine and she thought they overstated the situation. But by day three, her phone was lighting up like a Christmas tree. Kendrick was more than understanding with her situation and held no ill will toward her working, but she didn't want to hear it. And she loved him for it.

The first week she thought she had it worked out, that she would only look once a day and that was only if she was directly needed. By the second week, she was working while Kendrick slept and whenever he went to the store for groceries. Even then, she had a mountain of work when she came back.

It took her three weeks just to catch up, and even then she still felt like she's behind. Warm, familiar hands began to massage her shoulders from behind. The soothing caress of his hands felt so good she could cry. It wasn't until he started working out the knots, which she didn't realize were there, did she realize how tense she was.

She felt like she was floating on a cloud as he massaged away the tension that she carried on her shoulders. He told her that she needed to take ten minutes a day for her to stretch, meditate, or simply relax, and her body would thank her for it. Of course she didn't listen and now she's paying for it.

"How does that feel?" His voice was melodic in her ear, and his warm breath sent chills down her spine. She could feel him smiling against her as he knew he had her. "So I take it you didn't listen, again."

She got ready to make an excuse, but he would just see through it. She loved and hated that he knew her so well. "I got busy and wanted to, but I honestly didn't think I had the time." It was the truth, but she knew he was right. He never seemed to stress.

She turned around in her chair and began to kiss him like she hadn't seen him in years. Technically, it was three days, but it felt like forever. The world quickly fell away as she became lost in the man she loved as a simple kiss became more. She came to her senses when she had realized to her embarrassment that she had begun to wrap her legs around his waist.

She had forgotten she was in their favorite restaurant that they had their memorable ill-fated first date. Most people would have sworn off the place that they were almost killed in, but Kendrick wouldn't hear of it. He told her that she wasn't really in any danger because he had the situation under control.

As much as she wanted to believe it, there had always been an element of doubt deep down inside. What would have happened if he was in the bathroom for just two more minutes? What if he was able to take her out of the restaurant before he came back? She shuddered at the thought.

Kendrick had ordered drinks while she zoned out, and she was glad because she felt like she needed it. She looked to her right and saw an older couple that looked like they were in their early sixties; she smiled and waved hello.

The lady had waved her closer, and she leaned in so she could hear what she had to say. The lady's voice wasn't that strong, so she cupped her hand so she could hear her better.

She smiled and whispered, "He must be putting it down because you looked like you was ready right there on that bar stool." She chuckled.

Anika sat back in total shock and started laughing. "You kinda freaky there, ain't you, grandma? But you right, I've never had anything like that before. I can barely keep up half the time; I just sit back and enjoy the ride." Anika couldn't help but laugh because she reminded her so much of her own grandmother. They're gonna have to do lunch soon, she thought.

"What can I say? You're not the first lady to partake of the joys of excellent dick. My Clyde has been doing me good and proper since the seventies. And before you ask, yes, we still making it happen. Just because you old doesn't mean you stop."

Both ladies leaned in and laughed as they toasted to their fortunate turn of events. Kendrick and Clyde looked at one another and just silently shook their heads with mirroring smirks on their faces. Both couples spent the next hour laughing and enjoying each other's company.

Eventually, the hour became late and the elderly couple had to excuse themselves. Anika, being who she was, wrangled a promise out of them that they would do it again real soon. The couple was caught off guard that someone her age would want to hang out with them. She assured them that she really enjoyed their company and that it was a joy just seeing mature love. After hearing that, they readily agreed to meet up next week; maybe a little earlier. Anika couldn't have been happier as she waved bye to them from the bar.

Kendrick just smiled and shook his head at her. He knew that she was a people person and if he was being honest with himself, it was a good thing for him as well. He was always polite, but due to his life experiences, he tended to keep his guard up, which made it hard to make meaningful connections.

She turned toward Kendrick and wrapped her arms around his neck to bring him in for another kiss. "That was really fun spending time with them. I'm really looking forward to seeing them next week." She thought for a moment and suddenly turned toward Kendrick "I didn't ask you if you would be able to make it."

He just smiled at the woman that he loved. "Oh, so now you ask," teasing her. "I'll move some things around. Just so you know, I really enjoyed them too."

Anika became lost in thought as she imagined all the years that they have been together and yet they still love each other. "Do you think we will have that when we get old?"

He pulled her into a hug. "If it doesn't happen, it won't be because I didn't want it to. I'm in it for the long haul."

"Awwwwwwww, didn't you tell me pretty much the same thing?" ShaBree said as she sat several seats away.

Kendrick cursed inside. He didn't even notice her enter the bar. "I think you and I have totally different memories of that, ShaBree."

Anika turned to look as soon as she heard Kendrick's ex's name. She looked at her with a critical eye. ShaBree was about her height and, she had to admit, beautiful. She had big, beautiful light brown eyes, caramel skin, and long hair that came just below her shoulders. She had a shapely figure that most women would envy, but she could tell that she put in the work at the gym by her toned arms, flat midsection, and sculptured legs.

ShaBree had on a white dress that came just above her knees that wasn't revealing, but still allowed the eye the opportunity to catch a glimpse of what lay beneath. Her neck-line had the same effect and she wore a matching pair of white heels that matched her dress and carried a black purse that set the whole outfit off.

"Kendrick, we need to talk," ShaBree said, totally ignoring Anika. "I don't think you want to do this here, in front of your latest conquest." She turned to look at her as if she just now saw that she was there.

"I don't have time for your games, ShaBree. Why don't you just have a drink on me and enjoy the evening," Kendrick said as he tried to maintain his composure.

"That would be nice, but aren't you going to introduce me to your new toy?" ShaBree saw Kendrick's anger beginning to show and she amended, "I meant your soon-to-be ex."

The urge to beat the brakes off of this woman was starting to sound really good, but Anika knows how women are and she knew that she was just trying to push her buttons. But knowing that doesn't make it any easier, she thought ruefully.

She saw a smile spread across Kendrick's face, and she started to worry. Anyone who didn't know him wouldn't think anything of it. But she wasn't just anyone; she was his woman. His smile never touched his eyes as his stare never left ShaBree. "If I remember correctly, I believe anything free is good, right?"

Anika watched in silence as he leaned forward to order her the same drink he was having. He moved with an added grace that until now she had never seen. He was a moment away from action, and for the first time, she seemed afraid. She glanced over at ShaBree, who either didn't notice or was too dumb to realize that her life was about to end.

The bartender gave her the drink, and she took a sip and nodded her approval. "I see that your taste in liquor has improved. I suppose I have her to thank for that."

Now, Kendrick's demeanor was beginning to fray at the edges. "I need you to finish your drink soon or I might have to help you home." His words implied threat and from the look on his face, he meant every word.

She smiled at him with a hint of mischief. "I love it when you get angry. This reminds me of the last time I saw you. I never thanked you for that night. You fucked the dog shit out of me!" She tipped her glass toward Kendrick, then looked back at Anika. "I think you know all about that, am I right, girlfriend?" She put her hand up, waiting for a high-five that she knew wasn't coming.

Anika grabbed her drink from the bar and toasted with ShaBree, who couldn't hide her surprise. "Girl, you ain't never lied! I have to fight the urge all the damn time not to just hop right back on that dick. As a matter of fact, I took two weeks off just so I can fuck him every way I can think of. But you know all about that, right?"

She did her best to hide her smirk as ShaBree struggled not to let her emotions show. She reached for her drink and downed it. She shook her glass at the bartender, who he looked at Kendrick who gave a slight nod and he made her another drink. She grabbed her drink out of the bartender's hand and drank, but a lot slower than the one before.

Not one to give up easily, she looked at Anika in the eyes and said, "The way you're defending him, I guess he didn't tell you what we did. It's kind of sad really. . . he tends to string women along until he's done with them, and you're no exception. Tell me, how does my pussy taste?" She took a sip of her drink and then gave her a condescending smile as she shook her head in disappointment. "If you only knew. . ."

"That's just it, I do know."

ShaBree was about to take another drink when she paused with the glass inches from her lips, "What exactly do you know?"

Anika gave her a mocking smile. "You think my man and I don't talk? He told me all about you."

"I doubt it." she snorted.

"So he didn't tell me how you fucked his best friend and set him up to be jumped?"

ShaBree was at a loss for words. She looked to Kendrick for help out of habit, but he never looked her way as he sipped on his drink and watched the basketball game on the big-screen TV behind the bar. She knew he was listening in on every word, but he decided not to get involved. She saw an advantage in that. "I'm sure he didn't tell you all the details. He has skeletons in his closet that I'm sure he doesn't want out."

She thought she had effectively turned the tables on the situation. She was ready to drive the nail in the coffin, but was cut off; Anika raised her hand. She leaned in so that only ShaBree could hear, "When I say my man tells me everything, I wasn't saying that for effect. I know all about his reputation and how it was well deserved, if you catch my meaning. The one question I have is how in the fuck are you still here? I consider myself a Christian, but if you had done that to me, yo ass would have turned up missing."

ShaBree remembered how women were always trying to get at Kendrick when they were dating. She would ask him constantly if he was fucking somebody else, and he always said he wasn't. Finally, he stopped answering the question altogether. It was then she knew for sure that he had been with other women.

She noticed how, when Kendrick wasn't around, Lawrence would always find a reason to stand a little too close or say things that weren't necessarily of a friendly nature. He would sometimes come over at night when Kendrick was working or out of town. He said it was just to check up on her. She remembered how she wouldn't invite him in, but one night she finally did.

From that point on, they would fuck any chance they got. On a few occasions, they even did it while Kendrick was in the other room playing cards with his boys. She was getting her sweet revenge right under his nose, and he was none the wiser.

She recalled how Lawrence had introduced her to some of his boys from out of town who were looking to get a foothold in the neighborhood. They seemed pleasant enough; they always referred to her as "pretty lady," which she really appreciated. Although they were nice and always respectful, anytime they asked her questions, it always centered around Kendrick and what his habits were.

ShaBree wasn't stupid; she knew what they were getting at and ultimately what their intentions were. It wasn't until later that she found out that they were working for a bigger organization that was looking to test out a new designer drug in their neighborhood. They essentially were using them for guinea pigs. If she had known that at the time, she would have run straight to Kendrick and told him what they were up to.

But ultimately her pain stopped her from saying anything. She tried convincing herself that it was only weed; what could it hurt? They offered her a new handbag that wasn't available in their area yet as well as some spending money. Plus, they were going to knock Kendrick down a peg or two. That'll teach him for taking her for granted.

Looking back on it now, she should have seen the signs. After Lawrence introduced her to his friends, he started making excuses why he couldn't spend time with her. It was always Kendrick had him running errands or he thought maybe he was on to them and they needed to chill for a minute. He used to say hello even when Kendrick was there, but now he couldn't even meet her gaze. It was if he was distancing himself from her.

One day, she was on her way over to Kendrick's when several SUVs had rolled up on his home, kicked in his front and backdoor, then opened fire. A small army ran into his home and then came out several minutes later cussing. Apparently, Kendrick caught wind and left just before they arrived. She heard someone say her name, and she quickly hid in the alley. She stayed at a cousin's house for the next few days until things calmed down.

That night, the leader of the crew disappeared.

She got word from one of her girlfriends that the dudes who tried to kill Kendrick had left town and they never found their leader. She came home to find Kendrick and his boys sitting in her living room. She noticed that Lawrence was there too, and again he couldn't meet her gaze. She didn't have to be a mind reader to know what he was thinking.

She'll never forget the look of hurt on Kendrick's face. His eyes seemed tired and he looked like he had been crying. She wanted to run to him, but his stance told her that that may not be the wisest decision. He asked her to tell him the truth because he knew everything.

She lied.

Kendrick was many things, but stupid wasn't one of them. He took a few steps away from her and turned around to regain his composure. Once he turned back, she saw the look on his face and cold fear washed over her. At that moment, she realized there were no guarantees that she will walk out of the situation in one piece or if at all.

Kendrick walked up to her, gently placed both hands on her shoulders, and asked her again. She started to lie and felt his grip tighten like a vice, so she stopped midsentence. He asked yet again, but he held up a finger and said that if she lied again, he was going to kill her.

The truth rolled off her tongue in quick succession. She was talking so fast that he had to ask her to stop and then start over again, but slower. ShaBree took a deep breath and started over, but slower as he instructed.

She started from the first time she had met the out-of-town crew. She told him how they had started out nice and treated her with respect.

She told him how they started asking seemingly innocent questions about him. She didn't think anything of it at first, but then they slowly started asking more and more direct questions about him. They wanted to know where he was going and when he would be home.

She started crying as she tried to explain that she attempted to be more evasive with her answers. They continued to be nice, but she wasn't born yesterday and she knew that wouldn't continue if she didn't tell them what they wanted to hear. She even admitted that they gave her gifts and money as compensation. She turned her head away in shame, unable to meet Kendrick's intense glare.

"Is that all?"

"Yes, as far as I can remember, I swear." He released his vice-like grip and she started to move her arms, trying to return circulation to them.

Kendrick turned to walk away, but stopped. "How did you meet them in the first place? I know you pretty well and you're not the type of person to run with that type of crowd."

When he said "that type of crowd," she knew he meant hired killers. She thought it was rather hypocritical considering everyone in the room had killed more than their fair share, but she wasn't in any position to quibble.

"Well, how did you meet them?"

Fresh tears started to run down her cheeks as she began to tremble. "Please don't make me tell you! I'm begging you, Kendrick, I'll do anything. . . please don't. . ."

His jaw clenched as he fought the urge to strike her. "So, you'll protect him even though there's a real possibility that you'll die? ANSWER ME!"

"Yes." She said meekly, barely above a whisper.

He screamed as he grabbed a chair and threw it at the wall. People scrambled out of the way to avoid the debris. ShaBree felt her back smash into the wall as her senses reeled from the impact. He shook her and screamed, "Why would you do this to me?! What did I ever do to you?"

ShaBree's anger flared and with it, she found her courage. "You want to know what you did? You don't think I don't know about you and all those hoes you've been running around with?" She advanced on him and poked her figure in his chest, "I asked you repeatedly if you were cheating on me, Kendrick, and you just ignored me. I didn't deserve that, and you know it."

He said nothing as she continued on with her tirade, "But you know what, two could play at that game. Yes, I cheated on you. I didn't run around and fuck every guy in town. Lord knows I could have, and you wouldn't have ever noticed. No, I was better than that, better than you. I was with one man and he treated me with love and respect. More than I can say for you."

She gently placed both hands on his as she started to cry again. "I didn't know any of that was going to happen and that's the truth, but damn it, Kendrick, don't you think I deserve better than that?"

The look of hurt that was on his face broke heart. He looked to the ground and slowly shook his head. "You are a stupid woman. I never cheated on you, ShaBree. The reason I stopped answering you because it didn't deserve an answer. Why would I run around when the only place I wanted to run to was you? No matter what I did to show you how much I cared, you turned it into an excuse that I was trying to make up for something I never did."

"I don't believe you."

"Of course you don't. . ." He pulled his gun out of his holster, and she took a step back. She looked around to run, but there was nowhere to go. "The thing I don't understand was why you didn't just break it off instead of cheating on me with my best friend behind my back."

At hearing his words, the crew's eyes immediately found Lawrence. The look of shock at hearing that he had been caught was evident. His face screwed up with a look of outrage that someone would even suggest such a thing. He tried to rise, but multiple hands pushed him back down into his chair.

His eyes met Kendrick's and all he saw controlled rage. Not knowing what else to do, he tried to make light of the situation. "Look, bruh, I don't know what you heard but. . ."

Kendrick placed the barrel of the gun up against his forehead which caused Lawrence to swallow hard and go silent. "Don't even try and lie to me. As you can see, I'm not in the mood." He turned back to ShaBree, who looked resigned to her fate as she stood numbly. He grabbed her chin and lifted it so their eyes met. "So, out of all the niggas in the world, you had to fuck around with my best friend who was going to let you die." He turned away in disgust before she could respond.

Lawrence, realizing that he had no way out, tried a different approach. "We've been through too much to let a piece of ass get in the way of a friendship! We've known each other since diapers and baby bottles! Shit, Kendrick, I made you my son's godfather!"

"Yeah. . . I know. . . That's why you're not dead already. The fact that you fucked my ex-girlfriend pissed me off, but over time, we probably could have got past it. But that you would help some niggas from out of town kill your supposed best friend so they can sell drugs in a neighborhood that your son, my god son, lives in is unforgivable!"

Lawrence's eyes widened as realization settled in. "Yeah, I fucked her." He waved his chin in her direction. "But I wouldn't sell you out like that. You have got to believe me!"

"Believe you, huh. . ." He turned away from his friend before he lost control of his emotions. "You know Antwan from Flint, right? The dude who ran the crew who just left town?" He turned back to look at Lawrence, who shook his head no with vigor. "Uh-huh. . . well, he knows you. When I pulled out the blowtorch and started in on his balls, he began talking real fast. He told me you *asked him to come* and that all he had to do was to get rid of me and he had a nice setup." He walked over to stand in front of him until they were inches apart. "He said you paid him to kill me."

Kendrick looked at the two men who were holding Lawrence down and nodded. They hauled him to his feet and toward another room. He started begging and pleading for him not to do this. He told him that it was just a big misunderstanding and he was on his way to warn him, but they must have moved up their time-table.

All his pleas and explanations fell on deaf ears. Kendrick couldn't bring himself to do it no matter how he betrayed him, but, it had to be done. He watched as Lawrence struggled to break free, but was unable to as he was slowly being dragged toward his inevitable end. He looked to ShaBree for help, but she cast her eyes to the floor, knowing that if she was in the same position, he wouldn't have lifted a finger to help her.

Lawrence saw the door leading to the other room looming before him and he began to cry shamelessly. He began to squirm with renewed desperation as his life was measured in minutes. He knew his two executioners, and they were as close to Kendrick as he was. He knew without a doubt that they were going to make the pain linger before it was over. He passed the threshold and screamed with one last desperate plea, "What about my son?!"

Kendrick's heart wrenched at hearing that Steve, his god-son, would be without his father and it would be at his hands. He knew he would never be able to tell him every time he asked about his father and where he went. He couldn't live with it.

"Hold up." The two men looked to him with surprise but said nothing. He walked over to Lawrence as he hung loosely in their grip. He looked up to Kendrick with gratitude, which annoyed him to no end. The urge to break his neck right then and there was almost too tempting, but he reminded himself that he wasn't doing it for him; he was doing it for his god-son.

"You have one day to leave town. If I find you here one minute past that, you will wish that they had killed you now. Don't come back, don't call. If I find out that you've even tried to contact Steve, I will find you. We clear?"

He shook his head as he cried tears of joy. Kendrick gave the two men a slight nod, and they let him fall unceremoniously to the ground. Lawrence staggered to his feet on legs that felt like jelly. He had to grab a-hold of the wall until he was able to regain his bearings.

He slowly made his way toward the door. He wouldn't meet anyone's stare for fear of being attacked, but mostly, he felt ashamed. If he had it to do it all over again. . . would he?

Lawrence never got a chance to when Josh stepped in front of him and buried his fist in his midsection, which sent him crashing to his knees, fighting for breath. He felt a sharp pain when he tried to catch his breath and knew he must have broken a rib or two.

As he struggled to breathe, everything suddenly went white and he felt his head crash to the ground. He felt darkness closing in around him and fought to stay conscious. He didn't know what would happen if he passed out and he really didn't want to know.

Blinking back tears, he saw a pair of eyes devoid of any emotion other than rage and hate. Josh leaned in closely so he would be able to hear him. "If I catch yo punk ass *anywhere*, you's a dead bitch-ass nigga. I don't care if I'm on vacation with the family in Jamaica. If I see you, you still done." He started to grind Lawrence's head into the floor hard as his rage began to build. "Nigga, if I see yo ass at Disneyland singing it's a small, small, world with yo grandchild, I'm *still* gonna make yo ass disappear."

He snatched him to his feet and the room swam. Tears were blurring his vision as he tried to make his way toward the door and away from the man who would still kill him regardless of what Kendrick said.

He opened the door and stepped through when a huge hand landed on his shoulder stopping him in his tracks. "The only reason I won't do it now is out of respect for my best friend and a nigga you used to know. I know he told you that you had a day to leave, but if I catch yo bitch ass within the next two hours, you won't see the morning." He released his shoulder and then landed a vicious blow to his kidneys which caused him to scream in pain and stumble down the stairs.

He staggered to his feet and started running as fast as he could away from his former friends. He heard Josh yell, "Tic Toc, motherfucka, Tic Toc. . ." This only fueled his desperation as he left town within the hour.

Kendrick wanted to stop Josh, but what gave him the right? He not only betrayed him, but he betrayed all of them. He was sure when they shot up his house and they were there, they wouldn't have hesitated to kill them too. Not to mention this was their neighborhood as well.

He sighed and turned his attention back toward ShaBree and he found her sitting in a chair, crying silently. He looked around and everyone's eyes were firmly on her. They looked ready to pounce; all they needed was the word.

He needed to defuse the situation. "Hey, fellas, can you give us a minute and wait outside?"

They looked ready to argue until Josh spoke up, "Y'all niggas heard him, let's go." He waited until they were all gone before he turned back to look at them. "If you need me to do anything, just let me know," he said in a low voice so the others couldn't hear. He looked at ShaBree with a look of disappointment, and he went outside to join the others.

The way he said it more than what he said sent chills up her spine. Now finally alone, she tried to explain her situation again. Maybe this time he will see things from her point of view. "Kendrick, I'm so sorry I got you mixed up in that. If I had known that was the case, I wouldn't have gotten involved with them, I swear."

"You just don't get it." He shook his head. "Out of all the niggas you could've have chosen to fuck me over with, you had to pick Lawrence." It wasn't a question she realized, so she remained silent. He grabbed a chair and sat across from her so they sat face-to-face. "The problem that you had was that you don't love yourself enough. A relationship is supposed to enhance the other person, not become defined by it. You enjoyed the perks of being with me more than being my girlfriend. The reason you felt jealous of those other women was because you knew that you didn't love me like you should and felt threatened that maybe one of them could. But what you didn't realize and I'm willing to bet that you still don't; I only wanted you. I never so much as looked at another woman.

ShaBree was crying profusely, but Kendrick totally ignored it. "I'm not gonna lie, I hate you. The only reason you're alive is because a part of me still loves you." She tried to hug him, but he pushed her roughly away. "From this day forward, you're dead to me. Don't call me or; come by house or my families. If I see you again, I will kill you."

He stood to leave, but she grabbed his hands. The look he gave her was of such anger that she dropped his hands as if she had been shocked. He walked out of her home, not looking back once.

ShaBree remembered that as the worst day of her life.

As the years passed, she realized that he was never going to kill her. She was even able to seduce him into her bed on occasion. He fucked her rough like he didn't even know her. He would bend her over the back of her couch and fuck her in the ass.

She remembered how hard she came.

That was all the proof she needed. He still loved her; all she needed to do was to convince him of that fact.

She's looking at Anika and how smug she's being. Little did she know; that she didn't stand a chance. "You know what, for the most part you right, but we've gotten past that. He wouldn't talk to me if he didn't." She folded her arms in triumph.

Anika saw the look on her face and thought she was crazier than squirrel shit or dumb as fuck; she hadn't decided yet. "Look, I don't know what story you have going on in your head, but Kendrick is with me."

"Oh yeah, is that what he's telling you? I guess he didn't tell you about when I was over his house." She smirked as she took a sip of her drink. "Men keep secrets for a reason. . ."

Anika just stared at her, wondering what was wrong with her. Finally unable to hold it in anymore, she burst out laughing. She went on like this for a minute. This caused Kendrick to stop pretending like he wasn't listening to the whole conversation and look at her with concern. She waved him off as he tried to comfort her. ShaBree looked at her like she had lost it.

Anika wiped away the tears as she finally composed herself then she turned her attentions back to ShaBree. "So let me get this straight, you said you were over Kendrick's and your point is?"

"My point is, I shouldn't have to tell you. We're all grown here," she said as she gave her a wink.

Anika was stunned as she looked at her with amazement. "Does that really work? I mean, you telling me that you showed up at my man's house is that supposed to what, make me act a fool and start clowning and he runs back to you? That ABC shit only works on insecure, weak women who don't know their own worth. FYI, he told me how you showed up, after our first date, mind you, and tried to throw the pussy at him."

This wasn't how she thought this would go at all. ShaBree thought to herself. She tried to scramble for a way out of her predicament, but

Anika continued on. "I honestly can see why he would have wanted to be with you, but at the same time I can see why he left you behind. You're beautiful, have a great shape. You're obviously intelligent, educated, but exceedingly stupid.

"I mean what woman who claims she loves a man, hell, likes him would fuck his best friend and *then* try and get him killed? I'm at an absolute loss that a man you know was faithful to you and bent over backward for your ignorant ass. . ." Anika had to take a deep breath because she felt her anger rising. She couldn't believe that someone could be that cruel and narcissistic to a man like Kendrick and still have the nerve to smile all up in his face like they ain't do shit. "I tell you what, if I find out you've been sniffing after my man, I will personally beat the brakes off yo ass."

ShaBree grabbed her glass and tried to throw her drink in Anika's face, but she had read her intentions. As quick as a snake, she slammed her hand down on top of hers, driving it painfully into the lip of the glass. She tried to pull her hand away, but Anika had the superior strength.

"Please stop, you're hurting me," she said with her pride hurting as much as her hand was. Anika let go slowly, never taking her eyes from hers. She looked down and noticed that her other hand was balled up into a fist, ready to strike at a moment's notice. She saw the look on her face and knew there was conviction behind the threat.

"I think you should leave. My man and I have a date to finish." ShaBree, aware that Anika was watching her like a hawk, grabbed her drink slowly and downed it. She stood, beaten, and without a word walked slowly away. She didn't know if anyone was watching the scene at the bar, but she imagined that several people had to have seen it. She was sure that she knew that several people from the neighborhood were in there tonight, but right now she was too shell-shocked to care.

She walked outside with her head held low, and when she was out the door and no one was around, she let the tears flow. Part of her wanted to go back in there and fight for her man, but was he really hers? She hated Anika not because she was with Kendrick; she hated her because her words cut so deep and true.

ShaBree leaned against the building as the tears came of their own accord when a shadow blocked out the lamp-light. She looked up and once realization set in, she looked on with a mixture of confusion and fear.

"I don't know why you put yourself through the torture. You know you can do better than him."

"Fuck you." She said as her anger began to boil over.

"Nice to see you too, boo," Lawrence said as he gave her a wink and a smile.

ShaBree turned to leave when he grabbed her arm. "Let me go or I'll scream!"

He released his grip on her arm, then threw his hands up in peace and she started walking toward her car. "Where are you going?" he asked in an innocent tone as he followed behind.

"Home!" she said as she started looking for her keys in her purse.

"To an empty bed." He closed the gap so he didn't have to speak louder than he needed to.

She turned to regard him as he made his way over to her car. "I don't want to have shit to do with you. You almost got me killed, I'm not fucking with you. Besides, I lost the man I loved over that mess."

He rolled his eyes. "Oh please, I didn't force you to do anything that you didn't already want to. If you loved him like you keep screaming from the roof-tops, you and I would never have happened. You need to cut the bullshit and take off those rose-colored glasses."

She walked closer as she tried to look him in the eye, but it was difficult considering how much taller he was than her. It came across as comical, so she settled for just folding her arms and scowling. "What's to stop me from just going back in there and telling him that you're in town? I'm sure he would love to get reacquainted with you."

"You won't," he said with confidence as he looked at his watch as if he was bored.

"And why is that?"

He leaned against her car and waved her closer. "The way I see it, the only thing keeping you from him is her," he said, pointing at the bar.

She knew who he was referring to _Anika. "What do you know about her?" Her eyes started to narrow as her suspicions grew.

"That's none of your concern. Besides, why do you care?"

She knew she should go warn Kendrick that Lawrence was back in town, but old habits die hard. "What's in it for me?"

"Besides the man that you fuck yourself to sleep over at night I'm open to negotiations." She looked away, and blushed as his words struck home, and he knew he had her hooked. "And as an added incentive, I'll give you ten thousand dollars."

"That's it?" she scoffed. *That was too easy* she thought to herself. She knew he was holding out. Truth be told, she didn't need the money. She owned her own hair salon and tax preparation office, so money wasn't the issue. She hated to be played. "I want fifty thousand with half upfront."

He gave her a hard stare. "I'll give you thirty thousand with ten thousand upfront, that's my final offer."

She thought for a moment as she looked down the dark road leading to her lonely home and then empty bed. "Deal."

He winked and smiled as they came to an agreement. He didn't plan on paying her that much. She must have grown some common sense since the last time he saw her, but he chalked it up to the price of doing business. He was making more than ten times that amount, so he wouldn't miss it. "I'll bring it to you tomorrow and the rest after."

ShaBree knew she should ask what *after* meant, but frankly, she didn't really care. She smiled as she thought about having Kendrick all to herself once again. This time, things would be different. "Fine, meet me at restaurant Du Muet. It's over on Tyson an_"

"I'm familiar with the place," he interjected. He was just there earlier doing business with his new client, he thought to himself with a smirk.

"Aight. . ." She tried to shoo him away as she made her way over to the driver's side of her car to go home.

"Where are you going?"

"Home. I have to work in the morning."

He leaned against her car as he looked over the roof at her. "Want some company?"

She gave him a blank look. She stared at him so long that he thought she didn't hear him, and then she finally said, "Get in." He hopped into the passenger seat without another word. She started down the street and all she could think about as she made her way home with her former lover was, *it's been so long and I need this. This is the last time...*

CHAPTER FOURTEEN

"Wow" was all Kendrick could say as he clapped his hands in admiration.

"Oh, hush," Anika said as she started to blush. She looked around and noticed more than a few people who were nodding their approval, which only made her blush even more.

"I'm just saying, that was impressive. I've never seen her actually shut up and, to top it off, she left without a word. I think I'll buy you a drink," he said as he laughed.

"Oh, I think you can do better than that," she said as she started kissing his neck. "I've missed you," she whispered in his ear. She smiled as his breathing started to deepen ever so slightly, a telltale sign that her machinations were having an effect.

"You better stop playing. . . you gonna get yourself in trouble messing with me like that," he said in her ear as he nibbled playfully on her earlobe, which caused her to squirm ever so slightly in her chair. "I can't wait to get you home. Let's go. If you're good, I'll even let you drive."

When he said "drive," Anika shivered. She remembered the last time he said that, she was caught totally off guard as she got behind the wheel and he pulled her panties to the side and started to lick slowly up and down her slit until she couldn't take it anymore. He wouldn't let her pull over, and if she stopped, he would stop. She almost crashed twice as she came so hard when he buried his tongue in her hole. By the time they reached his house, she was a quivering mess. Now that they had reached their destination, he was able to give her the full service. He pulled her legs toward him as he removed her panties and threw one leg on the dashboard and the other in the backseat. She had several little orgasms as he ate her pussy thoroughly and completely. She almost hit the roof of the car when he placed his finger inside of her so he could lube it up, and then pushed it slowly into her ass. He moved it slowly in and out of her tight ass. She grabbed the back of his head and buried it between her quivering legs until she almost passed out.

Kendrick watched in silent amusement, wondering what was going through her mind as she chewed absently on her drink stirrer. "Hey, you still in there?" he said as he gently gripped her shoulder.

Anika looked up suddenly as she realized that she had zoned out. "I'm sorry, I was just thinking about some things." She got ready to take a sip of her drink through her straw and realized that she had chewed it up. She dumped it on the counter and took it to the head until it was gone. She let out a contented sigh. "There, that's much better."

"Uh huh. . ."

"What did I do?" Anika said as she looked totally confused.

"You're adorable. Kind of like a beautiful unicorn or some shit with razor-sharp teeth and a 9mm on your waist."

"Uh, that's not possible. Unicorns don't have fingers. I would probably have to use my horn to stab somebody or something, maybe step on them. Maybe if had I wings; I could sneak up on them from the air and then bite them. I think that might work. . ." Anika said with a completely serious look.

Kendrick looked at her with one raised eyebrow. "You kind of gave that a lot of thought there."

Unable to hold it in any longer, she burst out laughing. "I'm just messing with you! Besides, if I was a unicorn, I would shoot lasers out of my horn. Totally untraceable."

"You're a nut and quite possibly drunk."

"Yeah, that's why you love me." She kissed him on the cheek.

"That you're drunk or a nut?"

She looked up and thought for a moment and then said, "A little of both. You love me being a nut because I keep things interesting and a drunk so you can take advantage of all this goodness." She makes a comical parody of being sexy as she ran her hands up and down her body.

Kendrick laughed. "Is that an invitation?"

She looked him deeply in his eyes without a hint of humor. "It's an open invitation. That door will never be closed to you." She moved closer until she was standing in between his legs. "I love you in a way I've never known before now. I'm yours."

He was left speechless as her words moved him in a profound way. He touched the side of her face and pulled her in for a kiss. His lips said everything that he couldn't say and more. She knew without a doubt that this man loved her.

Kendrick pulled away reluctantly from their embrace. "Let's get the fuck out of here," he whispered huskily in her ear, which caused her nipples to harden and her legs to rub together slightly in anticipation.

Kendrick quickly paid the bill and they made their way toward his car. Anika stepped in front of him. "Let's take my car, I'll drive."

He gave her a crooked smile. "As the lady requests," he said as he followed her to her car.

They walked around aimlessly through the parking garage for about five minutes looking for her car. He laughed silently to himself as she held the remote up in the air looking for that all-too-familiar chirp.

Each click on the remote caused her frustration to grow. It was all he could do not to burst out laughing. She turned around accusingly as she stared at him for any sign of humor. She wanted to unleash her frustration and he was as good a target as the next.

They finally found her vehicle, and she let out an audible sigh. She unlocked the doors, and Kendrick made his way around to the passenger side and got in. Anika entered a split second after he did. She started the car and then stared off into space. She looked at him as if she was in thought and then got out of the car without a word.

He was puzzled at first until she reached under her skirt and removed her panties. She threw the soaking-wet garments into the backseat and sat back down. "Ahhh, that's much better. They were starting to get cold."

She started the car and they drove off. Kendrick offered to pay the parking fee, but she beat him to it. "I got this. Besides, you have your car here still. You can get that one."

They made their way onto the main street as the traffic was light due to the late hour. Anika pulled up to a red light and turned to Kendrick. "You still hungry?" She said as she slowly hiked her skirt up in the front.

He licked his lips sensually. "I'm starving. You have something in mind?"

"I think I might be able to whip something up." She pulled her skirt all the way up past her ass.

Kendrick stared at her with lust-filled eyes as he adjusted the growing bulge in his pants. His eyes traveled down to her glistening womanhood, and he had to swallow before he could speak. "You wanna tell me what you're serving?"

"Me."

"That's my favorite," he said as he leaned over and covered her drooling snatch with his mouth. He ran his tongue up and down her slit as her body went stiff and she began to shake. "Damn, that was fast" he chuckled.

"Oh, shut up, I think you left some food on your plate," she said as she pushed his head back between her legs. She let out a content sigh when she suddenly heard someone laying on a horn behind her.

Anika began to flush furiously as she dropped her head in total embarrassment. She started to drive away and bemoaned the fact that until she met Kendrick, she would have never thought that she would have done anything like this.

She lets out a sigh and Kendrick raises his head. "You okay?"

"I'm fine," she said as she pushed his head yet again between her legs and she bit the palm of her hand as he continued to explore her eager pussy.

They continued on their way until Anika looked up and noticed police lights behind her. She began to worry how long they were on as she pulled over to the side of the road. *A ticket was one thing, but getting arrested was another matter altogether,* she thought as her mind began to race.

Kendrick raised his head to look around as he wondered why they stopped. The lights were the first indication that something was going on. "Did you run a light or something?"

"I don't think so." She reached to the passenger side floor to grab her purse. "Even if I did, I think I deserve a pass due to the circumstances." She leaned over and gave him a peck on the lips.

As the officer walked toward the car, Anika jumped as she felt Kendrick's finger sliding into her still-wet pussy. He threw his jacket over her lap to keep the officer from noticing. She turned to look at him questioningly, but he just smiled. "It's okay, I won't move too much."

Before she could object, the officer tapped on her window with their flashlight. She couldn't make them out due to the bright light being shined on her face. The window rolled down and the officer asked for her license and registration, which she quickly handed over.

The light moved away from her face, and Anika had to blink a few times to regain some form of night vision. This was the first time that she had been stopped in over ten years. Normally, she would be racked with guilt, but Kendrick's finger moving inside of her was helping to take the edge off. Her body shook subtly as she had a mini orgasm. She started to grind ever so slightly against his hand as the pleasure built. He slipped a second digit inside which increased her pleasure exponentially.

She bit her finger to keep herself from letting out a moan. The officer noticed something was going on, and shined the flashlight back in the car. "What's going on in there? I need both of you to put your hands where I can see them."

Anika finally got a look at the officer and noticed that it was a woman. She was shorter than her, but she had full breast, a small waist, a round supple, butt, and luscious lips. She turned to look at Kendrick as a spark of jealousy struck. To his credit, he didn't even notice her.

"I said put your hands where I can see them!" She unclasped her weapon with her hand resting on the hilt, a clear indication that she was deadly serious. Anika quickly placed both hands on the steering wheel, but to her amazement, Kendrick continued to finger her. Her mouth opened in utter shock as he began to rub along her G-spot. He applied a little pressure and she orgasmed. It was so sudden that she wasn't able to hide it.

The officer drew her weapon as Anika moaned loudly. "Sir, what are you doing with your other hand?" He had placed his right hand on the dashboard but kept his other inside of Anika. "I asked you a question."

He leaned over Anika, so he could speak directly to the officer. "I could tell you, but I'm pretty sure you have an idea."

"Why don't you tell me?"

Anika noticed that the officer's tone had changed to less than official as she placed her weapon back in its holster. She looked at Kendrick out of the corner of her eye and saw the smile on his face that she wanted to rip off. She wanted to say something, but knowing him, she knew he was up to something.

"What fun would that be? I guess you could ask her if you're that curious." He started to move his fingers again, and Anika fought the urge to let him know how much he was affecting her. As hard as she tried, she felt her hips moving almost against their will.

The whole situation was so surreal. She was sitting in a car being finger-banged by her man as a lady, a police officer no less, was watching. Anika watched her from the corner of her eye. The police officer was watching Kendrick's hand administer waves of pleasure with rapt attention.

"I'm still waiting."

Pleasure was overtaking her as she felt another orgasm coming over the horizon. She looked her directly in the eye. "He's fucking me with his fingers."

"How do I know that you're telling me the truth?" She was leaning against the car with her head inside the vehicle. Never losing eye contact, Anika pulled the jacket out of the way, revealing the erotic scene.

"Is this what you wanted to see?" She spread her legs wider so she could get a good view.

"Yes," she whispered, "it's so pretty."

The scene was too much for Anika as she came again on his fingers. Now they were making wet noises as he continued his delicious assault on her nether regions. Anika reached her hand under her blouse and started caressing her own breast.

Anika was grinding against his hand like a wanton slut. A small part of her was revolted by her behavior while a larger, more urgent inner voice was screaming for her to continue. She let out a soft whimper as her orgasm took control over body.

Through pants and waves of pleasure, Anika had enough awareness to remember her surroundings. She looked and saw the officer absently caressing her breast through her uniform. "What's your name?" She was able to ask before her voice was cut off as Kendrick licked her wet slit.

"It's B-Beverly," she said as her breathing became shallow. It was obvious that she was being swept up in the spell as well.

Anika looked down at Kendrick as he nursed her sexual needs to new peaks. He looked up and saw the look on her face and shrugged. "Whenever you're ready."

She turned to look at Beverly. "Do you think I could possibly get my driver's license back by chance?"

Beverly was confused for a moment, not realizing that the moment had passed. She looked around, unable to meet her eyes. The embarrassment was more than she could bear at that time. She went back to the squad car and returned momentarily with her identification. It seemed almost silly to return to a professional environment, but what else could she do, she thought?

The officer tried to hand it back to her, but Anika held her hand up, which caused her to pause. "I need you to look closely at my license." She did as requested and looked back at Anika questioningly. Anika gave her a smile with a hint of mischief and said, "If you know a beautiful, sexy lady who may or may not wear a uniform and she happens to get off in the next couple of hours. . . It would be nice if she stopped by to play." She looked her up and down seductively to drive home her meaning.

Beverly didn't say anything, but she smiled as she walked away. Kendrick gave her a blank stare. "What was that all about?"

"You started it. Besides, that got us out of the ticket, didn't it?"

"Yeah, but what did you just get us into?" He sat up and put on his seatbelt as Anika got them on their way. He sat there for a moment and started giggling.

Anika looked over at him as her irritation started to build. "You wanna let me in on the joke too."

"You know she's gonna show up, right?"

"No, she's not. She just got caught up in the moment just like we did."

"Don't put me in that. I was just trying to get us out of a ticket." He threw his hands up as she looked at him with daggers. "I saw that she had undercover freak potential so I played it up a bit so she would let us slide." He rubbed her thigh sensually and Anika bit her lower lip as she drove on.

After a few moments, she turned to regard him. "What do you mean by undercover freak potential?" She came to a red light, turned completely toward him, and then leaned in. "So was you checking her out? I gotta say, if you were, I didn't catch it."

"Are you jealous, Anika?" he said as he gave her teasing smile.

"No. . .not really, yes. It's just that she was beautiful and, well, look at you." She waved her hand at him. "You're beautiful, ridiculously sexy, and intelligent beyond words. I'm just afraid that you might get bored with me."

"Isn't that my line? I'm the one who is worried that you might realize that you can do better and jump ship." He gripped her forearm gently. She had crossed her arms protectively, not knowing what he might say. "I wouldn't leave you unless you told me to leave you alone. Even then, I would bug you, hoping you might change your mind." He began to tickle her, and she jumped as she tried to shoo his hands away.

"Stop, you're going to make me pee on myself!" He stopped and then kissed the back on her hand, which caused her to smile. To her amazement, she was still aroused. She couldn't remember how many times she had cum, but she was ready for more. "I love you," she said with all sincerity.

"Not more than me." He kissed her gently on the lips.

The light changed and Anika turned left. He didn't say anything at first as she continued down the street, but after a couple of miles, he spoke up. "Uh, I thought we were going to your house?"

She looked at him as if he lost his mind. "Oh hell, naw. She might actually show up!"

He burst out laughing as they made their way to his home for a night of passion.

CHAPTER FIFTEEN

"Just a minute, I'll be right there!" Evelyn rushed to the door as the visitor continued to ring the doorbell incessantly. She pulled the door open, her irritation level on ten. "I said just a min_" she stopped as she looked up at a tall, handsome man with a huge smile planted firmly on his face. "What can I do for you?" she said as she pulled her robe closed at the top, trying to maintain her dignity.

"Hello, my name is Mr. Sampson and I work for your granddaughter's company's security firm." He extended his hand and she took it wearily. If he noticed the slight, he didn't let on. "I was wondering if you had a few moments so we can discuss a delicate situation."

Her heart jumped into her throat. "Is something wrong with Anika?" she said as she opened the door to let him in.

"Nothing is wrong at the moment, but that's what I wanted to talk to you about, to make sure that nothing does happen."

She stepped aside to let him pass. He stood by the door, waiting to take her cue. She led him over to the chairs in the sitting room, off the kitchen. He took a seat as she disappeared for a moment, only to return with iced tea and snack cakes. She handed him a small plate, which he accepted. She poured two glasses of tea and left them on the table at their leisure.

He took a bite of the cake and brightened as he nodded his approval. She gave a slight smile at the compliment "I'm glad you liked them, but what is it about my granddaughter that you wanted to discuss?"

Mr. Sampson set his plate down and put on his glasses as he opened his briefcase and pulled out some forms. Her reviewed them quickly and returned his attention to Evelyn. "It has come to our attention that your granddaughter, Anika Washington, was involved in a domestic violence incident."

She wasn't aware that Anika had mentioned the incident to anyone. She was under the impression that the fewer people who knew, the better. *Maybe she decided to err on the side of caution,* she mused. "Yes, she made us aware of the situation." She gripped her glass and squinted her eyes in anger at the thought of that man putting his hands on her kin. "I take it you are referring to Jay? I can't believe that man is still walking the streets. I hope he gets what's coming to him."

"We don't advocate violence, but we do what's necessary to keep our employees safe." He made a show of looking at his questions. "Do you happen to know the places your granddaughter tends to frequent?"

"I would assume you had all that information."

"Yes, but we like to be thorough when gathering information. We want to make sure that if anything possibly happens, we will be there to see your granddaughter home safely."

"I appreciate that, but after all this time, do you still consider him a threat to her?"

"To be honest with you, my bosses want me to do a simple interview, but I've never been one to do anything half measure." He took a sip of tea to clear his throat. "They don't think that he's still a threat, but I had a client a few years ago who was in a similar situation and things got bad. Her ex-boyfriend broke into her house and murdered her and her two young children. Since then, I've tried to do everything in my power to see that doesn't happen again."

Evelyn felt her pulse quicken at the thought of something happening to Anika. "I thank you for your due diligence. I would hate for something to happen and no one is there to protect her."

"I'm here to do my very best, Ms. Washington." He flipped through his papers as if he's looking for something. "I understand that your granddaughter is currently dating someone, I believe his name is Kendrick? I was wondering if you happen to have any information on him. We're currently trying to building a file on him as well, in the interest of protecting your granddaughter."

Her hackles went up at the mention of Anika's boyfriend. She was sure that she wouldn't have told anyone about her current relationship. She had always valued her privacy. "I don't know what I can tell you about him seeing as how I haven't had the privilege of meeting him yet."

"Don't you think that is strange? I mean, considering everything that's happened to her, she would want to at least keep you aware of her comings and goings?"

"She is a strong, capable woman who doesn't need to tell me her every move."

"Believe me, I wouldn't ask these invasive questions if I didn't have to. I see that she is rather young. Would you say that they frequently see each other? If so, how and where would they meet, and if possible, what nights?

"I think it's time for you to leave. If you have any more questions, I think you should contact my granddaughter," she said as she stood.

"Oh, I plan on seeing her very shortly, Ms. Washington. Do you mind if I call you Evelyn? I think Evelyn is a beautiful name."

She started to take a good look at the man who probably isn't "Mr. Sampson." He was tall, dark, and relatively good-looking. He had a lean muscular build, which could be easily explained away due to his supposed profession. What started to alarm her were the tattoos on the back of his hands that weren't uncommon, but seemed oddly out of place. But what really made her fearful were his eyes, they seemed devoid of compassion and they carried an almost palatable air of menace. He looked as if he could drown his own mother in a bathtub while he ordered Thai food over the phone. She took a step back as she tried to ease her way into the kitchen. "Who are you?"

He flashed a huge smile that never seemed to touch his eyes, which caused Evelyn to swallow as she began to shake slightly with fear. "Now, Evelyn, don't you think it's a little late for that now?" he said as he stood. "Don't beat yourself up over it. I would have just barged past you if you didn't willingly let me in." He grabbed another cake off the tray and bit into it. "This is really good. I wasn't lying about that."

He blocked her path to the front door, eliminating any attempt at fleeing. Even if she could move, she knew there wasn't a chance that she could win past him and to her freedom. "I'm not telling you anything else about my granddaughter. To be honest, there's nothing else to tell, but even if there were, you're not getting anything else from me. So, if you're going to kill me, we might as well get on with it."

He shook his head with a sad smile. "The day is still young. Let's leave our options open, shall we?" He started to pace. "The thing is, I believe you. I also believe that you probably don't know anything else as well."

She continued to ease slowly back into the kitchen as she tried to move away from him. She carefully opened the kitchen drawer and slid her hand in as she continued to talk. "You never answered my question."

"Which was?" he was still preoccupied with the cake as he ate it slowly, enjoying the taste.

"You never told me who you really are." She wrapped her hand around the handle and she let a slow breath out slowly as she thanked God for it still being where she thought she left it.

"My name is Lawrence. Pleasure to meet your acquaintance."

If she didn't meet him under these circumstances, she might have considered introducing Anika to him, she thought ruefully. He was very charming in a sadistic sort of way. If she didn't act now, her chances of living through this ordeal was nil. She bent over, feigning a cough, and pulled the stun gun out and placed it in her pocket.

Lawrence waved her toward him. "Evelyn, I need you to come out of the kitchen, please. I just have a few more questions and this will all be over soon."

She highly doubted that it would be. He doesn't seem like a man who would just walk away. He looks like he enjoys causing pain, and she wasn't going to be the exception. She walked slowly toward him as if she was resigned to her fate. She was terrified, but she did as she was told. She knew that he was faster than her, so her only option was to get close enough that he couldn't dodge and pray that he won't be able to stop her.

Lawrence had been in countless situations such as these. He'd experienced all types of people in his line of work. But what he'd taken away from these experiences is that there are two types of people: they either cower or fight. He could tell from the moment he met Evelyn that she was a fighter.

As she walked toward him, Lawrence saw her right arm tense. The average person wouldn't notice such a subtle movement, but fortunately for him, he wasn't one of them. Having a trained eye, he knew she was up to something. "Evelyn, I like you. I promise I won't make this worse than it has to be. But if you try and go through with this, it's going to go badly for you."

She hesitated only for a moment, but a moment was all he needed. Evelyn pulled the stun gun out of her pocket and tried to jam it in his chest. She was a lot faster than he first thought to her credit, but it wasn't nearly enough. He placed his forearm in front of her strike to protect himself. She gave a smug look of satisfaction, which quickly turned to a look of confusion, followed by panic.

Lawrence grabbed her arm and pulled it over her head. He twisted her wrist, and she cried out in pain as she dropped the stun gun to the floor. "Why did you have to go and do that? I told you, Evelyn, things would go bad for you." He punched her in the face, and her nose exploded in a spray of blood.

He wiped his hand off on her robe and fondled her breast, which caused him to grunt in appreciation. "I must say, the years have been very kind to you."

"Go fuck yourself," she said as she spit in his face.

He wiped it off with a snarl of disgust and backhanded her so hard across the face that she fell back and flipped over the chair, landing heavily on the ground. "Nah, I don't think it's physically possible to fuck myself but. . ." he slid his hand under her robe and found that she was naked underneath, "I think you will do nicely."

Evelyn started to cry as the enormity of the situation was starting to set in. "Why are you doing this?" she said through what felt like a cotton-filled mouth, no doubt from the swelling that was taking place. Mostly likely she had a fractured jaw and probably more.

"Well, there are several reasons, actually. You know the guy who roughed up your granddaughter?" she nodded as she looked away. He took that as acknowledgment. "He hired me to kill her. He said to make it hurt, which I plan on doing." He rubbed the side of her face affectionately. Evelyn wanted to squirm away in disgust, but she feared another blow. "Then, there's her boyfriend. See, he and I have a past."

Her eyes lit up in shock and tears started to fall. "No, killing your granddaughter doesn't have anything to do with him. I was hired to kill her slowly; that's just business. My reasons for wanting him dead is I just hate him, is all. He took away my life, and I want him to suffer."

Evelyn tried to struggle to get away, but Lawrence grabbed both of her hands into his one massive paw and pinned them over her head. She tried to squirm loose, but he had them in a vise-like grip. Struggling as she may, she couldn't move an inch. Her left eye was starting to swell shut and she knew with cold realization that she was going to die.

"My final reason for all this is unfortunately your' doing, I'm afraid." He gave her a sympathetic look. "I told you that things were going to go badly for you if you tried anything. My original plan was just to ruff you up a bit, leave a nice message for your granddaughter, but I guess a hard head makes a soft ass." He started to slowly untie her robe as she tried to struggle. A blow landed on the side of her head that sent her reeling, which caused her body to go limp and allowed him to continue his work unfettered.

If he was being honest with himself, he knew things would always end up here. She would have done some real or imagined slight, which would have given him license to do what it is that he knew he wanted to do all along. As her unconscious form lay naked before him, he ran his hands all over her prone body.

An evil smile started at the corners of Lawrence's mouth as he slowly started to remove his clothes. *"This is going to be nice"* he thought as he moved slowly toward her....

CHAPTER SIXTEEN

Anika had several messages waiting for her once she left her monthly organizational meeting. Several people, including Shawna, were trying to reach her, but security had locked down the auditorium due to a former employee crashing a previous meeting in a drunken state and pouring red paint on the vice president of the division. Since then, you were only able to attend if you were specifically invited and had to submit to a search.

She walked into her office, followed closely by Shawna, who closed the door behind her. She came to stand next to her and spoke in a soft voice, explaining what happened. Her grandmother was found by a neighbor unconscious on the living room floor. They had rushed her to the hospital, but she didn't know what her condition was.

Anika ran out of the office in a flurry as onlookers watched her in confusion and concern. She moved past them without a word as she made her way to the elevator. She used her key to turn the elevator off, so she can go to the ground unimpeded. She's never used it before because she always considered it pretentious, but today was an exception. Her grandmother was in the hospital.

After running several lights and near-miss accidents, she arrived at the hospital. She parked her car in the emergency entrance, which a part of her was sure that it would be towed, which she gave less than a fuck about at the moment.

Anika burst into the emergency room and ran frantically to the counter. The receptionist greeted her with a practiced smile. She looked as if she had played out this scenario thousands of times as she greeted her. "Hello, what can I do for you?"

"My grandmother, Evelyn Washington, was brought in about an hour ago. I'm trying to find out what room she's in."

"I will be glad to help. If you can take a seat, I will call you back up in a few minutes."

Anika was trying to hold her temper. She knew the lady was just trying to do her job. "I understand that you're busy, but I just need to know the room she's in. After that, I'll be out of your hair." She gave her a smile that she didn't really feel.

"I can help, but first you'll need to take a seat," she sighed.

Having reached the end of her patience, she leaned over the counter and stared at her in the eye. "Look, I don't have time for this bullshit. So, if you can't help me, find someone who can," she looked at her name tag, "Tammy."

Tammy dropped all pretense at this point. "Look, I said I would help you, but first you need to take a seat and *then* I'll call you up."

"Why do I need to take a seat? You could have typed up her name and gave me the information I needed in a few seconds. What's the deal?"

"Because I said so."

It took everything in Anika not to snatch her ass across the counter, but she fought off the urge. "Okay, I see you're gonna be that bitch today." She took a deep a breath and whispered. "So I guess I'm going to have to be that bitch. You can look up the information like I asked you to or I'll have your job before I leave this hospital today. I'm the wrong bitch to fuck with."

"Like I said, you ne_"

Without another word, Anika walked down the hall toward the elevators. Tammy called after her, but she kept walking. She went to the third floor, walked to the counter, told her she was looking for her grandmother, and was promptly given the information.

The fact that she was able to get the information so quickly and without hassle really pissed her off. She had threatened to get her fired, but now it was part of her to-do list.

Anika burst into her grandmother's room, saw all the machines hooked up to her body, and she screamed. She ran to her side and grabbed her hand. Her face was so bruised that she barely recognized her. There were bandages everywhere; her left arm was in a splint as well as her right leg. Looking at her like this, so frail and small, the tears ran unabated.

There was a movement in the corner, and to her shock, Kendrick was sitting there, watching silently. She was left speechless. To say that she was shocked would be an understatement. "What are you doing here?" was all she could manage to say.

"Your assistant, Shawna, called me when she couldn't contact you."

She wondered why Shawna would have called him, but then she realized she had him listed as an authorized person in case she couldn't get a hold of her. "I can understand you relaying the message, but you didn't have to come down here."

He looked away to hide his emotions, and she immediately regretted saying it. "She couldn't get a hold of you, so I came down to make sure she was okay and have someone here with her. If you check your messages, you'll see that I left several." He shook his head as he became lost in his thoughts. "You didn't see her when they brought her in. . . it was bad. I was leaving school when I got the call, and when I got down here, they had just brought her into emergency. I had only planned to check in on her to make sure she was good. Once I saw what the deal was, I wasn't leaving until I was sure she was going to be okay. They asked me if I was any relation, and I said I was her grandson."

He stood up to leave, and Anika ran and placed her hand gently on his chest. "Please don't leave. I was wrong to come at you like that. I know you only have my best interest at heart. Just seeing my grandma like that, it's no excuse." She placed her head on his chest, and he wrapped her into his arms, trying to shield her from the pain.

"You don't need to apologize to me. I can't begin to imagine what you're feeling right now. I wish there was more I could do."

"You've already done more than I ever thought a man would do for me." She leaned back to look him in the eye. "I just want to say thank you."

He kissed her forehead. "You're more than welcome."

Evelyn began to stir, and Anika rushed to be at her side as she took her hand. She looked frightened and confused as she tried to move. Tears welled up in her eyes as her bottom lip started to quiver. She tried to speak, but no words came out. Pain was evident on her face, and it broke Anika's heart.

"It's okay, Grandma. I'm here and I'm not going anywhere," she said as she rubbed her hand. It took everything in her not to break down, but she needed to be strong for her.

Evelyn began to rub her throat, and Anika grabbed the cup of water off the nightstand next to the bed. She turned the straw toward her, and she took a long sip. She tried to sit up again, but Anika placed a gentle hand on her chest. "Please Grandma, don't try to sit up. I'll get a nurse to help you."

"Please don't go." She grabbed Anika's hand with surprising strength. She saw a large dark figure move and her fears were renewed. "Is he here?!" She whispered as more tears began to fall.

"Is who here, Grandma?" Anika said as she was no longer able to hold it in any longer. The tears began to flow down her face.

She beckoned Anika closer and then whispered "I can't tell you," as if she was afraid he would hear.

Anika sat up with a look of confusion. "Why?"

She looked past Anika and at the dark figure in the chair. She had never had great vision, and it became even more pronounced due to the swelling and her lack of her glasses. "Who is that, baby?" she said as she tried to keep the fear out of her voice.

Anika looked over her shoulder and smiled. "That's Kendrick, Grandma. He was here when they brought you in."

"Kendrick?"

"Yes, Grandma. He's been here the whole the time."

The door opened and Evelyn almost jumped out of the bed in fear, but it was only the nurse coming to check her vitals. "Is he here?" she said as the terror was clearly evident on her face.

"Is who here, Grandma? Nobody is here except us and the nurse."

The nurse gave her a warm smile. "Don't worry, Ms. Washington. We're going to have you all better in no time. It was very nice of your grandson to stay with you all this time."

Evelyn waited until the nurse left before she spoke. "Lawrence," she said in a whisper.

"Who's Lawrence?" she said. She was starting to worry that maybe she was having hallucinations from the medication.

"He's the one who did this to me." She began to cry as her body shook from the effort.

"What do you mean he did this to you?"

At hearing the name Lawrence, Kendrick became very keyed in on the conversation now taking place. *'It can't be him'* he thought as the possibilities ran through his mind.

It took a moment for her to compose herself. After a great effort, she looked at Anika with her one good eye. "He told me that he needed to leave a message that can't be ignored for Kendrick."

Kendrick looked as if he was physically struck by her words. His worst fears were beginning to be realized. He feared that his past would come back to hurt the ones he loved, and now it was happening. "What was the message?" he asked, afraid he already knew the answer.

"Me," she said as she began to sob. "He-he did things to me baby. . . He hurt me." She completely broke down at this point. Anika tried to console her, but nothing she was doing was of any help.

"It's okay, Grandma, I'm here and I'll fix this." She turned to look at Kendrick with a fierce expression. "What's going on, Kendrick? What does all this have to do with my grandmother?" she said with accusatory venom in her tone.

Evelyn gripped Anika's to get her attention. "Don't blame him, baby. It's not his fault. He's just a part of the puzzle."

"I don't understand," she said as she tried to make sense of everything that was happening too fast.

"He came here to kill you. He said that Jay hired him to do it and that he was to make the pain last," she said as she broke down into tears.

There was a haunted look on her face that terrified Anika. It wasn't dying so much the scared her, but it was how he was beginning to make her suffer. She couldn't begin to imagine what was done to her grandma and to her shame. Her mind wouldn't even allow her to process the thought.

Kendrick stood silently as he shook with rage. He was full of guilt for not doing what needed to be done all those years ago. Who knows how many lives have been ruined by not following through with an act that should have been done long ago.

Now, he will correct his mistake.

He stood to leave and was at the door when Anika noticed. "Where are you going?"

"I think it's better that you don't know. I want you to stay here at the hospital until I call. If I'm not back by tonight, I'll call and send someone over to get you. If you don't hear from me and someone shows up. . ." he handed her a small gun that she would have thought was a toy if it wasn't for the deadly serious expression on his face, "use this."

"You're not going anywhere without me," she said as she grabbed her jacket and purse to leave. She looked over and saw that her grandmother was asleep as she made her way over to the door.

"You can't go this time, baby, I'm sorry." He held up his hand, barring her from leaving.

"The hell I can't. I told you that I'm with you and I meant that in every sense. When I die, I want it to be holding your hand. Whatever comes, let it come with us together as one, standing side by side."

The look of conviction on her face almost caused him to waver. But he knew what he had to do and he knew he had to do it without her. "Anika, you can't. I know Lawrence, and if he knows I'm out looking for him, he will come back here and finish things with your grandmother. I need you to stay here with her." He pulled her into an embrace as he whispered, "I know you love me and I can't tell you how much joy you've brought to my life, but I need you to be safe. He's after you, and he only used your grandmother as a means to get to you. If something were to happen to your grandmother while you're out running with me. . . Please stay."

She looked back at her grandmother's still form lying on the bed, and she knew what she had to do. "I'll stay, but I better hear from you every two hours, understand?"

He gave her a nod as he kissed her forehead and was out the door.

She sighed as the man she loved walked out into unknown danger. Every part of her wanted to jump up and go with him, but she knew her place was right here next to her grandmother. She sat down in the chair next to the bed and leaned in to make sure she was sleep.

She made her way silently to the door so she could call a nurse to watch her grandmother while she went to get a cup of coffee and make some calls. When she suddenly said, You still there, baby?"

She turned around and was quickly by her side holding her hand. "Yes Grandma, I'm here. Do you need anything, some more water?" She had the cup in hand just in case she wanted some.

Her grandmother waved her off. "No, I'm fine except for this pain." Anika was up in an instant, on to the door to call a nurse in. "No, baby, not yet. I need to talk to you."

Anika sat up in her chair. "Anything, I'm here, just tell me what you need."

She chuckled, "I just need to talk to you." She tried to sit up, but the pain was too much and she had to lie back down. "So, that was the mysterious Kendrick, huh?"

She blushed and dropped her head. "Yeah, that was him. I'm so sorry that I haven't brought him by. I just wanted to make sure this was real, you know?"

"I can completely understand that. I guess you on your grown woman shit now." She smiled as best she could. "I just wanted to tell you before they come back in to give me some more meds, you have yourself a good man."

"I know." She smiled as she rubbed her hand.

"I don't think you really do. I was pretty much out of it when they brought me in, but someone held my hand and whispered to me that everything was going to be okay the whole time. I didn't know who it was because I didn't recognize the voice, but once I heard him speak,

I knew it was him. Most men won't do that for somebody they don't know."

Hearing his simple act of kindness made her want to fall in love with him all over again. Without a doubt, she knew he was the man for her. She was brought out of her thoughts as her grandmother started to cough violently.

She ran to the door and called for a nurse, who came in quickly. She checked her lungs and said that her lung had collapsed, and she had to leave the room as a doctor and several more nurses hurried in. They were removing the bandages around her chest as her heart stopped.

Anika looked on in horror as the door closed. She tried to enter the room, but the nurse who came in earlier to check her vitals wouldn't let her in. "I'm sorry, but you can't come in. You will do more harm than good at this point. I know this is hard for you, but there isn't anything you can do at this point."

She pleaded. "What do you want me to do?"

The nurse paused as she looked over her shoulder and turned back to her with a look of apprehension. "Pray for her," she said as she closed the door.

Anika was left standing there as the tears began to fall. She dropped to her knees in the hallway and began to pray.

After she turned her problems over to God, she decided to go work on her "to-do list." She went to find the head administrator of the hospital and discussed Tammy. Some folks don't believe fat meat is greasy, and Tammy is about to find out that Anika is a woman of her word. . .

CHAPTER SEVENTEEN

Kendrick has tried everybody he knew for any clues to where Lawrence might be. Knowing him like he does, he knew that he won't find him in time by himself. One thing he's good at is not being found when he doesn't want to be. He slammed his hand against the steering wheel in frustration, lamenting yet again his failure to have killed him when he had the chance.

He pulled up at Josh's house and he already knew that he's going to hear it for not calling before coming by. They've known each other almost as long as he and Lawrence. He always said that if anybody came over his house without calling, he was going to put a bullet in their ass. He prayed that he was just joking. You never can tell with Josh.

He rang the doorbell and cringed slightly until his wife, Marile, opened the door with a smile. "Hey, stranger. How have you been?" she said with genuine warmth. "Hey, honey, Kendrick is here to see you," she yelled over her shoulder. "Don't just stand there and let my heat out. Come on in."

Marile might be the nicest person he'd ever met. She's a God-fearing Christian who went to church twice a week like clockwork. She even got Josh to go, which is a miracle in and of itself. In short, she'd made him a better man. How Josh ever lucked up on a lady like her back in the day is beyond his understanding.

Josh came out the back with a smile as he walked up to Marile and gave her a kiss on the cheek. "Hey, Mel, can you give us a minute to talk?"

"Of course, babe." Then she turned to Kendrick. "You staying or just stopping by?"

"Unfortunately, I can't stay this time. But I have wanted you to meet my lady for quite some time. I was thinking maybe we could make a night of it if you're interested."

Her face lit up. "That would be great. I never get to spend time with any of his friends. He says they're always busy."

"You win, Mel. We'll set something up soon, okay?" He kissed her on the cheek, trying to shoo her away.

"Thanks, honey. That's all I ask." She gave him a quick peck on the lips and turned and walked away, but not before he gave her a soft tap on the butt, which caused her to give him a wink. She strolled away with a slight sway in her hips.

As soon as she turned the corner and was out of sight, Josh turned to Kendrick. "What you want, nigga, and be quick about it. As you can see, I'm about to get some ass."

"Yeah, I noticed," he chuckled.

"Oh, so now you're staring at my woman's ass? Nigga, don't make me shoot you. . ."

"Wait, what?" Kendrick said as he was starting to wonder when things went sideways.

"I'm just fucking with you. What you need? I know you didn't just stop by to check on me."

"I have to ask you question. Have you seen Lawrence?"

"Nah, I ain't seen his bitch ass. What the fuck he do?"

"This dude who Anika used to fuck with put a hit out on us. Seeing as how we know all the hitters in town, he had to get somebody who ain't from around here."

"So he lucked up and found a nigga who wants you dead anyway," Josh said, finishing his line of thought as he chuckled bitterly. "I have never seen you with an ugly chic because yo game is tight, but damn if you don't pick bitches with problems."

"Watch yo mouth when you speak on my lady."

He held up his hands "No disrespect, but you see my point. So what you gonna do?"

"There's more."

Kendrick began to tell him what happened to Anika's grandmother and that she was in the hospital. He told him what Lawrence had done to her and his message he had her deliver.

Josh was quiet for a long time as he just stood there looking out into space. Kendrick was about to ask him if he was okay when he suddenly blurted out. "Really should have said fuck you and just killed his bitch ass back in the day. This whole situation is fucked up to the nth degree."

"I'm sorry bro. I wasn't trying to bring trouble to your door. I was just trying to find out if you might have heard anything."

Josh ignored his comment. "He's paying him to make y'all suffer. . ." He walked over to the hallway and yelled, "Hey, Mel, I gotta make a run right quick. I'll be back as soon as I can."

"You can't, man. You got a wife and kids at home. I can't ask you to do this."

"You didn't ask me to do shit," he said as he walked past him and opened a door into the garage. He opened a drawer and pulled out a key that looked like it was used to open cans of tuna, and then went over to a tile on the floor and popped it open where he removed a 9mm and its clip. He looked up and saw the look on Kendrick's face. "What? I'm not making the same mistake as I did last time. He gots to go," he said as he loaded the clip into the gun.

"Who has to go?" Marile said as both men turned, startled by her sudden appearance.

Josh hid the gun behind his back like a child, knowing that they've been caught. "I have to take care of something, and its best that you don't get involved."

Seeing that she wasn't getting anywhere with him, she turned her attention to Kendrick. "So, are you going to tell me or am I supposed to trust that what he's doing isn't stupid?" she said bitterly.

Kendrick just stood there. He didn't want to lie to Marile, but he also knew it wasn't his place to get in the middle of a wife and husband. "I don't want to lie to you Marile, bu_"

"One of the dudes we used to run with came back into town because he was contracted to do a job on his girl, Anika, and somehow Kendrick got mixed up in it too. The guy who hired him wanted to make them suffer, and he's already gotten to her grandmother; she in the hospital now and it's not looking too good." She said nothing as her eyes went big as saucers as he continued on. "The way I see it, the best way to make someone suffer is to take away the things they love. Seeing as how he's my best friend and you're my wife, it makes sense that we're not too far down that list."

She thought about Anika and her grandmother and her heart ached for them. She thought about her two little children in the house and she started to get scared. "Are you sure about all of this?"

"Yeah, I'm pretty sure. There's no love lost between us, so getting me, you, or the kids would be a plus in his book."

"Who is this man that you two used to run with?"

"Lawrence."

She didn't say anything, but a clear look of concern was evident on her face. No doubt, Josh had told her stories. "Do you really think he would hurt the kids?"

"I don't know, but I'm not putting anything past him at this point. I'm not willing to take that chance. You all are my life, and I rather spend the rest of my days in jail rather than to see any of you hurt or worse."

She was silent as she thought over everything she just heard. "What did he do to her grandmother?"

Kendrick couldn't meet her intense gaze. "It was bad" was all he was willing to say.

"I see" was all she said as she continued to deliberate. She turned to look at her husband as her eyes pleaded with him, searching his for the answer. "Are you sure there's no other way?"

"Yeah, I'm sure" was all he could say as he met her gaze. "I can't leave it to him. He'll probably fuck it up, again," he said as he turned to look at Kendrick.

"If you feel this is what has to be done, then go." She reached out, gave her husband a hug, and then leaned back to look at him. There was a steely gaze in her eyes. "If it comes down to it, don't be quick."

"I didn't plan on it," he said as he gave her a passionate kiss.

Kendrick stood slacked jaw, not knowing what else to say. *I guess they really are made for each other,* he thought.

They made their way toward Kendrick's car when Josh said, "We not taking your ride. Knowing you, you asked too many niggas too many questions, and I'm pretty sure by now somebody gave him a heads-up and he's looking for it. We're taking mine."

"Okay, since you got all this figured out, where we going?"

"The one place I'm pretty sure your friendly ass didn't think of," he said as they made their way down the street. "ShaBree's."

The doorbell rang repeatedly as ShaBree struggled to put some clothes on after her hot, relaxing bath. She spent most of the day putting out fires at her saloon, which contributed to her long, grueling day. They continued to ring the doorbell incessantly. They must have thought it was broken and switched to banging to ShaBree's annoyance. She slipped on a presentable top that coverd up her nipples and ran down the stairs to give whoever it is a piece of her mind. *This better not be that crackhead trying to sell me stale chicken again,* she thought as she grabbed the door handle.

As she started to open the door, suddenly it's removed from its hinges as she scrambled to get out of the way or risk being crushed by it. She looked up and saw a large black man that she immediately recognized as Josh came barging in, followed closely by Kendrick. She turned around to run, but was immediately grabbed by her hair and pulled roughly back.

"Bitch, I know you heard me knocking!" Josh said as he pulled her head back painfully to look her in the eye.

She looked to Kendrick and saw a cold detachment and knew that he wouldn't be coming to her rescue this time.

"Where's Lawrence?" Kendrick said casually as he stood by the door looking out.

"I haven't seen him since you told him to leave town. He's not stupid enough to come back here." She let out a moan as Josh applied more pressure.

"Man, you know she's lying. We don't have time for these games. Why don't you just let me talk to her. You can go get you a latte or whatever it is you soft-ass college niggas do."

Kendrick walked over so he could look her in the face. "Yeah, she probably is," he said to him. "Look, I don't have time to play games with you today. Have you seen him or not?"

"Oh so now you wanna ask," she laughed bitterly. "I haven't seen him, I told you!"

Kendrick played a hunch. "Fine," he nodded to Josh to let her go, and he did begrudgingly. "I can't find Anika, and somebody told me they saw some guy and her walking off. I'm just worried."

She rubbed her neck as she looked at Josh with daggers in her eyes. "I told you before, I don't know anything about no hit on your precious Anika."

Kendrick jumped to his feet and slapped fire across her face. "I never said anything about a hit." He looked down at her with rage as she scooted away in fear as she held the side of her face where he struck her. "Cut the bullshit. You ain't hurt! We had sex rougher than that." He pulled her to her feet by her neck. Her toes barely touched the ground as he pulled her closer. "If the next words out of your mouth aren't what I want to hear, I'm going to go to work on you. By that time, I'm pretty sure you're going to tell me everything I want to know, but, it'll be too late for you. See, I'm not going to stop; that'll be too easy for you. I'm going to kill you slowly and intimately. I plan on taking my time to make sure I do it just right. But don't worry, I won't mess with your face so you can have an open casket. I'll even send flowers."

She tried to swallow, but it was impossible because he had his hands wrapped too tight around her throat. She gave a slight nod and he loosened his grip, allowing her to finally breathe. "I'll tell you everything, okay?"

He released her. "Before you start talking, if you leave anything out, I'm going to let Josh at you, then you and I will go play," he said as he sat back on the couch.

The ease in which he spoke of doing unspeakable things to her sent a shiver down her spine. This time, she knew she might have gone too far. "He came up to me after I left the bar a few weeks back when we ran into each other."

She started to tell the tale of how she became involved in all of this. She explained to him how he offered her money to keep tabs on Kendrick, and Anika if possible. So far, all she gave him was stuff she figured he already knew.

To her shame, she even told him about the night they spent together, which turned into many, many more.

She told him everything she could think of and waited as he seemed to be processing everything. Not knowing what else to say, she blurted out, "Please don't be mad at me, okay?"

His eyes shot up as he looked her with pure hatred. "Mad at you? Bitch, is you crazy? It's taking everything in me not to kick your motherfuckin' forehead in!"

He took a calming breath as he stood and began pacing. Every time he looked at her, the urge to break her skinny neck was becoming harder and harder to resist. He had to calm down as he tried to piece everything together that he just heard.

"So let me get this straight, he's paying you spy on us, is that it?"

"Yeah, he offered me forty thousand."

Josh and Kendrick shared a look and then burst out laughing.

"Oh bitch, you dead. Who the fuck would pay your ass forty thousand just to snoop on a motherfucka? You is stupid," Josh said as he pointed and laughed.

As the laughter died down, Kendrick said, "Anika's grandmother is in the hospital, and your boyfriend put her there."

"That don't have nothing to do with me." She shrugged.

"The fuck is wrong with you?" He looked at her in shock, realizing that he didn't really know her at all. "Just so you know, he was hired to make her suffer."

"Correction, both of you. He was hired to make both of you suffer."

"Did he tell you who all might be on the list?"

"I told you all that I know. If he went after her grandmother, it's safe to assume that was her. Since he was hired to kill her too, who else could he possibly use to make you suffer. . ." She turned to stare at Josh. "Do you have any suggestions?"

He got up to strike her, but Kendrick told him to hold up, which he ignored as he punched her in the stomach. She doubled over in pain, which brought a smirk to his face. "I bet you want talk slick again."

"I knew you didn't like me. You were always mad that Kendrick listened to me and not you."

"Bitch I don't dislike you. I hate you. I hope you die."

"That's why he's going to kill your wife and probably your kids," she laughed.

He pulled out his gun as he loomed over ShaBree's suddenly frightened form. Kendrick yelled for him to stop as he put the barrel of the gun against her forehead and clicked off the safety. His finger was on the trigger when suddenly two shots rang out seemingly from nowhere as the impact sent Josh flying backward, tumbling over the chair.

Kendrick instantly dove for cover behind the couch as he tipped over the coffee table for more protection as more shots continued to ring out. ShaBree screamed as she curled into the fetal position on the floor and covered her ears. He saw the gun Josh had dropped when he was shot and reached out for it, risking his life in the process.

It was less than an arm's length away, but it might as well have been a mile. He reached out and grabbed the handle as more shots rang out. He retreated back behind the relative safety of the table.

"I know you're out there, Lawrence," he yelled from behind cover.

"Yeah, it's me, What's up? I take it you got my message, huh?"

"That was fucked up what you did to her grandmother."

A chuckle rang out from the other side of the wall. "I was just doing my job. Besides, have you ever seen her? She was kinda hot. . ."

Kendrick rose up while Lawrence was talking as he tried to get a bead on his location by his voice. He shot two times through the wall and was rewarded with a curse. "You know this isn't going to end well," he said. He waited for several minutes as he listened for any sign of Lawrence, but was rewarded with only silence.

He started to grow antsy as he waited. He knew Lawrence could be waiting for him to make the first move. He looked over at Josh's still form, lying face down in his own pool of blood that was spreading. At this rate, he'll bleed out.

Kendrick knew he was running out of time. He had to do something or his friend would be dead if he wasn't dead already. He tried to get ShaBree's attention, but she was crying and oblivious to her surroundings.

He cursed under his breath as he steeled himself. Rising with his gun at the ready, he stepped around his makeshift cover and made his way silently across the room. He took another look at ShaBree as she was lost in her own thoughts as her sobbing continued. *Useless bitch*, he thought to himself ruefully as he edged closer toward the other room. A dark thought crossed his mind: W*ouldn't it be hilarious if this idiot screamed out my name and gave away my location so her dick of the day could put two in my chest? Serves me right for dealing with these hoe ass bitches in the first place.'*

He crept closer as his pulse quickened. He chanced a glance around the corner and there was no one there. He did a quick check of the rest of the house and found blood on the door frame at the back door. He cursed under his breath, knowing he got away.

Kendrick cursed again, knowing that Lawrence was still out there. The good news is that he got hit, but he didn't know if his injury was serious or not. For all he knew, he could've cut his hand on a glass trying to get away. Now that he knows that he's after him, he likely will have to speed up his plans. He knew he had to call Anika and let her know what was going on, but first he had to see to his friend.

He rushed back into the living room and checked Josh for a pulse. There was a faint pulse, and he thanked God that he was still alive. He got ready to call an ambulance, but then paused; he knew there would be questions and he couldn't afford to be hamstrung by the police right now.

Kendrick looked over at ShaBree and gritted his teeth. She had completely fallen apart and was still sobbing on the floor. He walked over to her and pulled her to a sitting position. "Hey, you're okay. You weren't shot, you have nothing to worry about," he said as nicely as he could.

All kindness bled away as he continued to watch her. He thought about all the pain she was directly responsible for in his life and then he looked over to see his best friend bleeding out not ten feet away, and he snapped.

He reared back and slapped the dog shit out of her.

She looked up at him as if she was seeing him for the first time. "Why did you hit me?" She looked around at her destroyed home with bullet holes everywhere and she started to cry again.

Kendrick promptly slapped the shit out of her yet again.

"Will you stop hitting me!" she wailed.

"I'm glad I finally have your attention," he said without remorse. "I need you to call an ambulance for Josh now, or when the police show up, they'll find two bodies."

"I'm not calling_"

He wrapped his hands around her throat and started to strangle the life out of her, but stopped himself with great effort. "You will do what I said now or so help me God, I will break your neck."

ShaBree scowled at him as she rubbed her throat. She grabbed her phone and called 911. To her credit, she put on a show, crying and telling them that a stranger broke in and shot her boyfriend. By the time she was done, the operator had two ambulances, police, and even had a fire truck to boot.

"I need you to sit with him until they get here." He lifted her chin to make his point. "If he dies, I'm going to kill everyone you know, and everyone you love."

"It's not my fault if he dies. You shouldn't have come over here to begin with." She crossed her arms like a petulant child.

He wanted nothing more than to kill her right then and there, but she was still useful, but it wasn't an easy decision. He rolled Josh over slowly as he checked the wounds; they were bad. He couldn't tell the extent of them due to the amount of blood. He grabbed some towels out of the bathroom and applied pressure to the wounds.

ShaBree was about to object when Kendrick gave her a warning look and she wisely bit her tongue. He checked his pulse and it was still there. He couldn't tell if it was any weaker than it was before, but as long as it was there, he considered it a good sign.

"Come here. I need you to apply pressure to this until they get here."

"I'm not touching him; that's nasty." she said as she scrunched up her nose in disgust.

"Bitch, get yo ass over here now!" he bellowed.

She let out a squeal and hurried to do as she was told. He placed her hands over the now blood-soaked towels and she grimaced. She did as he requested until the ambulance arrived.

He hurried toward the back but turned around to retrieve Josh's gloves. The fewer questions asked, the better, he figured. Once he had them, he was out the door and gone. As he drove away, he heard the faint sound of sirens.

Kendrick spent the rest of the night looking for Lawrence with no luck. Truth be told, his heart really wasn't in it because he was worried about Josh. There was so much blood loss that they didn't know if he was going to make it.

He had Anika calling him every fifteen minutes with updates. She was so worried about him after what happened to Josh that she was willing to drop everything to be at his side. It wasn't without just cause; Lawrence was still out there and he's a legit danger. Who knows where he will strike next.

The night began to turn into day, and Kendrick was tired beyond belief. All he wanted to do was sleep, but there were more important things that needed to be done. He made his way to the hospital where he was greeted by Anika and Marile.

He could tell that they both had puffy eyes, no doubt from crying and lack of sleep. "I'm so sorry. We were talking and the next thing we know, shots came out of nowhere." He didn't know what to do to ease her pain as her tears continued fall.

"I know you did everything you could. How were you to know?" She gave him a smile that she really didn't feel. Even in her grief, she is trying to comfort him. It was all he could do to keep it together.

"But I should have known something. Me and Lawrence go way back to kindergarten, and I know how he thinks." Guilt was tearing him apart.

Anika was silent as she watched the exchange. She didn't know them and it seemed wrong to try and interject her presence into the situation.

She was there when they brought him in, and she stayed with her to try and provide some comfort. She was thankful for the support, but it was somewhat awkward considering the circumstances, not to mention they have never met before now.

Their conversation was interrupted as the doctor came out as they waited to find out the latest news. Marile held her breath as she was waiting to hear what he had to say.

The doctor looked over his chart before speaking. "It looks like the worst is over. He had a lot of blood loss, and if he had gotten here any later, we would be having a decidedly different conversation. There were two gun-shots: one to his side, which went clean through, and one in his chest, a few inches from his heart. If he wasn't carrying his Bible, which took the brunt of the impact, he would have died instantly."

Marile began to laugh as tears of joy ran down her face. "Can I go see him now?"

"Not just yet. He's still in ICU for the next couple of days to make sure there aren't any possible setbacks, and in his weakened state, he's prone to infection."

"Thank you so much!" She hugged the doctor, and he couldn't help but smile. "Thank you for taking care of my husband. Bless you." She noticed a policeman posted outside of her husband's room. "Why is there a policeman outside of his room?"

"That's standard procedure when there's a shooting involved. I'm sure when he comes through, they're going to want to talk to him about the incident. The good news is that there's someone to make sure that nothing happens."

"What do you mean?"

The doctor realized that he was going down the wrong path. He answered hesitantly, "We had an incident a while back where someone was brought in for a GSW, and the perpetrator came back to finish the job." He patted her hand. "We won't let that happen again. That's why there's a policeman posted at his door." He smiled and walked away.

The doctor left and they let out a collective sigh of relief. Kendrick's joy was tempered because he knew what he had to do. Anika saw the look on his face and immediately knew something was wrong. "What's wrong?"

Marile saw the change in the vibe and she knew something was wrong as well. "What's wrong, Kendrick? The doctor said he was going to be okay."

"You and the kids have to leave, now."

"What do you mean I have to leave? I'm not leaving my husband, Kendrick."

"It's not safe for you here." He looked around to make sure their conversation wasn't being overheard. "Josh wasn't shot by accident. He was his intended target all along."

Marile started to look around as fear started to set in. She looked as if someone was going to jump out of the shadows. "Why would he target him? I thought he was after you two?" She looked down in embarrassment once she realized what she had said. "I'm sorry".

"No need to apologize. This is a messed up situation all the way around," Anika said as she gave her an understanding look of sympathy.

"It's more than just that," Kendrick said, getting back to the conversation at hand. "You have to leave, now." He saw the determined look on Marile's face and he knew he had to convince her. He pulled them over to the side, away from prying eyes. "There is no love lost between Josh and Lawrence. We've all known each other as long as I can remember, and it was Josh who saw Lawrence for what he was long before I did. He tried to tell me, but I didn't want to hear it or I really didn't want to believe it; take your pick."

Kendrick took a deep breath as he continued, "When all that went down all those years ago, Josh tried to warn me that something didn't seem right. He said too many people we didn't know was hanging a little close. They all led back to Lawrence.

"We did some research and came to find out that they were some hitters from out of town looking to branch out. Lawrence had invited them to town and he even worked out a deal with them to get a cut."

"How did you know?" was all she could think to ask.

"When a man realizes he's about to lose his life, he tends to want to tell you all sorts of things."

There was an uneasy silence as the two ladies pondered the implication of his words. Anika spoke more to break the uncomfortable silence than anything else. "But that doesn't explain why he would go after his family."

"Like I said, they really don't like each other. But to go into more detail, Josh wanted to kill him, but I told him to stand down. I gave Lawrence until the end of the night to get out of town. But Josh being Josh, he stabbed him in the side to give him something to remember him by. I think he did it hoping that he wouldn't make it and he could have gotten rid of him for good."

Marile clenched her jaw as she listened to how things got to this point. Anika could see the rage building up behind her eyes and she was helpless to provide any comfort. She knew that if she was in her shoes, she would probably feel similarly.

Marile's head shot up suddenly as realization dawned upon her. "Was anyone else hurt besides Josh?"

Kendrick was confused as the conversation had taken a sudden change, but he quickly recovered. "No, no one else was hurt. ShaBree was scared, but ain't shit happen to her."

She nodded as relief washed over her "I'm glad, there's been enough pain for one day."

"Not by a long shot," Kendrick said as dark thoughts ran through his mind.

"So, what do we do now?" Marile said as she started to come to terms with the necessity of her and the children leaving.

He gave her a wad of bills and an address. "I need you to go here first for a few days. I will call you once all of this is settled." She nodded and turned to gather the children when he placed a hand on her shoulder. "Josh is my family, and that makes you family as well. I will never let any harm come to you or the kids."

She gave him a kiss on the cheek in thanks and turned to hug Anika. "Thanks for being here for me. I just wish we met under better circumstances."

"Likewise," Anika said as she hugged her in return.

CHAPTER EIGHTEEN

As the day wore on, Kendrick explained in detail the plan for Marile and the children to leave town. He had to convince her on more than one occasion that she needed to leave for the safety of the children, but she didn't want to leave Josh. After several hours of pleading and compromises, she and the children got in the car and left, but not without Kendrick promising to call her to give regular updates.

Anika sat with Kendrick for the rest of the night by Josh's bedside.

As the days went by, Evelyn was making a steady recovery. The doctors had said she was out of danger, but that she wasn't ready to go home for at least another week. Anika was determined to stay by her side the whole time, but Evelyn wouldn't hear of it. She had said that she had wasted enough time on her as it is and she has to get back to her own life.

Anika was afraid that Lawrence might come back again, but she didn't want to voice her concerns and cause her grandmother to worry. She conceded and went back to work, but not before hiring a private security firm to watch her around-the-clock. Her grandmother didn't say it, but she was still haunted by the ordeal and extremely grateful that she would provide her that peace of mind.

Things were still pretty touch-and-go with Josh. Kendrick's been in constant contact with Marile, who was worried sick over her husband. He was still fighting a battle with her that he was starting to lose ground. She kept asking questions that he couldn't answer, and he could tell that she was losing confidence. He asked her for another week, and if he didn't have anything by then, he would come up personally to bring them back. She was skeptical, but she finally agreed.

It's been days and there had been no change with Josh or in Kendrick finding Lawrence. Until now, there had been no sign of him. Kendrick stayed at his bedside whenever he could between school and searching for Lawrence. He was hoping he died, but he knew deep down he wouldn't get that lucky.

Kendrick's phone continued to vibrate in his pocket, and he turned it off for what seemed like the hundredth time. He could feel his classmates' eyes on him as he turned his ringer off yet again. He was finally in his capstone and graduation was only a few weeks away. His instructor had already warned him that he had missed a number of days and that he was on a short leash. He didn't want to make any more problems for himself than he already has.

His phone vibrated in his pocket yet again and his professor, Dr. Gillis, looked toward Kendrick. "Mr. Watts, why don't you take a moment and get that. The class will wait until your finished with your obviously more important business," he said sarcastically.

He bit his tongue and took a calming breath as he stood to leave. He gave the professor an apologetic look as he made his way into the hallway. He was never one for kissing ass, but he knew it wasn't the professor's fault that he missed so many days. But even with that, he knew that he was only going to be at the butt end of so many jokes.

Kendrick's face scrunched up as he looked at the unfamiliar number. He noticed there were numerous calls with several messages and they were all from the same number. He listened to several of them and could tell it was a boy, probably no older than twelve, telling him that he had that information he was looking for.

His first thought was it was a setup. There's no telling what Lawrence would do at this point, especially since he knows that he is after him. With what he learned about him over the past few days, nothing would surprise him.

Yet, there was something in his voice that didn't set his bullshit detector off. For one, the kid sounded like he was in a closet or basement and he was talking softly as if he wasn't trying to be overheard. Two, he heard loud voices yelling in the background.

He was running out of options and time, so he called the number back. It rang several times before someone picked up the phone. No one spoke at first and he was ready to hang up the phone when someone whispered, "Hello?"

Kendrick paused for a moment when heard the boy whisper in the phone and he sounded scared. "You got some information for me?"

"Yeah, hold on, don't hang up." There was yelling in the background and he heard the boy moving until he couldn't hear the arguing anymore. "I found out what you been asking around for."

"Aight, cool. What you got for me?"

"I'll tell you, but first you have to do something for me."

He knew this was coming and he was ready for it. "Yeah, I got you. I'll give you a hundred dollars."

The little boy smacked his lips. "I heard it was a thousand. Don't try to play me. I might be young, but I'm not dumb."

Kendrick chuckled. "You right, my apologies. But what is someone your age going to do with that much money?"

"Spend it like everybody else. But it isn't money I want from you. I need a favor."

Kendrick's patience was starting to run thin. "Look, I don't have time for these games. Either you have the information or you don't. Give me what I need and you'll have your money before the end of the day."

"I told you I don't want your money! I need you to do a favor for me. I heard that you were a good dude and I need someone like you."

He knew arguing wasn't going to get him the information any sooner, he so listened to the boy. "What type of favor do you need?"

He was quiet for a moment, then he said, "I need you to get rid of my mama's boyfriend."

"You need me to kill him?" He didn't like where this was headed.

"I didn't say kill. I said get rid of. He keeps beating her, and when the police come, they don't arrest him because he knows them. I ain't no punk. I tried to help her, but he broke my arm. My big sister tried too, but he started hitting her like he was hitting my mama." Kendrick could hear tears in his voice.

"What's your name?"

The little boy hesitated, then said, "Christopher".

"Okay, Christopher, tell me where you live and I will see what I can do."

"Are you going to help me? You have to promise first."

"I promise." Kendrick knew he was getting in over his head, but the only way to get the information was to help the kid. "Text me the information. I'm on my way."

"I will, but you need to go handle your business first. I overheard my mama's boyfriend telling that Lawrence dude you looking for over the phone that he can pick up his package at six."

He swore under his breath because it was already four thirty. He knew he would have to work quickly if he was going to get there and get set up. He didn't like going into unknown situations unprepared. "Okay, text me where he's going to be at and then text me your address. Once I handle my business with him, I will head your way. I need you to let me know when he's home."

He looked at his phone and he had two text messages. He recognized the first address immediately; it used to be where he hung out when he was a kid. It used to be an office building that closed a long time ago. He was familiar with the layout, and knowing Lawrence, he would park in a secluded area away from prying eyes.

He saw the second address and he knew exactly where that was and more importantly, who it was. One of the dudes he grew up with lived there with his wife and kids, but was killed while serving in the army over in Afghanistan. Word on the street was that she hooked up with a small-time arms dealer named Melvin, but they called him M Good. He knew him and wasn't impressed. He shook his head. He always thought that was a stupid name.

He looked at the phone and noticed he was still on the line. "Okay, I got your messages."

"Remember, you promised," Christopher said through the phone with a hint of desperation in his voice.

"I give you my word. As soon as I finish up I'll be on my way."

"Okay, I'll text you when he's home," he said and then hung up.

Kendrick started to go back into the classroom and explain to his professor that he had to leave, but he thought better of it. He knew there would be more teasing and he didn't have time for that. *Better to ask for forgiveness than permission*, he thought to himself as he ran down the hallway.

He arrived at the location that Christopher had given him in record time. It was a good thing too because he had to park two blocks away to make sure he wasn't spotted. He made his way over to the building and was careful not to be spotted.

Kendrick found a spot on an adjacent roof that provided him cover from prying eyes as well as allowed him to see who comes and goes through the building. The reason why this location was so coveted was because there was only one way in and one way out. There was a large gate that opened into a courtyard that used to be a circle driveway that would allow you to pick up or drop off someone. There were no windows; the previous "tenant" had enough presence of mind to brick them over.

That was an ill-advised plan on his part because he was gunned down by his own men when they found out he was hoarding money. They found his body in one of the back-rooms riddled with bullets. Word was that he was trying break through one of the windows, which ironically the noise he was making led them straight to him.

Looking around, he saw several noticeable upgrades to the area. For one, there was no debris anywhere in the courtyard. The grass was recently cut, and there was power running to the building. The gate had been upgraded to a solid steel, electric-powered version with a state-of-the-art identification pad that he would have trouble cracking even if he had the time, which he doesn't. He was surprised that M Good had enough juice to hold a spot like this. *"I guess he's not so small-time after all,"* he thought to himself.

Kendrick saw movement out of the corner of his eye, and he instinctively hunched down further. No need to blow his cover before his prize arrived. He chanced a look from his hiding place and saw several SUVs pulling up to the building. One of the men got out of the car and opened the gate, which led them into the courtyard. The vehicles flowed into the compound, and the gate promptly closed.

Kendrick sat back, looked at his watch, and realized that he was earlier than he thought. Lawrence isn't due to be here for another twenty minutes. He was infamous for being late, which everyone chided him for. But what they didn't know was that he was never late to any meeting.

Lawrence is a lot of things, but reckless isn't one of them. He made it a habit to scout out any location before entering the building, park, or anywhere for that matter. His "tardiness" had saved him and his crew more times than he was readily willing to admit. This caused a pang of nostalgia, followed by waves of bitterness and anger that he had to fight to bury.

The scrapping sound against the side of the building was all the warning Kendrick got when Lawrence's head popped into view over the side of the building. He hurried and ducked down quickly behind cover as his heart hammered in his ears. He wasn't sure if he was seen because he knew that if Lawrence suspected anything, he would call the whole deal off and he was back to square one.

Kendrick waited for what seemed like an eternity as the seconds ticked by. The urge to look was almost unbearable as the tension built. He heard more scuffling against the side of the building as the noise seemed as if it was moving away. He waited a few more anxious minutes, then chanced a glance. To his relief, there was no one there.

He took a look at his watch again and realized it was five minutes after the scheduled appointment time. He let out a bitter chuckle to himself as he realized that now was about the time that he would walk in and apologize for his tardiness with some ridiculously lame excuse. Now, all there was to do was wait. . .

CHAPTER NINETEEN

Lawrence walked up to the gate and rang the buzzer. A heavy door without a handle swung open. Lawrence silently cursed under his breath because under normal circumstances, he would have noticed it. *But this isn't normal circumstances, is it?* he thought to himself. Today is the day that he gets his life back. Today is the day that Kendrick dies.

The huge dark-skinned man at the door looked at him with dispassionate eyes as he stepped aside to let him in. Lawrence found himself standing in a dark-room as a dash of fear crept over him. The door closed behind him and he was standing in total darkness. He fought the urge to panic, but it was no sure thing. The door opened behind him, and he let out an involuntary sigh of relief. The man chuckled as he opened the door and Lawrence felt small.

He had an impulse to shoot the disrespectful lackey in the head when it dawned on him that he still held his weapon. He turned back to glare at the man who looked at him with a chuckle still playing on his face, but was starting to turn into a look of confusion. Lawrence felt his hand creeping toward the gun that sat in his holster, but stopped when a voice behind him spoke.

"Come on, dude, M Good is waiting on you."

Lawrence gave the still-confused man a smile as he turned to follow another one of M Good's lackeys. He didn't realize how close he was to catching two to the head.

"I don't know what you were doing, but he ain't in a good mood. He hates waiting."

He waved his concerns off. "I'm sure once I explain to him what happened, he'll let it slide this time." The man didn't say anything, but the look on his face told him that he didn't think it would work, but he kept his thoughts and opinion to himself.

Lawrence looked around and noticed how clean and well-lit the building was. The walls were recently painted an eggshell white, and the floors looked as if they were recently polished. He glanced up and noticed the light fixtures were new as well. If he didn't play in here when he was a child, he would have believed the building was relatively new.

They made several turns down different hallways until they came to a large door at the end of a long hallway. The lackey did a series of knocks and then someone responded with knocks in return. It was obvious that they had a system to ensure they weren't compromised.

The door opened and Lawrence was escorted through. In the middle of a large room sat M Good at a table that was so big that it bordered on comical. He was leaning forward on the table with both his hands visible, except he noticed a pearl white 9mm resting inches from his hand.

The look on M Good's face was not a pleasant one. "You're late, which is obvious. But the question is, *why* you are late?"

Lawrence looked around the room discreetly and noticed that every man instantly brought their hands near or on their weapons. He would have chuckled if this was anybody, but it's him in this situation. He moved his hands apart slowly to show that M Good made his point and he was properly chastised. "I got caught up in traffic, so I took another way here." He looked at his watch and everyone immediately raised their weapons and trained them on him. He quickly parted his hands again. "Man, I was only five minutes late this time. For me, that's pretty good."

M Good didn't see the humor in his self-deprecating joke. "How do I know that you're not working with the feds? Are you wearing a wire, nigga?"

Lawrence saw the look on his face, and he realized that he was in more trouble than he previously anticipated. The tension went up another notch, which was already high to begin with. He knew he had to do something quick or he was going to be riddled with bullets if he's lucky. Worst-case scenario would be for them to torture him and then put a bullet in his head.

"I'm not wearing a wire. I can strip butt naked if you want." A few men in the room let out a chuckle, which eased the tension a little bit but not enough for his liking. The look in M Good's eyes was still saying they'd rather kill him and lose some money than risk exposure.

Not knowing what else to do, Lawrence began to strip. He took his time removing his jacket, not wanting an overly zealous member of his crew to mistake his movements as a threat. He raised his hands in the air, removed his gun holster, and then his shirt. He started to remove his pants when M Good raised his hand to stop. "You good, nigga, I just wanted to make sure you weren't on no bullshit is all. Go ahead and put yo shit back on. We ain't trying to get a show up in here."

Lawrence had enough common sense to chuckle as he put his clothes back on. He purposely left the gun and holster on the floor as a gesture of trust, although if it came down to it, he was confident that he could kill M Good and several of his boys before their numbers overwhelmed him. He waited until he was given permission to come closer.

M Good waved him over to another table, which was significantly smaller. No doubt it was used to conduct business. The table was made of a sturdy metal which allowed them to place numerous weapons on it, confident it wouldn't collapse.

He opened the bag and got ready to hand it over to Lawrence when he pulled it back. "Who's the job?"

He knew this was coming whenever he buys from small-time dealers; they always want to know who the job is. He fought the urge to roll his eyes. "As much as I would like to tell you, it's not place."

"Then whose place is?"

"My employer's."

"Who's your employer?"

"I can't tell you." M Good was starting to get annoyed, which at this point Lawrence didn't care.

"Well, if you can't tell me, then I guess we're done here." M Good says with a shit-eating smile on his face.

All hint of humor left Lawrence. Another thing he hated about working with small-time organizations was that they didn't know when to quit. He reached into his jacket and everyone raised their guns in his direction. He ignored them as he pulled out an ink pen. "See, this is why I don't fuck with thugs. They always gotta push shit too far." He pushes down on the pen and there was an explosion, which shook the building.

M Good's eyes grew big as saucers. "Nigga is you crazy?! Do you know how much ammunition we got up in this bitch?"

"Do I look like I give a fuck? I suggest you lower your weapons and hand me what I purchased." He waved his hand in the air so everyone could see that he was still holding the pen. "I'm holding a dead man's switch and I rigged the entire building with explosives, so I suggest that cooler heads prevail. I don't want to have to kill anymore of you than I already have."

M Good passed the bag over to Lawrence, and he turned his back to inspect the contents, letting him know that he didn't consider him a threat. He grinded his teeth as he was tempted to kill him anyway and let the world be damned.

Lawrence turned back to him with the same pleasant expression that he had before, which grated M Good's nerves. "Looks like everything is here as we agreed upon, and if you'll check the account you gave me, all the money is there." He tooted the bag over his shoulder. "Wait ten minutes after I leave before you try to exit the building. I rigged the exit with a motion sensor and it will trigger the rest of the bombs if anyone tries to leave after me before then.

"Just get the fuck out," M Good said as he barely contained his rage.

Lawrence left without another word, *no need to dig the blade in any deeper*, he thought to himself as he made his way to the exit. He stepped over what remained of the guy who was guarding the door who thought he was funny. Guess the joke was on him since he didn't see when he dropped the mini explosive in the corner.

Normally, that size charge is enough to scare people, but not much more. But since it was placed in a small enclosed space, it unfortunately increased the blast radius, which was good for him but not so good for the guard at the door. He needed to make it convincing or M Good wouldn't have bought it, which would have made things a lot more interesting to say the least.

He had only the one charge and he was hoping he didn't have to use it, but circumstances made it necessary, he thought bitterly. Now if he needed to do business with him in the future, things could get tricky. He might have to use a go between, which can get expensive or just kill him, which puts him back at square one.

Lawrence thought for a moment and pulled out his phone. He contacted his people and had them reverse the transaction. He thought he was being charged highway robbery for what he requested anyway, so he felt justified.

Lawrence was in high spirits as he made his way back to his car. He thought he felt someone behind him, but before he could reach for his gun, he felt a blow to that back of his head and everything went dark.

Kendrick felt more than heard the explosion that was coming from inside the building. He realized with a start that the building was full of high-power ammunition, and if that was to get caught up in the blast, there's no telling what kind of damage that could do.

He scurried down from the roof of the building and made his way around the back, where there was a lesser chance of him being discovered. He knew he had to be careful because thanks to that explosion, M Good's men were going to be on their guard. He couldn't risk an altercation with his men, and Lawrence noticed. His intentions were to double back and find a more secure place to wait for Lawrence, but luck had other plans.

Kendrick made his way across the street, ducked down behind a car, and pretended like he was tying his shoe. He felt the barrel of the gun at the back of his head and he froze. He cursed under his breath for being so careless. He knew that if he tried to make a move, he would be dead before he got his hand up.

"Don't make a move or I'll have your brains all over this car. Now, get up and put your hands on top of your head."

Kendrick slowly placed his hands on top of his head as he stood. "I didn't do anything. I was just trying to take a piss and then I heard this loud noise, so I ran across the street."

"Nigga, did I ask you what you was doing? Turn yo ass around so I can see yo face."

He turned around and he saw a kid who couldn't be much older than twenty looking at him with cold eyes, which made him look older. He was a big kid, probably used to play sports, but now he's working for M Good. From the look in his eyes, he could tell that this wasn't his first time. He didn't look rushed or nervous. He knew that if M Good gave the order to kill him, he would pull the trigger without hesitating.

Kendrick knew that he couldn't let things play out much longer. After the explosion that just took place, he knew it wouldn't be too long before Lawrence made his way out of the building. If he missed his chance, all his friends would be in danger.

"Hey, bruh, I didn't do anything wrong. Can't you just let me go? I didn't see nothing or know nothing."

The young thug gave him a hard look, and Kendrick noticed his hand beginning to grip the handle of the gun tighter. His body tensed, but he knew that if he tried anything, the odds weren't in his favor.

"Look here, dude, if you keep running off at the mouth like that, I might just pop you on principle, you feel me?" Kendrick just nodded as he kept his hands in the air. "Give me yo ID. I need to know who I'm dealing with." He reached behind Kendrick and pulled his wallet out. He looked at the photo and then back at him. He saw the name and his eyes narrowed. "Yo name Kendrick? You not that dude Kendrick is you?"

He wanted to tell him the truth, hoping his name would buy him some clout, but he stopped. "Nah, bruh, my mama named me Kendrick. I heard about another dude with that name, but I never met him." He noticed that the young thug was buying his story. He held up his phone and took his picture. Panic set in as his mouth went dry. "Why did you take my picture?"

He let out a chuckle as if it was the dumbest question he heard all day. "I'm sending this to M Good. He knows all the players in the neighborhood. I can't tell who's who, so I send it to him. He'll know what to do."

Curiosity got the best of Kendrick. "What happens if he realizes I'm not this guy you talking about?"

He shrugged. "He'll probably tell me to put a bullet in your head. No loose ends."

Kendrick cursed under his breath yet again for being so careless. He knew what he had to do, but didn't feel good about it. He tried to get the young thug's attention by feigning tears. He succeeded when he gave him a look of contempt. "You haven't sent the picture yet?"

The young thug's eyebrows knitted together as he looked at him with suspicion. "Nah, I can't get a signal. This area has poor coverage for whatever reason." He lowered his gun toward Kendrick's chest. "Why the fuck you worried about whether or not I sent a picture? I'm starting to think you on some bullshit."

"Why the fuck would I be on bullshit? You gon kill me either way!" He winced inwardly at his harsh tone. He needed to gain his trust, if not sympathy. As things stand, he's just outside his reach. He needed him to be closer if he had any chance of getting out of this situation.

The young thug stepped closer as he pointed the gun at Kendrick's head. "Nah, you playing games. As soon as I get word back, we gonna deal with this situation."

Kendrick started crying in earnest as his body shook with the effort. He moved ever so slowly toward the young thug. "I didn't do anything! Why do I have to die for something I didn't do?!"

He gave a dispassionate glance as he continued to try and get the message to go through on his phone with no success. "Hey, it's just your lot in life. Take it like a man."

Kendrick continued to cry as he was finally inside his guard. He saw out the corner of his eye that he was looking at him as a non-threat, which could be nothing further from the truth. The young thug held the phone up and smiled as he was finally able to get a signal.

"I was finally able to get a signal. You better hope he says something good for your sake, but I wouldn't hold out much hope," the young thug said as he waited for the picture to go through.

Kendrick couldn't afford to wait any longer. He continued to cry, and the young thug finally realized how close Kendrick was, but it was too late. He tried to raise the gun up, but Kendrick was on him before he had a chance. He gave him a smirk as if he found his actions comical until Kendrick snapped his wrist, causing him to drop the gun. He let out a cry of pain, and Kendrick quickly covered his mouth.

"I'm sorry about this, young fella. You should have stayed home today." He snapped his neck and laid his lifeless body down next to the car, shielding him from prying eyes.

There was movement out of the corner of Kendrick's eye as he crouched down further behind the car. He looked down into the now lifeless eyes of the dead thug. He felt guilt nipping at his outer shell, but he quickly pushed it away. *"He would have killed me without a second thought"* he said to himself as his resolve began to return.

He looked up and noticed that it was Lawrence walking toward his car with a shit-eating grin on his face as his blood began to boil. He looked as if he didn't have a care in the world. He knew that was about to change.

Kendrick's emotions began to churn within him and he had to fight the urge to run out into the street and shoot him in the head. The fact that he's responsible for his best friend and the grandmother of woman he loves being in the hospital and he's walking around without a care in the world was almost more than he could take. He knew what he had to do.

Making his way around the back of Lawrence wasn't going to be easy. He was a cautious man and he knew how to handle himself. Kendrick knew that if he made a mistake, the chance of him being killed was a real possibility. He reached down, took off the dead thug's jacket, and grabbed his hat. He quickly put them on and started walking down the street. He knew that if Lawrence saw him, he would think that he was on patrol and not look too deeply into it.

But he was quickly running into two problems. Sneaking up on Lawrence was a problem all unto itself, but he was quickly running out of time, which didn't help matters. Lawrence will be at his car in mere moments and if he didn't get to him before then, he may never have another chance before it's too late. Lawrence turned the corner and Kendrick knew he had less than a half of a block to reach him. He started to run as fast as he could in hopes of catching up to him. He turned the corner and immediately ducked down when he saw him beginning to turn around. He was on his phone and was thankfully oblivious to his surroundings for once.

Lawrence turned around, heading for his car once again. Kendrick continued to make steady progress as he gained on him. He was a mere thirty feet away and he reached into his pocket for his taser, but cursed under his breath when he saw that the base was cracked. The taser was now useless, and he looked down at the gun in his hand and knew that all he had to do was pull the trigger and all this would be over. He was close enough that he knew that he couldn't miss. *Yeah fuck that, you not getting off that easy,* he thought to himself as he ran towards Lawrence.

He knew he only had one chance, and that was to catch him off guard. He thought he saw him reaching into his jacket and he panicked. He reared back with the gun and threw it as hard as he could. The blow landed true, and Lawrence collapsed unconscious to the ground.

Kendrick ran up and kicked him in the head to make sure that he was out. He didn't want to take any chances, but he was pretty sure he was out for the count. He rummaged through his pockets to find the keys and then he opened the trunk. He noticed a homeless man watching from the alley and he was pretty sure that he saw the whole thing.

He waved the man over, and he slinked toward him with his shoulders down, not meeting his gaze as he shook with fear.

"What's your name?" Kendrick said.

He didn't know if it was the tone of his voice, but the man looked up with a surprised expression on his face. "My name is Carl," he said as he met Kendrick with a full-on gaze.

"How would you like to make some money?" Kendrick said as he looked around to see if anyone else was watching.

"Sure," Carl said, not knowing what else to say.

"Great, you grab his feet and help me throw him in the trunk."

Carl gave a shrug and grabbed the unconscious Lawrence's feet, and they dumped him unceremoniously in the trunk. He winced as he saw Lawrence's head hit the side of the trunk. He turned to leave and head back to the alley when Kendrick called after him.

"Hey, don't you want your money?"

Carl waved him away, not wanting to have anything else to do with the situation. He just wanted to get back to his cardboard box and the half of pint of gin he had been saving for just the right moment. He figured if this didn't qualify, nothing else would.

Kendrick reached into his back pocket, but Carl cringed. He tried to give him a smile, but it didn't seem to help. He pulled out $60, which seemed kinda cheap for the work he just did. He immediately ran over to Lawrence and pulled out his wallet. He gave him the entire content, not bothering to count.

Carl's eyes lit up as he saw more money than he's seen in years. "Thank you" was all he could say as his mouth hung open in shock.

"No, thank you. I wouldn't have been able to do this without your help. I hope you can keep this just between us."

"Keep what? I didn't see anything."

Kendrick smiled, satisfied with his answer. "You stay out of trouble, Carl, and hide that money."

Kendrick went to get into the car when Carl walked up and asked, "Who are you?"

"Kendrick," he said as he looked him in the eye.

Carl only gave a nod and pulled the money out that he had just gave him. I can't take your money. I heard you were tough as they come, but also you were a good man," he said as he tried to give him the money back.

"Nah, you keep that, Carl. Try and get you a room because rain is coming and the temperature is supposed to dip tonight."

He nodded and turned to walk away when he stopped and turned back. "What did he do?"

"Too much" was all Kendrick would say.

Carl didn't say anything else as he made his way back to his cardboard box and disappeared inside.

Kendrick hopped into the car and sped away down the street toward his next location.

Kendrick dropped off Lawrence's unconscious body at one of his many "private" locations around the city. He strapped him to the chair with plastic tie wraps binding his wrist and arms, and with a metal band going across the front of his head, which will keep him from escaping. As much as he needed to find out what he had planned, he had to wait because he was still unconscious.

He noticed his breathing patterns beginning to change and he could tell from experience that he was starting to wake. He smiled inwardly, waiting to see the shocked expression on his face when he finally came completely around. His phone began to vibrate in his pocket and he almost knew without looking who it was _Christopher.

He answered the phone, dreading what he already knew he was going to say. "Yeah"

"He's home. You told me to call you when he got in." There was a silence and Kendrick could hear loud voices in the background and then there was a loud crash. "I don't know what happened, but I've never seen him like this. I think you better hurry before he kills one of us." There was more than a hint of fear in his voice when he hung up the phone.

He hated to tear himself away from his revenge, but he made a promise. The kid really was in trouble and he knew he had to hurry. He grabbed his bag and was heading for the door when he heard a groan over his shoulder. Kendrick turned around, knowing what he would find _Lawrence looking around with an amused look on his face.

"Wow, you must have gotten rusty since the last time we saw each other. I figured you would have tried something sooner. Although I have to admit I didn't think you would actually pull it off, kudos to you," he said with mock respect.

Even with him bound and unable to escape, you would think he would have enough decency to respect the situation that he's in. He's sitting there completely immobile without any chance of escape as he giggled silently to himself. He would shake his head in disappointment as if he wasn't the one strapped to the chair.

Kendrick felt his anger beginning to rise as he felt his control over the situation beginning to slip. "I don't think you fully grasp the situation that you're in, but you will." He grabs the cloth with the chloroform that he prepared earlier in case he woke sooner than he anticipated. Lawrence didn't even try to put up a fight as he placed the cloth over his face longer than he needed to. He couldn't take any chances of him escaping.

Kendrick looked down at his now still form and saw a slight smirk on his face. He couldn't tell if it was imagined or real, but at this point it, really didn't matter. He wanted to strike him, but he didn't know if he currently possessed enough restraint to stop himself. *"Even tied down and knocked the fuck out, you still find a way to get on my last motherfuckin nerve,"* he thought bitterly.

With an effort, he tore himself away to handle more pressing concerns.

CHAPTER TWENTY

The sunset was over an hour ago and there were few people on the streets. Kendrick had parked Lawrence's car around the corner and made his way to his old friend's house. As soon as he neared the walkway, he heard a woman scream followed by a loud thud. He ran to the door and knocked softly. The door swung open with a crash and M Good had a gun pointing directly at his face. "Who the fuck is you and why are you knocking on my door?"

Kendrick threw his hands up as a sign of fear and that he was unarmed. Truth be told, he really didn't have to pretend to be afraid; having a gun thrust in your face will do that all by itself. He took a step back, "I know your son, Christopher. I was stopping by because I was trying to pay him for some work he did for me."

M Good snorted as he lowered the gun, but not completely. "First of all, that little nigga ain't no child of mine. He belongs to this hoe I've been dealing with and he happens to stay in my house." He suddenly put the barrel of the gun on Kendrick's forehead. "Second of all, why is yo old ass coming around here asking about him in the first place? You a pedophile or some shit?"

He clicked the safety off on the gun, and he knew he had to come up with something fast or he was going to have an unwanted hole in his head. But before he could speak, he saw a woman stagger into view, looking barely able to stand. Her face was badly bruised, clothes torn and bloody, and she was holding her side like her ribs were broken. She held on to the wall as she tried to make it to the chair. It was then that he saw her leg bent in an awkward position and he knew it was probably fractured, if not broken.

She reached for the chair but under estimated the distance and went crashing to the ground. M Good turned around when he heard the noise and gritted his teeth. "Bitch, I didn't say you could move! Imma deal with you once I'm finished with him. And when that little nigga of yours come through, tell him to go to the store and get me some Black & Milds."

She lifted her head and her one good eye opened in shock. "Kendrick?" she said louder than she intended to.

She quickly dropped her head to the ground, trying to conceal her blunder, but it was too late. He turned toward her with murder in his eyes. "What the fuck did you just call me? I know you didn't just call me another man's name!" He kicked her in her broken leg, and she screamed and tried to scoot away. He pulled his leg back to kick her again when he paused as he realized that she wasn't talking to him. The name kept turning in his head, then it dawned on him when the name finally clicked.

He turned around to raise the gun, but was shocked to see Kendrick standing just inches away. Kendrick grabbed his wrist and twisted it as the gun went tumbling to the floor and then he smashed his forearm into the side of his head knocking him out cold. His body dropped heavy to the ground.

Kendrick made his way over to the sobbing woman. She lifted her head to regard him. "You shouldn't be here. When he wakes, things are going to get really bad," she said as her body shook from fear.

He didn't want to think about what she meant by *real bad* because things couldn't get much worse. "I owed your son a favor and I'm just paying him back." He tried to smile to reassure her, but she seemed to be in another place.

Her head snapped up as she looked at him with fear in her eyes. "My baby" was all she said as she broke down in sobs.

Kendrick immediately started to search the house frantically. He checked all the bedrooms until he found the boy's still form lying across the bed. He would have thought he was asleep except for the blood that was seeping out the nasty gash on the side of his head.

He began to shake him, trying to get him to regain consciousness. When he didn't, he started to shake him harder and his eyes fluttered open. "Why are you shaking me?" Christopher said groggily.

Kendrick let out a sigh of relief. "Man, I thought we lost you for a second there."

"Nah, he hits like a bitch," Christopher said as he tried to sit up, but swayed until he regained his bearings.

"If you think you can walk, I got a present for you in the living room."

Not knowing what else to do, he followed him into the living room, saw his mother sprawled out on the floor, and rushed to her side. When she saw him, she hugged him with surprising strength and didn't want to let go.

"I'm sorry," she cried as she continued to hug him.

"Sorry for what, Mama?" he said as tears began to fall.

"I should have protected you, fought back, but I didn't." More tears fell as her son tried to comfort her.

"No, Mama, I was supposed to protect you. I'm the man of the house."

Kendrick hated to break up the touching moment, but he was pressed for time. "As the man of the house, you got anything you want to say to your former tenant?"

M Good started to move slightly, and Christopher took a step back. He opened his eyes and looked around in confusion. "What the fuck is going on here? Little nigga, when I get free, Imma do you like I did yo mama!" He tried to move his arms, but they were tied behind him and strapped to the heater with plastic straps.

Christopher took another step back, but ran into Kendrick. Kendrick looked down at him with a smirk on his face. "You don't have to be afraid of him anymore. He can't hurt you. Why don't you tell him how you feel?"

"I hate you for hurting my mama and I want you to leave and never come back!" He screamed as the tears began to flow once again.

M Good began to laugh. "Oh, I'm gonna leave, but then what's your mama gonna do for money? If it wasn't for me, you would be out on the streets and your sister would be turning tricks on one of my corners." He tried to struggle to get free once again, but there was no use. He looked at Christopher with a sadistic look and smiled. "When I get free, I'm going to cut your mama into little pieces and make you watch."

The room was silent and the air filled with tension. Kendrick broke the silence as he chuckled. Christopher looked up at him like he was crazy. "I guess he wasn't really listening, huh?" Kendrick pulled out a lead pipe from behind his back. "Try talking to him with this, he might understand you better."

There was real fear in M Good eyes as Christopher took the pipe from Kendrick's hand. His mouth went dry as he struggled for words. "Hold up, young blood, I was just talking shit. I'm just going to leave and never come back, okay?"

Christopher looked over at his beaten and broken mother and then turned his attention back to him. "Was you just *playin'* with my mama too?" M Good's mouth opened, but no words came out. "Yeah, that's what I thought." He brought the pipe down crashing onto his ankle and he was rewarded with a loud grunt.

He raised the pipe again, but Kendrick asked him to hold up. He went over to M Good and spoke but only he could hear. "Why don't you tell me where you keep your money. I know you have bank accounts and safes all over the city."

He looked him in the eye. "If I give you what you want, you gonna let me go?"

"Oh no, I'm pretty sure you're gonna die. But how you get there is still up for negotiation. Quick and painless or we can take the other path. Strictly up to you."

"Nigga, fuck you!"

"Yeah, I kinda figured you would say that. Just so you know, you *will* tell me where everything is before it's all over, I promise you that." He stood up and walked back over to Christopher. "You need to swing through your blows; this way he can understand your feelings better. If you hear a loud crack followed by an uncontrollable scream, it just means you're doing it right."

Christopher nodded as he brought the heavy pipe down on M Good's shin and there was a loud crack followed by a scream. "That was for my mama!" He smashed the pipe into his other shin, breaking it. "That was for my sister!"

He raised the pipe over his head with a two hand grip, ready to deliver the killing blow when Kendrick took the pipe from him. "That's enough."

Christopher looked at him with rage clearly on his face. "Why did you stop me?! He has to pay for what he did to us!"

"And he will, but not like this. You're better than this, you're better than me. There will come a time when you will thank me for stopping you."

"I doubt if I will ever forgive you for this, Kendrick. I don't ever want to see you again!" he said as he ran out the door.

Kendrick watched him go, but didn't try to stop him. He knew he was full of emotion and just needed to clear his head. He remembered when he was his age and doesn't think he was nearly as strong as Christopher. If he had let him kill M Good, he would be sending him down a path that few people have ever been able to walk away from.

"Thank you for stopping him, I'm sure if you weren't there, he would have killed me," M Good said as he smiled at Kendrick.

He saw the look of adoration on his face and Kendrick felt sick to his stomach. "Oh, don't thank me. I'm going to kill you and it's not going to be quick."

M Good saw the murderous intent in Kendrick's eyes and tears began to fall. "Look, I'm sorry. I-I need help. If you let me go, I will leave and never come back again, I promise."

He stared at him intently. "I need the account information, M Good. . ."

"I can't do that, Kendrick. I got people who are depending on me. I have responsibilities. You understand, right?"

Kendrick looked down on the floor as he shook his head and then started to chuckle. "You don't really understand yet, I see. You are going to die and from the way things are going, you're going to experience more pain than I can honestly contemplate. I told you the only thing that's open to negotiation is how you get there."

M Good Hardened his resolve. "I ain't tellin' you shit. If today is my day to die, I'm going to go out like a G. Best believe that shit!"

"If I had a dollar for every time somebody told me they weren't telling me shit, I probably would have just killed you outright." He reached into his pocket and pulled out a cloth, but paused. He turned to the woman lying on the ground and nudged her slightly. She looked up with a confused look on her face. "I have to ask you something."

She raised her head the best she could. He couldn't imagine the pain she was going through with just that simple effort. She stifled a grimace as she tried to keep a strong face. "What do you want to ask me?"

"I need to go and I'm taking him with me. I trust that I can count on your discretion."

He gave her such an intense look of finality that she had to look aware from his glare. "I-I thank you for coming to my son's aide, but I don't think it's necessary for you to take him away. How are we supposed to live? I haven't worked in years and I don't have a degree. Who would hire me?"

Kendrick's mouth dropped open in shock. Of all the things that have happened recently, this might be the most surprising. "How are you supposed to live? He knocked your son unconscious, and if he had struck him a few inches to the right or left, he would be dead."

"I know you're right, but I'm sure he's sorry and didn't mean it. But my son isn't an angel either. He sometimes likes to antagonize him by not doing what he says or walking in front of the TV."

As she lay there beaten and broken, Kendrick found it increasingly difficult to find sympathy for this woman. She knew this man was abusive by the fact that he did it to her as well as her son. To say that the daughter left due to the abuse wouldn't be a stretch. More than likely, she was a victim as well.

Yet, this woman laying here with a compound fracture in her leg and can barely open one eye due to the abuse is defending this man and asking him not to take him. He had half a mind to leave him with her. No doubt she probably wouldn't survive the night due to the injuries that have already been inflicted. And if he were to leave him in the home, he would inflict more harm to her and her son.

"I understand that you don't want him to leave, but what about your son? You know that if I leave him here, he will hurt him or probably kill him, right?"

Her face hardened. "He shouldn't have involved you in the first place. Serves him right if he got smacked around a little bit. Maybe then he'll stay out of grown folks' business."

"Be that as it may, I'm taking him with me." Kendrick rose and placed the cloth over M Good's face, and he was quickly knocked out by the fumes.

"If you take him, I will tell. I'll tell whoever asks about him. I'll tell the police. Don't think he doesn't have friends on the force. They'll love to know who cut off their money train."

He was making his way toward the door and froze at her words. He knew without a doubt that she meant every word that she said. Now he had a decision to make; leave him here and wait for the inevitable retaliation that was to come or take him now and hope that they don't believe her story.

He had to admit that that was leaving too much to chance. All it takes is the wrong person to ask the right questions and it would all be over. As much as he loathed the idea, he had to let him go for now. He knew that if he waited long enough, another opportunity would arise. He was about to undo his bonds when he stopped. The thought of leaving Christopher here with this monster was something he wasn't willing to do.

Kendrick saw the look of determination on her broken face and he knew what he had to do. "Apparently, you don't give a fuck about nobody but your selfish, warped needs. But as luck would have it, I got just the thing for you." He gave her a hard look as he stood and made his way around the house. She heard noises coming from different rooms as Kendrick made his way throughout the house.

She tried to move, but she couldn't as her body was starting to go into shock. He made his way back into the room and picked up M

Good as if he weighed nothing. She saw that he was leaving with him and she spoke up, "I told you if you leave with him, I'm going to tell."

Kendrick dropped M Good's lifeless body like a sack of potatoes and squatted in front of her until they were almost at eye level. He looked at her face as if he was studying it. "Nah, I don't think you're going to tell. More than likely, you'll be dead within the hour."

"I don't believe you."

"Yeah, I figured you wouldn't. The thing is, your body is going into shock and you probably already noticed that you can't move."

Her good eye grew big as fear crept up her spine. She didn't want to believe him, but she felt herself growing cold and her vision is starting to blur. "I bet you're real proud of yourself, aren't you, big man? You're just going to leave me here to die. What kind of a man does that?"

"Well, to answer your question, I was going to leave you here to die. I cut the phone lines throughout the house just in case somebody happened to stop by after I left. But now that I look at you, I don't know why I even bothered. Your wounds are extensive, and coupled with the years of abuse, I'm afraid there's not much anyone can do for you."

"Will you let him go?" she said as a tear ran down her cheek, her last pathetic attempt for him to spare the man who killed her.

"No, but you can rest assured you'll be seeing him a lot sooner than you think." He stood and slung M Good over his shoulder. "For what it's worth, I'll make sure that your son and daughter are taken care of."

"I hope you burn in hell for this."

"Probably not, but when you see your husband I'm sure he might have some hard questions for you."

She watched as Kendrick left with M Good slung over his shoulder. She watched him close the door behind them and she was left there lying on the floor, left with only her thoughts. She tried to move again, but her body wouldn't cooperate. A powerful urge to sleep swept over her as she tried to fight it. She knew that when she closed her eyes, it would be for the last time. Her eyes closed as she dreamed of a life long ago when she still loved herself. A single tear fell as her last breath escaped her lips.

CHAPTER TWENTY-ONE

He woke with a start when he heard the outer door opening with a loud bang. He heard a pleading voice as he came back to his senses. He tried to move his arms, but found that they were bound. The memories and events came crashing in on him like waves on the ocean. He remembered how he bested M Good and his crew and how he got what he needed essentially free. Then he remembered everything going black and ultimately waking up in this abandoned building.

He knew it was Kendrick, to his irritation, who had put him in his present predicament. With all his planning and studying of the man, he was able to sneak up on him and knock him upside the head. If it was anybody but him, he would laugh. But it was him and he didn't find it the least bit amusing.

Lawrence heard a man screaming, which snapped him out of his self-deprecating train of thought. He heard sobbing, followed closely by pleading as his words trailed off to a whisper that he was no longer able to hear. There was an eerie silence that seemed to fill the air. Lawrence realized that he was holding his breath as he waited for the inevitable screaming to start anew. He didn't have to wait long as a low wailing filled his ears, which caused him to cringe involuntarily.

Lawrence's heart jumped in his chest as the door to his room swung open. Kendrick stepped into his room wearing a heavy leather garment that covered him from his neck to his feet, not unlike an apron that a butcher would wear. His feet were covered in footies, like the ones they wear in a hospital. He wore thick rubber gloves that came up to his elbows. There was a welder's mask sitting up on his head as their eyes met.

The first thing Lawrence noticed was a... *emptiness* in his eyes. He can't ever recall a time, even when he threatened his life in the past, when he ever looked at him like that. He fought, but failed to hold back the urge to swallow out of fear. His body tensed as Kendrick took several steps toward him.

Kendrick stopped just short of him as he grabbed a pair of pliers off the table that he was just noticed. "I always forget to grab these." He sighed as if he had left his cellphone on the kitchen counter. "Don't worry, I haven't forgotten about you." He winked as he made his way back into the other room.

Lawrence was grateful that he had enough presence of mind to close the door on his way out. Even with the door closed, he recognized the familiar snapping of bones breaking and he knew that he was breaking that poor soul's fingers. Whoever that man was, he found himself hoping that his heart would give out and just die.

He had more than his fair share of delivering the type of pain that Kendrick was now administering. Sometimes, he did it at a client's request; they usually wanted to watch. But once he started inflicting the pain and the scene became all too real, they would back out and want him to end it quickly. But every now and then, they would want him to make it linger and skip the details. Those were the days he enjoyed the most. But now that it looked like he was going to be on the other end of the entertainment, he was having a decidedly different opinion on the matter.

Lawrence cringed inwardly when he heard the man scream again. It wasn't that he cared anything about the man; it was the fact that his screams were a reminder of what he had to look forward to in the not too distant future.

He found himself slipping into despair. If he was a lesser man, his predicament would break him. But he wasn't a lesser man, far from it. He knew there was nothing he could do about being bound to a chair while a man he thought he knew was busy torturing someone who he thought probably deserved it.

Do I deserve it? Lawrence pondered as he tried to work the situation out in his head. He heard an especially bloodcurdling scream that he knew had to hurt. He started to wonder what he was doing to him to illicit that type of scream and he quickly chided himself for letting it distract him from the situation at hand.

Lawrence focused on his situation and did his best to block out the disturbing noises coming from the other room. He knew why he was there, that wasn't up for debate. He figured if the situations were reversed, he would feel some kinda way too.

After all, he did shoot Josh and as far as he knows he's probably dead. Then there was that sweet old lady that was Anika's grandmother. The thought of the things he did to her brought a perverse smile to his face. He allowed himself to become lost in the memory of the act as he felt his manhood begin to swell in his pants. He always did love when they begged and screamed for him to stop. It was almost as enjoyable as the act itself.

The pleasurable thought was ripped from his mind as another scream found its way into his room. His head shot up as he had an epiphany. He almost laughed at the simplicity of it all. He was looking at the situation and not the players involved.

If this were anyone else involved in this scenario, he knew they would be good as dead. This was apparently the case for the man in the other room as another scream echoed through the walls. But this wasn't any other situation and these weren't strangers involved in it either. *This is Kendrick and me,* he thought to himself as he began to relax his body and let his mind begin to flesh out the details.

If he really wanted him dead, he had ample opportunity to do it. He could think of a half dozen different ways off the top of his head that would have done the job without all the "theatrics." He never really understood why Kendrick went through all the cloak-and-dagger shit when it was just as effective to shoot a man in the head and leave him on his child's mother's doorstep. *A dead body with a hole in the head leaves a damn good message,* he thought.

Well, since I'm still alive, he must want something, he said as he brought his thoughts full circle. Then it dawned on him _the girl,

Anika. That's what this is all about? He would shake his head in shame if it wasn't for the fact that his head was strapped to the back of his chair.

All this for a bitch, Lawrence thought ruefully. Despite his dire situation, he was starting to think less of Kendrick. *Then again, it's just like him to fall for the wrong woman,* he thought as memories of all the times he used to fuck ShaBree practically right under his nose. Even when he found out, he was still willing to listen. *Hell, if they both said they were really sorry, he would probably have forgiven the whole thing,* Lawrence thought as he chuckled to himself.

After weighing all the facts, and no matter how much Kendrick had tried to cover up his actions, it's clear. There's an overwhelming preponderance of evidence that can't be denied.

He won't hurt him.

Oh, he'll put on a great show, to be, sure and do his best to make it convincing; he's sure of that. But when it comes right down to it, he doesn't have the heart. He may even go as far as to give him a good beating. Even he had to admit that he hasn't been on his best behavior. Lawrence knew that a beating was well within his right. After all, he did go a tad bit overboard with the grandmother and odds are that he probably killed Josh. *Yeah, a solid ass whopping is in order,* he thought with finality.

He found himself drifting back to the time he spent with the grandmother. A smile threatened to spread across his face as he savored every intricate detail. The way her body shook with pain as he did unspeakable things, how she tried to hide her face as he told her how all of this was her fault as he continued to repeatedly assault her fragile form. A lewd smile began to appear as he closed his eyes as the memories caressed the darkest parts of his soul.

"I told you everything you wanted to know! Please, you promised!" The sound of the man's voice startled Lawrence from his pleasurable thoughts. It wasn't so much the screaming that caused him to jump. It was more of the familiarity of the voice that sent a chill up and down his spine. He strained to hear more as the voices began to fade.

"Stop, please stop! You're a good man. You don't want to do this! I'm begging you from the bottom of my soul. You don't want to kill me! I'll be good. I'll do anything that you want. I don't want to die! I know where you ca_"

The sounds suddenly stopped, followed by gurgling noises. Lawrence's imagination took over as he imagined the dark acts being performed that should never be done to another human being. He knew all too well the things that could cause that sound. He's done them more than a few times and he knows intimately the details of such acts.

There was silence. The only sounds that could be heard was his heart pounding in his ears. He vaguely reminded himself to breathe as the silence became almost too much. There was a sound that followed that chilled him to his bones. It was a wet sound, almost like someone was chewing. . .

Suddenly, the door to his room swung open and Lawrence screamed. He saw Kendrick standing before him covered in blood. There was a vacant look in his eyes that he's never seen before. That alone was enough to cause tears to begin to pour from his eyes. In those eyes, there wasn't a glint of compassion. It was almost as if his soul left his body and the only thing that remained was the human shell of his former friend.

He tried to process the image before him, but he couldn't seem to make his mind work. He's known Kendrick all his life and never in his wildest dreams did he ever imagine a look like that.

All he saw was death.

He looked down and saw something in his hands and he began to mumble as fear caused his body to tremble. He wanted to beg for his life, but no words were able to escape his lips. He was paralyzed with fear. As Kendrick made his way into the room, he was able to see clearly what was in his hands. He knew before his mind was able to fully comprehend the situation before him what it was. . .

It was a man's head.

It wasn't the fact that it was a man's head that traumatized him; it was the fact that he knew him that caused him such consternation. It's was M Good's head.

Lawrence wasn't a weak man. He'd faced life or death situations more times than he can count and walked into them not knowing if he was going to live or die with a smile. But this was different. Now, he was beginning to understand who Kendrick really was. He wanted to beg for his life, but the look in his eyes told him that it was pointless. If anything, he would make him suffer longer just for asking.

Kendrick looked at Lawrence as if he was looking into his soul, and this chilled him to his very core. He started to slowly make his way toward him as he casually tossed the head into the corner as if it was an old pair of basketball shoes. It made a wet, dull sound as it hit the floor and rolled into a dark, unseen corner.

Fresh tears began to fall as he slowly began to realize that he was going to die.

Kendrick began to remove his gloves as he made his way casually over toward Lawrence. If this was an attempt to calm him, it was having the opposite effect. His heart was threatening to jump out of his chest as Kendrick stood within arm's length of him. He tossed the gloves on a table out of his field of view.

He bent over so that he was at eye level and gave him a smile. If he wasn't in his present situation, he would think that it was one of affection. This bothered him because it was how he *always* looked when they greeted. He never dreamed this version of Kendrick existed. "Hey, how you doing in those restraints? I wasn't sure if I made them too tight or not." He didn't wait for a response as he continued. "You heard all that commotion from next door, I take it."

"Yeah" was all he could manage to say. He didn't trust that his voice wouldn't crack from fear.

"Sorry about that. For what it's worth, I did give him a choice. But you know how it is, some folks don't believe fat meat is greasy." He began to remove the rest of his bloody equipment until he was standing in a pair of jeans and a button-up shirt.

"So, where does this leave us?" he said as he stared his executioner in the eye. He wasn't in any hurry to take his turn, but waiting was almost as bad.

"That's what I'm struggling with. If you did all of this to just me, we could probably have worked out something. An ass whoopin' and a couple of million would have squashed all of this. But you shot Josh and really *really* fucked up Anika's grandma in a bad way. This shit, I can't let slide, bro."

Lawrence still remembered M Good's screams as they echoed through his memory and his body shivered. He licked his lips as his mouth went dry. "Look, we're both gentlemen. I'm sure we can come to some type of understanding."

Kendrick paused as he considered his proposal. He looked down and was quiet for a longtime. He was so quiet that Lawrence thought he had fallen asleep. Finally, Kendrick looked up at him with a smile. "I thought it over. I want all of your money or you die."

"All of it?"

"All of it. You have thirty seconds to decide."

"All of it? How am I supposed to get home?"

"Nigga, that's yo problem. Twenty seconds."

Lawrence's head dropped in resignation. "You're not going to let me go, are you? I can't say I blame you. We both know that if the situation was reversed, you would already be dead."

"You talk too much. Five seconds."

"Man, fuck you!" Lawrence said with as much venom as he could muster, knowing they would probably be his last words.

"Some niggas just don't get it. . ." Kendrick shrugged his shoulders as he pulled a gun from his back and pointed it at his head. Lawrence closed his eyes as Kendrick pulled the trigger.

The gun went off, and Lawrence had a loud ringing in his hear, followed by white pain. He wasn't dead, and for that he was grateful. But the pain he was currently feeling was making him have second thoughts. "Fuck, man, you can't shoot straight anymore!"

Kendrick looked at the gun and then Lawrence and began to laugh. "Nah, dawg, it's not that. I can't kill you. Believe me, I would love to, but I can't."

Lawrence saw Kendrick laughing and he felt all the stress leave his body. Despite the situation, he began to laugh as well. "Okay, I had to admit, you had me there. I really thought you were going to actually do it."

"Nah, I can't" was all he said as he continued to laugh.

I was right, Lawrence thought as he buried a smug look. *No need to rub his nose in it,* he thought. "All right, you had your fun. Come on let me go and we can forget this ever happened. I'll even tell that pussy-ass nigga, Jay, that the deal is off. Imma keep the retainer, though." He thought for a moment. "You know you can have it. My way of saying I'm sorry."

"I really appreciate it, thanks," he said as he made no attempt to free him.

"Okay, cool, let me go."

"I said I wasn't going to kill you. I never said anything about letting you go. At least not yet. The choice is yours, of course, on how the next few hours would go."

Lawrence was so close to freedom that he could almost taste it. But to have it snatched away from him at the last moment was worse than cruel. "What do you mean?" he said, crestfallen.

"Well, I wasn't kidding when I said I wanted all of your money. I want all of it, Lawrence. This is checkmate. I hope you realize that."

"Checkmate? You already said you weren't going to kill me. There's not much more you can do. It seems you played your hand too soon, my friend."

Kendrick gave him a puzzled expression. "There are things worse than death, my friend. I only tell you this because of what we shared in the past. Make the smart decision. I'm going to offer you two favors. This offer now counts as one and one more when I finally let you go."

He walked over to the counter and picked up a tray. He came back and Lawrence saw that it held two syringes. "Before we get started, I need you to understand a few things. You more than likely won't live through this. No need to argue and say anything, really. This is a foregone conclusion. Secondly, you *will* give me anything I want before I'm done with you." He held the tray close so that he could see. "Now, the one on the left is epinephrine or adrenaline, depends on who you ask. If I give you this, no matter what I do to you, you won't be able to pass out from the pain. But if you decide to play nice, I can give you the one on the right. That one is bupivacaine hydrochloride. It basically kills the nerve endings in your body." He held it closer to his face. "This right here is probably the most precious thing in your life at this very moment."

"You must think I'm a young punk or something. I ain't buying it."

"So is that your final answer?"

"Nigga, you deaf or stupid? I ain't given you shit. Now, let me go!"

Kendrick just gave him a sad smile. "I really wish you had thought this through. You probably will come to regret that decision very soon. Hopefully, you won't make that same mistake with my second favor."

"And what's that?" Lawrence said smugly.

Kendrick rolled a cart in front of him. He pulled back the tarp and Lawrence could see there were several hammers and various sizes of metal rods ranging from the size of a pencil to as large as a policeman's' baton. What was odd was that they were all rounded off smooth. They looked round and smooth, like a miniature bowling ball on the end.

Kendrick noticed that he was looking at them strangely. "I guess you noticed my little invention. See, when I first started doing this, I was killing them before I got all that I needed out of them because they always tended to bleed out. But we won't have to worry about that anymore."

Lawrence was beginning to sweat. "I don't suppose you would be willing to let me have that good shot now. . . please?"

He completely ignored his request as he ran his hand lazily over the different types of hammers. "Which one to choose. . ."

"Please, I'm sorry! You don't have to do this. I promise I will go away and you will never see me again. Please!" Lawrence screamed till his voice was raw as tears ran down his face.

Kendrick still couldn't decide on which one he wanted until he reached behind a shelf and pulled out a sledge hammer. "I was going to start small, but for you, I'm going to make an exception."

As Kendrick raised the hammer over his head, Lawrence knew in that moment why he was feared. As the blow came down on his femur in his left leg, shattering it, the pain was so intense that he lost all sense of self. Thanks to the injection that he was given, he knew without a doubt that he was going to be totally aware of each and every strike that followed.

He knew beyond a shadow of a doubt that this was just the beginning . . . and he screamed.

CHAPTER TWENTY-TWO

Anika stared at the phone every few minutes waiting anxiously for Kendrick's call. She'd been like this since yesterday when he called her in a hushed and urgent tone, and then quickly hung up. Now she's sitting in a monthly meeting that was scheduled for her team, but she might as well be a million miles away. It's been hard for her to concentrate on anything lately and she doesn't see it getting better any time soon, not until she hears from him.

She had the feeling that someone was staring at her, and when she looked up, her suspicions were confirmed. Her whole entire team was staring at her expectantly. She realized that they must have asked her a question and were waiting for a response.

Normally she would be embarrassed and give a bashful smile, but she has too much on her mind. "Sorry, I missed whatever it was that you said. Could you please repeat it for me, please? And thank you."

Deshaun, the team member who was slated to lead this week's meeting, looked at her as if he wanted to say something, but he continued on with the meeting. "I was asking, due to the change in the way we process credit apps, do you think we should focus on more weighted areas or continue to process them as we have always done?"

Anika could have kicked herself. Normally, she is on top of, well, pretty much all aspects of the business. But lately, she had to admit she had been slacking. Yet with what had been happening lately, who could blame her? Unfortunately, that didn't fly in the business world. If you can't get the job done, they'll soon replace you with someone who can.

No matter if you have a psycho ex-boyfriend who hired a hit man, who raped your grandmother and plans on killing you at any moment or not. Business is business.

"Let me do some research on that and I'll get back to you with that tomorrow." She noticed the team was less than thrilled with her response and she honestly couldn't blame them. "I'll tell you what, let's table this for tomorrow. Deshaun, I want you to lead tomorrow's meeting as well since this one got cut short." He gave her a tight nod as he began to pack up his things, clearly not happy with today's outcome.

As the team made their way out of her office, she indicated to Deshaun that she wanted him to remain behind. She also gave Shawna a look, letting her know that she was to remain as well.

She waited until the remaining team members made their way out before she spoke. It wasn't until the door closed that Anika released the breath that she didn't realize until then that she was holding. With that, her composure seemed to crumble right before their eyes.

Shawna ran over and placed a comforting arm around Anika's shoulders, which she gratefully accepted. Deshaun, not knowing what to do, just stood by her desk, hoping that his just being there would be of some help to her.

"I asked you two to stay behind because you're really my only friends that I can talk to." She noticed Deshaun's mouth hung open, but no words came out and she couldn't help but smile. "Yeah, you too. We admittedly haven't spent a lot of time together, but I can tell that you are a good man and was raised right. Why else do you think I hired you?"

She didn't give him a chance to respond as she continued. "As I'm sure you are aware, I've been seeing someone."

"Okay. . ." was all he said. It was obvious that she was seeing someone. *Nobody comes to work with that kind of glow and not have someone*, he thought to himself.

"Well, what you don't know is that I've. . . ran into some difficulties with an ex-boyfriend and it's kind of spilled over into other parts of my life." She thought about her grandmother and what was done to her and shivered inside. She looked at Deshaun's face and it was a mask.

The only sign she caught was him clenching his fist at his sides, then quickly released them.

Shawna gave her a questioning look, and Anika shook her head as she looked out the window, trying to reel in her emotions. "As you probably guessed, Shawna already knows pretty much everything. I can't tell you too much because I don't want this coming back on you."

"I understand."

"I'm sure you probably do, but I need a favor from you."

"Whatever you need," he said as his back straightened a little more. "Just tell me and I'll make sure it gets done."

She could tell by his tone that he wasn't just referring to work. This made her feel a small measure of relief knowing that he had her back. "I'm asking if you would walk me and Shawna to and from our cars. Maybe keep an eye out for people who don't belong in the office." She noted that he had a deadly serious look on his face. "I don't need you playing hero. Just let me know if something out of the ordinary is going on. Or if I'm not here, call the police, okay?"

"Not a problem. As I said before, whatever you need." He glanced at Shawna and noticed that she was looking at him in return and he gave her a slight smile which she returned in kind.

"Ugh, about damn time!" Anika said as she fell back into her seat and threw her hands up in the air.

"Huh?" Shawna and Deshaun said simultaneously.

"You two!" By the looks on their faces, she could tell they weren't getting it. "The fact that you two *finally* hooked up. I thought I might have to get involved. I mean, it took y'all like forever to finally get out of the way and just let it happen."

"Well. . . If he wasn't so damn dumb, this would have happened a long time ago." Shawna said as she glared at Deshaun, and all the while her cheeks burned read.

"Hold up, you've liked me all along? Why didn't you just say something instead of treating me like shit?"

"She's a girl, Deshaun, she's a girl," Anika said as if it was the most obvious thing in the world. By the look on his face, she could tell that he wasn't quite there with the conversation yet. But he had enough common sense not to push it.

"I know that isn't what you called us in here for. What else is it?" he said as he blushed furiously. Apparently, his mind caught up with the conversation after all.

"I finally got approval from on high to hire a new associate. And I'm going to need you to train them, Deshaun."

"Wow, are you sure I'm the one you want? I've been with you less than a year. Wouldn't you want to put them with somebody more seasoned?"

"Nope. You're the best man for the job. You haven't been poisoned by the short-cuts like the majority of my seasoned staff members. You do things the right way, and that's how I want them to learn. You think you can handle that?"

"Yeah, I'm sure that wouldn't be a problem."

Anika eyed him. "You may have to work longer hours than you're accustomed to and this may cut into your home-life."

He glanced at Shawna. "Okay, I'll make it work," he said quickly, but a lot less enthused.

"Uh-huh. . ." was all she said as she watched him closely. She turned her eyes to Shawna. "I hate to do this, but. . . I'm going to need you to train your replacement. I would have somebody else do it, but I don't have anyone better than you. I'm going to hate losing you."

"What?" was all she could say as tears threatened to fall from her eyes.

"I know. I feel the same way too. But this is something I've been thinking over and I think this is what's best for the company and this department. Wouldn't you agree?"

"Wait, you just fired me, asked me to train my replacement, and you have the nerve to ask me if I agree? What kind of fuck game you playing, Anika? I thought we were better than that?" Shawna said as her voice threatened to crack. Tears were starting to fall as her breathing increased. "Out of all the people here, I've always had your back. Thanks for nothing." She said as she stormed across the room toward the door." She wanted to look at Deshaun one more time, but she was too embarrassed.

"Hold up, why do you think I'm firing you? All I wanted you to do was train your replacement because you just got promoted."

Shawna had her hand on the doorknob as her words started to sink in. "Promotion?"

"Yeah, I promoted you to associate. But if you don't want it, I can open it up to people outside of the organization. . ."

"Hell, yeah, I want it! Why you have to play games? You could have just said that from the beginning instead of having me get all pissed off and shit."

Anika's mouth fell open in shock. "What did you think I was talking about? I just said that you were promoted and that I needed you to train your replacement. I didn't think it was that big of a deal."

"That's not what you said. You said that you hired a new associate. You never said it was me. But it's cool; I see how you are. . ."

Anika looked toward Deshaun for help, and he just shrugged. "Hey, don't put me in the middle of this. This is between y'all. My name is Bennett and I ain't in it. But you never said it was her, I'm just saying," he added quickly.

"You ain't any kind of help."

"And you're welcome."

She threw daggers with her eyes as Deshaun became suddenly interested with something on the floor. She looked at Shawna and saw that she was giving her the same look. "I'm sorry. You know my mouth takes a minute to catch up with my brain sometimes."

Shawna just stared at her with an intensity that made Anika want to take a step back. She had tears welling up in her eyes as she began to shake. She dropped her head as her shoulders shook with the effort to hold it in. Anika felt her heart go out to her friend. She placed a tentative hand on her shoulder and gripped it reassuringly.

Anika saw Shawna looking at her as she said "gotcha" and then she burst out laughing.

Anika was completely caught off guard. She looked at Deshaun accusingly, trying to determine if he was in on it. He just shrugged as if he had nothing to do with it. "Oh, that was good. You know payback is in order, right?"

"Hey, you started it. How you gonna try and get back at me?"

"I told you it was an honest mista_ "She heard her phone vibrating on her desk and she made a beeline towards it. She ran into a chair and it threatened to topple her over, but at the last moment, she regained her balance as she reached her desk. She ignored the snickers from Deshaun and Shawna as she answered the phone. "Hello?"

"Yeah, it's me, babe."

"Where have you been? I've been dying over here because I haven't heard from you. Everything okay?"

"Everything is going to be fine from now on. I just have one more thing to take care of, but not tonight. I need to see my woman. Why don't you meet me over at the hospital and then we can go have dinner after that?"

"Your woman needs her man too." She glanced out of the corner of her eye to see if they were listening. She knew they were, but they had courtesy to pretend as if they weren't. "Should I bring somebody with me?" she said as she held her breath.

He knew what she meant by that. "I think it should be okay. Word probably hasn't got back yet. Tonight, should be fine. We'll reevaluate in the morning."

"Okay love, see you soon."

"All right, I love you, Anika"

Her heart skipped a beat at hearing him confess his love for her. She never gets tired of hearing it. "Love you too. Bye." She hung up the phone as she started to grab her things.

Shawna looked at her watch and chuckled. "You're leaving early today, I see. And when I say early, I mean on time."

Anika looked at her watch and noticed it was 5p.m. as she grabbed her jacket. "Yeah, today is going to be an early day for me. I'll catch up with you two tomorrow," she said as she made her way to the door.

Deshaun stepped in front of her, causing her to stop. He placed his hands out in front of him. "Hold on, you just asked me to walk you to your car. Let me do it."

"Oh, you don't have to today. I think today should be all right," she said as she tried to make her way past him.

"What happened that all of a sudden you don't need me to do it anymore?" he said with a hint of suspicion in his voice.

"Fine, you can walk me to my car. I'm just in a hurry is all." She didn't want him to start asking questions, so she agreed.

"Yeah, let me grab my things and I'll walk out with you too," Shawna said as she walked over to her desk to gather up her things.

Deshaun beat them to the elevator as he held the door. Anika and Shawna stepped through. They ignored him as the started talking excitedly in hushed tones. He stepped in the elevator, and as the doors started to close, he realized that he didn't have his keys. He smacked his head for being so forgetful. He pushed the open button and the doors reversed course. The two women looked at him questioningly. "I forgot my keys," he said sheepishly. "Just hold the door and I'll be right back, okay?" they both nodded with a smile as they continued their conversation. He stepped out of the elevator and hurried toward his office.

Shawna stood between the doors, keeping the elevator from closing. It started making a buzzing noise because the doors were held open for too long. "You wanna just wait for the next one?"

Anika, in her rush to get going said, "Nah, we can just ride it down to the garage and wait for him there."

"Okay." Shawna looked back one more time, hoping to see Deshaun coming, but she knew he wouldn't be back for a few minutes yet, so she let the doors close and they rode the elevator down.

The elevator grew quiet as it seemed to take longer than normal to reach the garage. *Maybe it was the anticipation,* Anika thought to herself. There were so many questions she wanted to ask Kendrick, but she knew over the phone wasn't the best time. She could tell by his tone that something was different, but she couldn't quite place it.

"So, is everything okay now?"

Anika was pulled from her thoughts as she looked at the mixture of concern and curiosity on her friend's face. "Hell, I sure hope so" was all she could manage to say as her mind began to let her fears run wild.

"Look, I know there's more going on than you're letting on. I'm not asking you to tell me your business. We all have our secrets, God knows I do. I'm just saying, if you need to talk, I'm always here. We don't even have to talk about what's bothering you. We can just talk. Sometimes, talking is enough to get you through the rough patches. Trust me, I have more than enough experience."

Anika just looked at her friend and she could see the pained look in her eyes as she thought about the times better left in the past. She could see the emotional scares play across her friend's face and for the first time, she realized that she didn't know that much about her. "You know that goes both ways, right? I might be your boss, but I'm your friend, first and foremost. Don't forget that."

Shawna nodded as she looked torn over whether to confide in her or not. But before she could say more, the elevator came to a stop as the doors opened. Both women paused as they considered whether to exit or not. They looked at each other and neither one moved, each one waiting until the other took the first step.

Anika looked at her watch and saw that it was a little after five. She could hear the traffic noise as voices and sounds carried through the parking structure. As she looked out at the parking structure, an ominous feeling started to creep in. She looked over at Shawna, and that did nothing to ease their anxieties. She looked downright terrified.

Never being one to let her fears get the best of her, she made a decision. She composed herself and stepped off the elevator. She looked back at her friend. "You coming?"

Shawna stuck her head out of the elevator and looked around. Not being completely convinced, she stepped back. "Don't you think it would be safer if we all went together? Maybe wait until Deshaun comes down?"

"Oh, stop being a chicken. My car isn't more than fifty feet away. I'm sure we'll be fine." She sounded more confident than she felt as that ominous feeling came back.

"Good for you. My car is on the second level, and once you leave, I'll be by myself. I'm a white girl. Everything happens to us."

"Fine, I'll give you a ride to your car. I can't have anything happening to my new junior executive."

At hearing her new title, she smiled. That seemed to be enough to get her feet moving again. "Okay, I'll go with you this time. But let me just call Deshaun and let him know what we're doing. You saw how intense he was."

"Yeah, I know, right! Is he *always* like that?" Anika said with devilish grin.

"Hell, yeah, but I ain't complaining." Deshaun's phone rang and then went to voicemail as she let out a frustrated sigh. "Hey, babe, Anika and I are just going to walk to her car since its right by the elevator and she's going to give me a lift to mine. Call me when you get this." She looked at Anika and shook her head. "I swear he got the oldest cell phone known to man. He never gets signal and it's the size of a flip-flop."

Both women laughed as they finally made it to Anika's car. Neither one of them said it, but they were both relieved. She finally realized why the garage seemed so empty. The majority of upper management had to go to Dallas for a conference this week. Seeing as how this whole level is reserved for senior executive members on up, it made sense.

Anika unlocked the doors. "Get in so I can drop your scary butt off. I got a man I need to see," she said as smiled.

"Yeah, too much information for my taste," Shawna said as she feigned covering her ears.

"What do you mean? I didn't say anything."

"No, you didn't say anything per se, but that shit eating grim is saying a lot."

Anika blushed. "Oh hush, and get in."

Shawna opened the door and froze. "And where do you want me to sit?"

She just noticed a stack of files in the passenger seat. She had taken them home over the weekend to try and catch up on some work. "Could you be a friend and put them in the trunk for me?"

"Do I have a choice?"

"Oh yeah. You can walk in the spooky garage all by yourself, you a cute white girl. I'm sure nothing bad will happen to you."

She rolled her eyes and stuck out her tongue as she grabbed the files. She yells for Anika to pop the trunk which she quickly did as she smiled sheepishly.

"Sorry!"

"Uh-huh."

Anika started the car as she waited for Shawna to close the trunk. She looked out the rearview mirror and began to wonder what's taking so long. More than likely, the box tipped over and she was trying to put everything back in its proper place. She threw the car back in park with an exasperated sigh and goes out to check on her to see what the holdup was.

"Don't worry about it. I'll fix whatever's messed up later but I gots to go_"

"I was hoping you could make time for an old acquaintance."

Anika's blood ran cold as she heard Jay's voice. To see him standing there was terrifying to say the least, but the fact that she couldn't see her friend was worse. "Where is she, Jay?"

"Who?" He smiled.

Anika looked around frantically for her friend, only to find her lying on the ground unmoving. "Is she dead?" she said weakly as her mouth ran dry.

"How the fuck should I know? I didn't ask her when I split her skull." He waved the gun in the air so she could see. "But I can check if you like." He didn't wait for a response as he rammed his cane in her midsection. She let out a groan as he delivered several more vicious blows. "Huh, guess I didn't kill her after all." he said as he delivered one more accompanied by a grunt.

"I will kill you!" Anika lunged at him, but he calmly pointed the gun and fired. She stopped dead in her tracks as ten thousand volts racked her body, causing her to fall to the ground, racked with spasms.

"I don't think so. . ." he moved closer so he can see her face. "You have no idea how long I've waited a long time to see you like this." He studied her body as he licked his lips with clear intent in his eyes. "I have all sorts of things in store for you."

Anika struggled to move, but her body just wouldn't cooperate. She was lying on her side as drool ran out the side of her mouth, pooling on the ground. She could follow him with her eyes, but if he stepped out of her view, she wouldn't be able to see him anymore. She tried to relax her body as much as possible in the hopes that some movement would return. She hoped sooner rather than later because she had a feeling that her life depended on it.

Jay made his way over where Shawna's still form laid. He looked at Anika to make sure that she was still incapacitated. Satisfied with what he saw, he continued. "You know, your friend ain't half bad. I probably should have hit you in the head instead of her. Of course, if I had hit you, there's a chance I might have accidentally killed you. Can't have that now, can we?" He used his cane to raise Shawna's skirt and smiled. "I love when a woman is Open for business," he said as his eyes lingered on her pantyless womanhood.

Anika tried to speak, but only unintelligible garble came out.

"What was that you said? You think I should include her in our festivities too? What a wonderful idea!" He looked at her and smiled. The look of her helpless form only fueled him further. "Or would you rather we leave her here?" He placed the end of his cane on her throat and began to apply pressure. Shawna began to wheeze as she tried to draw in air, but unable to. Her face started to turn a light shade of purple as her chest began to rise and fall rapidly as she struggled in vain to draw in air.

Jay looked at her with an intensity that she had never seen before. "Come on, Anika, you know what I want. Say it!" He began to apply more pressure "You can make all of this stop. All you have to do is beg me." He knew that she couldn't move or talk at that point, but it didn't seem to matter. "The cat got your tongue, huh? Let me provide you with a little more incentive." He removed the cane from her throat and replaced it with his foot. He began to slowly apply pressure to her throat as her face immediately turned a dark purple. "If I was you, I would make up her mind quickly because from the look of your friend, she doesn't have much time."

From the way he had his foot positioned on her throat, she knew that he could easily crush her windpipe. "Yes, please bring her." Anika struggled to say. It took everything in her just to speak, but it seemed it was effective as Jay removed his cane from her throat, glaring the whole time.

"I'm glad you decided to join the party. Having two of you should make this more interesting." Then, he removed his foot from her throat. He reached into his pocket and pulled out a cheap phone, a burner more than likely. "Bring the van around," he said as he quickly put it away.

"Where are you taking us?" she croaked.

He stood over her with a look of pure hatred. "I bet you think you're so smart, don't you? You want to bring her along so you can live a little bit longer, but it's not going to help you." He squeezed the trigger and sent another ten thousand volts through Anika's body as she flapped around on the ground like a fish out of water as tears stung her eyes. "If you're a good girl, I might let you watch some of the biggest, blackest dudes you've ever seen fuck your girl to death before we start in on you."

Anika lay on the ground immobile and helpless. She felt her mind clouding over and she knew unconsciousness will soon overtake her. She tried to focus as she fought to stay alert and awake. The smug look of triumph plastered on Jay's face helped fuel her anger as she felt a surge of adrenaline flow through her body.

She knew better than to let him even think she might be able, to move and in truth, she wasn't all that sure that she could. There was tingling in her extremities that bordered on painful, which was a tell-tale sign that movement was returning to her limbs.

He gave her a hard stare full of hate as he bent down mere inches from her as he looked into her eyes. "All of this could have been avoided if you just stayed in your lane and been a good hoe. But you had to go and cause me problems that I didn't need, and for that alone, I'm going to make you suffer in ways that words haven't been invented for yet," he said as he seethed with rage.

"When I'm done with you and your friend, I think I'm going to have to teach my wife a lesson or two as well. She's been talking all crazy and shit that she's going to take the kids and leave me. She even had the nerve to tell me that she's going to ask for half of everything."

Anika, unable to move, looked into his eyes and saw madness. She knew that he had a short temper, which was part of the reason she wasn't sad to see him go. But this is so beyond anything she thought would ever happen. She wished she had just followed her own advice and waited for Deshaun. All of this could have been avoided. She wanted nothing more than to cry, but she would be damned if she would let him see her do it.

She was brought back to her present situation when Jay gave her a vicious slap across her face. "Bitch, look at me when I'm talking to you! I see I'm going to have to teach you some manners," he said as he wrapped his hands around her throat and began to squeeze.

Anika felt her airway close immediately. She wasn't sure if he was trying to strangle her to death, but from the blank look in his eyes, her well-being wasn't very high on his list of priorities at the moment. She tried to pry his fingers from around her throat, but she lacked the strength.

Her vision started to go dark around the edges as she felt her consciousness beginning to fade. She saw a shadow behind Jay and figured it was one of his hired thugs come to transport them to God knows where. All of a sudden, she was able to breathe as Jay was pulled violently off her. She tried to make sense of the scene before her but was having a hard time due to the lack of oxygen.

As her senses came back to her, she was able to see Deshaun holding Jay in a choke-hold. His eyes began to bug out of his head as she saw Deshaun continuing to apply pressure to the hold. She tried to warn him as Jay reached inside of his jacket and pulled a gun out.

But he saw the same thing as he grabbed his wrist and twisted. There was a loud pop followed by a scream as Jay dropped the gun. Deshaun now had his left arm wrapped around his throat while he had Jay's arm extended out to his side as he continued to apply pressure to the now-broken wrist.

Jay reached into his jacket with his other hand and pulled out something shiny.

"Watch out!" Anika screamed as Deshaun tried to leap out of the way but too late as Jay slashed his left side with a knife. Deshaun fell back against the car as a red stain began to appear on his left side.

Jay wasn't a small man. Although not a bodybuilder, he wasn't a stranger to the gym. He had a powerful build that was only enhanced by the damage done to his legs as he was required to use more of his upper body to adapt. He found his cane and pulled himself to his feet. He made his way over to Deshaun as he lean against the car clutching his side.

"Looks like you stepped into grown folk's business, young buck. Sorry about your luck, but your time is up." he said as he swung the blade in a cross stroke, trying to cut his throat. But before he could make contact, Deshaun brought up his hand to block the attack.

"You talk too much," he said as he slammed his foot in the side of Jay's knee, causing him to go crashing to the ground. He made his way over to him as he grabbed his left arm and pulled it back until he dropped the knife followed by a scream as Jay's shoulder popped out of socket.

Deshaun struggled to his feet as he eyed Anika, "Next time, follow your own advice and fuckin' wait for me!"

She just stared at him dumbstruck. "Okay, won't happen again."

"Where is Shawna?" he said as he tried to regain his composure. Anika was unable to look him in the eye as she pointed behind the car. Upon seeing her, he lets out a heartbreaking wail at seeing her still form. "I'm here, babe. No one is going to hurt you ever again," he said as he cradles her to his chest. He reaches in his pocket and pulls out his phone then he calls 911 and hangs up. He gives her a hard look. "So are you going to tell me what this is all about, or are you going to keep trying to do this all by yourself?"

"There isn't much to tell…" The look on his face told her that he expected an answer. Realizing that he was right, she struggled to sit up and then with an odd sense of relief, she told him the whole story.

She told him everything from the beginning, but left out anything to do with Kendrick. She wasn't ready to put his name in another person's mouth without running it by him first. "That's pretty much it," she said when she finally finished.

Deshaun was quiet for a longtime as he tried to process everything he had just heard. He absently stroked Shawna's hair as he looked out at nothing in particular. At what seemed longer than she had anticipated, he chuckled. "Wow, you don't do anything half ass, do you? Most women just find out a guy has a wife or chic at home and they leave you alone, hoping you don't dime them out. But you had to find a guy who turns out to be bat shit crazy," he continued to chuckle and shake his head.

"I'm so sorry, this is all my fault," Anika said barely above a whisper.

He looked at her with rage clearly on his face. He took a deep breath and let it out slowly as he gathers himself. "It's not your fault. You're not responsible for another person's actions."

"That's kind of you but, it is. If I never left the building and waiting on you like I said I would, we all could be on our way, no harm no foul."

Deshaun thought for a moment. "Maybe. Or instead he could have simply thought it was more than he could handle and shot all of us. This way, he didn't account for me and I was able to sneak up on him." He paused for a moment as if he was considering something, but said nothing.

She picked up on his hesitance as he looked away. "What is it? I know we're not that close yet, but you can talk to me."

He thought for a moment then looked her squarely in the eye. "What do you want this outcome to be?"

"I don't follow," she said clearly, not grasping the question.

He hesitated as he thought about what he was going to say. Finally gathering his words, he continued. "There are two outcomes here, but only one will truly bring you peace." He looked at her to make sure that she was following along. Confident that he held her attention, he went on. "We can wait for the police to arrive, and they can arrest him. Judging by his clothes and that watch_" after quick consideration, he promptly removes the watch. "Well, besides the watch, the clothes tell me that he isn't a stranger to wealth. He more than likely will get the best lawyer in town and be out on bail within twenty four hours.

Depending on his mind-set, we could be doing a remix of this same situation tomorrow."

Anika gave a slight shiver as he continued, "The other option is. . . it doesn't have to get to that point. We could end this right now."

"What do you mean?" She feared she already knew the answer.

"Just- just turn around and this will all be over."

"I don't think I would be comfortable with that. . ."

He nodded his head more to himself than anything else. "I understand, I really do, but there's more to consider here than just you." He looked down at Shawna's unconscious form and swallowed as a lump formed in his throat.

There was a giggle that broke the silence as Jay spoke up, "Of course, your friend is right. When I get out, and I will, I won't make the same mistake again, you can bet on that." His giggle turned into a manic laugh. "I knew you didn't have it in you. Not only are you a bitch, you're a stupid bitch."

Deshaun delivered a vicious kick to his testicles followed by several wicked kicks to his ribs. This was more than enough to shut him up as only moans and shallow pants escaped his lips. "Sometimes people don't know when to shut the fuck up," he said as he let out an exasperated breath followed by another kick to Jay's midsection.

Anika recoiled at the sheer ferocity of Deshaun's attack on the now defenseless man lying on the ground. "Do you think that all that is necessary?"

"Yes" was all he said as he picked up Jay's cane. He stood over him with a look on his face devoid of emotion which chilled her to the bone.

"Please don't do this," she said as she tried to stand but fell hard to the ground. Deshaun dropped the cane as he rushed to help. She still was too weak from the Taser attacks so she sat back down and leaned against her car.

"Why did you hire me?"

She was caught off guard by the sudden change in topics, but she recovered quickly. "I thought you were the best person for the job at the time, and I trust your judgment. Why do you ask?" she said suddenly feeling nervous.

"The same van has driven by us twice and never looked in our direction once," he said as he picked up the gun lying next to her leg.

"That doesn't mean anything, they could be lost."

"Two things_ who gets lost in a private garage?" He picked her up off the ground as if she weighed nothing and placed her behind the car with Shawna. "Secondly, I know those dudes from back in the day. They some heavy hitters and they don't come cheap."

"But you don't know that for sure, they could be here for someone else. Besides if that was the case, why didn't they stop?"

He gave her a look as if she lost her mind "you willing to bet your life on that? Besides, we all have a past right?"

Deshaun ducked away before she could say anything else. She tried to see where he went, but it was like he disappeared. She heard a vehicle coming, and she scooted further behind the car, pulling Shawna with her. She held her in her arms as she rocked silently, hoping the police came soon.

It was too quiet, Anika thought to herself. The vehicle should have passed by now, but she hadn't heard anything. She chanced a look, and all the color drained from her face. She saw a mountain of a man standing over Jay trying to help him to his feet.

Jay must have said something to him because he started looking around for something. Anika tried to move silently to the other side of her car while taking Shawna with her. Her hand ran into something hard, and when she looked down, she realized what he was probably looking for, his cane. It must have rolled under the car when Deshaun dropped it.

She tried to push it under the car but froze when she heard a voice that was deeper than any she'd ever heard and devoid of any form kindness "what do we have here?" He held a humorous smile on his face as he pulled her to her feet by her hair. Anika gave a muffled scream as pain shot through her head.

"Let me go, the police are on their way." She looked at him defiantly in the eye.

If that was meant to garner a reaction, he didn't show any indication as he turned to Jay who whispered something that she couldn't hear. He released his grip on her hair, and she fell heavy to the ground, barely missing Shawna.

"Looks like we ain't got time to play," he said with a hint of disappointment. "But it looks like you still gonna die." He picked her up by the throat, and she tried to claw at his hands but it was like trying to scratch steel. He ignored her futile attempts as he began to tilt her head to the side. She felt an unbearable pressure on her neck as he tried to break it.

Anika tried to release some of the pressure off her neck as she pulled on his arm but she knew that was only delaying the inevitable. Suddenly, her face was wet followed by a loud noise. She instinctively closed her eyes as warm fluid ran down her face. Her body fell against the car as the huge man fell heavily on top of her.

She rolled him off her, but he still had a grip on her collar as they went crashing to the ground as he fell on top of her. Not knowing what else to do, she instinctively used his shirt to wipe the fluid off her face. When she opened her eyes, she realized that the warm fluid that she was covered in was blood, and the huge man was lying dead on the ground with a hole in the side of his head.

A part of her recoiled at the site before her, the shock of seeing a man who was alive only a few seconds ago lying at her feet with a whole in his head mind numbing to say the least. But as bullets started to fly, she had more pressing concerns like finding cover from the onslaught of artillery that was being brought to bear. She chanced a look from behind her car, hoping to find some sign of Deshaun. A bullet hit a mere inch or two, give or take, from her head. Flakes of paint flew into her eyes, and that was all the incentive she needed to seek cover.

Things suddenly went quiet as the sound of gun fire ceased. She heard multiple voices coming from the van, no doubt trying to determine if they hit their unseen assailant. She chanced a look and saw that three men similar to the man lying at her feet were conversing among themselves. The driver tried to start the van, no doubt turned it off once the bullets started flying.

The van started but before he could let companions in on that bit of knowledge, a single shot rang out and his brains were sprayed all over the interior windshield of the vehicle. The other two men began to fire aimlessly, hoping to hit their unseen assailant. The attempt was futile as the man standing at the rear of the van was taken down by a shot to the head; he was dead before he hit the ground. The last man standing threw his gun to the ground, hoping that now he was unarmed, he would let him live. His hopes were dashed as another shot took him in the knee, causing him to fall out of the van, crashing to the ground head first. He brought his head up, hoping to beg for mercy yet again and was reward with a bullet to throat.

He didn't die quickly as he drowned on his own blood.

Anika looked on in horror as four men lay dead on the ground in her company's parking garage. She's had her run in with violence in the past when she was robbed and potentially worse but that pales in comparison to what she is currently witnessing. There is blood everywhere and bullet holes all over her car and in the walls mere inches away. She shivered at the thought at how close she was to potentially being shot.

She reached out to check and make sure Shawna was okay and was relieved to find that she was okay. She starts to look for her phone to let Kendrick know what happened when someone grabs her wrist painfully. She tried to pull away but their grip is too strong.

"You didn't forget about me that quickly did you?"

Anika froze as she felt something cold and sharp in her side. She couldn't believe that she was so careless that she would forget about the man who put all of this in motion and turned her life into a living hell. "The police are coming and you have no way of getting out of here. If you let me go now, I will tell them that you had nothing to do with all of this. We can go on with our lives like nothing happened."

He gave a slight jab to the side as it drew blood. "You think I give a fuck about going to jail? Apparently you haven't been listening at all, just like a hoe," he said as he pushed the blade in deeper, drawing more blood. "When all of you are dead, I will be the one to tell the story of how you hired these men to get revenge on me for spurning your affections."

"And you think anyone is going to believe that bullshit?" She fumed as he gave her another poke as she tried to ignore the pain. Apparently he wasn't ready to finish her just yet.

"And exactly who do you think they're going to believe? I'm a respected member of the city with friends in high places. I've got enough dirt on key officials that they just might give me the key to the city as thanks for stopping a delusional black woman from running amok."

"Fuck yo weak ass, you should be glad that I even acknowledged your existence." She closed her eyes for what she knew was about to happen.

"Nice knowing you, slut," he said as he drew the blade back to drive it home. As he began to thrust, a shot rang out and hit him in the shoulder, causing him to drop the blade. He looked around for the culprit as he seethed with rage.

"I can't let you kill my boss I need a job, and she was the only one hiring," Deshaun said as he held the still smoking gun pointed at Jay.

"I'm so glad to see you. I tried to look for you but I couldn't find you."

"That was the whole point of hiding_ so you can't find me." He smirked.

"You know, you've gotten real snippy lately. Saving my life doesn't get you off the hook."

"The way I see it, you owe me a substantial raise. Besides, the woman I plan on marrying someday is lying on the ground unconscious because of you." She dropped her head, and he knew he had gone too far. "I'm sorry, you didn't deserve that."

"Deserve what?" Anika and Deshaun turned to see Shawna sitting up against the car rubbing her throat in obvious pain. "What did I miss?"

Deshaun grabbed her in a tight embrace, as if he never wanted to let her go. She had a confused look and hugged him with the same fierce passion. "You scared the shit out of me. Don't ever do no shit like that again."

"I promise." She looked over his shoulder at Anika looking for help. Anika just looked away, unable to meet her friend's questioning stare.

Shawna felt movement next to her, and she jumped when she saw a man lying on the ground. She tried to see if he was okay but was snatched away by Deshaun.

"Stay away from him" was all Deshaun said as he put himself between her and Jay.

"You want to tell me what's going, or do I have to start guessing?"

"He was the reason you woke up on the ground. He knocked you out" Anika said, still unable to look at her.

"Oh" was all she managed to say as she tried to wrap her head around what she just heard. "But why does it look like he's been shot?"

Jay started to laugh. "Because your weak-ass boyfriend shot me. He didn't even have the balls to finish what he started. But his mistake, I'll be seeing all of you very soon." He struggled to his feet attempting to regain some of the dignity he lost.

"What did he mean by see us very soon?" Shawna said as anxiety crept into her voice.

"That's Jay," Anika said finally meeting her gaze. "I'm sorry, this is all my fault."

"We're not going over that again," Deshaun interjected. "You know what needs to be done."

"We're not killing anyone. Let's just let the police handle it."

"Wait a minute, this is the motherfucker responsible for hurting your grandmother and you want to just let him go." Anger causing her voice to rise. "Fuck that shit, he gots to go!" She rises to her feet on shaky legs. She looks around for something to use, eyeing the gun that sat near the back of Anika's car.

Shawna grabbed the gun off the back of the car and aimed it at Jay's head. He gave her a smirk as he continued to wait for the police to arrive. "Little lady, we've been over all this before. None of you have what it takes. Just have a seat before you embarrass yourself further."

Deshaun grabbed the gun from Shawna and had to lunge after her to keep her from attacking Jay. Jay looked over his shoulder and gave another chuckle as he shook his head at the scene.

"I'm going to need you to calm down, and then I'll let you go okay?"

"I will after I put a bullet into his head." Jay chuckled again, and Shawna had to be restrained once more.

"I think you're a beautiful person, and you don't need to tarnish your soul for the likes of him." Shawna didn't say anything, but she stopped struggling. When he released her, she sat quietly on the ground next to Anika.

Anika wrapped her arm around Shawna's shoulder "I'm glad we finally can agree to let the police handle this. Everything will work out in the end, you'll see." She knew that if he did manage to get out, Kendrick would more than likely be waiting for him.

"I'm sorry but that doesn't work for me. You can fire me later."

Before Anika realized what Deshaun had said, he had rammed the butt of the gun into the back of Jay's head. He crumbled to the ground in a heap. He looked up with look indignation, and in response, Deshaun slammed the butt of the gun into the side of his head, caused a wide gash to open as blood poured out of the wound.

He tried to put up his one arm that was still halfway functional, but it was useless due to the broken wrist he suffered earlier. Deshaun continued to rain blows down on his head until he fell back, semiconscious from the attack. He looked on the verge of passing out but Deshaun slapped his face until he regained consciousness.

Confident that he was as lucid as he was going to get, Deshaun stood up and shot him in both knees. Jays screamed out in sheer agony as he tried to clutch his shattered legs. Deshaun leaned down to peer into his eyes as Jay struggled to move away. But with his broken wrist and dislocated shoulder, it was a futile attempt. The smug look of superiority was replaced with unadulterated fear.

"Apparently you've run out of things to say." He checked the magazine in his gun and shook his head. "Looks like you lucked out. I'm down to my last bullet." He pointed the gun at his head.

"Please don't kill me," Jay pleaded as his tears ran down his face and his body trembled.

"You're kidding, right?" Deshaun pulled the trigger, and the bullet entered through his forehead. Jay's lifeless body fell to the ground.

Anika's mouth fell open in shock.

Of all the things she thought could happen today, Deshaun killing Jay wasn't even remotely anywhere near the list. She looked at Jay lying on the ground with a hole in the middle of his head and his blank eyes staring out at nothing. She thought she would feel sadness, but the only thing she felt was satisfaction. The fact that he was dead left her numb, but the fact that he suffered for his hand in what happened to her grandmother, that was good enough.

She was brought out of her thoughts as several police cars pulled up to the scene, and soon they were surrounded. Several officers jumped out of their vehicles with their guns drawn as they began to canvas the area. The three of them sat quietly as the officers gathered to discuss what they've discovered.

Anika recognized the lead detective immediately, Anthony. He saw her making eye contact, and he makes his way over. "What the fuck happened here?!" he said under his breath. "I was on my way home on time for the first time in God knows how long, and this bullshit falls in my lap." He looked down and recognized a familiar face. "Tell me this isn't that piece of shit from that thing, Anika?"

She said nothing as she looked away, pretty much telling him that he is.

"Fuck," he looked over the body and whistled to himself, "he suffered, that's for damn sure. Couldn't have happened to a nicer guy if you ask me." He eyed the three of them hoping to get to the bottom of what happened here. "Do any of you have any idea how he happened to come by his unfortunate condition?"

"I did it. He was trying to hurt Anika," Shawna said as she stepped forward. "He snuck up behind me and knocked me unconscious, and when I came through, I saw that he had Anika on the ground and was standing over her, so I crept behind him, hit him with a stick, took the gun, and shot him."

"Uh-huh. . ."

"You don't believe me I take it. I'll sign whatever you need me to."

Anthony didn't try to hide his skepticism. "So what you're telling me is that you snuck behind a man over six feet tall, and 230 pounds, hit him with a stick, and then shot him. Really."

"That's the story I'm sticking to."

Deshaun tried to speak up, but Anika cut him off "I did it. Everything she said was true except for the last part. She hit him with the stick. The gun fell, I grabbed it, and shot him."

Anthony's partner walked over, but he waved him off. He looked at Deshaun and asked, "I take it you want to confess too?"

"Nope."

"Why not?"

"Because you might actually believe me."

He chuckled. "I see your point".

Anthony looked over the crime scene and started to put two and two together. He recognized a couple of the faces as known criminals in the area. Word on the street is they were hit men who specialized kidnapping and murder. They were wanted for questioning in several murders and missing persons. Until now, no case has stuck to them because the witnesses usually got scared and wouldn't testify or turned up missing themselves.

Anthony looked down at Jay, and his blood began to boil. He thought about how his friend, Brian, the police officer from the night he first met that piece of shit went missing. In all likelihood, he was dead, but without having a body, the department is being a dick about paying out his life insurance claim. To make matters worse, he knew that if he told, they would probably pay his claim, but it would've opened him up to a whole other world of problems.

He had did some research on Jay when his friend first went missing. They found his squad car abandoned in a known gang area, and there were signs of a struggle. He started asking questions, but he kept running into dead ends. It wasn't until he found out just how connected Jay really was when things started to click. He rubbed elbows with the mayor and some of the most influential people in the city and no telling who else he was on a first-name basis with.

He had no choice but to drop his lines of questioning and to stop checking into Jay or they were going to start going over his career with a fine-tooth comb which he had no doubt they would find something because he was no angel. And even if they didn't find anything, he was confident something would show up, fabricated or not.

It wasn't until he started being followed that he realized just how much trouble he was in. First it was a random car that seemed to be following just a little beyond the norm. Then it was a strange car sitting outside his home, and when he would go outside, they would drive off. Things were starting to happen, and he knew it wasn't good. He was out of options, and he had only one move left.

Hide.

Anthony was no coward, far from it. But he wasn't stupid either. He had a wife and two little girls to think about, and once he thought it over, there really wasn't anything to consider. He told his boss that he needed a few days to take care of some personal matters. He hoped that wouldn't draw any attention as he tried to keep some of the heat off himself and hopefully his family.

His plan was simple_ lay low and off the grid. At least that's what he kept telling himself. What he really had planned was to kill Jay. He figured that was the only way he would be able to live his life without having to constantly look over his shoulder. What he did find out about Jay was that he was a man who didn't forget or forgive easily. That was all the incentive he needed.

He found it's easier to plan than it is to execute seeing as how he's been laying low for the past two weeks as he covertly hunted for the sonofabitch with no luck. Today was his first day back to work, and he was afraid that if push came to shove, he knew in his heart that he would pull the trigger. *To hell with what happens to me*, he thought as long as the three people who matters the most to him are okay, he's okay.

Anthony is brought to the here and now as he vaguely hears an officer trying to get his attention. He absently nodded his head to his question, and the officer rushed off to do whatever it was that he just agreed to. He stares at Jay's lifeless form and his rage is fanned again as he thought of all the shit that he's done from his attack on Anika to the disappearance of Brian and God only knows what else.

"I hope they have a special place reserved in hell just for you," he spit on him and was half tempted to take a piss. He noticed Anika's concerned look, and he stopped, not wanting to cause her any more pain than she's already feeling. He looked at him one last time and turned away before he did it anyway.

"You okay?" Anika said as she never took her eyes off him.

"Yeah, nothing a few drinks won't cure." He looked at the three of them, the worse for wear, and just shook his head. "So I have two confessions to the same murder, and only one of you seems to be smart enough not to say shit." He gave Deshaun a knowing look. "You all can go, but don't go too far, understand?"

They all shared a look, and without much prodding, they gathered up what they could and was trying to leaving the seen as quickly as possible. Anthony grabbed Deshaun's arm causing him to stop in place. The two women turned to see what the holdup was. "Y'all gone ahead. Seems he still has some questions for me." He gave Anthony a withering stare.

Anthony pulled him off to the side away from ear hustlers and then brought him around so they are face-to-face. "Cut the bullshit. I know you did it. More importantly, I know who you are."

Deshaun said nothing as Anthony continued. "Yeah, you didn't think I would recognize you. But I don't give a shit about any of that. We all have shit we rather leave in the toilet, you feel me. What I want to know is if you are working with Jay and shit just went bad."

Deshaun looked at him with such rage; Anthony thought he was going to strike him. His featured soften, albeit slightly. "No, I don't get down like that. If you know anything about me, then you should know that."

"I did, just needed to hear it for myself. I know bullshit when I hear it, and I haven't heard any yet so we still good."

"Glad to hear it, can I go?"

"Not just yet. I got a few more questions."

Seeing that he was going to be there for a while, he leaned against the wall and crossed his arms. "Apparently I have nowhere to go."

"Can she trust you?"

He knew who he was talking about immediately. "She helped me out when she didn't have to, has kept it real with me from jump. You don't do people dirty who only show you kindness." He saw Anthony was looking for a better answer. "I wouldn't let anything happen to her on my watch. I'll take a bullet for her before that ever happens. She's like family to me whether she feels that way about me or not. She's my big sister."

Anthony extended his hand and Deshaun tensed until he looked down. "Thank you for looking after my friend. If you need anything you call me first, understand?"

"Definitely top two, but I hear you." He took his hand in turn and shook it. "I would appreciate it if you don't mention this to your friend. I like this job, and I'm kind of good at it. I'm not looking for any other opportunities, you feel me?"

"You keep your word to me, I keep my word to you."

"I can get behind that." He turned to leave but stopped. "I saw how you looked at him. You don't do that just for anybody. All I'm saying is, if I can help, let me know. If I can't, I'll find out what I can."

"We'll see."

Deshaun looked nervous, like a young man unsure of himself as he said, "Thanks for everything."

"Yeah, I think the ladies are waiting on you to carry some boxes or some shit."

He smiled. "I guess I better go catch up with them," he said as he hurried to catch up.

Anthony allowed himself a slight smirk as he turned back to the crime scene. His smile quickly disappeared as he tried to figure out how to make all of this go away without it blowing back on Anika, her friends, or himself. He would probably have to call in more than a few favors, but it was well worth it. He knew at the end of the night he was going home to his family, which is all that really matters.

CHAPTER TWENTY-THREE

Josh sits in his hospital bed restless as a caged tiger. He has been in here for over two weeks, and he was ready to go home to his family. He has threatened more than a few doctors and nurses, but nobody would give him his release. His patience was starting to run low. He figured he'll give them a couple more days before he gets up and walks right out that bitch; damn a security guard.

He didn't hear the door open as he's lost in his dark thoughts. "Sup."

Josh looked up and gave a slight scowl, which is the closest he'll come to a smile for his best friend, Kendrick. "Damn nigga, you act like you can't come see a nigga and don't give me that shit that you had to work either because I know you work when you want to."

If Kendrick didn't know any better, he might think he was upset? "I would have been here, but I had to go back down memory lane." Josh immediately knew what he was referring to and adopted a more serious demeanor, if that were possible. Kendrick continued, "I hit a few bumps along the way, but I'm no worse for wear." He smiled.

"Uh-huh, let you tell it. You could have a hole in your head, and you would tell me it was just a scratch." Josh scowled.

Kendrick saw where the conversation was heading, and he quickly changed the subject. "So when are you getting out of here?"

Josh looked as if he was ready to continue the previous conversation, but he dropped it for the moment. "I don't know. I keep telling them I'm fine, but the bitch-ass doctors won't sign the release forms and Marile is being all stank acting about it. Can you believe she's cosigning on all this bullshit. I'm ready to go!"

He did look like he was ready to climb the walls. Kendrick could only imagine all the hell he was giving his doctors and nurses. Frankly he was surprised they didn't release him already. But with all the lawsuits the hospital has been experiencing lately, it's no wonder he's still there.

Which works for what he was about to do.

"Hey look, I got some more stops to make. I left you a gift next door if you think you're up for it?"

"Nigga, I ain't gay, why you buying me gifts and shit?"

"I think this is just what the doctor ordered." He smiled as he left a roll of fifties on the nightstand and left.

Josh was about to talk some more shit but money is money and he let it drop. He took the roll of fifties and put them under his pillow, but after some consideration, he decided to keep it on him. He figured the nurse might come in and fluff his pillow or some shit and sneak out with his money. Fuck that.

He then remembered Kendrick said something about a gift next door. He hoped it wasn't no surprise party because he hates surprises. Then he thought maybe it was Marile and the kids which brought a smile to his face despite his best effort to hide it. Can't let nobody see him being all soft up in this bitch.

Josh cracked the door and peeked out. Ever since he made a scene and tried to leave, causing him to pass out from the effort, they have been keeping a close watch on him. He stuck his head out and took a quick peek. There wasn't any hospital staff walking around which he found odd this time of day.

He chanced another look, but this time, he looked in the direction Kendrick indicated and a saw a police officer standing by the door which made things seem even stranger. The officer noticed him looking and waved him over.

Not having shit else to do, he walked over. Normally he wouldn't be caught dead with a police officer unless he was dead, and even then, he wouldn't like it. "Yeah, what's up? Why they got you standing by the door, he wanted or some shit?"

The officer just stared at him for a moment before he spoke, "I don't know. I just go where they tell me to go as long as the checks cash on Friday, you feel me?"

Josh couldn't help but chuckle at the comment "Yeah, I feel you. We don't work for free no mo." This time the officer laughed with him.

"Hey, I have to run to the bathroom right quick. That Mexican food I ate ain't setting too well. I'm probably gonna be in there for a while, about half an hour."

"Okay, why you feel the need to tell me? We chuckled over some words, don't mean we go together" Josh said as he looked at him like he lost his mind.

The officer ignored the comment. "I believe you have something for me? Your friend told me to check with you."

"I don't know what the fuck you talking about. We don't know the same people. I assure you of that."

This time the officer narrowed his eyes. "Nigga, if you don't give me my money, we're going to have a problem." he said as he rested his hand on his gun.

The move didn't go unnoticed by Josh. Under normal circumstances, he would have knocked his ass the fuck out and go on about his business. But none of this shit seemed normal.

Then everything clicked into place.

"You motherfucka," Josh mumbled under his breath. He handed over the role of bills he had stashed on him and gave them to the officer. *Easy come, easy go,* he reasoned within himself as he tried to swallow the bitter pill of disappointment.

The officer's eyes lit up as he saw the wad of bills. "Remember, you got thirty minutes," he said as he walked off, leaving Josh standing there with a perplexed look on his face.

Not knowing what else to do, he walked into the room. The first thing he noticed was a man wrapped up like a mummy. He looked as if he was in traction, probably some fucked-up car accident or something he wagered. There were all types of wires and machines that were running to and from him. Josh felt a twinge of pity for the man as he lay there in obvious pain.

He began to look around the room, and he saw a card addressed to him on the nightstand next to the bed and he rolled his eyes. "Nigga always gotta do this cloak-and-dagger shit. I wish just for once he would just come right out and say what the hell is on his mind," he mumbled to himself again.

The card said: *I picked up a little something for you while I was out. I hope this makes you feel a little better. One more thing, I left something on the nurse's tray for you as well, but don't look at that until after you read the chart.*

"I swear he is the most thoughtful, borderline gay ass nigga I know," he thought as he went to look at the chart at the foot of the bed. He saw the name, and his breath caught in his throat as he staggered back in shock.

Lawrence Mikelson.

He shivered involuntarily at the site before him. He couldn't imagine how he wound up in the condition that he was in. The chart said that almost every bone in his body was broken in multiple places. The only reason he was still alive was that none of the major organs or spine was broken.

He had to pinch himself more than once to be sure that what he was seeing was truly real. He made his way over to the tray, and there was another note.

I left you two syringes. The small one is full of adrenaline; I figured you would want him to know it was you. The large one is full of Pavulon which causes paralysis, I don't think I need to spell it out for you.

Have fun.

Josh read the note several times, and he came to the conclusion that Kendrick is not someone he would ever want as an enemy.

He grabbed the small syringe and injected it into the IV, and Lawrence eye's popped open as wide as saucers. He looked around as his eyes focused on Josh. He let out a low moan as he shook his head ever so slightly.

"Hey, nigga, you remember me?" Before he could say anything, he injected him with the final syringe which caused the slight movements to stop. The only thing still able to move was his eyes. "I told you the next time I saw you I was gonna kill you. I guess a hard head makes a soft ass," he shrugged as he grabbed the scalpel that Kendrick was kind enough to leave for him. He stopped as if he was considering something. He left the room but returned shortly with his cellphone.

"All right, let's get this party poppin'!"

Kendrick arrived at the diner where Melvin said he was to meet his top lieutenants. He grabbed his package and made his way toward the building. There were about five men sitting in the corner facing the door. They immediately noticed him as soon as he walked in. One of them leaned over and whispered something in the ear of the man next to him; he obviously knew who he was.

That was going to make things easier he hoped.

He turned to the man behind the counter who looked like the owner. "You're closed for the next two hours." He threw a wad of money on the counter and continued on.

He walked directly toward them as one of the men stood to bar his way. He ignored him. "Which one of you is second in command?"

"That would be, fuck you want to know for?" the man who was sitting in the middle said.

Kendrick didn't say anything as he shot him right between the eyes. The man standing next to him reached for his gun and was elbowed in the face, and he went down in a heap. Before anyone else could move, he dropped his package on the table as he trained his gun on them and said, "Open it."

The man closest to the package was hesitant to do it. Kendrick placed the nose of the gun to the back of his head, and that seemed to motivate him into action. He opened the bag with shaky hands, and once he saw its content, his eyes grew big as saucers. The look on his face didn't make things any easier for his associates as they all started to scoot away; their former second in command was all but an afterthought.

"Now pull it out."

The man shook his head as he continued to try and move away from the package, regardless of the gun pressed to the back of his skull. He preferred being shot in the head rather than touch what's in the bag.

"You." Kendrick pointed at another man who looked as if he was about to pass out when he looked at Kendrick with such fear, it bordered on comical. It took everything within Kendrick not to laugh. "Open the bag or you're next."

To the man's credit, he was made of better stuff than his friend who was willing to die rather than face what was in the bag. He opened the bag and looked to Kendrick.

"Now take it out."

He pulled the contents of the bag out and laid it on the table. The head rolled around a bit until it settled right in front of the man who was too scared to do it originally. M Good's vacant eyes stared at him, condemning from the grave for his cowardice. They all looked at the head in shock as their boss's head lay on the table like a discarded piece of meat.

Kendrick let the scene settle in before he spoke. He gave it a couple of minutes, satisfied that his point was made. Several eyes fell on him with looks of contempt but he ignored them. "As you can see, there's been a restructuring of upper management." No one said anything, and he continued. "These streets aren't kind to the weak, and the way things were going, you wouldn't have lasted with your former employer. I gave it less than a year before someone else decided they wanted what he had and took it, leaving you all to become collateral damage."

The man who opened the bag was the first to speak. "Fuck you mean, collateral damage? I was making more money than I ever had in my life plus, we had this city on lock. What you know about that?"

Several of his friends nodded their heads in agreement. Kendrick knew on a certain level their views held merit. "Okay, I see your point, and on some level you might be right. But let me clear up a few misconceptions. First of all, you never was considered anything of consequence in this city. No one of any importance even knew your names, or they didn't consider you enough of a threat to bother. If they did, you would've been dead a long time ago. More than likely, they would've killed your families first and then came after you."

"Another misconception, M Good didn't have a direct supplier. He got all his weapons from somebody who is known as a joke in the arms community. So where do you think that puts you in the grand scheme of things? Y'all weren't even considered shit. More likely you were the toilet paper that wiped the shit off the clowns' asses."

The man who spoke before piped in. "So what you gonna come up in here and just talk down to us because you're the mighty Kendrick? We ain't you. We gotta go where the money is if we want to survive out here. Man, if you came here to kill us just do it, but please spare me the lecture."

He regarded the man for a moment. "What's your name"

"Carlos."

"Okay, Carlos, I'll cut to the chase." He sat the gun on the table. A few eyed the gun as if gauging their chances of getting to it before he could. He didn't worry about it because there was only one bullet, and he already used it on their second in command. Also, he had another gun with a full clip sitting in a holster behind his back.

"I came here to offer you an opportunity to work for me."

A few of the men stole a glance at the two dead men at the table and cast their eyes toward the ground. No doubt they've heard this speech before. These were the men who were thrown at a problem as cannon fodder without a second's hesitation. They weren't missed because there was always five more waiting in line to take their place. But he was looking for more than just cannon fodder. He was looking for men.

"So, what's it gonna be? Drugs, women, weapons, or do you reinvent the wheel in your spare time? Please enlighten us," Carlos said with sarcasm dripping from every word.

"Nope, nothing like that. I need men to work for me, not just tools who are easily disposed of. I promise you respect, not just from the people around you, but when you look in the mirror."

"We heard all this before. But you still haven't told us what we'll be doing."

One of the men at the table grabbed the gun and pointed it at Kendrick's head and fired. Nothing happened. He pulled it repeatedly and still the same result. He looked around for help that wasn't coming. Kendrick shook his head and pulled out his other gun and shot him in the head. His body fell ironically on top of the other man.

He continued as if he wasn't interrupted. "As I was saying, what I'm offering you is something that you've never had before, a cause. Now before we go any further, everybody on board? You can leave here alive and there will be no hard feelings or you can stay." He held up a finger. "If you betray me, you will think what I did to your last boss was me being nice." He leveled them with harsh stare. "Do I make myself clear?" Everyone to a man nodded, and he continued as he laid out his plan.

CHAPTER TWENTY-FOUR

Kendrick spent the better part of the day laying out what he had in mind. He was bombarded with question after question that he answered with patience and honesty. When he told them that he expected them to go back to school, he had more than one begin to tune out. But once he laid out the grand scheme and the financial incentives that came with it, smiles started to spread across their faces. He explained to them that if they knew anyone else who was tired of the same old shit to come and see him. He will make the same offer to them that they received. If they have "obstacles" keeping them from coming aboard, he will take care of it. He wasn't looking for minions: he needed soldiers.

In all, the day was successful, but that was only the beginning. Now comes the hard part _making all of this work while carving out a life that included Anika.

As Kendrick drove down the street, a realization dawned on him.

Kendrick was back.

In truth he never really left.

As the following weeks went by, everyone's lives started to get back to normal. Anika was swamped with work as the fiscal year came to an end. She spent the majority of her time trying to catch up on work from when she was off as well as trying to hit the new fiscal year running.

Not to mention help, Deshaun train Shawna in her new position. Truth be told, she was a fast learner and needed very little instruction on the basics of the job. It helped that she watched and learned while she was working as Anika's assistant. The hardest part was trying to keep up with her fashion. She couldn't let her new junior analyst show her up.

The downside was that she barely had time for Kendrick and their budding relationship. They had to get creative and steal precious moments whenever they could. On more than a few occasions, he would stop by and "consult" on a few problems she was having. It took everything in her not to scream out when he was torturing her with his tongue or pounding her tight little pussy on top of her desk, couch, floor, and against her window.

One time, Anika forgot to lock the door, and Shawna walked in with a question about the new report that she hadn't seen before. She had to threaten her with a shoe and a demotion just to get her to leave. She was teased mercilessly for weeks. But she never said a word, not even to Deshaun about what she observed. But she had plenty to say when they were in private.

When Shawna wasn't teasing her, she talked endlessly about her relationship with Deshaun. He finally told her that he loved her. She figured it was about time considering he did everything but said it. He was even discussing moving in together. He said it would be more convenient for him to help train her considering how many late nights they were working.

But she knew better.

Sometimes Shawna would get so graphic with the details of their love making that she would have to schedule an "extra consulting" meeting with Kendrick, sometimes twice a day. She suspected that she was doing it deliberately so she could catch them in the act, but Anika vowed never to get caught slipping again.

Kendrick was burning the candle at both ends with school, work, and getting his new project off the ground. Sometimes he would go on for days with little to no sleep as he tried to be all things to everyone.

His cousin had fallen down the stairs at his home and had broken his arm which made it impossible for him to work. He was the owner of the shop, and if he didn't work, he didn't eat. Kendrick took up the slack and worked extra, sometimes double shifts to make up for the lack of help.

His cousin came in one morning to check on the shop and found Kendrick sleeping at a work station with him face down in a political science book. He sent Kendrick home much to his objections. He told him that he rather be broke than to let something happen to him because he wasn't getting enough sleep.

His cousin came in the next morning and found three young men working in his shop. At first, he was going to call the police until one of them convinced him to take the phone and Kendrick was on the line. He explained to him that these were some kids who had been caught up in a gang, and he promised them a fresh start. He told him to pay them out of his wages, and he would cover anything that came up short.

With the extra help, he was able to take on more jobs and was able to hire the three young men on permanently and pay them a fair wage. With the extra influx of business, he was eventually able to build on additional garage space on to the shop. There was even talk about opening another location. Business had never been better.

Now that Kendrick was freed up from working at his cousin's shop, he was able to spend more time with his growing organization. He set-up study groups for those who were struggling with school. The vast majority of the ones who decided to join his cause needed little instruction. They had dropped out of school not because of grades but rather they were "encouraged" to leave school behind and join the gang full time, ensuring that they had limited options and the gang being ultimately the only one. These were the ones that Kendrick relied on to help those who were struggling in school to pass.

Kendrick got word that one of his new recruits was in the hospital. He was beaten pretty badly because he wanted to leave a neighborhood gang. They weren't willing to let him go easily. They even threatened his mother and his young child's life if he didn't come back.

Kendrick showed up at the hospital to check on him and see how things were going. He told him his version of what happened and what they did to him. He listened without comment. He told him he would take care of things and not to worry.

That was the last anyone heard from the gang leader or his lieutenants.

Word got out on the streets about what happened to those who chose to bar those who tried to join his organization. From that point forward, there was little to no resistance. People were coming to join up in droves. There was a record number of drop-outs returning to school, and crime was virtually nonexistent in the areas that Kendrick now controlled. For the first time in years, people were able to walk down the street without fear of being robbed, raped, or killed.

Josh was released from the hospital after a few days. More than likely, he finally threatened the right person, and they were too scared to make him stay. They said he was stable enough to recover at home as long as he followed the doctors' orders and went to physical therapy regularly.

He was questioned repeatedly by the police about the stabbing death and execution of the man next door. They figured he had to have heard something and threatened to take him to jail as an accessory to murder. But with nothing to tie him to the crime, they had to relent and let him go. They threatened to keep an eye on him, and it took everything in him not to laugh in their faces.

When he left the hospital, Mel and the kids were waiting for him outside with smiles on their faces. He tried to maintain his menacing expression, but even he couldn't hold up for long as tears of joy and relief ran down his face. The orderly who wheeled him out of the hospital had heard enough rumors to make himself scarce during the tender moment. Josh went home with his family with a genuine smile on his face. He couldn't remember the last time he was so happy.

Evelyn was moved from ICU and was eventually released from the hospital. The doctor recommended that she shouldn't be left alone. She was still recovering physically and to continue her counseling sessions. Anika had her grandmother stay with her, much to her objections.

Evelyn was a proud woman, and she felt she could handle things on her own.

It was the first night out of the hospital, and she awoke screaming. Anika came running into her room and wrapped her arms around her as she cried herself back to sleep. Things went on like this for weeks as she tried to cope with what happened to her. She had many more nights of awaking screaming as she kept having the same reoccurring dream. Lawrence had bound her hands overhead as she hung suspended in the air as he repeatedly assaulted her.

With the counseling sessions and the help of the church, the dreams became less frequent until she hardly had them at all. Even when she did, they were never as intense as they were in the beginning, and she was able to manage. Over time, she was able to gain a semblance of a normal life.

One of the scariest moments of Evelyn's life was when she was ready to move back to her home. She expected Anika to fight her tooth and nail on it, but she didn't. She told her that her door was always open, and she will check up on her every day. She made Evelyn promise that if she's having a bad day, she will call for help and not try and fight through it alone.

She agreed.

After a few days of being back in her home, there came a knock at the door. She barely heard it since she was on the back porch beating the rugs that accumulated dust in her absence. She made her way to the door but paused as her hand was inches from the handle. *I won't let fear rule me,* she thought to herself as her shaky hand turned the knob.

When she opened the door, there was a man walking away. Likely assumed no one was home considering it took so long for her to answer. "May I help you?"

The man seemed to consider something before he said, "No ma'am, I think I have the wrong house."

"Who are you looking for? I've lived here for over forty years, and I know pretty much everyone."

"That's okay, sorry to bother you." He turned away quickly as he made his way toward a large black SUV.

"Stop." and he did. "I know you know who you came to see. Why don't you spit it out? I've been through too much lately, and my normal friendly demeanor is running low these days. Why don't you come back over here and tell me what's on your mind?"

The man seemed to consider her offer. He seemed to sigh to himself as he closed the door and made his way back to her porch. "If it wouldn't be too much trouble, I would like to speak with you if that's okay?"

She regarded the man who now stood on her stump. He had to be over six and a half feet tall and unlike most people his height, he wasn't slim. He had the build of a professional wrestler. She could tell by the way he carried himself that he was used to causing people fear. But the thing that stood out most was his eyes. They looked. . . lost. Now that she studied him more closely, she could see a hint of pain coupled with fear. It seemed strange to see a man of his stature show that level of vulnerability. She recognized the look because it's the same look she saw every morning since the incident happened to her every time she looks in the mirror.

"My name is Evelyn." She extended her hand in greeting.

"My name is Joshua, but my friends call me Josh." He took her offered hand and swallowed it in his as he returned the gesture.

"Well, which one is it?"

"Ma'am?"

"Which name should I call you. Joshua or Josh? I can't decide for you."

"You can call me Josh." He gave her an awkward smile.

"Not used to smiling I see, my late husband was the same way. Well, come on in. No need to stand out here for no reason. It looks like it's going to rain."

He followed her into the house. She led him into the living room and offered to take his jacket. He hesitated at first but eventually relented. She offered him a cup of coffee, and he nodded. She handed him a coffee mug as opposed to a cup because she was sure his hands were too big to hold it properly.

After everything that's happened to her, she should be terrified of this man. Everything about him screamed dangerous. She knew that he wasn't gentle, at least that's what she assumed. When she thinks back on it, she knew all he needed was someone to talk to.

"So what brings you by today?"

He looked as if he was trying to get his words together. He finally seemed like he was ready to talk. "I heard about what happened to you, and I wanted to say I was sorry."

"How would you know about what happened to me?" She looked at him warily. She felt fear slowly creeping up her spine.

He seemed to notice it too. "I'm a friend of your granddaughter's boyfriend, Kendrick."

When he said that, things seemed to click into place. "Oh you're that Josh. I met your lovely wife at the hospital. She would sometimes stop and see me after she went to see you in the hospital. We would talk and pray together. I found her to be a lovely woman."

"Thank you for the kind words. A lot of people say that about her. But they don't want to get on her bad side though," he chuckled.

"I suppose not," she chuckled as well. "I'm sorry about what happened to you. I'm just glad that man got what was coming to him. I just wish I was able to see him suffer like he made me suffer," she said as thunder flashed in her eyes.

"He hurt me too," Josh said in a small voice.

"He did? I thought no one knew who did that to you." She was referring to him being shot and almost dying. She didn't want to come right out and say it because he still seemed to be dealing with it himself.

He nodded. "Yes, ma'am. I would sometimes wake up in the hospital sweating and crying and shit." He realized that he swore, and he covered his mouth. "Sorry for the swear words."

She waved it off. "Sometimes every day words aren't enough. Please continue."

He gave her a grateful smile. "Well, like I was saying, I would wake up sweating and shit from a bad dream. I would dream about Lawrence holding a gun to my family, and they would be screaming for me. I realize I can't move to help them. He would look at me and smile as he shot each one of them in the head. The sick thing was he would wait for me to look at him before he shot each one. I tried not to look, but for some reason I couldn't look away," he said as tears started to flow down his cheeks.

Evelyn found herself crying as well. "I had similar dreams as well. I take it you know what happened to me?"

He nodded, unable to look her in the eye. "Yes, my wife filled me in when I got home. Again, I'm so sorry that happened to you."

"It's not your fault. Sometimes bad people do bad things to us good folks." She wiped the tears from her cheeks and then offered him a refill on his coffee, and he nodded. Both cups were more than half full, but based on the level of emotions that were flying around, now seemed like good a time as any to take a break.

They spent the rest of the afternoon just talking. They both hated what happened to them but were glad that they had someone that each other could talk to. They both were hurt by the same man who ironically brought them together. They decided to keep meeting at least once a week and to call one another if things seem too hard.

The day was winding down, and Josh had to get home before his wife started to worry. Neither one realized how late it was. Evelyn had to get to church because it was her turn to lead the choir. She didn't want to be late because she had missed enough time as it is.

Josh unexpectedly gave her a hug. She was caught completely off-guard but quickly warmed to it and returned the hug in kind. "Thanks for letting me come by to see you, Evelyn. You don't know how much this meant to me."

"It was my pleasure. We both needed someone to talk to. It seems God always give us what we need."

"Amen."

"You have my number?"

"Yes, ma'am, I saved it in my phone as soon as you said it. I put you in under Grandma if that's okay?"

She couldn't help but smile. "That is more than fine. I hope your grandmother doesn't get jealous," she teased.

"No, ma'am, she passed before I was born. I never got the chance to know her."

"Well, you have a grandma in me then." She smiled and winked.

Josh started to blush. "I think I would like that."

"You're a big ol' teddy bear, aren't you?"

"Only my wife and kids ever get to see that side of me. I guess I can add you to the club too." He reached into his jacket and handed her a DVD that read *whenever you feel helpless, press play*. "If you don't call me again, I'll understand."

She didn't know what to make of it. "Thank you. I will play it, I promise."

They chatted for a few more minutes, and then Josh left. As soon as he was gone, she suddenly felt all alone. She looked at her watch and realized that she had to hurry, or she was going to be late for choir rehearsal.

Evelyn returned home a few hours later that evening, and the old feeling of dread returned. She started to call her pastor, but he had gone to the hospital to see the Deacon who became ill while on a cruise. She thought about calling Anika, but she didn't want her to worry. She had enough on her plate as it was.

She saw the DVD still lying on the coffee table. She decided what the heck and put the DVD in and pressed play. The picture was kinda blurry, and she could tell it was done on a cellphone. It must have been one of the newer ones because it had auto focused. She noticed that it was a video in a hospital room, and there was a man all wrapped in bandages like a mummy. . .

The day was shaping up to be a hot one. It was unseasonably warm for early May, and it was a telltale sign that it was going to be a blistering summer. Anika was sure that when the planning committee was deciding on where to have the graduation, it seemed like a good idea to have the graduation outside. But the way she was sweating from every orifice of her body, she wasn't so sure.

CHAPTER TWENTY-FIVE

Outside of the temperature, it was a beautiful spring day. There wasn't a cloud in the sky. The all-white theme for the graduation was spot on, except for the heat. She was really feeling some type of way about the heat.

The graduation was set to take place around 4:00 p.m. Anika looked at her watch and saw that she had nearly two hours before the commencement was to begin. She figured that this was going to be an all-day affair. She sighed in defeat, knowing that her hair wasn't going to survive the day.

She looked over at Shawna dressed in her best southern belle white outfit complete with the big bonnet hat. Deshaun was sitting next to her in a white suit looking all kinds dapper. She noticed that he was struggling with the heat too as beads of sweat roll down his face. They shared a look and just shook their heads.

He gave his head a nod in the direction of the lounge area, and she jumped at the chance. Shawna waved them away as they made their way toward shelter and hopefully relief from the swelter heat. She remained smiling and talking with the crowds, oblivious to the heat that ran off her man and best friend.

Deshaun held the door for Anika as she rushed inside. She paused in the doorway as the cool air blew from the vent directly by the door. She stayed there basking in the cool relief until Deshaun cleared his throat and she begrudgingly moved into the building.

Anika found a tub full of complimentary waters and other beverages. She passed one to him as she opened hers and greedily drank it down. She didn't stop until it was almost empty and let out a sigh full of relief. Deshaun did something similarly as he tried desperately to lower his body temperature.

They, each, had another bottle of water and grab one to take with them. Deshaun, forever being the dutiful boyfriend, Deshaun grabbed one for Shawna just in case she needed it. She had her suspicions that he grabbed an extra one for himself, but she didn't voice it.

"How is it this hot, this early in the year?"

"Tell me about it. I just did my hair and look at it." She threw her hands up in the air in defeat.

"Eh, I've seen worse. Besides, it doesn't look bad at all. Kinda looks like you meant to do it."

Anika looked in the mirror behind her and realized it wasn't as bad as she feared. And he was right, it kinda did look nice the way it was. She shrugged to herself and turned back to Deshaun. She regarded him for a moment "Hey, remember when we first met at that club?"

"Yeah, the tip you gave me was more than I probably would've earned in a week." He smiled fondly, remembering the moment. "That was the day that my life truly began and I started to live."

"I can take credit for that. You're very gifted, and I'm sure if you didn't work for me, someone else would've noticed the same things in you that I saw."

"You're not giving yourself enough credit. I might have some skill but in this business, you have to know somebody or have gone to the right school. I was lacking on all counts."

"Maybe. I still think you would've been successful regardless."

"But you're forgetting one thing. I never would've met Shawna if it wasn't for you. That one is something else. She wants me to meet her parents before we move in together."

"What's wrong with that? Most women want their parent's stamp of approval before they take that big step."

"Yeah, but there's one problem with all of this."

"And that would be?"

"I never asked her to move in with me. I told her that she should stay over my house while I'm still training her because we both work late hours, and it's just easier all the way around."

"So what are you going to do?"

"Oh, I'm going to ask her to move in with me."

"But you just said. . ."

"I said that I never asked her. Look, I already know how this story ends, and it will be with us living together. To be honest, I kinda like the idea. I can't think of anyone else I rather wake up to. Besides, you know how she is when she's pissed off. I'm not trying to relive those days." He cringed as he was remembering how things used to be.

"Oh yeah, she has some issues when it comes to that, no doubt. I hate to even bring up a topic if I think she *might* get upset over it, and I'm her boss." They both laughed.

"Man, it's hotter than a motherfucker up in this bitch!"

They both turn around to see a mountain of a man standing behind them. Deshaun fought the urge to take a step back as Anika reached up to give the big man a hug. "I'm so glad you made it, Josh." She gave him a kiss on the cheek as he tried to hide his smile behind a scowl.

"Nah, I couldn't miss this. My boy is graduating today to become a full-fledged sellout. If I catch him on the streets rocking a sweater wrapped around his shoulders, I might just have to jack him on principal alone."

Everyone except Josh chuckled at the comment which dissolved into awkward silence. He glanced out the corner of his eye at Deshaun. "You look really familiar... aren't you_"

He cut him off. "I don't think so, besides, the woman you was just all hugged up with is my boss." He gave him a pointed look.

Josh seemed to catch the hint. "Yeah, okay, small world though," he chuckled more to himself than anything else.

They sat around making small talk until they noticed everyone making their way back out to the field as the graduation was starting soon. They stepped back outside, and it seemed even hotter than before. They saw Shawna waving at them, and they made their way over. She had a total of three seats reserved, but when she saw a fourth person walking up, she asked the person next to her to slide down one seat.

They mumbled that they were there first and she can't make them move. She tried to reason with them, but they refused every overture. She turned to her group with an apologetic look as she looked around for more seating.

"Man, if you don't slide yo little ass over_" Josh never got the chance to finish his threat as the man realized who was speaking to him, he promptly slid over three seats and stared intently at the ground in front of him. Seeing that he was properly cowed, he slid over to the seat on the far end, allowing the three to sit together.

Shawna leaned over and introduced herself. "Hello, my name Shawna, and you are?"

"Josh."

She was expecting more, but she just shrugged and reached out her hand and he shook it, swallowing her hand whole in the process. "My you're a big one, aren't you?" She smiled.

"That's what everybody keeps telling me." He turned to face the stage, letting her know that the conversation was over.

She noticed them walking also and turned to watch as well. Mentally noting that the conversation was not over, just postponed till a later time. She noticed Deshaun sitting stiff in the chair next to her. "Hey, you okay?"

"Yeah, I'm good."

"You don't look like it." She gave him a concerned look.

He hesitated for a moment, not sure just how much he wanted to say in front of a crowd. He glanced over at Josh. "We can talk about it later."

She seemed to catch the hint. "Fine, but we will finish this later, okay?" He gave her a noncommittal shrug. She looked at him and crossed her arms. "We can talk about that, or we can talk about color patterns for the house _your choice."

"House?" was all he could manage to say as a haunted look crept across his face. He looked up and noticed Josh trying not to laugh. "What's so funny."

"Not a damn thing. Watch the ceremony."

Everyone rose to clap as the graduating class made their way on to the field. Some cried while others waved at their friends and family. Others just looked on as the moment seemed to overwhelm them. Everyone sat once the graduating class took their seats.

Anika craned her neck as she tried to find Kendrick among the crowd. She almost gave up when Josh said, "Third row from the front, four seats in from the aisle."

"Thanks, I probably wouldn't have found him until they called his name."

"No need to thank me, we're family."

To say that she was shocked by his words would be a monumental understatement. A smile spread across her face. "Thanks, that means a lot coming from you."

He nodded and let a rare smile escape. "You're welcome."

She sat back in her seat as she started to watch the ceremony begin. Then realization crept into her eyes as they shot wide open and she sat up bolt straight. She turned to regard Josh with a look of shock. "You're the grandson she was talking about?"

"Oh, you mean Grandma Evelyn?" he said casually as if he were talking about the weather. "What did she say?"

She hesitated as she tried to remember exactly what her grandmother had said, "She said that she really enjoyed your talk and look forward to the next time you stopped by. She wants you and the family to stop by for dinner."

"Cool, I'll let Mel know," he said with a barely contained smile. "You and my boy is gonna to be there too, right?"

Anika narrowed her eyes and said, "what's up with you and my grandma? You bed not be up to no bullshit with her. So help me God, I will_"

"Hold up," he raised his hand to cut her off. She flinched slightly, but she did her best not to show how scared she suddenly became. "It's true, I will crack a nigga's head before I would tell him the time, but you seem to have some false impressions about me. First of all, I wouldn't ever do anything to so much as to make *OUR* grandmother frown. Second of all, I consider you and her family now and I guess if you marry, my boy too. But he was already grandfathered in, so he was good regardless. The point is, I'm not always like that. If I find out that somebody so much as dropped a piece of paper on her lawn, they got hell to pay. But outside of that, you have nothing to worry about from me or anybody I roll with. So we cool? I would like to watch my boy, *your boyfriend,* graduate, okay?"

This wasn't the first time Anika was glad she was of a darker complexion; she was blushing so furiously that she could barely make a reply. "Whatever, I'm not calling you my brother, so don't think about it." She mumbled as she crossed her arms, unable to look up at him. If he gave any indication that he had won the argument, she couldn't tell.

Anika was brought out of her full on pouting session when she heard them call Kendrick's name. Their group rose to their feet and began cheering and shouting as the moment finally arrived. Although everyone in attendance was cheering for that special person and to a lesser extent, everyone else, Anika's group was by far the loudest. A few of the people in their area gave them disapproving glares, but when Josh gave them one of his own, they quickly diverted their eyes.

After the graduating class walked across the stage, things moved on quickly from that point. The school president gave a rousing speech about how the world is their oyster and so and so. . . It wasn't until the class threw their graduation caps into the air did she finally make her way toward the stage. She fought her way through the crowd as it seemed as if everyone had the same idea.

In her haste, Anika tripped over someone's foot, and she began to fall. A strong pair of hands reached out and rescued her from an embarrassing moment. She would know those hands from anywhere _Kendrick.

"You okay, babes?"

She looked into his smiling face, and before she knew it, she was smiling right along with him. "I am now." She looked up and saw that he still had his cap on. "You know tradition says that you're supposed to throw it in the air."

Kendrick looked up and moved his tassel back to the proper side. "Nah, I paid good money for this. Tradition is going to have to wait for the next brutha to roll through."

"You know you silly right?"

"You love me anyway." He smiled.

"Damn Skippy." She slid into his arms as their lips found one another. Her body instantly began to respond to his simple touch. All she did was give him a small kiss and already her body was on fire. "You keep that up and we might not make it to dinner."

"You are my dinner." His eyes smoldered with sensual intent.

She felt her knees go weak.

It practically killed her to say the words, "No, we need to wait. We have friends who want to celebrate with us."

Kendrick looked up and saw Josh followed by Shawna making their way toward them. "Hey, thanks for coming. I really appreciate you all coming out her to see me." Shawna gave him a hug and a sisterly kiss on the cheek, congratulating him for his accomplishment. Josh followed that up by giving him a man hug followed by a respectful nod.

"I don't know about you all, but I'm about ready to melt. Let's go get a few drinks before dinner?" Anika said as everyone seemed to like the idea.

Kendrick looked up and smiled. "I didn't think you was going to make it."

Anika gave him a quizzical look. "Who you talking to, babe? I didn't know anyone else was coming." She looked around to see who he could be talking about.

"My cousin."

Everyone looked around to see who he was talking about.

"Who's your cousin?" Anika and Shawna said in unison.

"I would've called you, but nobody got your number. I didn't find out until Mama told me you had stopped by." Deshaun emerged from the crowd and smiled at Kendrick.

Kendrick walked over and grabbed him in a big hug. "Damn, man, I haven't seen you since your graduation. How's everything with you?"

"Ummmm, pretty good, I got a good job" he grabbed Shawna's hand and pulled her to his side "also got me a pretty good woman to boot. Apparently we're moving in together." He winked. Shawna elbowed him in the side. He extended his hand toward Anika. "And this lady right here is my boss."

Kendrick laughed. "Yeah, I think we've met." Anika had a shocked look on her face as she tried to process everything she just heard. He leaned in and kissed her. "This is the lady I was telling Auntie Lynn about. I think I'm going to keep her." He gave her a wink.

"I thought I knew you. They used to call you little Shaun when you was younger," Josh said as he made his way into the conversation.

"I remembered you, but I didn't want to say nothing in front of my boss. I didn't know how she would take it." He gave a sheepish look.

"I'm pretty sure she's taking it very well."

Everybody just stared at him.

"What? All I said was that she looked happy." He shrugged.

They stood around talking for the next few minutes as everyone commented on what were the chances that everyone, directly or indirectly, had a bond with one another. The events over the past ten months were more than any of them imagined. The fact they came out on the other end albeit a little bruised and battered; they are stronger for the experience.

Everyone decided to go down to Ed's Southside Bar off Main and Oakford. It was an out-of-the way place, but they made strong drinks and the majority of them were familiar with the place. Kendrick had called ahead to let them know he was coming with a few friends and if they had someplace they could chill that was a little more private. Everyone piled into the limo Anika rented for the occasion, and they were off.

When they walked into the bar, Anika was pleasantly surprised by what she saw. The bar was larger than any bar she's been to, and it was nicely furnished with antique furnisher that looked as if it was recently remodeled. The light fixtures were similarly refurbished as well. The original floors were a dark wood which were resurfaced and waxed which gave it a stylish look. It was like she took a step back in time when things were simpler.

"This place is beautiful," was all Anika could say as she glanced over at Shawna who had the same awed expression that she held.

She looked around at the patrons, and it was a mixed bag. One side of the bar was an older crowd; no doubt they had been coming there for years. On the other side of the bar was a young posh group who saw the same charm in the place that she did.

A small part of her felt a tinge of sadness for the longtime patrons. She saw the relatively small group of loyal clientele versus the younger hip crowd. The way things have been going, this will probably cause the prices to go up, which will effectively cause the once vital lifeblood of this bar to become obsolete. She wasn't so sure that was a good thing.

Someone walked up to their group and led them to the back of the bar and through a short hallway. Their guide opened a door and led them into a dimly lit room. It took a moment for Anika's eyes to adjust to the lighting.

Once her eyes adjusted, she saw they were in a small cozy lounge with a large circular table in the corner surrounded by a half circle couch. There were several other tables that were stationed throughout the room that allowed for a little more privacy, but didn't take away from the intimacy that the room had captured.

"How come I've never heard of this place before? I would've been here way before now," Deshaun asked, and several other people nodded in agreement.

"Well, it used to be a hole in the wall not too long ago," Kendrick said as he walked behind the bar and grabbed a bottle of red wine out of the wine cabinet which didn't go unnoticed by Anika. "You probably passed it more than a few times but never paid it too much attention to it because of the gangs in the neighborhood. The owner had wanted to fix up the place for years but didn't want to put money into it because of the crime in the area. He was getting robbed about once a week. And when one of the gangs offered protection for a *small fee*, they wound up drinking up almost all of the liquor and robbing the patrons, then ultimately robbed him anyway. He figured why put good money after bad, so I heard."

"Yeah, I get all that, what happened to get it like *THIS*?" He waved his around at the complete transformation.

"Well, there aren't any more gangs in the area. It seems as if they found something more constructive to do with their time." He poured each one of them a glass. "Now let's toast."

Kendrick was being deliberately coy, and it was grinding Anika's gears. If there was one thing that drove her crazy about him, this was it. "Hold up, aren't you leaving out something from this story?"

"What do you mean?"

Anika almost lost it, but she somehow held her composure. "Like how did all this happen with the bar, where did the gangs go, and more importantly, how is it that you walk around this place like you own it?"

"Co-owner."

"Huh?"

"I'm a co-owner. The original owner and I came to an understanding, and in return, he offered me forty percent ownership in the bar."

"I'm going to need more than that this time, Kendrick. I need the whole story."

He gave her an intense look. "Another time."

"No, I need to hear it now."

The tension in the air was thick as everyone seemed to be holding their respective breath, waiting to see the outcome of their battle of wills.

"I'll tell, just not right now, okay?"

"No, Kendrick, I think you need to understand a few things. Everyone here," she pointed to each person in their group for effect and then finally at Kendrick, "has been down for one another whether they knew it or not from day one. Josh has been with you since you guys were kids. Deshaun is your cousin, and from what I gather, that's a whole other story that needs to be told, but not now. Shawna has been on your team since she first heard about you. She's been holding me down when you were nowhere to be found."

He flinched at that, and she felt shame begin to trickle in. She knew exactly what he was doing: he didn't deserve that. But now was not the time for apologies. She continued, "What I'm trying to say is, we got each other backs. We all have a stake in all of this. You're going to have to trust somebody sometime."

Kendrick was quiet for a longtime. He sat there staring off into space as he thought about what she had said. He drained his glass and then poured another one and drained that one as well. He let out a sigh as his shoulders dropped in defeat. "You . . . you're right." He looked at Josh, "I owe you an apology. You are always there to help me, no questions asked. I was telling myself that I was trying to keep you out of all of this, but the truth is, I was scared to let you in. After everything that happened before, I didn't know if I could trust like that again."

Josh knew exactly what he was referring to: Lawrence and ShaBree. "I feel you, my nigga, but you wrong as two left shoes. But you knew that already, please continue."

Kendrick couldn't help but chuckle. "That just illustrates my point, I was wrong. I can't keep living in the past. It's time I let go and move into the here and now." He looked directly at Anika, and she immediately began to blush. She bit the corner of her lip, and it made his heart jump in his chest.

God he loved that woman.

"So y'all wanted the whole story?" Everyone nodded in agreement. "Okay, here goes. . ."

Kendrick started from the beginning. He told them what happened with the young thug who had caught him dead to rights at M Good's place when he was looking for Lawrence. That is where the seeds for his plan first started to hatch. Then he let all of them in on his long-range plans, and when he was finished, everyone was speechless.

"Look, I know I've probably bit off more than my ass can handle, but I have to at least try. I've seen too much and done too much in my relatively short years on this earth. I want to give something back to my community and those who reside in it. I want to help those on both sides of the law."

The room fell silent as everyone seemed to ponder what his plan meant to them. They all have experienced what he was trying to fix in one way or another. They all knew the system was broken, but no one ever thought to try and actually fix it until now.

A silence had taken hold over the room that everyone seemed reluctant to break. But it was Josh who had spoken up first. "I ain't gonna lie, I'm pissed than a motherfucka that you left me on the side-lines."

"I know I should've told you as soon as_"

"Hold up, I wasn't finished." Josh held up his hand cutting Kendrick off. "I know all that shit that went down in your past was some fucked-up shit. To be honest, that wasn't your fault. It was mine. I knew you always had a blind spot for those two, even though you knew deep down they probably weren't about shit. Even still, you kept them around, hoping that one day they might change for the better. I knew that shit was never going to go down the way you hoped. If I was a better friend, I would have put two in both their heads and told you some bullshit ass lie that your gullible ass would've probably believed. And for that, I'm sorry."

If anyone was shocked or appalled by what Josh said, no one said anything. He looked around to see if anyone objected to what he said, but the looks he saw on everyone's face confirmed what he already knew; he should have killed their asses way back, and none of this shit would've happened.

"I appreciate you saying that, man, I really do. But I'm a grown-ass man, and I don't need anyone fighting my battles."

"See, there you go again with that fucked-up ass logic. Haven't you figured that shit out yet, my nigga? When you bleed, we bleed. There's no other way to look at it. I know beyond a shadow of a doubt that if I called you on some real shit, you would be there, no questions asked. Why can't you let somebody do the same for you? You got this fine-ass bitch all in love with yo ass_" He turned quickly toward Anika and said, "No disrespect, just trying to prove a point."

"None taken and. . . thanks?" She shrugged, not knowing what to make of what just happened.

"The point I'm making is, we got you. Not just because we know you got our back. It's because we know you're a good man." He looked around, and everyone was nodding in agreement. "Just' cause I said you was a good man, don't think I'm gonna hold your hand or some shit."

Kendrick smiled. "Nah dawg, never that."

"So what time you want me there tomorrow?"

Kendrick saw the challenging look that Josh held. He looked around, and he could see that everyone was waiting on his answer. He knew he really had no choice in the matter. "Come through around eight and we can work through the details."

Anika gave him a tight look and shook her head.

"Make that about ten?"

She thought for a moment and shook her again.

"Damn, woman, you trying to kill me. Make it around 2:00 p.m., I promise I'll be ready by then,"

"Aight cool. I'm gonna head out. I gotta stop by my grandma's house and then go take the kids out for ice cream. Those little mofos always want something." He tried to hide his smile. He said his goodbyes which consisted of a head nod, and then he was gone.

"You got a strange friend there, Kendrick, but I like him. He seems genuine." Shawna smiled as she intertwined her fingers with Deshaun's.

"You have no idea."

Deshaun grabbed a bottle and began to pour everyone a drink. "I believe a toast is in order." He raised his glass, and everyone followed in turn. "To Kendrick, we couldn't be any more proud of you." Everyone cheered and drained their glasses.

Deshaun began to top everyone's glasses off again, but Shawna placed a hand on his arm, stopping him. "Remember we got that thing to do tonight?"

He gave her a blank look until realization began to dawn. "Oh yeah, I almost forgot. I'm gonna go call a cab." He hurried out of the room.

Anika smiled as she realized what they were doing. "You guys don't have to run off just yet, I thought we were doing dinner?"

"Nah, we'll just pick something up on the way home. Besides, we have some things to sort out as far as the house goes."

"I thought you were getting an apartment together?"

"Oh that. I just said that so he wouldn't get scared. No, we're getting a house."

"Good luck with that. I know my cousin, and he's as stubborn as they come." Kendrick chuckled.

"Oh, I have my ways. I'm pretty sure he'll come around sooner or later."

"And how do you plan on doing that?" Anika smiled.

She looked at Anika like it was the most obvious thing in the world. "I'm going to fuck him silly. That pretty much does it every time. If that doesn't work, I'll cook him his favorite meals. What kind of southern belle would I be if I couldn't make my man happy with my cooking?"

Anika glanced over at Kendrick, and he seemed suspiciously preoccupied with his glass of wine. Very smart decision on his part. "Have you done that thing we've talked about?"

Shawna's eyes went as big as saucers. "Oh, I don't think he's ready for that just yet. He hasn't even gotten *I'm sorry for not cooking tonight* fuck. I'll pull that out when I think he's ready to make me an honest woman." She looked at her toenail polish and then turned to regard Anika. "Do you think this polish matches my walls?"

"And why would I know that? Just check it out yourself when you get home."

Shawna shrugged. "Yeah that makes sense, I'll compare my toenail polish to the ceiling tonight. I'm sure I'll have plenty of time." She gave each one of them a hug and hurried off to catch up with Deshaun.

Kendrick waited until she was gone and then burst out laughing. "My cousin doesn't have a chance, does he?"

"Not even a little bit." Anika joined in with his laughter. She wrapped her arms around his neck as she straddled his lap. "You don't suppose you could help me check out my toenail polish tonight too?" She batted her eyes as she gave him her best innocent look.

"Shit, that goes without saying." He thought for a moment "You two don't talk about what we do in the bedroom, do you?"

Anika's mouth fell open as she was caught completely off guard. "Huh?"

He chuckled. "Yeah, I figured as much."

"You mad?"

"Nah, its cool, I trust her."

"As well you should." Anika looked down as her phone began to vibrate. She looked at the message, and it was Shawna. It said, *We'll be there tomorrow at 2pm, you want us to bring any snacks?* She shrugged and put her phone back in her purse.

"Bad news?" he asked, looking concerned.

"No, Shawna wanted to know if we wanted snacks at tomorrow's meeting."

"What meeting?"

"The meeting we're having tomorrow at 2:00p.m. at your place, remember?"

"That wasn't for everybody. I was going to go over some things with Josh."

"Correction. With all of us. When Josh spoke, he spoke for everyone. We're a team now."

"I don't know. . ."

Anika hopped off his lap. "Do I need to convince you?"

"How do you plan on doing that pray tell?"

"Stand up." He did as instructed. She pulled his pants down to his knees and pulled out his rapidly rising dick. "I can think of a few things."

"Hold on, baby, just let me go lock the door."

"That's okay if somebody walks in. I don't mind an audience." She swallowed half his cock down her greedy throat as she began to run her tongue along the shaft.

Kendrick leaned back against the wall as the woman he loved more than life itself began "convincing" him to include the whole gang. Truth be told, he had decided to include them in before she even began. But who was he to interrupt her?

This was the beginning of one of the best nights of his life.

Epilogue

The phone rang, and ShaBree rushed to answer it. She looked at the caller ID, and it said anonymous. She answered the phone, but no one was on the line. She hated when people called her anonymous. She let out an annoyed sigh as she threw the phone back on the counter as she continued to pack for her vacation.

She heard what happened to Lawrence, and she decided it was in her best interest to get out of town for a while. She felt bad that happened to him, but at least, she got her money up front. *The price of doing business*, she thought to herself.

But she sure was going to miss that dick.

It wasn't as good as Kendrick's, but it would do in a pinch. He wasn't kind and gentle like Kendrick. He would fuck her hard and rough like she was an object to be used and discarded afterward. She absolutely loved it.

The thought of Kendrick made her throb in between her legs. It's been too long since she's had a piece of that. She made it a top priority to ride that dick the first chance she gets.

His girlfriend be damned.

She was fairly confident that he was still upset with her. But she was a patient woman. Besides, if he was that upset, he would have come over to confront her by now. She wasn't so much worried about him doing to her that she was pretty sure he did to Lawrence. She was more worried about that animal he calls friend, Josh. If Josh caught her alone, that would be that. Good thing Kendrick kept him on a tight leash.

Of course, she will never say this to Kendrick, but she was more than a little disappointed that he didn't die.

She was almost done with her packing. She decided to bring two more bikinis for the trip. You never know when you might need them. The prices they charge at resorts are almost criminal.

ShaBree was standing in the kitchen going over her checklist to make sure she wasn't forgetting anything. She heard a horn blow and checked her watch. It must be the cab that she had called to take her to the airport.

She started to grab her suitcase and then stopped. Better to let the help do it. Besides, if he wants a tip, he'll have to earn it. Even then, she knew that she more than likely wasn't going to give it anyway.

ShaBree heard a rustle behind her; but before she could turn around, someone had grabbed her head from behind, pulled it back, and ran a blade across her throat.

Her mind couldn't seem to process what had just happened to her. She realized she couldn't breathe but couldn't understand why. She brought her hands to her throat, and when she pulled them back, they were coated with blood.

Her blood.

She saw movement in front of her. It was becoming difficult for her eyes to focus due to the lack of oxygen and loss of blood. What she saw didn't make sense. Someone kneeled down in front of her, and she was able to make out the face. She tried to speak, but she realized that they must have cut her vocal cords as well.

"I wouldn't try to speak if I were you. You'll only bring the end on sooner. I want to actually enjoy this a bit a longer." They pulled up a chair and sat down right in front of ShaBree.

"I bet you're wondering how this could happen to someone like you right about now. Well, it's simple really. You fucked with mines. Did you really think I would let something like that go? I mean seriously. . ."

The killer grabbed ShaBree's hands and placed them against the gaping wound. "I can't have you dying just yet. I still have some things I need to get off my chest, woman to woman. I promised God that I would leave this life in the past. But for you, I'm sure he'll make an exception. Okay, now you can die." She pulled ShaBree's hands away from her throat and the blood began to pour out unimpeded. She looked her in the eyes until the light went out of them.

Marile stood up and admired her handiwork. It's been a while since she's had a chance to use her talents. She put that life behind her when she met Josh. She wanted to be the woman that he deserved. But when he told her about what happened with Lawrence, she figured why not? The bitch had it coming.

She looked around to make sure that there was no evidence leading back to her. Confident that she had a clean kill, she took a photo and went to leave. She stopped at the door, suddenly not sure that she covered all her bases; it has been a while after all.

She grabbed a can of green beans out of the cabinet and shook her head at all the sodium listed on the container. She preferred fresh green beans for her family. She placed the can in the microwave and then ripped out the gas line from behind the stove.

She removed the plastic bag that she was wearing and threw it on the floor next to ShaBree's body. And just for good measure, she poured powder sugar and flower all over the crime scene to ensure there was no way anything could be linked back to her. Very few people know that sugar and flour are highly combustible.

She turned on the microwave and left.

Marile opened her car door as she heard a loud explosion followed by smoke and flames that shot into the sky. She regarded the scene in front of her, confident that she had a successful outing.

She looked at her watch and realized that she was running behind schedule. Today was Thursday, which means it's steak night. It looked as if it was going to be a nice night. Maybe she will cook on the grill. With any luck, she probably could get Josh start a fire, and they could have s'mores later.

A satisfied smile spread across her face as she raced to the store to pick up dinner for her family.

The End

Lightning Source UK Ltd.
Milton Keynes UK
UKHW041039240219
337503UK00015B/14/P